BAD COUNTRY

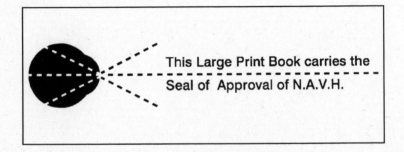

This Large Print Book carries the
Seal of Approval of N.A.V.H.

BAD COUNTRY

CB McKENZIE

THORNDIKE PRESS
A part of Gale, Cengage Learning

GALE
CENGAGE Learning®

Thorndike Press® Large Print Crime Scene.
The text of this Large Print edition is unabridged.
Other aspects of the book may vary from the original edition.
Set in 16 pt. Plantin.

LIBRARY OF CONGRESS CATALOGING-IN-PUBLICATION DATA

McKenzie, C. B.
   Bad country / by CB McKenzie. — Large print edition.
     pages cm. — (Thorndike Press large print crime scene)
   ISBN 978-1-4104-7743-9 (hardcover) — ISBN 1-4104-7743-6 (hardcover)
   1. Private investigators—Fiction. 2. Murder—Investigation—Fiction.
3. Indians of North America—Crimes against—Fiction. 4. Arizona—Fiction.
5. Large type books. I. Title.
PS3613.C55566B33 2015
813'.6—dc23   2014047316

Published in 2015 by arrangement with St. Martin's Press, LLC

Printed in Mexico
1 2 3 4 5 6 7 19 18 17 16 15

This first published novel is for
my parents,

Ann Williams McKenzie and
Charles Benjamin McKenzie,

As they have suffered the longest with
me for this.

As instructed, the man stopped at a certain landmark in the desert, stripped and used the cheap folding knife to cut his dusty khakis and T-shirt into small pieces. He tossed his old clothes bit by bit into a hard wind, unpacked the plastic trash bag and re-dressed in new clothes. He squatted in the skeletal shade of a creosote bush, sliced his last apple and chewed and swallowed each piece slowly then sipped bleach-treated water from a recycled milk jug through the heat of the day. Near sundown he cut the jug into small pieces and threw them and the knife into a steep-sided arroyo, took his bearings and then tore his map into small bits and broadcast these as he walked north. When he neared the meeting place he hustled through slanting shadows and hid behind the large boulder so that he could espy in both directions the sparse traffic on Agua Seco Road. As he waited his eyes strayed toward a solitary cloud towed north by invisible forces. A call and response from a pair of falcons hunting late he took as a good omen.

During the night a vehicle stopped in the middle of the turn-out. Muffled by closed doors and raised windows, the music from the SUV sounded like something the waiting man might hear when he stood outside a cathedral. When the vehicle shut down it was as if a trapdoor had opened on the surface of the world and all extant sound fallen through it. When a door unlatched, the dome light in the cab of the SUV illuminated a passenger in the backseat as a dark face under a white hat. The figure that emerged on the driver's side had on a billed cap, dark glasses and a plastic coat that glimmered in the moonlight.

This is your ride, hombre. The command was a hoarse whisper aimed directly at the hiding place. Levántate. Into la luz.

The waiting man stepped into the glare of the headlights.

Tienes algo? the driver asked.

Nada, the man said. He spread his arms wide with his hands open. He had nothing but the new clothes on his back and the old boots on his feet, had no identification, no keys, weapons, cell phone or any paper with writing or numbers on it. He had no photographs of family, no money, no tattoos or identifiable scars, wore no jewelry and had never been arrested on either side of the border. He did not even know the name of his employer.

Eres Indio? the driver asked.

Si, soy Indio, the man said.

The man lowered his arms and waited for words that made more sense to him.

Has estado esperando mucho? the driver asked.

Si. Todo mi vida.

The bill of the driver's gimme cap tilted down and then up.

I have been waiting my whole life for this too, the driver said.

The back door of the SUV opened and the man moved out of the headlights and toward his ride.

Adonde va? he asked.

Trabajar, hombre, said the driver. We go to work now.

Rodeo and his dog drove over "Elm Street," which was but a collection of ruts and potholes, streambed cuts and corduroy stretches that led from the paved Agua Seco Ranch Road into a small dead end of southern Arizona called El Hoyo, The Hole.

Where the man and his dog lived was supposed to have been a full-service, upscale trailer park with concrete pads radiating like the segmented spokes of a big wagon wheel from the hub of an Activities Center, and wound through these spokes like a gourd vine a nine-hole golf course. But the investment venture had been mistimed and misplaced and so remained as only a concentric grid of blade-graded dirt roads marked at random intersections by unlikely green-and-white street signs now aimed into all compassed directions and bent by gravity to all angles of repose, mostly a collection of unpaid property taxes and dirt off the grid.

The old dog on the shotgun seat whined when he scented blood. Rodeo slowed as he approached the "gates" of his place, two jumbled piles of cinder block on either side of the dirt road with a sign advertising VISTA MONTANA ESTATES — AN ACTIVE LIFE COMMUNITY skewered on a splintered pole like a reminder note to do something later.

Cállate, Rodeo said.

The dog was quiet at his man's command.

The corpse was facedown in the dirt, his jeans-clad legs widespread, boot toes pointed back, arms outstretched like a small, misguided Superman buried in a dead-end earthly mission. The back of his red, white and blue shirt was blown into shreds. Hung up on a piece of rebar, a pristine white straw cowboy hat twirled slowly in a breeze.

Rodeo sat for a long moment with a boot vibrating on the clutch pad, then he shifted the truck into neutral and stomped on the emergency brake. When the dog started barking Rodeo reached below the bench seat, pulled the 9mm from its stash site, jacked a load into the Glock and stepped out of the truck.

A cottontail hopped around a pile of vent bricks and froze and twitched and stared at

11

the man with the gun. Rodeo waved his pistol but the rabbit moved toward the dead man where it sat trembling in the pool of congealed blood. Rodeo reached back through the open window and pounded the truck's horn and the rabbit hopped away, his white paws tracing red across the desert. Vultures drifted overhead. Crows defined the margins of the crime scene by picking at spattered flesh and bone.

Rodeo reentered his vehicle, re-holstered his hideaway, calmed his dog, made a U-turn and headed back to the nearest place where cell phone reception was dependable.

Where you at, Garnet?

The voice of the Los Jarros County sheriff sounded in the cell phone like creek gravel sifted in a tin mining pan. Rodeo sat in the shade of the gas pumps island of Twin Arrows Trading Post, which establishment along with the handful of trailer houses scattered around it, passed as a village in a small county in Southern Arizona mostly uninhabited. He stared out the cracked windscreen of his truck at a sky that was blue-white as an old blister.

I'm at the Store, Ray. Where you at?

I'm up to my ass in a crime scene right

12

now over at the Boulder Turn-Out, so spare me the details if that's possible.

Dead man by my front gates, said Rodeo.

Well, that's a short story, said the sheriff. You know him?

I don't know him, Ray. He's a little man, probably Indio but probably not local. What have you got at the Boulder Turn-Out?

Some sort of death by misadventure, the sheriff said. And the body's been here a while, so it's tough for Doc Boxer to figure some theory out that will fit the evidence at hand.

What is the evidence, Ray?

Another dead Indian is the long and short of it.

What's the official theory about these dead Indians in Los Jarros County, Ray?

We are understaffed and official theory–short about Major Crimes in Los Jarros County Sheriff's Department recently, said the sheriff.

Rodeo said nothing.

You got some idea, Garnet? Official or otherwise?

State should send somebody down from Major Crimes Department to deal with my trouble out at the Estates, said Rodeo.

I doubt it's just your trouble, Garnet, said the lawman. And I'm still the sheriff of Los

Jarros County, so I'll decide what needs to be done when I see what this new trouble is.

What do you want me to do, Ray?

You just sit tight at the Store, said the sheriff.

Hypothetical . . . Rodeo said. He was on the pay phone outside Twin Arrows Trading Post talking to his lawyer, Jarred Willis, who was in his well-appointed office in downtown Tucson.

I got my own shit to do, Chief, so put me out of my misery already.

You know where my place in El Hoyo is at, said Rodeo. You hid a Jaguar XJ with Texas plates in my storage shed last year, a vehicle that was later found in East Tucson with a dead cholo and his pit bull in the trunk.

That car was never registered in my name so don't get on one of your Indian warpaths or this will be a very short conversation, Tonto. The lawyer paused. So what's got up in your Hole out there most recently?

A dead man nearby the front gates of my place, said Rodeo. And The Hole's not someplace you get to be dead in usually unless it's by starvation or dehydration.

And these were not the case?

Death by shotgun would be my guess.

You didn't touch him?

No point, said Rodeo.

When was he killed, do you think?

When I was away on vacation this last week sometime.

How many times I got to tell you to call the cops first, Tonto? It just looks real bad when you call your lawyer first thing because modern law enforcement can track these cellular phone shit conversations like Pocahontas could track short white dick in deep dark woods.

This is a pay phone. Ray's on the way.

Well, if you're smart as all that, Chief, then you don't need a lawyer, do you?

I've often wondered about that myself, said Rodeo.

Rodeo's lawyer laughed really loud.

Well, play it straight as you usually do then, Chief. And remember Law Enforcement don't do Citizens favors, so don't admit nothing to Police and don't let them anywhere without a warrant and don't invoke your lawyer's name until you are firmly behind bars.

Good to know my lawyer's got my back like that.

Save the sarcasm for the rodeo clown you rode in on, cowboy, said Willis. And you got about thirty seconds left on your retainer to tell me if you been in any shit lately.

I did that thing in New Mexico a couple of months ago and then found a lost kid and a lost husband and did a bit of divorce snooping in the last several weeks. Rodeo paused for a moment. Then right before I went on vacation I served papers on several minor characters for A-2-Z Bailbonds, but no criminals. So it's been nothing major or personal for a while.

Then the dead man in your driveway's probably nothing major or personal, Tonto. So just stay out of trouble on this and let Law Enforcement do their business.

Can I call you if Law Enforcement hauls me in?

You're welcome to drop by my office in the Old Pueblo if you bring beers, said Willis. But you're too low-rent for me these days, Chief. And since this phone call took care of what was left of your retainer fee I'll just have to say hasta la vista to you as a client.

The lawyer hung up before the private investigator could.

Rodeo pulled back the Mexican screen door and peered into the gloom of Twin Arrows Trading Post. The place smelled of dry rot and swamp cooler mold and cheap goods extracted from mothball storage, soured milk, spilled beer, stale cigarette smoke and of the old man scent of trouser piss and necksweat.

The plank floor of the Territorial Era store was warped by permanent dry heat and grooved by a century of footfall. The pressed-tin ceiling sagged against the weight of faded piñatas and unraveling Pancho Villa hats hanging from it. A large metal carousel packed with "Native American" and "Southwestern" and "Biker" T-shirts dominated the center of the room. Neon-colored polyester blankets and other tourist-trade goods were piled against a side wall cattycornered to a rickety table where vintage computers were available to rent-by-the-minute.

The moneymaker of the store, a big glassfronted cooler that advertised COLD BEER, hummed phatically. A bumper sticker on the side of this industrial-sized refrigerator promised FREE BEER TOMORROW. The fourth side of the room was a long glasstopped counter behind which the storekeep sat on a rolling stool.

Sa'p a'i masma, Luis. This simple greeting was the only phrase in Tohono O'odham Rodeo had memorized for the owner of the trading post, Luis Azul Encarnacion.

Rodeo took his usual seat on his usual barstool at the glass-topped counter that served both as display for wares and elbow space for regulars. His dog insinuated himself around his master's legs and took his place in the spot under the bar rubbed shiny by his occupation over the past six years. The storekeep reached his good hand back to lift a cowboy coffee pot from an electric burner ring, poured coffee into a speckled mug and slid it toward the only customer in the store.

Glad you made it back to El Hoyo, Brother Rodeo, Luis said. I always think you'll go away one day and won't come back no more and then I won't have nobody intelligent left to talk to in this hole in the world.

Where's your Locals at? asked Rodeo.

They found a dead man at the Boulder Turn-Out this morning, so I think the Locals they are laying low in their trailers today.

There's a dead man out at my place too, Luis.

This is bad country down here, brother. Luis made this statement without affect. People die here all the time. Especially us Indians. Luis held up a fifth of Patrón Silver.

18

You need something stronger, brother?

Just coffee, Luis. You got any fresh?

That's fresh in front of you from just two days ago.

Luis poured a swig of tequila into his own mug. Rodeo drank his old coffee. The pair shared a silence for a few minutes. As if suspended on strings, bottle flies bounced in the uneven flow of the swamp cooler. The dog snored.

Were you expecting somebody out in The Hole, brother? Some of your Wets coming through?

He's nobody I know, said Rodeo. And he's dressed up in new Walmart gear with no pack or trash bag, no candy bars, no water bottle even. So I don't think he's an Undocumented that came through La Entrada from the Sonora side. He was brought to my place from the American side.

Why would he be? asked Luis.

I don't know, Luis.

Sheriff coming by here?

Ray said he was coming this way after he attended to the dead man at the Boulder Turn-Out, said Rodeo. He rubbed at his eyes. Who found that dead man?

The Bread Man came by here this morning and bought an Olde English so I guess he was having an early Forty at the Turn-

19

Out and when he went to take a piss there was this dead man in the ditch behind the Boulder pretty rotted up. And there was another murder while you was gone on your vacation to the Whites, Luis said. Last week some Hand from Slash/M Rancho found a guy up under the overpass with his head half blowed off.

You keeping track of these on the wall?

Luis had painted a mural on the interior adobe wall behind the counter and labeled the map "AMexica" — West Texas, New Mexico, Arizona, SoCal, Chihuahua, Sinaloa, Sonora. The map was now mostly covered by newspaper clippings dealing with crime or Indian Affairs or Border Issues.

Nobody's interested in nothing I got to say, said Luis.

You talked to Police lately?

Apache Ray, he's high most the time now on oxy from Old Mexico, Luis said. You should run for sheriff, Rodeo. You got some connections with Statewide Law Enforcement and a certain sort of good reputation when you killed Charlie Constance. Ray, he's having heart troubles I heard so he might not last long in his current position anyhow. And Sheriff Sideways likes you so he might even support you if you run.

Ray dropped me from his radar when

Sirena dumped me and he's had heart troubles for thirty years, said Rodeo. You should run for sheriff on the "Free Beer Tomorrow" slogan, Luis.

That slogan does play good with the Locals, Luis said.

The store was quiet then save for the steady thump of the swamp cooler cylinder and the asthmatic mumbling of the overworked refrigerator cooling down sweaty tallboys of malt liquor and broken up sixpacks of "Ice" beer and "Drink Very Cold" wine, quart cartons of whole milk, blocks of margarine and Oaxaca cheese, boiled eggs in plastic sandwich bags. Rodeo picked up his coffee cup and took a polite sip, stared out a dirty plate glass window at a dozen thin beeves across the road testing the dust for edible vegetation.

A late model Crown Victoria Special Edition arrived ten minutes later and Sheriff "Apache" Ray Molina labored out of his green-on-white cruiser and moved toward the store. Though in the face he still looked like the third lead in a classic Western, the senior lawman had ridden a lot of wild horses, eaten a lot of tough steaks and drunk a lot of hard liquor in his day and so was flat in the ass, fat in the belly and his

21

Southwestern patrician nose was webbed with broken veins. He pushed back the Mexican screen door with some care, and nodded at the entire room as if he might have a large audience even though only Luis and Rodeo were in the place.

I sent Deputy Buenjose over to your place to have a look-out, Garnet, the sheriff said. But I doubt he's even got out of his car.

Where's the medical examiner?

Doc Boxer's at the Turn-Out with some State Patrol and CSI from Special Investigations Unit who are down here to help us out while we're shorthanded.

Follow me out to my place then, Ray, said Rodeo. And have a look at the new addition to your troubles.

The sheriff tipped his hat at an invisible crowd and walked back to the county cruiser.

Rodeo pulled out a hip wallet thick with calling cards and IDs and scrimps of paper and old receipts. There was not much fungible in the wallet, but Rodeo thumbed through the various pockets and crevices in the trifold and managed to find an assortment of hideaway money, which he laid out on the countertop. Luis flattened the bills with his good hand.

With the price of gas these days this cash money won't half fill one tank of that old horse you're riding, said the storekeep. Luis tapped the glass countertop under which were assorted valuables, many of them from Rodeo, including several of his smaller firearms and rodeo prize buckles, much of Rodeo's mother's old turquoise and his diamond wedding ring. Pawn Shop is always open, brother.

I need some work, Luis.

I got something for you over on Tuxson Res, your home turf, Luis said. An old woman she wants you to look out about her grandson's killing. Familia name's Rocha.

I don't know her, Rodeo said. She know me?

She knows about you at least.

All the Indians I ever known on the Res are poor, said Rodeo.

You got anything better to do, brother?

Rodeo shook his head. The 800 numbers attached to his listings for "Private Investigator" in the Yellow Pages of Tucson, Casa Grande, Phoenix, Scottsdale, Tempe, Nogales, Los Cruces, Silver City and El Paso had not rung in weeks though his renewal payments for these advertisements were past due.

What's the job, Luis?

23

This kid's death, it's probably just a drive-by and not much you can do about it anyway, Luis said. But it should be a day or two cash wages.

What killed him?

It's a mystery, Luis said. Some cowboy found the Rocha kid up under some brush in the Santa Cruz riverbed near the Res. The kid might have been shot off the Starr Pass Road bridge or just fell off.

Rodeo shook his head.

For ten dollars I can get you a folder together on the whole thing if you'll come by tomorrow? Give you something to do.

Rodeo sat for a moment staring at his hocked objects under the glass top of the counter.

I'll have to owe you the ten for the contact, he said.

I'll put it on your tab, little brother. Luis pulled a pencil stub from behind a cauliflower ear and scribbled on a notepad. You staying out at the Estates then? Even with a dead man in your yard?

They'll move him eventually, said Rodeo.

The sheriff's car horn honked and Rodeo whistled up the dog who stirred himself with great effort.

That old dog he's driving you to financial ruin, Luis said. For ten dollars I could shoot

24

him dead for you. Be painless for you both.

I'll shoot my own dog and save the ten dollars when it comes to that, Rodeo said. He scooped up the dog in two arms and carried him out of the trading post. The sky was clear but for one small, silvery cloud suspended over El Hoyo like a weather balloon. Rodeo established the dog in his regular depression on the bench seat of the pickup. The dog went immediately back to sleep as he always did when he was tired or bored.

Rodeo moved to the double gas tanks of his pickup, uncapped one and plugged in the unleaded nozzle, set the pump on automatic. He added a quart of Dollar Store forty weight to the crankcase of the F-150 without even checking the dipstick. When he looked at the tally on the pump he did not fail to notice that Luis Azul Encarnacion had allowed him twice what he had paid for. He recapped the rear gas tank, hopped in the truck, rubbed his dog's head for luck and aimed his pickup at the county road. It took fifteen minutes to get back to the murder site where vultures and crows feasted on and fought over the corpse dressed in a shirt of blue, white and mostly red.

Rodeo parked his truck well behind a black-on-black Los Jarros County SUV that was parked very near the corpse. Ray Molina parked in front of Rodeo and unfolded out of his county cruiser as if he were measuring the number of moves he made and could not go beyond a certain allowance for the day. Rodeo stayed in his vehicle. The dog stayed where he was in the shotgun seat, whining still about the scent of blood. Deputy Buenjose Contreras did not exit his black 4×4 but talked on his cell phone and smoked a cigarette. There was no crime scene tape in sight nor had the deputy made any attempt to fend off the carrion fowl.

The sheriff drew the big Colt revolver from his holster and fired in the air two times quickly and all of the crows and but one of the vultures flew away. The sheriff aimed and fired in the general direction of the remaining vulture and winged the feasting bird, which started flopping and screeching.

Oh for chrissake, the sheriff said. Even the birds out here in The Hole are stupid as shit.

Ray Molina killed the recalcitrant vulture

with a headshot from ten yards. Rodeo exited his pickup and leaned a hip on a fender.

You can still shoot, Ray.

The lawman acknowledged this compliment with a nod then turned and pointed the revolver at his deputy in the black SUV. He rolled his wrist and the revolver around and then re-holstered his six-shooter as his underling rolled down his car window and stuck his pale brown face into the world.

Raise Doc Boxer, Buenjose, and call State to see if they got somebody extra to help out around here, said the sheriff. And just keep me informed about the incoming from your air-conditioned perch in the county taxpayers' vehicle if that suits you all right?

That suits me just fine, Sheriff.

The deputy rolled up his window and picked up his radio receiver.

It suits my deputy just fine to stay in his vehicle during this situation, the sheriff said. After he damned near parked on top of a murder victim and ruined a crime scene to no end. The sheriff sniffed at the foul scent in the air. And that's the deputy around here who covets my job and wants to be sheriff of Los Jarros County one day. Probably one day soon if he has his way. Sheriff Molina glanced over at Rodeo. What do you think

27

about that, Garnet?

I think good help's hard to find, Ray.

I think that's what Jesus said at Gethsemane, the sheriff said. He surveyed the scene again and shook his head. I can see these asshole victims getting killed on the paved roads around here, he said. That would make some sense to me. But there's not any good reason for a dressed-up man like this to be out here on a dirt road in The Hole, Garnet. You're the only one ever crazy enough to live out here. The Apaches gave this place up without a fight, the Spanish gave it up without a fight, Mexicans don't want it, Anglos wouldn't have it when it was free land grant and even dumbass Snowbirds from Canadia won't move down here with three hundred and sixty-six days of sunshine a year.

You know your Bible and local history, Ray.

The sheriff looked at the ground as if it were moving under him.

You all right, Ray?

I'm fine, said the sheriff. Old. Tired.

It happens to the best of them, Ray.

You never expect it to happen to you, the sheriff said. Ray Molina rubbed the back of his creased neck as he surveyed the scene again. Did you hear anything when this happened, Garnet? Any piercing screams in the night or random gunfire or like that?

I just got back from my yearly vacation in the Whites, Rodeo said.

What have you got yourself into this time, Garnet?

You know I don't answer trick questions, Ray.

I know you don't, said the sheriff. And that's a sure sign of your intelligence.

The sheriff backed off from the cruiser, made a dramatic turn all around then stared for a while at the dead man.

Well, if he didn't walk out here then it looks to me like your little man in the U S of A flag shirt was in some vehicle, and if he was in some vehicle with people who might want to kill him he probably wanted out of that vehicle. The sheriff assayed the surrounding area again. And he'd only have the one way to go because on the northside of this so-called Elm Street of yours there's just a hell's deep arroyo to fall to death in, so he heads south, trying to get off the road and get to some cover. But your little man wasn't fast enough to get to cover and got just about exactly as far as he is before he was dropped with some pretty goddamned large buckshot. Ten gauge or twelve?

That seems about right, Rodeo said.

Except he's not my little man because I got nothing to do with him.

The sheriff lifted his nose to the stench and sniffed again. Well, whoever's he is he's ripe, idn't he?

The dog smelled him from a quarter mile away, said Rodeo.

You got any ideas about this rompecabeza? Or does your dog?

Like you say, it's a puzzler, Ray. But I will say that this man got here after I left for the Whites and before I got back from the Whites, so he'd be killed sometimes this past week.

The sheriff walked over to the corpse and crouched with obvious pain to examine what was left of the dead man. He raised his voice as he spoke over his shoulder.

So, who is this little fella, Garnet? asked the sheriff. You know most of the hands and half the stock in Los Jarros, don't you?

That's probably about the right percentages, Ray. But I don't know this one.

Looks sorta like an Indian but he's not an Apache or Pie Face from around here. He's not one of your Pascua Yaqui, is he?

No. He doesn't look like one of my tribe, said Rodeo. He's a Mexican Indio, would be my guess.

He's a Wet then, said the sheriff. But I

can't see one of your Illegals walking across Sonora and keeping his new clothes clean. The sheriff stood and stared down at the dead man. Jeans have still got a Walmart sale tag on them, don't they.

Rodeo nodded and adjusted his lean against the truck so his sore back absorbed some of the heat stored there.

The sheriff glanced around again. Why not just drag him back across the road and dump him into the arroyo and let this country work him down to bones with nobody the wiser?

Maybe somebody wanted him found, said Rodeo.

Goddammit. Less than five hundred murders in all the state last year, said the sheriff. And now we might have almost a handful of Unsolveds in the last few weeks just here in Los Jarros.

Buenjose Contreras honked the horn and rolled down the window of his SUV.

State Highway says they'll send a grunt from Traffic over here for crime scene perimeter if you want, Sheriff, and then SIU can get an evidence van over here but not for two or three hours, said the deputy. Medical Examiner is getting around to getting out here asap as soon as possible too, but Doc Boxer and them are all wrapping

31

up at the Boulder Turn-Out just now so . . .

Hell, it'll be dark before any of them gets here, said the sheriff.

Nothing I can do about that, Sheriff.

Nothing you can do about anything, Buenjose, said the sheriff.

The deputy rolled up his window and the sheriff tipped his cattleman's to block the westering sun and looked at Rodeo's casita in the near distance.

You say your house was locked or unlocked when you got back home here, Garnet?

I didn't say, Ray. I hadn't even been over there yet.

Anybody else got a key to your house?

Luis does. My lawyer had a key to the storage shed but I changed that lock . . . Rodeo hesitated.

And Sirena Rae? Did my daughter ever get a house key to your place out here when y'all were living together in Tucson?

I never gave her one . . .

Rodeo quit talking.

But you wouldn't put it past Sirena to lift one and make a copy?

No, I wouldn't, Ray, said Rodeo.

I wish that girl had just stayed in school, said the sheriff. He took in and let out a big breath of hot air. She had a full free ride academic scholarship at Arizona State, you know. The ones reserved for genius level. But she was too damned lazy to even go to her classes.

I know about her, Ray, said Rodeo.

Water seeks its own level, doesn't it?

Usually at the lowest point, Ray. Rodeo changed the subject.

Why would anybody in particular want in my place anyway? he asked. Even with keys to the one door you'd only be in a old house full of worthless shit except for the gun safe.

Which is uncrackable, right? asked the sheriff.

My safe's rated T-30 but there's nothing an intelligent person can't do with enough time and the right tools, Ray, you know that. He thought for a moment. But no Law Enforcement, not you or your deputies or State or Federal ever comes around here. Not even the watchdog vigilantes ever comes to The Hole, so anybody could operate out here at their leisure when I'm on my yearly vacation if they had a mind to.

You got all your guns in that safe?

I got guns all over the place, Rodeo said.

That's another sure sign of your intelligence, Garnet.

What're you looking for, Ray?

At this point I'm looking for anything, the

sheriff said. Because I seriously cannot make hide nor hair out of the killings around here in Los Jarros lately. Mostly all killed by shotgun and all left near roads not dragged out into this desert. He looked around at the barren landscape and shook his head. They're not drug hits, I don't think. And they're not relative-murders. All's I can figure is that they're all Indians of one type or another that are getting killed. But Conquistadors and Cavalry are all gone now, so who'd want to kill Indians just to kill Indians these days?

I don't know, Ray.

All right then, said the sheriff. Just sit in your truck till the Medical Examiner and Special Investigations and State Highway Patrol . . . and God knows who-all else in Law Enforcement get out here. Then we'll see what in hell everybody in the world has to say about this here.

It's getting late, Ray. I want to go home.

Humor me, Garnet.

Rodeo reentered his pickup, leaned his head back on the bench seat, laid a hand on his agitated dog and within a couple of minutes both the man and his dog were asleep.

The Arizona Department of Public Safety

Highway Patrol "grunt" arrived in a blue-on-white Ford Crown Victoria with no siren on but bubble lights swirling red and blue. The AZDPS cruiser parked behind Rodeo's truck. The single patrolman got out, put on his stiff Statie hat and walked to the Sheriff. He jerked a thumb at the corpse.

Looks like one dead man and one dead vulture, Sheriff Molina. Was it a shootout?

The sheriff ignored the joke.

Where's the CSI van at, Ted?

The Special Investigations Unit is still on scene at what you all call the Boulder Turn-Out, said the policeman. I came to secure this scene but I see you already got your Number One Lady Detective on the job. The state trooper inclined his flat-brimmed hat at the County 4×4 where Deputy Buenjose Contreras was talking into his private cell phone and lighting a fresh cigarette. You're not in a big hurry with this investigation, Sheriff Molina?

He'll keep, the sheriff said.

It's your county, Sheriff, said the trooper.

It is that. The old lawman scratched his chest as if his heart itched. For better and for worse.

Rodeo stepped out of his truck and walked over to Sheriff Molina and the AZDPS cop.

Do I know you from somewhere? the

35

patrolman asked.

I don't know who you know or where you been, Officer, said Rodeo. So I couldn't say.

The sheriff grunted. You two jokers ought to get along just famous, he said. This is Ted Anderton. The sheriff looked at the state trooper and then nodded toward Rodeo. And this is the homeowner near the scene of the crime as it were, name of Rodeo Grace Garnet.

Neither man attempted to shake hands.

Do you work in this area, sir? The policeman's voice was artificially polite. His stare at Rodeo also verged on the impolite.

Garnet here is a famous private eye, Ted. You know the drill. Citizen goes online, takes a test or two and gets a bounty hunter license, buys some handcuffs, lots of guns and Tasers and a flak jacket then starts calling himself a cop —

You're the private investigator who beat Charles Constance to death several years ago. The state trooper interrupted the sheriff and stared at Rodeo.

Garnet's also the man who found Charlie Constance out when nobody else in Law Enforcement could, including your own Arizona Special Investigations Unit and the entirety of the USA FBI, said Sheriff Molina. And so some down here in this county consider what Garnet did to Charlie Constance a public service. The sheriff moved half a step closer to standing between the Statie and the PI. But however you see it, since no charges were ever filed against Garnet the Constance Case is dry water under a old bridge we don't speak of anymore around here. The sheriff squinted at the state patrolman. If that suits you, Ted.

The Statie turned to look at the corpse near the gates.

Can you identify this deceased, Mr. Garnet, or do you have knowledge of the other recent murder victims in the area?

Who's that, Officer? asked Rodeo.

One, the recent victim found under the interstate overpass. Two, the vic at what you local people call the Boulder Turn-Out on Agua Seco Road. There was also a third death, down in Sells a few weeks ago, a young man shot with an unidentified .38. Plus this vic makes four. All these murders within the last few weeks are within the boundary of Los Jarros County. That's an inordinate number of murders for such a small, isolated area and in such a compressed time span.

That kid down in Sells that was gutshot near the Dairy Queen, he was from up at Lake Havasu, Ted, said the sheriff. You know how shorthanded we are in Los Jarros but I did my diligence and sent Pal Real up there to the Lake to interview the vic's people.

Did Deputy Real make any pertinent discoveries?

No he did not, said the sheriff. That victim was just a regular kid for nowadays. Had some little job at a convenience store and spent the rest of his day playing those video games they play and jacking off to porno, Pal Real said.

What was that vic doing in this area? asked the state trooper.

Kid had some cousins on South Tohona O'odham Res and was down here in our country for a little powwow somebody had going on near the border, said the sheriff. His cousins and kin in Los Jarros and up at the Lake were all clean too, except for DUIs of course. They all said the kid was just going out for a walk and to have a smoke, probably some reefer he was smoking, and he never came back. The sheriff wiped a hand over his face. They found the kid a few hours later, bled out in the barditch not far from the Dairy Queen. But with no computer matches on the slug in his guts and with no way to separate tire tracks and with no witnesses, no motive, no gang connections and nothing on the kid we got nada but drive-by, culprit or culprits unknown. Apache Ray jerked his head toward the nearest dead man. But it's sure not a .38 gutshot on this one here.

Do you think this vic on Mr. Garnet's property is an Undocumented Alien? The trooper pointed his thumb again at the dead man in the shadow of the Vista Montana Estates sign.

You might ask Garnet that one, Ted, said Sheriff Molina. He puts water and supplies all over The Hole all the way up to La Entrada on the top of the mountain because he says he don't like people dying in his own backyard.

And yet here is one, said the trooper. A dead man practically in Mr. Garnet's backyard.

So he is, said the sheriff.

This crime scene is not on my property, said Rodeo. My property doesn't start until past these gates here.

You mind if I have a look at the deceased, Sheriff? asked the Statie.

Have a gander, Ted. It's still a free country for Police.

Officer Anderton removed a squeeze tube of Mentholatum from his shirt pocket and spread a smear under each nostril then moved around the corpse. He pointed at an object just under the right thigh of the dead man.

You recognize this, Sheriff? he asked.

The sheriff moved next to the Statie and looked carefully then shook his head.

Looks like a wing of something, said the sheriff. Wood? Or is it metal?

Is it yours, Mr. Garnet? Ted Anderton asked. Something that could have been in your yard or in your house or could have flown out of the back of your vehicle? An angel wing perhaps from a religious icon? the state policeman asked.

I'm not religious to speak of, said Rodeo. And Apache Ray's the only icon we got around here.

Anderton stooped near a teddy bear cactus beside the body and touched his gloved fingertip to a small bit of blue plastic.

What you got there, Ted? asked the sheriff.

Butcher's apron maybe? Anybody doing a slaughter around here lately?

They're always killing goats for the Mexican meat markets over at Slash/M, said the sheriff.

You know anybody at the Miller Ranch, Sheriff Molina?

There's not many people in this little county so I pretty much know everybody there is to know, Ted. That's why I'm still sheriff.

We'll need to bag this as evidence. Anderton stood and put his hands on his hips. Because if there's blood other than human or alongside human on this plastic that might be interesting.

It might be, Ted, said the sheriff. It's always funny to me what you procedural types find interesting.

I want to get to the house and get my dog fed and my AC turned on so we can sleep tonight, Rodeo said. So unless y'all need my services further or want to arrest me I'd care to be on my way now, if that's all right?

I'm just a traffic cop, said Anderton. Here to stretch out some yellow tape and wait for the Big Boys from the Special Investigations Unit.

Just come on by the courthouse tomorrow, Garnet, and make your statement to Pal Real, said the sheriff. If my other deputy even shows up to work, that is.

You gonna be in the office tomorrow, Ray?

If I'm feeling better I will be. Mercedes might be bringing some chicken and fry bread for lunch I heard, the sheriff said. I'll tell her to save some for you either way, so ask after it.

All right, Ray. Rodeo nodded at Ted

Anderton. The state cop nodded back and watched Rodeo leave.

Rodeo and his dog rode the quarter mile to the casita and parked next to the "front" door on the side of the house. Rodeo got out and began unlocking the stainless steel gear box in the truck bed to get to more of his weaponry. The toolbox was standard heavy duty from Sears but was welded onto the bed of the truck and protected by heavy gauge Master locks defended in pig-iron cages. Rodeo raised the box lid on well-oiled hinges and pulled a modified 10-gauge Browning pump loaded with rubber buck-shot from a pile-lined nylon case bolted to the cabside of the storage box. He also extracted from the truck lockbox his compact defense pistol, an aluminum frame NightHawk .45 and slid its nylon clip holster onto the back right side of his tooled leather belt. He shut down the gear box and relocked it, jacked a 10-gauge shell into the chamber of his abbreviated shotgun, slung his Leica binoculars around his neck and began his reconnaissance.

He walked around the house. Several new rabbit corpses were curing in the dirt at the bottom of the dry swimming pool alongside the turquoise remnants of the fiberglass diving board and a couple of deflated basketballs. The basketball goal he had set up on the shuffleboard court was still leaning sideways where his former girlfriend, Sirena Rae Molina, had plowed one of her sheriff daddy's vehicles into it and the plywood backboard was strafed with shotgun pellets where she had unloaded a double barrel.

Rodeo unlocked the storage shed, filled his generator with gasoline from a fifty-five-gallon pump drum, removed the air filter, cleaned and replaced it and then primed and started the antique Coleman. He left the barn doors of the shed open to allow ventilation and fetched the ladder from the hooks on the side of the shed, extended the aluminum ladder up a wall of his casita and climbed to the top. The game camera affixed to the raised edge of the flat roof of the casita seemed in order and fully charged by the solar cell. The weatherproof digital camera aimed at his side yard was typically used to record the activity of game animals around a feeding site or salt lick so that guides could gauge the regularity and type of animal activity in a very circumscribed but representative area in order to plan their hunts with intelligence but, along with a motion-activated spotlight directed at the side yard, the camera constituted Rodeo's poor man's version of security surveillance. The camera recorded digital images that were fed through a cable strung from the roof into a kitchen cabinet, where they were stored on a compact hard drive.

Rodeo leaned over the four-foot-high adobe wall that ringed the rooftop and looked down at the kitchen garden, which was mostly used to grow ingredients for Pico de Gallo — tomatoes, carrots, onions, cilantro, chives, peppers. He had planted it for Sirena when she had been in an "organic foodie" phase and when he had decided to leave her, for a while or forever, the woman had plowed through the little garden in one of her father's biggest 4×4s. Rodeo had replanted in the spring, though he did not much tend his garden other than to sit on his roof and shoot rabbits away from it. Monsoon season officially started on June 15 and ran until September 30 and since tanked-in water was so expensive, the garden lived or died according to the weather. According to weather reports it hadn't rained in El Hoyo during the last week, so the garden should have been nearly dead. Yet the garden seemed relatively lush. The gauge on the gravity-powered water tank read significantly lower than it should have but there were no leaks in the tank. He wondered who had come to his place and watered his garden while he was gone.

Rodeo switched his Leica binoculars to 10× magnification and glassed the golf course which remained mostly as the original owners had laid it out, with fairways still only defined by survey stakes in the dirt and "greens" made of flat-topped mounds of oil-soaked sand with plastic pickle buckets Rodeo had buried in them to serve as holes. When he played golf Rodeo hit balls off a driving range mat attached to the tailgate of his truck, using the pickup as both golf cart and fairway.

When Rodeo noticed a reflection flare from near the entrance to the Estates, he adjusted the Leicas and used the laser range finder to spot the state trooper who was glassing him through his own binoculars from the gate. Rodeo lowered himself gingerly down the ladder.

The building that was Rodeo's home had only been the on-site sales office of Vista Montana Development Corporation and so was never intended to be a residence. Though it had no regular plumbing or a septic tank, the rectangular adobe had a room in the middle with a dining area and a kitchenette and a bathroom in which there was a seldom-used portable chemical toilet and a rusty tin shower stall that was gravity-fed water from the rooftop tank. The gray water from the sink and shower drained directly into the garden, the chem toilet was dumped at the trailer park Luis operated behind Twins Arrows Trading Post. Another room of the small house served as sleeping quarters for the man and his dog and the third housed a mechanic's bench and shell-loading equipment, gun safe, punching bags, weights, saddles, tack and gear and all the library books and LPs Rodeo's mother had stolen over the years from libraries. The only door and the several windows of the casita were protected by Mexican screens since the developers had feared vandals and thieves. But not even vandals and thieves had ever been interested in Vista Montana Estates.

Rodeo removed the rest of his travel guns and gear from the truck lockbox and took them to his house and replaced them in his gun safe. He turned on the swamp cooler in the work room and the AC window unit in his bedroom and then investigated the house thoroughly. When he found nothing amiss he swept the floors and wiped down all the surfaces inside the house, fed and watered the dog, locked his door, took a short, tepid shower, re-dressed in an old sweat suit and heated a can of SpaghettiOs mixed with a can of ranch beans. He percolated a fresh pot of coffee, then removed the compact hard drive from the cupboard, plugged it into his laptop and examined the week's worth of images from the game camera as he ate his dinner and drank his coffee.

Rodeo deleted through dozens of shots of cottontails and jack-rabbits and coyote packs until he stopped on an image captured two days into his vacation at 23:09 hours, a single shot of one oversized tire and then one shot of a boot and jeans' leg. It was only one cowboy boot in a country full of cowboys, but he saved it, then shut down his computer, checked his window screens and door locks and peered under his bed and in the several small closets of his casita. He had a spoonful of Eagle Brand, brushed his teeth at the kitchen sink, then he carried the sleeping dog into the bedroom and placed him on the pile of blankets near the foot of the cot. He had replaced all his armament and ordnance in the gun safe but for his father's old revolver. He spun the load in the .38 S&W Special and placed it atop his mother's Bible on the bedside table, stripped naked, crawled under a thin sheet, flipped his pillow to the cool side and within minutes was asleep.

At five the next morning Rodeo woke, dressed, splashed water on his face and had his first cup of coffee. He filled two recycled plastic jugs with tank water and dripped enough Clorox into the jugs to keep the water potable for at least a week. All he could afford to give away with the water was a bag of Dateland dates, a bag of marzipan, a few hard apples, an empty garbage bag and half a roll of duct tape. He packed these provisions into his daddy's old Vietnam-era rucksack then slung his holstered snake gun on the right side of his belt. Then the man and his dog hiked slowly but steadily until they achieved their destination just as the day was heating up.

La Entrada was a shallow cave in a natural gap between two unnamed peaks of the Theatine mountain range of southern Arizona. The cave had a south-facing vista and on a clear day Mexico was visible from the vantage. The surrounding sky billowed like an overwashed blue bedsheet on a clothesline suddenly snapped belly up by a gust of wind and still solid blue in the middle but faded white and gone ragged along the edges where it was more in contact with the dirt of the world.

This was one of the emptiest places in the world but there was still a lot to look at.

Rodeo stood on the rim of this world for a few minutes just staring into desert space with his bare eyes. Then he glassed a far ways into the Sonoran Desert, scanning with his binoculars for human movement or the trash bags and empty jugs, clothing and other discards that would mark the comings or goings of human beings. When his eyes wearied he moved back into the shade of the cave and ascertained what had been taken from the Army surplus ammo boxes — a water jug, a garbage bag and the hard apples. He left what little he could afford to give and headed back down the mountain.

Halfway down the steep trail the dog whined and Rodeo stopped and doffed his hat, wiped sweat off the headband with two fingers then licked that sweat off his fingers. He replaced his battered straw and squinted toward the sun, which seemed moving that day fast and with destructive purpose as if trying to get on top of Arizona Sonora and do the most damage it could as soon as it could. The temperature would reach over one hundred and twenty degrees Fahrenheit on the basin floor by afternoon, which would be hot enough to kill a weak man.

The dog circled three times and then assumed his resting position with his chin on his paws.

So that's it, Rodeo said. That's the exact spot idn't it.

The dog raised his head toward the sound of his man's voice. The dog's eyes were cloudwhite with cataracts.

Lay down then, the man said. I don't care what you do.

The dog settled and the man twisted off his GI rucksack. His khaki shirt was soaked down the back in a wide wedge where the pack had been and in dark stripes down his chest where the shoulder straps had hung and under his arms to the elbow where his shirtsleeves were rolled up. His Wranglers were soaked through at the crotch and at the backs of his knees. He used the edge of a walking boot to smooth level a spot on the faint sidecut in the mountain then hitched up his jeans and squatted on his bootheels. The dog yawned.

What I want to know is how you pick the exact right spot to lay down on every time? Rodeo asked.

The dog whined his answer as the man drizzled water from a blanket-sided canteen into his cupped hand and pressed it against the dog's dry muzzle. The dog lapped the water until he was licking the sweat off the man's skin. The man turned his hand over so the dog could lick more salt then withdrew a piece of fry bread from the army pack and unwrapped it from wax paper. The paper was ripped out of his hands by a gust of wind and kited out over the precipitous yawn of canyon below them called The Hole. Rodeo tore off a piece of bread for himself and chewed it slowly while watching the wax paper sail up and down on thermal drafts. He tore off a bigger piece of bread and fed it to the dog, drank from the canteen and then poured a little more water into his hand for the dog. He capped the canteen and rubbed the dog's head. The spot where he rubbed was almost bald to the dog's skullbone.

Whole world to lay down on and you circle around like it's one place better than any other, Rodeo said. For fifteen years you been thinking picking a spot to lay down on is some great and unusual talent you got on me, don't you? The man said this like it was part of a longstanding and ongoing argument between the pair. The dog barked feebly his side of the argument. But you are right per usual. This is a good spot, said

Rodeo. Nice sight lines.

The man extracted his binoculars from his pack and just held them for a moment near his chest like he was divining. Rodeo was looking for humans walking through El Hoyo and to the roads that would lead to the interstate, but Rodeo did not know exactly where to look because the immigrants often did not know where to go. Even with official maps and electronic and federal and state and county backup nobody on government salary would venture into The Hole except on forced overtime much less vigilantes come there on their own free time. Even drone planes, public and private, seemed repelled by the local airspace, got disoriented by the heat, lost their bearings in this isolation and often simply drifted up and down in airspace until they crashed. Still, poor people entered the USA through The Hole because it was the hardest place to get caught in.

And Rodeo had been informed lately that a small group of Undocumented Aliens were soon due through La Entrada to meet their Americanside coyote and get trucked out on the nearby interstate to parts unknown around the USA. That was why the man and his dog had risen before the sun to set supplies in the shallow cave in the landmark gap in the mountains. The day had turned from tolerable to hot. Anyone walking in that heat would suffer, so Rodeo was glad to see that no one obvious traversed the steepsided valley.

To reorient himself Rodeo looked toward his own property. A vehicular dust cloud moved from Agua Seco Road down Elm Street and toward his homeplace. Rodeo watched the dark SUV until it stopped abruptly near his isolated casita. The dust the vehicle had raised swirled over it and rolled past the casita to dive into the empty swimming pool. Only after the dust had fully settled did the driver exit the vehicle.

Rodeo refocused his Leicas. The visitor was dressed in khaki slacks and a dark T-shirt, wore Aviator sunglasses under a gimme cap. The visitor walked to the house and knocked, waited and then peered through the available windows, then went to Rodeo's truck and looked into the cab and into the bed, tested the locks on the lockbox. He then walked the ten yards to the storage shed and disappeared into that space for several minutes then exited the shed and continued a slow circuit around the house until he stopped again at the side door of the casita where a crooked REAL ESTATE sign still hung.

When Rodeo shifted his position his binocular lens flared and the visitor stopped and looked up the hill, returned to his SUV, leaned past the open door, pulled out his own pair of binoculars and aimed them at Rodeo. When the driver waved his gimme cap broadly from side to side, Rodeo recognized State Highway Trooper Ted Anderton and walked down the hill until he stopped several yards from Anderson's SUV.

This is not official business, Mr. Garnet, the state cop said. It's my day off from Traffic and I was just touring around the area.

Why?

The cop thought for a moment. I like the desert. This simple statement he delivered as if profound.

Rodeo turned away from the cop and waited for a minute for his dog to catch up to him, bent and scratched the dog's ears.

You are a real trooper, aren't you, boy? Rodeo asked.

Yessir.

I was talking to the dog, Mr. Anderton.

Rodeo stood. His dog whined. Rodeo turned to the state policeman. You running a rogue investigation, Mr. Anderton? Rodeo asked. That what you're really doing out here in the middle of noplace? You think

Sheriff Molina's not doing something he ought to be doing?

I didn't say anything against Sheriff Molina, said Anderton.

You here for some specific reason then?

I want you to take a look at something, Mr. Garnet. The cop reached into his vehicle and pulled a manila folder from the dash.

Rodeo opened the screen door of his casita and followed his dog inside and left the door open for the state trooper. The cop entered the little house and moved around the central room, peering where he could until Rodeo motioned him into a straight-backed chair at the table. Rodeo put fresh water in the dog's bowl and tipped what was left of a twenty-pound bag of generic dog food in the dog's dish. The dog sniffed at the powdery food but didn't eat any of it, only lapped wearily at the bowlwater and then looked up at Rodeo and whined. Rodeo pulled a fifth of Green Label Jack Daniel's from a cabinet and tipped a taste of the light liquor into the dog's water then recapped the bottle and put it away without offering it around.

You give your dog liquor? asked Anderton.

They say it's bad to drink alone, Rodeo said.

The dog drank for a while then walked under the kitchen table, circled three times, lay down and went almost immediately to sleep on the floor. Rodeo lit a propane burner with a wood match and watched the cowboy coffee pot. He slid the .357 magnum out of the leather holster on his belt and placed it on the countertop.

Have there been any rubberneckers around the vicinity this morning, Mr. Garnet? Anderton asked. Has anyone driven out to view the murder scene by your gate? Spectators of the crime scene?

Just you, Mr. Anderton. Coffee?

I have water in my vehicle, Anderton said.

The AZDPS cop opened the folder and extracted a single sheet of color photocopy paper on which was a set of photographs. He stood and moved forward to place the set of images on the kitchen table.

Can you identify any of the objects pictured here, sir?

Why are you asking?

I understand your caution, Mr. Garnet. But this is not part of any official inquiry.

That makes it less likely not more likely that I'll discuss this evidence, said Rodeo. If this is crime scene evidence you're showing me, Mr. Anderton?

Anderton tapped one of the photocopied images with a buffed fingertip. This is the object we discovered under the body of the man who was murdered near your property line, the cop said. You'll remember Sheriff Molina was asking whether it was wood or metal. Actually it's ironwood. Tourist trinkets are made of this material and sold by the Seri Indians, who traditionally inhabit areas around Kino Bay on the Sea of Cortez in Mexico. Seri are typically diminutive people, as was the vic by your gates.

Rodeo drank his coffee. The traffic cop tapped the page again.

This is a comb, he said. Probably something the Navajo would use making wool. The policeman pointed at another image. And this is a fragment of a water jar, probably an antique one. Virtually all Native American tribes have made water jars over the centuries, so it would take an expert to identify the specific mud used in order to verify the production site. He touched another image. And then this one is a small gourd rattle. Again, a wide variety of Native American tribes have and use these for ceremonial purposes like the sweat lodge ceremony or traditional dances, though mostly they are produced for the tourist trade currently.

Were these objects found at the current murder scenes in Los Jarros? asked Rodeo.

I can't say, said the policeman. I was just wondering if you had any ideas, Mr. Garnet, about any of these artifacts? Do any of them seem familiar to you?

Why are you bothering me with this? Rodeo asked.

The cop slid the photocopy back into the manila folder.

This is off the record, Mr. Garnet. But sometimes people who apprehend and . . . The policeman hesitated. Prosecute violent offenders are themselves traumatized by that violence and it . . . Their violent actions, even if done for good and even legal causes, as in war or law enforcement, may affect them . . .

Rodeo interrupted. Affect them how?

In negative psychological ways. The policeman delivered this education with due seriousness but he was sweating under his tan.

What's your point, Mr. Anderton?

On occasion men who are forced to perform violent acts as part of their job, say like law enforcement officers or soldiers, turn to violence themselves as some sort of compensatory psychological mechanism, said Anderton. If you understand what I mean?

You got a degree in criminal psychology or something? asked Rodeo.

No, sir. But my associate's degree is in criminal justice.

So I guess you have studied up on the Constance Case I was involved in, Officer Anderton? So you know about how I apprehended Charlie Constance and what I did to him and what the case was against him?

Yes, the cop said. And I admire your detection work on that case, sir. But I also know that no one was ever certain how many vics Charles Constance murdered or whether he had an accomplice or not and once you . . . killed Mr. Constance . . . whether justified or not . . . such information could probably never be fully known. The state cop wiped sweat from his upper lip with the back of his hand. What you did to Mr. Constance egregiously breached standard protocol for apprehending criminals.

Rodeo drank coffee and stared at the AZDPS cop.

So you think because I found and "prosecuted" a serial killer three years ago that I have now, three years later, taken to acting out and serial-killing on my own just to blow off some bad psychological steam, Mr. Anderton? Or else you think that I was Charlie's accomplice?

The cop was very still.

If that's your theory about these recent murders in Los Jarros, it's pretty weak, Officer Anderton.

The trooper eyed the revolver beside the coffee pot.

I don't have a theory at the moment, Mr. Garnet. I am just trying to analyze the pattern of this most recent series of murders in Los Jarros County. But be assured sir, that I'll be in touch with you if I construct a plausible theory. The cop stood and backed toward the door of the casita, his eyes on the gun on the kitchen countertop. And I apologize for the imposition if that's how you interpret my visit here today, sir. Thanks so much for your time, Mr. Garnet.

The Statie left the house and drove off in a new cloud of dust.

Rodeo held open the door of Twin Arrows Trading Post and followed his dog inside the store and to the bar. Luis reached back and poured a cup of coffee from the blue speckled pot into a rusty tin cup and slid it down the countertop. Under the glass-topped counter a slightly new variety of human artifacts from priceless to worthless were now displayed.

Free coffee today, brother. Free beer tomorrow.

Rodeo ignored the coffee as he took his usual seat.

A Highway Patrol name of Ted Anderton came by my house just a while ago to show me some photocopied pictures of some artifacts, Luis. Rodeo described the objects as thoroughly as he could. You deal in Indian artifacts, legal and illegal, so what can you tell me?

Well, the rattle that might be from anywhere in Indian Country, Luis said. Who knows which tribe? You go to sweat lodge anywhere these days and every drunk in the tent has got a sad story and a goddamned rattle of some kind. Pots a lot of us got too. Somebody at the Pottery Center over at the University would have to tell by the type of mud, you know, where something like that comes from. The comb, that's probably a wool comb from the Dine, the sheep people. An ironwood carving would be from the Seri. That's them down at Kino Bay and that's about the last place that pueblo are. Back in the day the Seri they fished from little boats made out of sticks and ate turtle eggs and cactus so they was a pretty backwards bunch, but they gave the Spaniards a hard time and wouldn't go Catholic and you got to hand it to people who won't get civilized without a fight. Like your Yaqui, right, brother? They never went down on the Spanish either.

My tribe was too little for the Spanish to bother with, Luis.

Sometimes little is better, Rodeo.

You would know about that better than me, Luis.

I'm not the one living alone, little brother.

You know this kid from State Barracks, Luis? asked Rodeo. Ted Anderton?

I seen him a few times, the storekeep said. He camps out with his radar gun near the overpass and picks up drunk Indians when they try to drive onto the interstate. He comes in here sometimes but don't ever buy nothing but Doublemint and bottled water. I think he's one of them Church People. The blond ones.

Mormons?

Yeah. I think this Anderton he's a Mormon guy, Luis said. That's why he can't buy nothing good in here. His church they would excommunicate him if he did.

What's he want with me?

He's a badge-and-haircut, brother, so

maybe he's trying to break some case so he can get out of Traffic? Maybe he's ambitious that way like they all are, brother. All them Anglos are ambitious. Luis paused. He asked me about what you did to Charlie Constance back in the day.

What did you tell him?

I told him to read the papers like everybody else.

Rodeo looked at the AMexica News Wall.

Was there anything in any of the newspapers about Native American artifacts found at any of these recent crime scenes in Los Jarros, Luis?

Not that I read of. So maybe you just learned something, brother. You know Police they always hold some things back, some evidence nobody would know about but the killer. They're sneaky like that.

Rodeo nodded. You got the folder ready for my job on the Res?

Luis slid a manila folder down the counter. The folder contained newspaper clippings and hardcopies of downloads from the Internet which concerned the death of Samuel Esau Rocha, aged nineteen of Tucson, Arizona.

Is this dead kid one of your relations, Luis?

You know Second Wife Silk Snowball she's related to half the Indians in southern

Arizona someway, the storekeep said. And then my Encarnacion tribe they got Indian-Mexican connections from Texas to California. But this Katherine Rocha woman, I don't think she's Apache or Tohono O'odham. I think she's registered Pascua Yaqui like you so you can be tribal on this and give her a good rate, but I heard that this old woman, she's a piece of work and tight as Dick's hatband so don't take no checks from her.

Thanks for the referral, Luis. I owe you ten dollars.

Story of my life with you, the storekeep said.

Rodeo lingered for several minutes saying nothing. Luis out-waited him.

You seen Sirena Rae lately? Rodeo asked.

Luis pulled a Bull Durham pouch and papers from his faded and stained shirt pocket and rolled a cigarette with his weird assortment of fingers, licked it shut, lit it and put the lighter on the counter. He stared at the Marines' insignia on one side of the brass then turned the lighter over and read silently the inscription there — WHEN HE DIES I KNOW THIS MARINE IS GOING TO HEAVEN BECAUSE HE HAS ALREADY BEEN TO HELL. Luis took a long drag and sighed out smoke.

Sirena Rae she came by here a few times when you was gone up to the Whites, Luis said. She was dressed like a Hand and driving that big black 4-by from her daddy's rancho.

What did she have to say for herself? Rodeo asked this almost reluctantly.

Said she'd cleaned up. Said she'd quit stripping for good. Said rehab had changed her life. Said she'd hooked up with somebody in Tuxson for a while.

Who?

Some Anglo professor type from California with family money she said. But that didn't work out.

Rodeo kept his face neutral.

How did she seem?

Clean and sober, said Luis. But otherwise same's usual. Luis smoked for a minute and Rodeo stared at the junk under the countertop. Just remember, brother, that as dangerous as she is drunk, that woman she's more dangerous when her head is clear.

Rodeo nodded.

Stay away from the Sirenas of this world and get you a plain, fat woman who thinks a hot dog and popcorn at Walmart's is a dinner date. That's my counsel, said Luis. Sirena she's messed up more good men around here than Marine Corps recruiters.

And she tried to kill your dog. A man shouldn't forget who tries to kill his dog.

Thanks for the sage counsel, Luis.

The advice around here is like the coffee, brother.

Rodeo left Twin Arrows and drove to the small town of Jarros, Arizona, stopped at the Records Office at the Los Jarros County Courthouse to make a partial payment on his outstanding land taxes, then went to County Jail to give his account of the discovery of the dead man near his property. Despite his greasy looks and a reputation as a lounge lizard, Deputy Raul "Pal" Real was efficient and capable and processed Rodeo's statement in less than ten minutes.

Ray coming in today, Raul? Rodeo asked.

Not that I know of, pal. What you want with Sheriff?

Just wondered what anybody knows about anything.

Your man was dead probably about five days from yesterday, pal. Autopsy on him will take some days more since our pre-emminent Medical Examiner Doctor Boxer has got some backlog of unnecessarily deceased just recently.

I was on vacation in the White Mountains for the whole of last week, said Rodeo. And he's not "my man."

Not that I asked you where you were, pal. The deputy grinned. But I already did call up to Show Low and got you resided in Kiva Inn on Deuce of Clubs Road most of that week. Motel clerk up there said you was some drunk up there too, pal. What's with that?

Relatives.

You know what they say, pal. Everything's relatives.

They get anything off that piece of blue plastic they found on the scene?

Butcher's apron. Victim's blood was all that was on it though.

Sheriff leave anything for me? Rodeo asked.

Nope. Came by this morning and then left but didn't mention you at all, pal. Are y'all dating or something?

Rodeo ignored the dig. Where was Ray headed? he asked.

Going to a job fair in Scottsdale to try and recruit us some new hands. The deputy shook his head dramatically. But even an infamous used car salesman like Apache Ray Molina ain't gonna have no luck with that pitch since working for Los Jarros County Sheriff's just too hard a job for too low a pay these days like everybody knows.

67

Sometimes it doesn't pay to be on the side of the Law, Pal.

Rodeo left the courthouse and bought a few groceries from Safeway then drove back to his casita and shot his guns for a while. When he was tired of killing tin cans and scaring rabbits, he put some beans to soak in a cast-iron lid skillet on his propane stove and then took a long siesta. Late in the afternoon he got up and poured the soak-water off the beans and started cooking the beans in fresh water with some hogback and then studied gun bibles for a while as he listened to his mother's LPs, mostly opera neither he nor she had ever understood. When the heat of the day had dissipated, Rodeo put on a pair of ragged gym shorts from his Ranger College days and a pair of old Chuck Taylors and jogged from his house down Elm Street to the Agua Seco Road with the dog lagging behind him. On the way back Rodeo stopped at the pile of concrete building blocks from which yellow crime scene tape now fluttered in shreds. He stood for a minute staring at the killing spot, then he sprinted the last quarter mile to his house where he sat on the side steps of his casita until his breath and the dog returned.

Rodeo fed and watered the dog and gave

him his vitamins and medicines. He pulled the bean pot off the stove and let it sit while he took a short tepid shower, then he re-dressed in Wranglers and a white T-shirt and ate his dinner, drank one Tecate and then spent the rest of the evening reloading spent shotgun shell hulls at his workbench. At ten o'clock he took a spoonful of Eagle Brand for dessert, then brushed his teeth at the kitchen sink and read the Bible in bed until he fell asleep.

The next day Rodeo got up well before dawn, took a sink bath, dressed in tub-washed, line-dried clothes, packed a big duffel including the ten-gauge riot gun with rubber ordnance, the Colt .357 revolver in a perforated leather sidearm holster, a two-shot derringer in a chamois-lined ankle holster, ammo, a Kevlar vest, metal and plastic handcuffs, two Tasers and an adjust-able neck brace and stowed these all in the stainless-steel gear box of his truck. Rodeo also carried away from his casita a pair of creased Wrangler bootcuts and two heavy-starched Larry Mahan snap-button shirts on hangers and in plastic dry-cleaning bags, a tooled leather belt with RODEO embossed on the back and his Professional Rodeo Cowboys Association National Finals trophy buckle on the front, a pair of alligator Luccheses and his 100X Beaver riding hat, both in plastic form-molded cases. Into his El Paso Saddleblanket Company saddlebags went his Toughbook laptop, an assortment of regional maps, his camera, eavesdropping and recording gear, binoculars, pepper spray, a sap, a Tony Hillerman and a Little Green New Testament. In his toiletries kit was a chunk of Ivory in a silver-plated soap travel dish, Crest and a toothbrush, a twenty-tooth comb and a bottle of Porter's Lotion.

Rodeo loaded the dog in the truck, checked the Ford's oil, topped off the radiator with coolant and slammed the hood of the pickup closed. He checked the load in his 9mm and slipped the Glock under the driver's side of the bench seat, inserted an eight-track cassette of Bill Monroe into the tape player and drove to Tucson, arriving there just in time to encounter the second wave of morning work traffic.

To strains of "Y'all Come!" Rodeo pulled off I-19 and drove east on Valencia Road, steered the pickup into the parking lot of Denny's, settled the dog, grabbed up his saddlebags and then went into the restaurant, ordered a Grand Slam and an "endless-cup-o' " coffee and for most of the next hour used Denny's free Wi-Fi to double check Luis's research.

He found stories about the death of Samuel Rocha in the archived Web editions of The *Tucson Citizen* and The *Arizona Daily Star* but these were the same reportage as in the file Luis had assembled for him. Carillo's Funeral Home had provided the memorial services for Samuel Rocha but no next of kin for the young man were listed. In a minor way Samuel Rocha's death had also figured in a larger piece in the local liberal rag, The *Tucson Weekly,* which article also came up in a Boolean search for "gangs *and* Tucson." In this extended report, Samuel Rocha's death was only mentioned as "another recent victim of South Tucson gang-related violence," a violence that, according to the *Weekly* writer, "had become a chronic epidemic stealthily creeping north of Twenty-second Street, the historic demarcation of South Tucson from Tucson Proper" and that was indicative of "the spread of the Drug Wars from the lawless borderlands of Sonora, Mexico, into the very heart of middle-class America that is downtown Tucson, Arizona."

The name "Samuel Rocha" also achieved one hit from the Web site of *SandScript the*

Journal of Creative Writing from Pima Community College where his poem, "Burn What Will Burn," had achieved publication. But otherwise he didn't learn anything Luis hadn't already told him.

Rodeo paid his bill, exited Denny's and continued west on Valencia.

Rodeo passed several strip malls, a trailer park, scattered San Carlos Indian Reservation housing and then pulled his truck to a stop in front of the Circle K on Mark Street a half mile from Casino del Sol and less than a quarter mile from the house in which his mother had killed herself. A blue-and-yellow on white Chevy Tahoe tribal cop car occupied the handicap spot. Rodeo parked between two pickups in worse shape than his and stepped into the convenience store. The big, flat-faced Indian clerk behind the counter looked aslant at him.

Is Mark Street around here pretty close? Rodeo wanted to start a conversation but the clerk was not interested.

There's Tucson city maps for sale right over there. The clerk pointed at a magazine rack. We're not supposed to give out directions. Management's orders.

Rodeo glanced around the convenience store. A Bud man stocked beer into a cooler and two men in work clothes assembled their breakfasts of burritos and coffee. A big cop walked out of a room behind the counter marked PRIVATE with a men's magazine in his hand.

What's up, Gilbert? the cop said. This guy giving you some grief or something?

The clerk shrugged as if that might be a possibility. The cop brushed past Rodeo to reinsert the *Maxim* into the periodical rack near the door, turned back to glare at him.

You looking for something around here, guy?

Katherine Rocha? asked Rodeo. Samuel Rocha?

You got some ID or something, guy?

Rodeo pulled out his huge billfold and extracted his Arizona driver's license and handed it over. The cop flipped the card back to front.

This is what you got, guy? A ten-year-old driving license?

It's good for another fifteen years, said Rodeo. Do you need a passport in Arizona now?

The big cop slipped the license into a flap pocket of his shirt.

Why don't we step outside and have a talk, guy? the cop asked. And let Gilbert get back to his business.

Rodeo followed the cop out of the store to stand near the phone kiosk. The cop stood very large on widespread feet as if ready to deliver or repel a blow.

So, what's up, guy? You a comedian or something?

I'm a PI hired to investigate the murder of the kid that got killed over on Starr Pass Road near A-Mountain a little while back, said Rodeo. The victim's name was Samuel Rocha.

I know who the kid was, the policeman said.

How do you know him? You related?

His dad is Alonzo Rocha, a cousin. What's it to you, guy?

You know his abuela, Katherine Rocha? She lives nearby here on Mark Street.

What do you think you're investigating around here, guy?

Just to see what's up with Samuel Rocha's death, said Rodeo.

Drive-by is what's up, the cop said. Open and shut. The punk's gang name was Smoke so what do you expect? The lowlife probably pissed somebody off on a bad drug deal and got shot for it. Happens every day, doesn't it, guy.

Just looking for some local information, Officer. . . . Rodeo glanced at the name tag

74

badge of the tribal policeman. The tag simply read MONJANO. Rodeo asked, do you have a first name, Officer Monjano?

I probably do and you probably don't want to know it, guy. The policeman pulled the driver's license out of his shirt pocket and tapped it against Rodeo's chest. Rodeo stood very still. I heard about you but I don't know you, guy, said the tribal cop. So watch yourself around here on my Res.

The policeman let go of the license which fell to the ground, went to his SUV, entered the vehicle and spoke for a minute on his cell phone. He jerked his head at Rodeo then drove off. After the cop drove off in the direction of Casino del Sol, Rodeo picked up his driver's license and returned into the Circle K and selected from a freezer a "Giannormous Gigantor" and placed the burrito supremo in the extra-dirty microwave. He pressed a button on the stove, and while he was waiting poured and drank an extra-large cup of Colombian coffee and then tossed the Styrofoam cup into a trash can and used his credit card to pay for only the burrito. The clerk processed the purchase but said nothing.

Rodeo walked out of the store, resettled in his truck, peeled back the wrapper from the burrito and fed his good dog a bad

75

breakfast.

Katherine Rocha's house on Mark Street was a small, red-brick ranch on a single lot.

Rodeo parked on the hard-packed dirt that served as sidewalk in the neighborhood. He exited the pickup and let the dog out and they both walked to the six-foot-tall adobe fence. Rodeo tipped up on his toes to look over the solid fence. Bright white gravel covered the yard. Attached to the house was a prefab carport. In the shade there was parked a 1980's-era Buick Le-Sabre. The car had an incongruous aluminum spoiler bolted amateurishly to the trunk lid and a new paint job. There was nothing alive in the yard but for the old lady who raked the gravel into neat furrows.

Rodeo moved to the gate, which was composed of lengths of barbed ocotillo branches wrapped in baling wire. As the old woman backed toward the concrete walk that led from the house to the gate, she raked meticulously over her own footprints until they had completely disappeared. She hung the yard broom tines-up on a nail in the front wall of the house, brushed her hands together and disappeared inside the little house. She came back out in three minutes and walked slowly and somewhat unsteadily down the concrete walkway, unlatched the gate and stood aside as the man and his dog entered her space. She closed the gate behind Rodeo. He smelled alcohol vapor around the woman's head.

He estado esparándote.

Yes ma'am, said Rodeo. Thanks for waiting for me.

You don't speak Spanish.

I get it mostly, but don't speak it much, Rodeo said. My daddy didn't allow any Spanish at home.

Buck liked to play at being an Indian and a Mexican when it suited him, but he was White, wasn't he?

I'm not really here to talk about my daddy, Mrs. Rocha.

That's why your mother married him, you know. She married Buck because she wanted to be White. His potential client appraised Rodeo from top to bottom. You're taller than I thought you'd be. Take after her, I guess. Your father was pint-sized and mean.

Rodeo did not comment.

Katherine Rocha shrugged. Apples don't fall far from their tree, do they? she asked.

If you say so, Mrs. Rocha. I don't know much about apples.

The woman squinted at him. And I see

you still dress up like a cowboy even at your age. But you looked better as a little kid dressed up like that for the Tucson Rodeo Parade than you are as a grown man dressed up like that. Little Indian kids in cowboy outfits are always so cute in parades but then they grow up, don't they.

Some do, Mrs. Rocha.

You don't remember me, do you? she asked.

No ma'am.

But I remember you, the woman said. San Xavier kid. Went to Mission School then Tucson High then got some college scholarship for rodeo later on, didn't you?

Yes ma'am. I went up to Highlands in New Mexico for a while and then to Ranger College, out in West Texas.

But you never graduated, did you?

No ma'am. Not yet.

Little late for you to do it now, idn't it?

Depends on how you look at it, Mrs. Rocha.

The old woman looked at Rodeo's dog. Don't you dare let that dog off the concrete or in my house, she said. He's your responsibility to clean up after if he messes. I am tired of cleaning up after dogs. And cleaning up after men with dogs.

He's a good dog, Mrs. Rocha.

Every man in the world says that about his dog. Katherine Rocha shook her head at the mongrel. That dog looks like every other dog I ever saw or worse.

The dog circled a spot on the polished concrete porch several times and laid himself down. The old woman entered the house, directed Rodeo into a folding lawn chair in the front room and left. She came back in a little while with a coffee mug in her hand and settled deep down into an ancient Barcalounger that was parked five feet from a giant TV. Rodeo moved his lawn chair sideways in order to be in the woman's range of vision.

I knew your mother, Katherine Rocha said. I was in Food Service with her at Mission School. That is your mother, idn't it? Grace Peña?

Yes ma'am. Grace Peña Garnet. But she passed six years ago.

I know all about it. The woman said this surely. She stared at the TV. Rodeo looked at the screen and saw his reflection there beside the woman's. I always wanted to meet his son grown up and now here he is. The woman said this to herself. Rodeo waited for her to explain this statement but she did not, only stared at the television.

How you been then, Mrs. Rocha?

The woman shrugged. I was a lunch lady at Mission School for a long time after your mother was fired for stealing from the library. I never heard from her again even though she lived just a little ways from here. But then we never had anything in common. She always thought she was above the rest of us because she had some sort of schooling. I guess that's why she killed herself. Just too smart for this life, she thought. But then she didn't have much real sense at all, did she. I remember she spent all her money on that worthless trailer lot down there in Los Jarros, thought that was a good investment, then died penniless without a soul around. She hung in that cheap trailer house for days and days with nobody to cut her down. It was like an oven in that trailer house they said.

Rodeo flinched.

What did you do after Mission School, Mrs. Rocha?

I went to the casinos and cleaned up after other people until I could retire. Now I go back to the casinos and let people clean up after me.

I guess all that worked out for you then, Rodeo said.

Nothing worked out, the woman said. She drank her coffee as if it were bitter. They built those casinos on our land, but you know Yaqui don't get any cut of the casino money. Just build firehouses and worthless . . . The old woman stopped and took a long drink from her cup. And I am Yaqui. Pure bred from Sonora on both sides, one of the Fourteen Thousand Registered up here. But your mother never had you registered did she. This was a statement and not a question from her.

My mother did have me registered, said Rodeo. I am Pascua Yaqui.

The old woman turned from the TV image to the man nearby her and stared at his face for several long seconds then looked back at the screen.

But your mother wanted you to be White, didn't she? That's the only reason why she married your father, because Buck passed as White. Claimed he was Irish. Black Irish, he said. That was a load of . . . Katherine Rocha stopped herself from cursing by taking another drink. That little man was Mexican as the day is long.

Rodeo nodded very slightly at this truth.

I remember when he left her she moved into town so you could go to high school with the Anglo kids. Thought maybe it would rub off on you, I guess.

My mother wanted me to go to the best

high school in Tucson, Mrs. Rocha. She thought that was Tucson High, so that's where I went.

The old woman sniffed and said nothing for a while. When her head nodded onto her chest, Rodeo shifted in his aluminum chair and cleared his throat.

You're looking to hire somebody like me, a private investigator to look into your grandson's death, Mrs. Rocha? Rodeo asked. Is that the case?

I wanted you, the woman said. She gulped coffee and stared at Rodeo as if at beef on sale. Her voice quavered. Another drink steadied her and she sat up straighter and changed her tone of voice. They said you could find out things. Is that the truth?

Mostly it is, Mrs. Rocha. Though I get paid the same whether I find out something or not. I never gyp anybody that hires me but I don't always get results my employers care for, Rodeo said. Sometimes I don't get results much at all. Just depends on the case.

That'd be fine that way, the old woman said. If you didn't find out anything, I mean. If that's the case.

Rodeo shifted in the flimsy lawn chair and leaned forward to ease the pressure on his herniated discs.

Is there something about your grandson's

death in particular you're interested in finding out about, Mrs. Rocha? Rodeo asked.

Who's that?

Your grandson Samuel. The boy who got killed on the bridge.

He was probably killed by one of those dope friends of his, the grandmother said. She waved a hand in Rodeo's face. I know how my husband was and so I know how my children are. And I know how my grandchildren are and now even my great-grandchildren probably. All but the one of them. She paused. But I'm at the point now that I don't really give a damn what people think about me, my family included. What do you think of that?

I think it's still a free country, Mrs. Rocha. More or less.

What did you say your Christian name was again?

Rodeo.

That's right. Buck always did want you to be a cowboy, didn't he? she said. A little Indian cowboy.

I guess you knew my daddy, Mrs. Rocha.

The woman looked sideways at Rodeo. You don't look much like him. He was little. And handsome.

No offense, Mrs. Rocha, but I just came here to see about a piece of work on offer.

Did you mean to hire me to investigate your grandson's death? Rodeo tried to keep his voice level. Because it seems like your grandson died in a bad way, so maybe you're like some people who want to hire me just in order to pay respects to someone who's died, to do the right thing by their dead but don't expect to find out too much about how they died or why?

I'm not paying respects to anybody. Why should I?

The old lady rocked herself out of her chair and stalked away. When she did not return in several minutes, Rodeo followed her into the kitchen where she was leaning against the sink having a glass of brandy in plain view. The room was neat but it had a stench of old grease, propane gas, wet pipes and dry rot.

You drink? the woman asked.

Not to speak of lately, said Rodeo.

Your parents were both drunks. Your mother was a Bad Drunk. Katherine Rocha poured another shot of Christian Brothers into a jelly jar, tossed it back and set the jelly glass down. Buck and her deserved each other.

The old woman looked at Rodeo then rubbed knuckles the size of golf balls into her eyesockets. She poured coffee from an antique percolator and spooned sugar and nondairy creamer into her coffee cup, stirred.

I can hire you if I want to, can't I? the woman asked.

If you got three hundred dollars a day plus expenses you can, Mrs. Rocha. Even though Rodeo had given her the family and friends rate, she still coughed and put her hand over her mouth, clearly shocked by this number.

I usually stay at Arizona Motel when I work in Tucson and that's as cheap as it gets, said the PI. Plus three meals a day and gasoline. And if you want to get your money's worth it would help to know a few things that I can't get from the papers or off the Internet, Mrs. Rocha.

Things like what?

Like who Samuel hung out with. And why he was living here instead of with his parents.

He lived with me because his parents kicked him out and he had no place else to live but with that girlfriend of his and I don't think she wanted him around either.

What girlfriend was that? Rodeo asked.

Just some trashy girl, she said. Anglo, I guess. How can you tell these days? Rings in her nose and tattoos or whatever you call it all over her. Pink hair.

You know who this girl was?

I don't know anything about her, said the woman. Except she came by here one time to pick him up when I wouldn't let him have the car. But it's my car. I paid for it.

Where did this girl live or work or go to school?

She was just nasty trash that kid brought around to bother me with, the grandmother said. I never trusted that kid. He was just as worthless as Alonzo.

And Alonzo is your son? And Samuel's father?

Yeah. We know whose padre was that kid's at least. Since they are both of no account.

What do you mean by that, Mrs. Rocha?

The old woman drank her coffee to keep her mouth shut. Rodeo proceeded.

So Samuel was living with you because his parents kicked him out. Why did they kick him out, Mrs. Rocha?

That kid was bad, she said. Her eyes got misty. But his mother had another child. A good child . . . The voice of the old woman trailed off. Rodeo waited, but no more words from her seemed forthcoming.

I don't want you to take this the wrong way, Mrs. Rocha . . . said Rodeo. But you don't seem all that cut up about your grandson, so I'm curious why you are even interested in me investigating Samuel's death.

Katherine Rocha stared at Rodeo. Her eyes were obsidian, almost unnaturally dark from iris to eyelid. Rodeo had to look away from the old woman's gaze.

You sound like Buck, she said. But you don't look like him.

Rodeo nodded because he did sound as his father did, exactly. Their voices were the same, father and son, though they were different men.

Do you have children? the woman asked.

No ma'am. I don't. Rodeo said this with some hesitation, but the woman did not notice.

Well, you're lucky then, because I had nine children with my husband but not one of them pretty or smart or good in rodeo or Indian dancing or sports or school or married good . . . And then we had her, a perfect little child finally. That was the saddest day of my life . . .

The woman stopped and took in a deep breath as if she had run out of oxygen, then put a fist on her breastbone as if to calm her heart. She pointed to her refrigerator, where there was Scotch-taped a studio photo in a cardboard frame of a little girl with obviously dyed blond hair and fake blue eyes staring in an animated way into the camera, her baby teeth like little white spikes. REST IN PEACE — FARRAH KATHERINE ROCHA was printed in Gothic script above the dates of the child's birth and death. The child had lived less than six years. This mass-produced copy of a studio photograph was a souvenir handed out at Farrah's funeral. The funeral home was CARILLO's, which was the same as Samuel's.

That's a granddaughter of yours, Mrs. Rocha? Rodeo asked.

The old woman lowered her chin to her chest.

Is Farrah related to Samuel?

Sister.

Did Farrah and Samuel have other siblings?

Katherine Rocha shook her head.

You've had a lot of troubles, Mrs. Rocha.

This should be Indian Country. By rights it should be. The woman said this as if it explained something in the world, maybe everything to her. But instead it's mostly Mexicans who want everything and Anglos who own everything. The woman shrugged and shook her head in scarcely controlled anger. My husband was Mexican. And he made me have all those kids but never had any money or talents for them or me either.

Rodeo had spent much of his early life on San Xavier Reservation and was Native-American, Mexican-American and Irish-American, so he understood this common domestic dilemma.

Can I trust you? The woman said this abruptly, as if it had just occurred to her.

Rodeo presented his regular sales pitch to a reluctant client.

Mrs. Rocha, hiring a private investigator is something of a trust issue in general. There's just no way around that. But you pay me, so I am a professional. And because I am a professional you can trust me to do my work. I investigate to the best of my abilities and then I report to you honestly what I find out. It's just a business deal. Rodeo tried to smile in a winning way but his teeth had always been bad.

The woman took a seat at the kitchen table and looked into her coffee cup as if divining in the dregs of nondairy creamer floating in Folgers some portent.

So you will tell me everything you find out? she asked.

You can have it that way if you want it that way, Mrs. Rocha. Or if you think I might find out something you really don't want to know and you don't want me to tell you about it, then I won't tell you about it. Unless it's something to do with Law Enforcement, then you have that option. Rodeo paused. The woman just stared into her coffee cup. Like I said, Mrs. Rocha, some people just hire me because they feel like it's the right thing to do. And often it is. Because an objective investigation into a suspicious death demonstrates respect for the dead by trying to find out what killed them.

But you can't just turn your ideas over to the police, can you?

Honestly, Mrs. Rocha, there's not much likelihood that I'll find anything the police didn't find anyway. Not in the short period of time you could probably hire me for.

I don't want the police involved, she said.

Rodeo rubbed the back of his neck and tried to keep the frustration out of his voice. Within common sense and the law of the land, I do what you want me to do, Mrs. Rocha, for as long as you got three hundred a day plus expenses.

A day, the woman said.

Rodeo sighed very quietly. We'll just need to fill in a contract and sign it then, Mrs. Rocha. You can get a witness if you want. A relative or somebody.

There's nobody, the old woman said.

Rodeo filled in a standard contract and under "services contracted" wrote "Investigate death of Samuel Rocha for one day and relay information accumulated to Mrs. Katherine Rocha." Rodeo put a Bic pen on the kitchen table beside the contract. His new client attempted to read the contract but was obviously losing focus. Rodeo guided her pen to the signature line and she signed in a shaky hand. Rodeo folded the contract into his pocket and slid a sheet of clean note paper in front of her.

If you would give me the full name and address of Samuel's parents that would help me get started, Rodeo said.

The old woman scratched violently on the paper and then thrust it away from her and slammed the pen down on top of it. Alonzo and her rented a house close to here, she said. But I don't know if they are even there. And I don't know anything about their business or that kid's business.

Can I get in Samuel's room, Mrs. Rocha?

The woman gestured toward the darkened hallway of the little house. Down there on the right. The police were in there but I don't think they took much out.

So I need my day rate plus fifty up front for expenses right now, Mrs. Rocha. That's the deal.

How do I know you won't just take my money?

Because I am a professional, Mrs. Rocha. Like I said. I always do my job.

I'll pay you the fifty for expenses then, she said.

It's not going to work that way, Mrs. Rocha. I need three hundred and fifty dollars.

A hundred.

When Rodeo shook his head, the old woman put her face in her hands and rubbed her eyes with her big knuckles, pressed a hard little fist against her chest then rose so abruptly she knocked over her chair. She moved on swerving slippers to a kitchen drawer and pulled out a plastic shopping bag from Food City and carefully counted out from it one hundred dollars in small bills, her swollen hands sure with the cash. She seemed now totally drained, spent completely. She held out the partial payment in a clenched fist.

Rodeo shrugged and shook his head but accepted the partial payment and put the money into his big billfold. That's one hundred, he said.

Katherine Rocha pressed a hand against her breastbone again.

Are you feeling all right, Mrs. Rocha?

Whoever cared about how I feel. This was a rhetorical question as she intoned it.

Why don't you go lay down while I look over Samuel's room, said Rodeo. If I take anything from Samuel's room I'll leave a receipt for that.

There's nothing in that pack rat's nest I want, the old woman said. Take it all. Cart all that kid's junk off in the back of that trashy brown truck of yours. That'd be a way to earn all that money you're charging me at least.

Have a rest now, Mrs. Rocha.

She did not resist as Rodeo took her elbow and steered her back into the living room, reestablished her in her Barcalounger. Rodeo stood stock still behind her chair and out of her sight. The old woman started snoring in less than three minutes. He went to work.

The carpet in Katherine Rocha's house was a mixture of browns and reds that partly camouflaged many stains. The walls were painted and overpainted several shades of tan except for the ones in the bathroom that were faded rose, and in that room most objects were either pink or fuzzy or both. The walls of the short hallway seemed sagged by the weight of framed photographs, many of which were faded beyond recognition with but few recent, as if the promise of Katherine Rocha's past had been unfulfilled by later generations. Dominating one wall of the hallway was an eight-by-ten studio glossy of Farrah, framed in faux weathered wood that was washed with pink paint. The child had regular features but was not especially pretty. Her eyes were cerulean and bright yellow hair was piled up on her head so high it could not be contained by the picture frame.

There were also on the hallway walls candid and studio photos of brown-skinned people in cowboy and Indian outfits, ill-fitting suits and prom gowns and oversized basketball uniforms, though very few of people in graduation robes and mortar-boards. Rodeo knew what Samuel looked like from newspaper images and there were no photos of Samuel on Katherine Rocha's Walk of Family Fame, not of him as a kid or teenager at least. All the babies on the wall looked pretty much the same except for Farrah, who had been framed theatrically from her earliest days. There were several candid shots of the little beauty queen with what must have been her parents jointly holding her at different stages of her growth. Standing beside the parents of

Farrah and Samuel in one large photo was the tribal cop Rodeo had encountered earlier that day at the Circle K. Officer Monjano held the baby Farrah, who was garishly overdressed in all pink. Farrah's mother was strikingly attractive except for her fat. The father, Alonzo, looked slightly like Monjano but was older and sloppy in his khakis with his shirttails out and his eyes puffy and red. There were also four other photographs of Farrah in later years, in her contest makeup and outfits, that always included the Reservation cop named Monjano prominently in the frames, often holding the little beauty queen in his big arms.

Since his client was still soundly asleep in the living room, Rodeo moved into Katherine Rocha's bedroom for a quick tour.

The smell in the old woman's room was of talcum powder and piss, patent medicines and packaged bandages, muscle rubs, and the odor of the seepage that accompanies the decomposition of vitality into decrepitude. On the bedside table were a number of pill bottles including the blood thinner warfarin along with lisinopril and metoprolol for hypertension and lithium for depression. There was another framed glossy photo of the favored dead child, Farrah, on Katherine Rocha's dresser and

95

several old photos featuring Katherine Rocha herself, in her late teens and early adulthood. In one of these Katherine Rocha wore a traditional Mexican dress and posed in front of Teatro Del Carmen. Her pose was as dramatic and alluring as a professional actress's. In another photo from the same era, Katherine Rocha lounged in front of El Minuto Café with some slick pachucos. An earlier photo showed Katherine Rocha as a smiling girl with curves in a cowgirl outfit standing in front of Western WearHouse with a Tucson Rodeo Parade prize banner draped over her chest. In these old photographs Katherine Rocha's long, round chin always tilted to the left and her thick, sculpted eyebrows arched above deep-set eyes that were luminous even in these old photographic reproductions.

Also on Katherine Rocha's dresser was a computer-enhanced reproduction of an old snapshot, the grain exploded large as if the eight-by-ten had been derived from a much smaller original snapshot. In this picture a small cowboy on a paint pony faced Black Mountain. Rodeo recognized the location of the snapshot as the practice rodeo arena near the San Xavier Mission, just yards from the house in which he had spent most of his youth. And though the rider's back was to the camera, from the way the cowboy sat his cutting horse Rodeo knew this was a photograph of his own father, a picture of Buck Garnet in his prime. Rodeo stood very still for a moment and then moved on.

Samuel's room was obviously the lair of an adolescent. Stale smoke residue coated the whole room, the odor refreshed by a hubcap brimful of cigarette butts, mostly Kools. There was no computer in the room and no cable connections for one. On a bedside table were a cheap cassette/CD/radio boom box and a small pile of CDs, mostly classic rock, the CDs so old the jewel cases were opaque. Rodeo opened them all and found nothing but liner notes.

Posters covered the walls — Ray Mysterio, Nine Inch Nails, Insane Clown Posse, a shirtless Brad Pitt. Scarface aimed his machine gun at Dirty Harry, who responded with his trademark .357 magnum in the corner near the head of the single bed. Dirty and soiled sheets and T-shirts were twisted and spread over an uncovered, stained mattress. The floor was littered with men's magazines, Mountain Dew and Red Bull cans, energy bar wrappers and Fritos bags. The drawers of the bureau disgorged dirty underwear, baggy jeans, graphic T-shirts that promoted Old School headbanger bands like Metallica, Whitesnake and Poison.

The back of Samuel's bedroom door was covered in concert ticket stubs from a wide variety of acts, mostly from the Rialto Theater, representing artists ascending to stardom or receding from it — Aimee Mann, The New Pornographers, Peter York, Queensrÿche, Bela Fleck, Sergio Mendoza, 2 Live Crew, Monkey Arte, Acoustic Alchemy, Tech N9ne, Lucinda Williams, Animal Collective, The Robert Cray Band, David Sedaris, Slammin' Poetry, Tucson Poetry Festival, Dark Star Orchestra, Squirrel Nut Zippers, Raúl Malo, Ken Nordine, Missy Higgins, Japonize Monkey, Morrissey, John Legend, New Found Legend, Styxnaseua, Old Timey Times, The Way Back Machine, Madansky Folk Ensemble, Franz Ferdinand, Three Red Neck Tenors, Big Bad Voodoo Daddy, Nicky Cruz, Badfish, Craig Ferguson, Ice Cube, Lamb of God, Indigenous, Authority Zero, Los Lobos, Wilco, Atmosphere, The Fucking Kennies, The Breeders, The Whistlers, The Wrongs, The Hives, The Faint, The Fainters, The Zombies, The Dead, A Live and Calexico.

In Samuel's closet was one set of neatly pressed pleated khakis and one long-sleeved, button-down baby blue dress shirt scarcely worn and many hooded sweatshirts that promoted colleges or professional sports teams — Pima Community College, La Universidad de Arizona, Phoenix Cardinals, Arizona Diamondbacks, Colorado Rockies, Chicago White Sox, The Tucson Javelinas, Gila Monsters, Mavericks, Sidewinders, Scorch, Heat and IceCats and one sweatshirt that had airbrushed on the chest ROSESMOKE.

Under the bed was nothing but a roach clip on a leather thong tied to a fragment of a hawk's feather. Between the mattress and box springs were two abused pornographic magazines, one gay and one straight. And a small spiral notebook filled with poems, a whole bookful of poems. Rodeo flipped through all the poems and read several of the shorter ones.

ROSE HAIKU

Pink hair is the prettiest,
  Unlike the man-stink,
Because it's not natural.

I'm supposed to be guilt-free
  After a guilt sweat.
I love your pink hair the best.

The tattoos that reach around
   Your wrists are etchings
Not even God could dream up.

I miss my little sister.
   You know how to make
Her come back to life with words.

WALKING TO THE PALACE

It's always night
When I'm walking
To the Palace to collect
The Bitchwitch is only her empty winnings
And heavy breath from
Christian Brothers.
Part cross, part hammer, all death
Knell, life
Sentence.
Whatever
Birds of prey dream
Of devouring in the brush,
Split and bloody,
Holds no candle
To what I'll do
To the BitchWitch is only her bones.
Once I burn her flesh
Clean off, I might let her
Breathe my smoke
A few hours more

Before I kiss her goodnight
With a straight razor
And cup of bleach.
Then, I'll grind her bones
And snort them. To complete
The exorcism,
Performed with the last of her
Christian Brothers, her only family left,
I'll make fire leap
From my mouth so my face
May be burned clean
Of any resemblance
Of her, even in the dark.

I AM SMOKE

I am smoke
   and you're a cloud
      and we float

through each other
   and trade colors
      become each other

and now you're good
   and now I'm bad again
      and gray is roseate

and black is white

        and wet is dry
            and earth is sky

    where the MIA
        are all at home

Folded into this book of chirographic
poetry was a copy of Farrah Katherine
Rocha's obituary. The six-year-old child's
obituary was longer than many of those
marking the deaths of octogenarians, most
of the copy detailing the girl's many wins,
places and finishes in Little Miss beauty
pageants. No mention was made of her only
sibling, her brother Samuel, as a survivor of
hers.

Rodeo closed the small notebook and
stuck it in his shirt pocket, turned his attention to the teenager's books. Though the
rest of the room seemed well-tossed by the
police, the books seemed undisturbed but
by gravity. The shelves were made of splintered pallet wood and were not even held in
the dry wall by expansion screw sets but
only with nails scarcely sufficient to hold
the pressure of the paperbacks resting on
them. Many nail heads were bent and
pounded into the walls in obvious frustration. The thin metal brackets were sagging
from the wall under the weight of words.

Each shelf had a theme. Science fiction, fantasy, true crime, government conspiracies, alien visitation, zombies, vampires and werewolves, satanic cults, Vietnam, guns, serial killers, Harry Potter, Stephen King and Poetry. There were six books on the assassination of John Fitzgerald Kennedy, so Rodeo studied these with some care. All had the pages containing the well-known diagrams of the Book Depository on Dealey Plaza dog-eared. A number of these diagrams of the ballistics report also had notes scribbled on them, distances from shooter to target and ballistics information. In a margin of one was drawn a Smiley Face and written beside it "not a hard shot!" In another book, on the most famous photograph of Lee Harvey Oswald, CE-133A, a halo was penciled in above Oswald's head, and near Oswald's mail-order rifle was penciled "Carcano 6.5 millimeters, ask RR about getting one for our 'job.' "

There were also two books detailing the lives, the pursuit and eventual capture of the Washington, D.C. "Beltway" serial sniper killers John Allen Muhammad and Lee Boyd Malvo.

Rodeo quickly flipped through the rest of the books and then replaced them one by one. He found only a single scrap of paper, in a book of Alexander Long poetry, a homemade business card that had ROSE RITE.COM embossed on the front and handwritten on the back a local telephone number and *the Kettle.* No wallet, keys or personal items but several framed photos were on the battered chest of drawers. One photo was of little Farrah, not in one of her competitive Little Miss costumes, but simply smiling in a candid shot looking like a plain little Mexican-American girl with natural brown pigtails and brown eyes. There was a blurry shot of an Anglo girl with pink hair as she was leaving a chain restaurant. Samuel had also taped to the bureau mirror several of his own cropped school pictures. Though the photos represented several different school years, Samuel consistently had acne spots on his face and long greasy hair, a downy fuzz on his upper lip, and was a very ordinary-looking mixed-race kid except for his eyes, which were as luminous as his grandmother's had been.

Also taped to the mirror was a photo of a group of Goth kids standing in line outside the Rialto Theater including the girl with pink hair again. Another snapshot had been taken in front of El Charro Café of a similar bunch of tattooed and pierced kids but in cheap prom gear. They stood beside a 1980's-era Buick sedan with a spoiler bolted unevenly on the trunk lid and "Stretch Limo" soaped on the side panels of the Le-Sabre.

Beside this photo was one Samuel had apparently taken of himself, as his skinny arm was partly in the picture as he held the camera in front of his face. Rodeo placed the location of this image as the nearby sweat lodge, which was within a mile or so of Katherine Rocha's house. The men's lodge was partly visible as a dome of rags with a low, shadowed entrance. Smoke rose behind the young man, partly obscuring Black Mountain in the near distance. A dark figure also drifted in the background behind Samuel's head, a thin, dark-skinned man in shorts.

There was also one blurry photo of a thin man in camo gear standing with a large and well-scoped rifle on his hip in the middle of a large field of grass. Rodeo removed the photo from the mirror. "White Mountain" was scribbled in ink on the back of this snapshot. A related snapshot also on the mirror was of a group of six dark-skinned grown men with one teenager easily identified as Samuel Rocha. All of the men in this photo were armed with rifles and held cigars and beers and all were smiling except for the central figure, who scowled at the camera as he aimed his large caliber, scoped hunting rifle at the head of a mature elk bull with a trophy-sized rack. Samuel Rocha stood beside this central shooter and looked up at the older man, the same man as in the solo hunter photo. Rodeo recognized one of the grown men in the group hunting shot as someone he knew very well.

The PI tucked all these photos and the ROSERITE.COM calling card into his wallet and returned to the living room where Katherine Rocha snored laboriously, a fisted hand clutched to her chest. Rodeo stood over his new client for a several minutes, staring at her faded beauty. Her thick eyebrows were now gray and unruly, her once long, round chin was disappeared in jowls. Her skin, once perfectly brown, was now sallow, her face marred by frown lines.

Rodeo returned to the kitchen and extracted his client's cash stash from the kitchen drawer, counted out another two hundred and fifty dollars and stuffed it in his pocket, replaced the Food City bag. He wrote a receipt reflecting this full amount for a day's pay and expenses as Paid In Full, put it on the table, left a RODEO GRACE GARNET, PRIVATE INVESTIGATOR business card atop it then left the house.

A few blocks south from Katherine Rocha's house on Mark Street was the local sweat lodge near Black Mountain. At the Fire Station Rodeo steered off pavement onto a faint dirt road and onto holy ground that looked like a dump with mattress carcasses and car seats deteriorating in the heat. Glass glittered the ground. Plastic shopping bags flagged creosote bushes like the Res equivalent of prayer flags.

Rodeo parked between the men's and women's sweat lodges and sat his truck for a while looking at the fire pit charred with remnants of half-burnt shipping pallets, the scroungy half-sphere sweat huts covered in carpet scraps and blue plastic tarpaulin and at Black Mountain overshadowing all this neighborhood and the Reservation.

Rodeo exited the truck and walked to the twelve-foot-wide, four-foot-deep fire pit. Some heating stones that had cracked too much to be carried into the tent, cracked too soon to serve, rimmed the fire pit. He kicked at one of these stones until it turned nearly to dust and then he moved to the men's lodge, got on his knees and peered into the round tent and searched the low-slung bent branch rafters.

Rodeo looked for the mobile of aged deer bones he had made when his mother died. The prayer bundles had been held together with leather thongs chewed between his teeth. Depended from these bones had been small canvas sacks filled with tobacco and each bundle tied by a separate ribbon — black for west and yellow for east and red for north and white for south, blue for father heaven and for mother earth green. But Rodeo's prayer bundles were gone, stolen by culture poachers as "art" or by local kids for the high-priced tobacco in them or the costly feathers on them.

Rodeo crawled backwards out of the men's lodge and stood and then trudged all around the fire pit and walked past the women's lodge without looking in. He paused under the crude ramada ten yards away and pulled the small spiral notebook of Samuel Rocha's poetry out of his back pocket and read.

THE GUILT SPIRITS

Are all around within and beyond
Waiting for me always waiting always

I breathe them in as I breathe them out
They soak my brow and crack my throat

And coat the length of my arms and legs

My shoulders shoot lightning
My spine is molten lava
My guts spew white fire
My lungs twin lodestars exploding

They carry me out

A mystery of big, black crows were hopping in a circle nearby the men's sweat lodge. Some birds picked at raw bones of fried chicken but others only cried their call and their raucous caw-caws awoke the dog in the truck who barked, straining hoarsely to make his old presence in the world still felt.

Cállate!

When the dog stopped barking the crows lifted in unison like a ragged black curtain. Rodeo pocketed Samuel's poems and kicked through a pile of household garbage and went back to his truck, laid a reassuring hand on his dog and drove back to pavement.

Tucson Famous Pets and Aquarium Design Center had been for most of Rodeo's life a general farm and ranch store called Salge Feed and Seed. There was only one other vehicle parked in front of the Quonset hut, a flare-side Dodge pickup with copper plates designating it as a Historic Vehicle. When Rodeo cut his truck's engine the dog woke and sniffed the air.

You do still got a good nose, Rodeo said. He laid a hand on the dog's head. Let's go get some overpriced food for you.

The dog wandered the several aisles of the pet store until he came to a stop in front of the Orijen display and started to whine. Rodeo hefted the largest bag of "Adult Formula" to the checkout counter where the store clerk sat on a barstool browsing through a veterinary supply catalogue. She pulled white-blond hair behind her ears and looked at Rodeo in a friendly way.

That's good dog food for an older dog, the woman said.

You know a lot about old dogs? Rodeo asked.

I should, I guess. The woman closed her catalogue. I ran a sort of hospice for old dogs. That's why I don't practice pet medicine anymore because I was just mostly putting down old dogs nobody wanted to deal with. The woman again fiddled with her hair. I had a little breakdown if you want to know the truth. My name's Summer Skye. I'm from Ojai, she said. In California? My girlfriend and I just moved here last year.

This place used to be owned by Roy Salge, Rodeo said. Mr. Salge was one of my first sponsors when I started rodeoing.

I don't know who owned this place before my girlfriend Hudson bought it for me, the young woman said. She frowned but in a friendly way. And I don't really like rodeo. It's not a real sport and it's cruel to animals.

I know it was cruel to me, Rodeo said. He put a credit card on the bag of Orijen.

The erstwhile veterinarian checked out the name on Rodeo's MasterCard and crinkled her nose as she processed the card purchase and slid the receipt toward him to sign.

You are from around here, I guess? she asked.

Born and raised out on the San Xavier Reservation near the Mission.

Well, it was nothing personal, the woman said. She showed off the gap between her central incisors as she returned the credit card. What I said about the rodeo I mean. I'm sure there's some nice people in the rodeo.

Not many that I ever noticed, Rodeo said.

The clerk leaned over the counter like a yogini and stroked the dog's head. His tongue lolled out of his mouth. When the woman resumed her seat the dog whined. The storekeep leaned over the counter again and spoke to the animal. Well then, you and your old master come back and see me again, won't you. The dog attempted a bark and wagged his chewed-up tail.

Rodeo left the pet store, loaded the dog food in the back of the truck and the dog in the front, took his own seat then frowned at the dog.

You just plain embarrass me sometimes, Rodeo said. Did you know that?

The dog barked and stuck his head into the breeze as the pair aimed back at Arizona Motel.

Back in the golden days of automobile travel, Arizona Motel had been a real tourist oasis of palm trees with swimming pool and barbeque and playground, rooms complete with kitchenettes and air-conditioning and wall-to-wall carpeting. But the horseshoe-shaped motel with parking in front of each unit was now mostly low-rent, semipermanent housing for those without start-up money or backup funds.

When he was working in Tucson, Rodeo stayed at Arizona Motel because it was cheap and located near the bank where his little bit of money was, the police station where his few official law-enforcement contacts were and Barrio Historico where his (former) lawyer was. But Arizona Motel was also a contact spot for Rodeo, a local depository of information for the private investigator, bounty hunter and warrant-server because amongst The Regulars at the motel was always some variety of retired military, local cowboys and Indians, dopers, derelicts and day laborers, prostitutes and a pool hustler who had lived at the motel for twenty years. And since these people often had nothing better to do than drink and gossip, cruise the Internet all day and the bars all night, they were about as likely as anyone to know what was going on in and around Downtown and Armory Park, along the Santa Cruz River around the Reservations and especially in the separate smaller municipality inside the city called South Tucson, "the pueblo inside the city" where a high percentage of local crime occurred and bail jumpers and missing kids on dope were most often found.

Rodeo let the dog precede him into the lobby of the motel. The air inside was just slightly cooler than the outside air. An old man slept in a wheelchair, an oscillating fan on the wall raising and lowering the American flag duct-taped to his Vietnam Vet cap.

A cracked voice called to the dog, who wandered into the "billiards room and loungette" area. No one was behind the reception desk, so Rodeo pushed past the swinging partition and peeked into the one-room apartment where the manager, Abishiek Chandrakar, was soundly asleep on a Budweiser beach towel spread on the unfinished concrete floor.

Rodeo selected his preferred room key and went to his room leaving the dog to visit with the old people, who seemed to consider him a gift from God. In #116 Rodeo turned on the anemic air-conditioning, stripped and flopped onto the bed then stared at the water stains on the ceiling until he drifted deeply into a shallow afternoon nap.

Two hours later Rodeo sat on the edge of the pool at Arizona Motel. He wore a pair of old gym shorts he kept behind the seat of his pickup and otherwise was naked. His skin was naturally dark but much darker from elbows to wrists and in a V around his neck. His feet were blanched virtually colorless since he had worn cowboy boots almost every day of his life since he was only months old.

The rectangular swimming pool was crystal clear but Rodeo didn't know how to swim, so he was only wet below the knees. The dog, a great swimmer, was curled up beside his master, his wet pelt steaming stink in the hot sun. It was early in the day and late in the summer, so the motel was mostly empty except for the marginally solvent, semipermanent residents, mostly male, who rented rooms at Arizona Motel so they could be near the VA Hospital a few blocks south on Sixth. In the evening, action at the motel would pick up as the transient workers who bunked six or seven to a room returned to share twelve-packs and prostitutes but for now it was a peaceful place to be.

Local traffic cruised down Sixth and the roar of interstate traffic sounded a few blocks away not unlike waves breaking continuously ashore. Rodeo kicked at the water with his fish-belly feet and used his cell phone to call Luis at Twin Arrows.

You started your job already? asked Luis.

More or less, said Rodeo.

What does TPD say?

I hadn't called Tucson Police yet, said Rodeo. Thought I'd call you first, Luis, just to make sure you didn't mind me digging around in this case because when I searched the old Rocha lady's house I found a photograph of a bunch of Res types elk hunting in the Whites and one of these Indian types is you. So I was just wondering if you got something to tell me, Luis?

You know all us Indians look alike, brother. So that might be a picture of me and it might just be an Indian that looks like me.

Who're these guys in the photo with you and Samuel Rocha? asked Rodeo.

Just some guys, said Luis. Some of us who used to powwow back in the day. A couple of us old ones we were in Nam together and a couple of the others were vets from the Gulf. But mostly just powwow pals, you know. This one time we camped up near Springerville and shot at some elk. That's probably that picture you got.

Who is the one that shot the big elk?

Ronald Rocha they call him, said Luis. Nobody really knows who he is or where he comes from. Says he's related to the Rochas on the Res but none of the Rochas claim him. He used to work some for the Millers down here in Los Jarros on Slash/M Rancho a few years back. Maybe Ronald he served with Randy Miller that politician guy in the Gulf War. Some kind of Special Forces sniper guy or something what they say.

What do you say, Luis?

I say the man can shoot, said Luis. So don't get to be a target around him.

You seen this Ronald Rocha character lately? Rodeo asked.

Me and him we met up again at a pow-wow in New Mexico a few months ago, Luis said. And he still had this kid Sam Rocha with him, tied at the hip. Ronald said this kid was his nephew but it didn't look like all they were sharing was turkey around Thanksgiving.

And it seemed odd later on when this kid Samuel Rocha turned up maybe shot off a bridge and there was this sniper guy, Ronald with the high-powered rifle, who maybe was a different sort of uncle to this Samuel Rocha . . . ? asked Rodeo. Is it like that, Luis? Was Ronald a different sort of "uncle" to this kid who got shot off the bridge?

They struck me queer.

Where is Ronald Rocha to be found recently, Luis?

When he wanted company Ronald he used to like The Buffet on Ninth, near Fourth.

Who does Ronald hang out with?

He hangs out with the government conspiracies, personal-rights wingnuts. But Ronald he's not really political. Not like a regular person is at least. And he don't want company as a usual thing and usually just lives rough what I hear.

Is Ronald a character, Luis?

Don't get in no pissing contest with him, brother, or you will definitely get your boots wet.

Water stirred around Rodeo's calves and feet as the swimming pool filtration system kicked in. The traffic hurtled by on Sixth like it had to get north or south before all the lights in the world turned red. Rodeo looked up at a sky free of clouds. The old dog slept peacefully beside his man like there was no place to be but where he was.

Anything else you want to tell me, Luis? Rodeo asked.

Badge-and-Haircut he came by this morning and this Anderton of yours he wanted to look at the AMexica Wall. He was taking notes and asking after you. This Statie's got some ideas, I guess, about there being another serial killer loosed in Los Jarros County. And I think he's got a hard-on for you or something, brother, so maybe he's one of those groupies like came after you once you got famous for taking care of Charlie Constance.

What did you tell Anderton? Rodeo asked.

I told him like I would tell anybody who asks that I don't know nothing about you or anybody else, Luis said.

Was anybody else around Twin Arrows asking about me, Luis?

Nobody that's good for you to know about or care about, Rodeo.

If Sirena's looking for me, she'll find me, Luis.

Second Wife Silk Snowball she's got a couple of cousins in Tuxson ready to date, said Luis. Both easy in bed and the fat one she's got a job with Social Service, so that would be a paycheck. And that fattest one she can cook.

Thanks for thinking of me, Luis, but you and me are tied up enough together just on the pawn shop level as it is without me hooking up with one of your second wife's relations. Hasta luego.

Always hope so, brother.

Rodeo led the dog back into their room, sprayed him with Lysol then rubbed him down with a motel towel, fed and watered him and forced supplements and medicine down his throat and then got himself dressed in his Wranglers, snap-button short-sleeved shirt and walking boots. He put his old straw hat on and walked the dog out of the motel room, loaded him into the truck, drove north on Sixth several blocks to

Twenty-second Street, turned west until Twenty-second became Starr Pass Road at the bridge over the Santa Cruz under which Samuel Rocha had died his slow death.

The Santa Cruz had been a running river until the end of the nineteenth century, but after multiple diversions and many decades of drought the river was bone dry except for when the monsoon rains flashflooded the riverbed. Now a place for homeless men and women to camp, kids to smoke dope and horse people and ATVers to ride, it was not unusual to see a bobcat wandering down the streambed right through the middle of Tucson.

There was a pedestrian walkway on the south side of the Starr Pass Road bridge with a sidewalk and five-foot-high walls and high chain-link fencing separating walkers from both traffic on one side and a fall on the other. But on the north side of the bridge there was no pedestrian sidewalk or protective walls, only a narrow ledge of concrete beside a low concrete bank topped by a six-inch-diameter metal pipe running the length of the bridge. The newspapers had reported that Samuel Rocha had fallen off the northside of the bridge, the un-guarded side. Where he would have most likely fallen there were small clusters of random trash but no permanent bushes or brush or large accumulations of monsoon, rushriver trash large enough to hide him from general view.

Where the Starr Pass Road bridge terminated on the east side was a parking lot. At an edge of the parking lot were two permanent public restrooms, so Rodeo walked to the parking lot and entered the men's room. On the walls around the toilet were advertised in Sharpie scribbles and knife scratches directive missives, most with dates or days attached — *"Blow Jobs Sour Apple Impala Tuesday, Well Hung Hippie Looking for Emo Action 8/11, Me @ Lazy Eight after ten, Big Trucker with $10/11, White Meat looking for Brown Meat, Silver Bell after six, look around and nod, want method? Eat the Rose special at Kettle, not cheap but yng blue eyes. If you need a jump raise hood . . ."*

Similarly hopeful directions were in the public restroom for women. Rodeo fetched the dog from the truck and walked him down the paved path along the east side of the riverbed. A fat Hispanic man in short shorts and a frayed Tour de Tucson jersey rode by on a Sears Free Spirit ten-speed and yelled, Pura Vida Loco! at the dog who barked.

121

Rodeo and his dog walked down a long ramp that led from the riverbank to the riverbed where the sand was soft several inches deep. Under the bridge the temperature was twenty degrees cooler than in the sun. From below, Rodeo aligned himself directly with the edge of the bridge and paced from bank to bank dragging a bootheel. The line in the sand was serpentine but averaged out accurately enough for him to judge more or less where a small man dropped directly off the bridge would land if he did not leap out.

They headed back up to street level and a quarter mile north on the bike path they met a curved concrete bench surrounding a water fountain. A man sat on the bench, reading an upside-down newspaper. The man's face was so darkly leathered it was difficult to judge his ethnicity or age. The bags under his eyes appeared filled with fouled blood and he stank of fabric soaked in urine and dried feces and old, spilled booze and a pathological level of cigarette smoke. Rodeo took a seat on the bench near the man, extracted his big wallet and pulled out one of the high school class photos of Samuel Rocha and held it in front of the benchman's face.

You know this kid, mister?

You could ask me my name first.

What's your name, mister? Mine's Rodeo Grace Garnet.

Billy, said the man. I'm from El Paso, Texas, I have a good memory and I'll suck your dick for one cigarette if it's Marlboro Red.

I'm not interested in that sort of business, Billy. But I am interested in whether you know the kid in this photograph? Rodeo asked.

Are you Police? Billy asked.

No, Billy but I can sure go get Police if you got something to tell the cops that you won't tell me.

Billy picked up his folded newspaper and handed it to Rodeo. Whether he could read or not, the man did recognize Samuel Rocha because he had found and saved the young man's obituary in The *Tucson Citizen.*

Died to death, Billy said. Right here. That's why I kept it. The man touched the newspaper.

You know anything about this kid's death, Billy? Were you around here on July twenty-seventh?

What day is it?

I think the day Samuel died was on a Wednesday.

No, what is today is?

123

Today is Tuesday, Billy.

I am inna choir practice in El Paso, Texas, onna Wednesday every time. That's tomorrow.

Where does this choir meet, Billy?

Here.

So you might have seen something on that Wednesday back in July?

I saw a Chevrolet Impala a lot, Billy said. 1967. Green. With spinny wheels that was driving back and forth and back and forth a lot back then.

You didn't see a license plate did you?

Those copper kind.

Rodeo studied the man for a moment trying to assess his reliability as a witness. Billy sat calmly on the stone bench but for the slight quiver that seemed to animate his whole body as it searched for alcohol. He stared at the dry river and then his eyes moved to the bridge as a vehicle passed over it. From his side-vision the private investigator watched Billy carefully tracking the car on the bridge, then Rodeo turned to look at his witness in the face. The whites of Billy's eyes were jaundiced but the pupils were sharp and clear.

Could you repeat that information for me please, Billy?

Chevrolet Impala. 1967. Green with copper wheels spinning back and forth and back and forth over the bridge. Billy seemed very confident about this recollection which seemed firmly implanted in his mind. And the repetition of his account was fairly accurate.

Anything else you remember about that day or around that time when the kid . . .

Sam.

Did you know him, Billy? Did you know Samuel, Sam Rocha?

Billy nodded. My friend, the man said.

So when Sam got killed did you see this green Impala? Did somebody shoot a gun around here that day?

Sometimes he comes to this side and meets a man on a Kawasaki 125 and they go over there and park under the letter A.

Rodeo frowned.

Who does this, Billy? Sam, the kid who fell off the bridge?

Yes, Billy said. In 1969 when I was born in El Paso, Texas.

Rodeo nodded. So the kid in the newspaper you showed me . . .

Sam. He's the girl and the other man he's the boy. Billy interrupted Rodeo with this information and then shifted gears again to point across the dry river at the small mountain with the big pile of organized

125

rocks that created the letter "A" for Arizona on its flank. This symbol of the University was fading after a year in the sun but would be refurbished by fraternity boys once autumn arrived as part of their dedicated and necessary service to the local community. I don't know where the rest of the letters are, said Billy.

What letters are those? asked Rodeo.

The alphabets letters. The man pointed at A-Mountain. It's just the "A" so far.

Rodeo looked at the defaced mountain Indians still called Sentinel Peak. I don't know, Billy.

They might be on the other side, said the man. But I never go over there to that side. That's not my side.

Who is on the motorcycle, Billy? Rodeo persisted. You said "he" comes over here and meets somebody on a motorcycle . . . Rodeo paused to point over his shoulder toward the public parking lot. You mean Sam comes over here to your side and meets a man back there in the parking lot?

Inna bathroom sometimes, Billy said. He inserted a filthy index finger into his mouth and pantomimed fellatio. When Rodeo cringed Billy took his finger out of his mouth.

So, Sam and some man they meet here on

this side and then they go on the motorcycle to the other side and go up on the mountain with the "A" on it . . . ?

Billy nodded.

And then what, Billy?

And then they walk down the hill with some suitcase and hide in the bushes and shoot bullets into the sand in the dry water.

Like target practice? Rodeo asked.

Billy nodded.

Who is the fella with Sam, Billy? Is he a real grown man or another teenager like Sam?

Like you, Billy said. Old. But he's a soldier Injun. You're a cowboy Injun.

Rodeo slid the photo of the elk hunters out of his wallet and held it up for Billy to examine.

Which one is the soldier Injun? Rodeo asked.

Without hesitation Billy pointed at the hunter standing beside Luis Encarnacion and Samuel Rocha in the photo from the White Mountains, pointed directly at Ronald Rocha. Rodeo showed Billy the group photos of young people.

You know any of these other people, Billy?

They're not people, said Billy. They're pictures of people.

You're right, Billy. But just take a look at

the pictures and see who looks familiar to you.

The man tapped the picture in the newspaper obituary again. I know Sam. He was my friend, so I saved him.

That's why you saved his picture from the newspaper you mean? Rodeo asked.

Billy's head sunk into the folds of clothes on his chest and he started to nod and his shoulders shook as if he were crying but he was so dehydrated no tears came forth.

I've got a ride, Rodeo said. Can I take you somewhere, Billy?

El Paso, Texas, Billy said. Sister said I could come home when I got straightened up but I never did get straightened up.

Rodeo extracted his wallet and pulled from the bulging tri-fold one of Katherine Rocha's ten-dollar bills and gave it to Billy.

You want me to suck your dick?

No, Billy. This is payment for the information you just gave me, Rodeo said. This is honest work money.

Billy crammed his money directly into the front of his fouled pants, stood and walked off without another word. Rodeo let him go.

Rodeo headed with the dog to the top of A-Mountain.

■ ■ ■ ■

Tucson is a buggy wheel, the rust brown rim of which is composed of the Catalina, Rincon, Santa Rita and Tucson mountain ranges which encircle the hub of an urban center. Strip malls and wide streets and avenues like neon and asphalt spokes emanate from this Barrio Historico. The best view of the Old Pueblo and surrounds is from the top of Sentinel Peak where a city-maintained road terminates in a curve of parking lot. Near dusk on any day there are sightseers, mostly local, come to watch electric lights crystallize the valley as it darkened. But in the middle of the day in the middle of the summer the parking lot was empty.

Rodeo aimed his binoculars toward the only skyscraper in the city and from that point of reference he swung the glasses south to recognize the Tucson Convention Center, a drab collection of industrial buildings whose rise was the demise of many square blocks of Territorial adobes. Rodeo watered the dog and drank some water himself, then paced the length of the parking lot until he found a footpath that would put a hiker in view from Billy's perspective.

When the dog veered off the well-worn track and into mesquite brush, Rodeo followed to a five-foot-high boulder where the dog had stopped to sniff at trash. A hooded sweat shirt had been chewed by pack rats but the graphic image on front was clearly METALLICA and part of a symbol for "chaos." Rodeo whistled the dog back from the scene then searched the area thoroughly. He found a small pile of Kool cigarette butts, three empty Mountain Dew cans, an empty bag of Fritos and half buried in the dirt at the base of the boulder one spent .30 caliber rifle cartridge with clear extraction marks. He left these things in situ, returned to his truck, fetched his point-and-click camera, returned to the sniper's nest and took a variety of photos then hiked back to the truck again.

Rodeo drove a few blocks east of Starr Pass Road bridge to Parade Liquor. Two Indian men and an Indian woman were sitting on a guardrail across the street from the convenience store. Rodeo braked nearby them and leaned toward the alpha male, a Res local he recognized.

Howdy Isidro, Rodeo said.

Hey, fella, the man said.

You seen that fella called Billy? Rodeo asked.

Been here and gone. Isidro said this as if he knew. You want to leave a message for Billy's message service?

Tell him "ten dollars" is looking for him again, said Rodeo.

Hey, fella, the woman yelled. Her voice was loud and flat. Give me ten dollars. My sister's sick in the hospital and I need a beer.

The Locals laughed at this joke as Rodeo pulled into the parking lot of the store and went inside, bought two six-packs of Milwaukee's Best, paid cash and returned to his truck, backed out and pulled into the middle of the street, held one six-pack out the window.

Tell your sister to get better, Rodeo said.

The woman leapt up as if electrocuted and scooted into the street, snatched the beer and started walking away as fast as she could. The men hurried after her. Rodeo cruised slowly through the Barrio Historico where some houses were still occupied by working class Mexican-Americans though most were now owned if not occupied by trial lawyers and cardiologists and real estate moguls.

Rodeo did not look at the house he had rented with Sirena Rae Molina for six tumultuous months the year before but he stopped a few houses farther down Convent Avenue in front of the house he had shared with his mother, a Territorial era adobe that Grace and her son had moved into after Buck Garnet had deserted his family. The people who had owned the house when Rodeo and his mother were living there still owned it and quite a few of the Dotas continued to occupy the big place judging from the number of cars, disabled and functional, in the driveway.

A middle-aged Hispanic man sat on a riding lawn mower on the hardpacked dirt that was the narrow front yard of the place and official sidewalk of the neighborhood. An open newspaper was balanced on his thick head of hair, a beer can inserted between his legs with one withered hand resting on top of it to keep out the flies. Rodeo stopped the truck.

Where's your dog at? the man asked. He shook his head and the newspaper fluttered in stages to the ground to gather there with other newspapers and beer cans, cigarette butts, car parts. You finally put him down?

The dog stuck his head out the shotgun-side window, barked hoarsely and lolled his tongue at the man on the tractor.

I'm glad to see you haven't killed him yet,

said the man on the lawn mower. He did not indicate whether he was talking to Rodeo or to Rodeo's dog.

Rodeo exited his truck and walked over to the man. When he leaned in for a quick bro hug he could feel the hard muscles bunched under a layer of fat on just one side of the man's body and the other side slack as bacon, the effects of a drug-induced stroke many years before. The screeching of the TV inside was muted, a curtain fluttered and a chair scraped in the front room as Mother Dota moved closer to the window to eavesdrop.

How you doing, Tomas?

Still a D-O-T-A, the lawn-mower man said. Denizen-of-Tucson-Arizona. Still handsome and horny as ever. Still upholding the family traditions. He finished off his crotch beer and crushed the can in his good hand, tossed the empty on the ground, turned expertly and pulled a fresh beer out of the cooler strapped on the seat behind him, popped the top and took a long swig.

Just dropped by to see how your mother was, Rodeo said.

Mama had a stroke herself a few months ago. Took her medicine wrong and the doctor said that would be the last time she did that and if she didn't straighten up and fly right from now on she wouldn't last the year out. Tomas shook his head. But she still eats fry bread and carne all day, ice cream sandwiches all night and fights like a cat with anybody that tries to take care of her. She won't let nobody help her, so I quit trying to help her. It's too much stress.

Where's your wheelchair at? Rodeo asked.

Got a DUI and Social Services took it back, Tomas said.

You got a DUI in an electric wheelchair?

That's what I get for living next to the police station.

Where'd you get the lawn mower?

It's a garden tractor. Henry got it for me at the Salivating Army where he works at now.

Henry's out? Rodeo was asking about the twin of Tomas, an inept but well known local criminal.

He got out of Florence a few months ago but he don't do nothing but just go to work every day at the SA Outpost down on Sixth and then he rides a dumbass bicycle all the way out to Holy Hope on Oracle to visit his Miguel, Tomas said. He's lost forty pounds riding that stupid bicycle to the cemetery every day. But he don't have nothing else to do except to visit his shot-dead son.

Miguelito's been passed now, what, almost

a year? asked Rodeo.

A year in a couple of weeks, Tomas said. You were living with Miss TaTas over here when it happened, so you remember it good don't you? Miguelito's gangbangers spray-painted the whole 'hood after his funeral. If Mama hadn't come out of the house and Eryn Hage hadn't fired off her shotgun a few times they would have graffitied every house on the block that buncha greaser beaner cholo pachuco assholes.

Henry still dealing?

That last time was Strike Two for Henry, Tomas said. And you remember he was in when his kid got popped and that hit him hard. So now he just spends all day going to the cemetery being the good dad to Miguelito he should have been when the kid was alive. Henry's a great dad now that his boy is dead. It's a sad story, brother. Another sad tale in the annals of Denizens of Tuxson Arizona. We're just snake bit, that's what it is. Tomas pulled on his beer and belched loudly. I'm glad I'm not in that shit anymore myself. Tomas held up his beer can. Legal beagle, that's me. Beeraholico no problemo.

Unless you get caught DUI in your electric wheelchair, Rodeo said.

There is that, thanks to PUTAs — Police-

Upchucks-of-Tuxson-Arizona.

Tomas finished the beer, crushed the can, dropped it on the ground and again reached back to snag another.

You need something, brother? he asked. You're making me nervous.

You know the Rochas? asked Rodeo. Over near Casino del Sol?

Yeah, I know them Rochas, Tomas said. I went to school with one of them at Tucson High back in the day before it was a magnet school for yuppy shitheads. The one my age his name was Alonzo. He married some pretty fat chick who can't keep her pussy to herself and he's still out there in that Res 'hood near the Casino. His kid got killed a little while ago too. Little guera girl got hit-n-run. Some asshole ran over a blond child and runned away, can you believe it? And Alonzo's other kid was shot off the Starr Pass Road bridge in a drive-by. Tomas shook his head again. Fucking degenerates around these days, Rodeo. No law or order any-where. I blame the Colonialists.

You know any of the rest of the Rochas besides Alonzo?

Yeah, I know one big asshole for sure. Tomas slurped his warm beer. This Alonzo he's got a cousin who's a tribal cop. Name of "Monjano," first name Carlos but they call that one "Caps" 'cause he threatens to put a cap in everybody. Used to be a South Tuxson gangbanger and now he's a Tribe cop if you can believe it. Total hound dog Caps Monjano is. Screws everything on the Res he can get into the back of his patrol car. If you need to know these assholes I can introduce you for a monetary exchange. You know I still got lots of connections from my days when I worked for the Tribe running that halfway house for drunk Indians.

I think I met this Res cop fella Carlos Monjano already, Rodeo said. Big guy, bad attitude?

That's him. Caps played football on the practice squad at ASU but one of his bitches got a little bit pregnant and then she "fell down" some stairs at the Sun Devils' stadium and miscarried then Caps he came back here and joined the Tribe cops. Tomas drank his beer again. My friend from AA, Gilbert says all Caps usually does is hangs out at Circle K all day jacking off in the bathroom and eating free burritos.

You know anything about the kid that got killed in the hit-and-run? Rodeo asked. The little guera girl, Farrah?

Yeah. I do know something.

Tomas raised his bushy eyebrows. Rodeo reached for his wallet and pulled out a ten, folded it into Tomas's shirt pocket.

I heard that little guera girl she might have been this tribal cop's, this Caps Monjano's real kid, said Tomas. But you didn't hear it from me. I think she was some beauty queen or something.

She was in "Little Miss" pageants, Rodeo said. They dyed her hair yellow and put contact lenses in her eyes to make them blue.

Yeah, that's her, Tomas said. Caps used to carry her around the 'hood when she was dressed up like that. He always said he was the godfather or something supposedly. Tomas tilted his head in a skeptical way. But like I said, Caps Monjano was this little blond girlchild's actual baby daddy is what I heard.

Not Alonzo?

Not Alonzo Rocha, said Tomas. I don't think Alonzo has got it up in ten years. So you know Caps Monjano was that little beauty queen's real baby daddy. And if you ever saw the kid she did looked just like Caps in the face. Tomas shook his head. Them Monjanos is assholes. Caps and his cousin Alonzo and his cousin Xavier they used to beat shit out of everybody when we were at Tucson High. And as bad as Caps Monjano is Xavier Monjano is the actual

138

major criminal asshole in that familia.

Where is this Xavier Monjano?

He ran most of the weed and speed in Bisbee and around there for long time, but then he got ratted out and was supposed to be in Florence on a twenty-to-life but he ran off to Mexico before they could get him.

Was Caps in the drug trade with Xavier?

I could ask Henry, he'd know. But I don't think Caps has the stones to hang with Xavier. Xavier Monjano is hang you up in the shower and carve you with a chainsaw himself bad. Caps is only push your pregnant girlfriend down the stairs or shoot somebody in a drive-by bad.

Is Caps Monjano on the take?

I think I been talking too much for ten dollars. And I'm thirsty. Tomas tossed his empty on the yard and with his good hand tapped his shirt pocket into which Rodeo slipped another ten.

I think I heard Henry say that Caps the Monjano cop and Xavier the Monjano drug dealer they have probably got some working relationships if you know what I mean. They have lots of very cartel relatives in Chihuahua with real gangster reputations, I do know that, Tomas said. And I actually wouldn't want to fuck with Caps Monjano or Xavier or any of them Monjano tribe.

The Rochas is just losers, but the Monjanos is killers. If that's what you were thinking of doing create a change of plans.

I'm looking into the death of some distant relative of this Caps Monjano, probably a cousin like everybody is around here, Rodeo said. I wasn't planning on messing with anybody serious on this one. I got no interest in Xavier if anybody asks.

What relative of Caps? There's lots of dead Monjanos. Not nearly enough yet though.

This kid is a Rocha not a Monjano. Samuel Rocha. He's Alonzo Rocha's son. The older brother of the little guera beauty queen.

Samuel Rocha is the one that got shot in the drive-by and died up under Starr Pass Road bridge? asked Tomas.

Yeah.

I know this kid too, said Tomas. Yeah, Samuel Rocha. Called himself Smoke which is a stupid name for a dope dealer if I ever heard one. Tomas shook his head again. And you know that kid was Alonzo's real son because he was just as stupid and ugly as Alonzo. Tomas laughed. Them Rochas are all that kind of stupid loser. Men who fall off bridges.

You know anything about Samuel's death, Tomas?

I heard he got shot in a drive-by and originally fell out in the sand where somebody should have seen him pretty quick. But somebody — probably the shooter — dragged that kid under a rock or under some bushes or something to hide him and then left the stupid kid to bleed out. Which is a very bad way to go, especially in this summer heat. Tomas smiled, showing off an assortment of mismanaged teeth. But it is a dry heat.

Who said the kid was dragged under cover out of sight? asked Rodeo.

Tomas shrugged. Just something I heard from a bum.

Any of your regular bums around?

I hadn't seen them bums around here lately, said Tomas. The City came in last week or so ago and moved all those mattresses and shit from behind Jerry's Lee Ho Market and I don't know where that bunch of bums went after that. Maybe the shelter over near the VA or maybe over to Parade Liquor where they got some places back near the river that are hard to get to and nobody bothers them. Go look around there if you're looking for some bums these days.

Rodeo nodded. So you think that Rocha kid's death was a drive-by, Tomas?

What else? Like diabetes ain't enough for

us to worry about now this bunch of gang-banger cholo wannabes is shooting kids in the street and running over little girls, so what else could have killed that Rocha kid but pachuco gang violence?

Was Samuel Rocha ganged up?

I got nothing to do with nobody from the Life anymore now that Henry is out of the trade, I think permanently this time. I hope he is at least because all this fucking drug business is ruining my fair city. Hard to be a Denizen of Tuxson Arizona no more. If a good Mexican like me farts he gets a strike against him and if he farts while he's high he could get the death penalty in Arizona.

Don't drink and drive, Tomas.

It's political, Tomas said. You know how they hate us Mexicans in Arizona. Even the Mexicans hate the Mexicans in Arizona. Good thing we're also Indian, brother, because even a half-breed Indian is better than a poor Mexican these days in Arizona. Tomas sounded fractious now that his beer buzz needed refreshing. At least us Indians are Native Americans and got papers so the assholes can't deport us. We should deport all you Anglos and the Tucson Police putas should be first in that line.

Tomas ran out of steam. The street was quiet and still in the afternoon heat as only a fully inhabited street in Tucson could be. Even the noise of the nearby interstate seemed but a distant sleeping beast. Though no workers were on site at that moment, there was obvious construction ongoing across the street where the old grocery store was being strategically dismantled.

What's up with Jerry's Lee Ho Market? Rodeo asked.

Turning it into a ecology clinic or some crazy Anglo shit like that. Saving the whales in Tuxson. They don't tell us or ask us Mexicans nothing of course, just come in and cheat us out of our places for centavos then put some paint on these old shithouses and sell them for a million dollars to a bunch of Anglo assholes.

A mid-1970's Toyota Land Cruiser with faded original green paint was parked in front of one of the apartments across the avenue. The vintage SUV bore the copper AZ license plates issued to Historic Vehicles over twenty-five years old, an automotive milestone which, considering the pollution generated by the rattletraps and their paltry gas mileage, should not probably have been rewarded.

Somebody living at Eryn Hage's now? Rodeo asked.

Some professor type is in her end apartment, said Tomas. He's a archaeology guy at the U he says. Name of Tinley Burke which is a stupid name for a college professor if I ever heard one, Tomas said. He's related somehow to that Right Wing asshole Randy Miller, the one who wants to be in Congress or President or something. The Professor don't talk too much. He has some noisy pussy over there sometimes but mostly he keeps to hisself.

Rodeo moved back to his truck, scratched his dog's ears and pushed him back onto the seat.

Since you're such a big pussy, I'm glad you're gone out of this 'hood, brother, said Tomas. But I miss having you as a ride. Nobody sober around here since you left to take me to the liquor store.

Maybe you ought to quit drinking so much, brother.

Maybe you ought to just suck my dick like you know you want to, brother.

Rodeo reached into the cab and retrieved the second six-pack of Milwaukee's Best and placed it in the tepid water in the cooler on back of the garden tractor.

You're still one step ahead of everybody aren't you? Tomas asked.

Or one step behind, said Rodeo. He turned to his truck and spoke over his shoulder. Tell your mother I asked after her, Tomas.

Mama Dota already knows everything you said. And probably knows everything you're thinking too. Tomas winked. But you know she's happy you came by to ask after her, Rodeo. For some reason Mama always liked you. I don't know why since you're such a big pussy.

Rodeo moved around the truck and got in.

You know Sirena's been back around. Tomas raised his voice as Rodeo started the cranky engine of his Ford. I seen her in some big ass negro truck cruising the neighborhood blasting that bullshit classy music she likes. What should I tell her from you after she quits fucking my brains out?

Tell her she needs to improve her tastes.

Rodeo rolled slowly to Cushing Street then drove east two blocks where he parked under shade near the Tucson Police Department building then went to Old Pueblo Credit Union where he rained his change into the coin counter. He took the slip to the window and deposited half of the fee Katherine Rocha had paid him into his near-empty account. He then crossed Sixth Street and stepped up to the walk-up window at Midtown Liquors drive-through liquor store where there was a short line of men on foot, all in fragments of GI gear with commemorative patches from theaters of war including several intergalactic. All the men were heavily tattooed and none over forty years old.

The men sized up Rodeo quickly and turned back to the walk-up window where a thirty-pack of Keystone Light appeared. The trio hurried toward wherever they drank with the suitcase full of beer cans between them like luggage. A thin white face appeared on the clerk's side of the walk-up window.

Long time no see, the face in the window said. A Green and a Blue?

You got a good memory, Rodeo said.

Nothing else to do around here but remember is it, the clerk said.

The Foster's oil cans appeared on the counter in less than a minute and Rodeo laid out the cash for the two beers and added an extra dollar as a tip.

Where's your old truck at? the clerk asked.

In shade.

How's your old dog?

He's pretty good considering how bad he is, said Rodeo.

Where's your old girlfriend at?

That, I don't know.

I miss seeing that girl around, the clerk said. You don't get to see women like that too often without paying for the pleasure. She still dancing at Richard Dick's clubs?

I don't know what she's doing these days.

How you ever get used to being around some woman that looks like that woman looks like I don't know.

Men get used to the way their women look, said Rodeo.

Rodeo walked a block west and knocked on the door of a beautifully remodeled adobe the color of lemon pulp trimmed in the color of lime rind.

Come!

Jarred Willis, Esq. was sitting behind his mahogany desk moving papers around under a gold Phantas ink pen. Two fresh Cuban Diplomáticos were clipped and laid out in a Waterford ashtray on the desk. The lawyer's Brooks Brothers suit was custom made for his paunch. His face looked freshly baked from Miraval Spa.

Sit, the lawyer said.

Rodeo settled into a distressed leather armchair that was soft as veal, unpacked the Foster's and put the Green in front of Jarred Willis and the Blue between his own knees.

What's the occasion, Chief? asked the lawyer.

Just visiting, said Rodeo.

That's horseshit. You always want something. Something for free usually.

The men popped their beers and drank off an inch or three.

Why you all dressed up, Jarred? What's with the twenty-dollar cigars?

The gentleman coming in after you is as rich as the Pope's pimp, so poor you just shut up about my three-thousand-dollar suit.

You are a piece of work, Jarred.

Seriously, Chief, just look at you on that side of the big desk like something the cat dragged in and then look at me on this side of the big desk like one million dollars in cash money. We went to Tucson High together, Tonto.

I get your point, Jarred. There's no justice in the world.

You just here to annoy me or you got some business in town?

A little, said Rodeo. A Mrs. Katherine Rocha hired me to look into her grandson's death by misadventure.

Don't know the case, said Jarred Willis. The lawyer studied Rodeo, his brow wrinkled in exaggerated concentration. Oh.

148

I get it, Willis said. You want the neighbor-hood rundown? Always the seeker of infor-mation. Willis pounded the remainder of his bitter, aimed the can at a wastebasket across the room and tossed it surely in. Well, Sirena got out of rehab and was downtown lately, shacked up with somebody in the neighbor-hood. She's serving at BoonDocks on the weekends, said the lawyer. And she might be shagging your old football buddy Tank Hage. At least Tank's shagging somebody at the club and he and Annabeth are splitting. I heard that from a divorce lawyer friend of mine. And from my real estate buddy I learned that Sirena's former employer Rich-ard "Nine Inch" Dick has bought up most of that block of Convent he lives on for reasons unknown. The lawyer took a breath. And now you are up to speed, Chief.

Thanks for the update, Mr. Cronkite, said Rodeo.

Speaking of local affairs, how's all that shit going down at Los Jarros with the murder at your place? asked the lawyer.

I made my statement, said Rodeo. I didn't have much to say but that I found the dead man and so that's what I said and nobody's bothered me about it yet. Special Investiga-tions Unit was down there.

Apache Ray called in Special Investigations? asked the lawyer.

Or SIU called themselves in, said Rodeo.

You think a few Undocumenteds dead in the desert amounts to anything serious, Chief? The lawyer asked this question as if he were really interested.

That would depend on who is killing them and why, wouldn't it? Rodeo asked.

Do you think something major is going on out there in your hole in the world like Federation Cartel or major smuggling of UAs? You think that's why State is getting involved and taking over from County?

It's not my business, Jarred.

The lawyer nodded. That's a good attitude, Chief, he said. Maybe you ought to keep that attitude and just stay low on this one. Maybe you should even think about extending your vacation this year.

There was a brisk knock on the office door, and Willis Jarred, Esquire smoothed his pale hair, stood, walked around his huge desk and ushered Rodeo out a side door. Rodeo lingered a moment but could hear nothing through the bulletproof steel, so he strode across the street to the Tucson Police Department.

Rodeo passed through the metal detectors, got his big belt buckle and jeans frisked then signed in to see Clint Overman and sat down. The detective came out to the waiting area ten minutes later and waved Rodeo through to his small, over-tidy office.

What's up? The big lawman eased himself into his captain's chair behind a metal desk. On the desk was a "participation" trophy for youth soccer and a framed photograph of the detective's teenaged son, an only child murdered three years before by the serial killer Charles Constance. The policeman adjusted the trophy so that the player kicked the ball directly at his guest.

Just in the neighborhood, Clint, said Rodeo. Thought I'd suss you out about the thing over at Starr Pass. The Rocha kid that went off the bridge.

Overman leaned forward in his chair and aligned his calendar blotter so the edges were exactly perpendicular to the edges of the desk. He put his hands down on the blotter. On one hand three fingers were severely misshapen and on the other a thumb and the ring finger were altogether missing, the effects of prolonged torture. His eyes were swollen and bloodshot and he smelled slightly of alcohol.

Nothing to suss out, the detective said. The Rocha kid got hit in a drive-by, fell off the bridge, busted himself up pretty badly but managed to crawl under some brush and rock overhang when nobody saw him for days and he died.

Bled out? asked Rodeo.

The kid's wound was relatively superficial, just a flesh wound to his shoulder. Enough to weaken him but nothing that would have been deadly if he'd been found soon enough. He died of exposure the ME said. Dehydration.

Was he paralyzed? Rodeo asked.

ME says so but that seems unlikely to me since he crawled up under some bushes to get shade. Must have seemed like a good move at the time but he hid himself where he couldn't be seen and got too weak to call for help.

There's shade under the bridge, Rodeo said.

Maybe he was trying to get out of the creek bed.

With all those busted bones? asked Rodeo.

You know yourself what people can do when adrenaline kicks in, the policeman said. It's not always rational. But then when that buzz wears off they can be totally disoriented and disabled completely.

Could somebody have dragged him under the brush?

Could be. No proof of it if they did.

Riverbed is totally tracked up, so we didn't find any drag heel marks as I recall.

No cell phone on the kid? asked Rodeo.

Not that I recall.

And y'all didn't find a slug? asked Rodeo. The one that hit the kid?

We didn't find any slug that I recall. The policeman jiggled his head as if something were loose in it. We don't even know for sure that the kid was shot and TPD doesn't have the manpower to search a river of sand for a slug that might not even exist.

You think Samuel Rocha just fell off the bridge? asked Rodeo. Was he high?

The kid had drugs in his system and had dope on him when he was found.

But he wasn't high.

The detective shrugged. He did time at the Pima County Juvie Center for selling nickel bags at a couple of high schools and middle schools, so he's probably connected to a gang, said the cop. It's still an open case and will stay that way, so don't think we're covering anything up.

I didn't think that, Clint.

The detective realigned the trophy on the desk slightly.

What gang does anybody think Sam Rocha was in? asked Rodeo.

I could check with Detective Haynes, who

heads our gang task force, but he's up at John Jay in New York City at some criminology conference at that college of justice. The policeman shifted in his seat and looked directly at Rodeo. What's your interest here? Overman asked. Maybe we need to get that straight first off.

I got hired to look into this Rocha kid's death is all, Rodeo said.

Hired by who?

I'd prefer to keep that under my hat since it's just a routine follow-up. I'm in and out in a day.

Overman shrugged. Like I said it's an open case, so anything you get is ours by law anyway. You got anything yet?

Rodeo shook his head.

Well, if you do come up with something it comes right to me, got that?

You handled the Samuel Rocha case? asked Rodeo.

I did.

Who found the body?

Horseman, said Overman. And there's nothing there. The guy who found the dead body is just a guy who rides the river every Saturday morning. Horse got spooked by the smell . . . The detective brushed at his eyes. That's all in the papers. He readjusted the soccer trophy on his desk again so that the little striker aimed the ball out the window. The policeman looked out the window too as if following the potential path of the prize ball. And I can tell you there's not much in the file that's not in the papers, so don't ask me to see the file. Overman aimed his watery eyes back at his guest and adjusted the kicker so that his foot was aimed at the door. I'm busy now, so . . .

I guess my free pass is about run out around here? Rodeo asked.

Nothing personal, said the lawman. It's just that I'm trying to put all that behind me and you remind me not to.

You don't owe me anything, Clint.

I never said I did. The detective sighed and pressed his fingertips into his bloodshot eyes. But as bad as it was for me, the Constance Case was still a potential career maker for me, the cop said. So I might still get to Phoenix on that one high-profile case if I can keep my shit together. He paused. So I won't forget you for the career boost, at least. But this Rocha kid, he's just a drive-by and you know how prosecuting a drive-by can be. If all the assholes and related persons keep their mouths shut there's not much we can do. The cop stared at his shaky hands and then stood. I need to get back to work now.

Rodeo stood and held out his hand but Overman walked past him and opened the office door.

Call next time, the TPD detective said.

Tucson, Arizona, is a schizophrenic place, a small city that feels like a big town divided into discernible sections based mostly on money and ethnicity or occupation or some hybrid admixture of these with most of the conservative Anglo retirees on the northern edges, protected in gated communities around golf courses, and with the liberal intelligentsia and college kids huddled around the University more or less in the middle of the valley, with military spreading out from Davis-Montham Air Force Base on the east side and with Mexicans and low-riders and cholos in South Tucson and increasingly in EastSide, and with bars and saloons and dives everywhere there were people, and a few places where there weren't even many people.

The Buffet opened early for the chronic regulars and stayed open late for the acute frat boys and sorority girls who liked to slum. Rodeo established himself near one end of the horseshoe bar, took off his hat and laid it crown down on the carved-upon wood. He put his saddlebags with his laptop and maps and notebooks on a stool beside him. A middle-aged woman was behind the horseshoe bar, her glass eye fixed at some spot slightly above Rodeo's left shoulder. Rodeo ordered a shot and a beer. The waitress slid a shot of house brand between his hands and placed an iced stein of beer on top of his twenty-dollar bill and moved away to wait on another customer. Rodeo threw back the shot and chased it with a long drink of Coors Light. There was not much custom in the place, not enough people to require conversation, so he pulled a spiral notebook from his bag and a Bic and started to work.

First he sketched the layout of Sam Rocha's death with Starr Pass Road bridge as one boundary and A-Mountain as another with the Rio Santa Cruz in between. He drew an arrow showing Sam's path across the bridge and Xs where the kid had most likely been hit on the bridge and where he had landed under the bridge. He drew a line from halfway up A-Mountain to the X. He drew a B for Billy on one side of the dry river.

You an artist, cowboy? the barkeeper asked.

She had crept up on him. She raised an eyebrow above the glass eye at the shot glass but Rodeo shook his head and she plopped the shot glass in the wet sink.

Just thinking, said Rodeo.

You draw pictures to think? the woman asked. You dyslexic or something?

My daddy said I was just plain retarded.

Join the Bad Daddy club, the woman said. She moved off to the other side of the bar where two summer school college boys were testing their afternoon limits against a pair of cougars working on multiple margaritas. A patron fed the jukebox old school rock and roll.

When Rodeo looked away from the barmaid and her patrons he noticed an angular Anglo wearing an MIA-POW cap covered in red, white and blue buttons. The man's beard was long and yellowed with nicotine, his eyes were beach glass gray. The old Vet raised his mug in a salute.

Hot one today, idn't it? the man asked.

104's not so hot if you're inside with a cold beer, said Rodeo.

I'm not going to say it's a dry heat though, the man said. Then people will know I'm not from around here.

That a fact? Rodeo asked. You're not from around here?

Nope. Idaho.

What brought you down here?

158

Dry heat, the man said. The man laughed again and pulled on his long beard. 'Struth though. I loved Idaho. I loved the attitude up there, you know. Independent. Survival of the fittest. But the winters are real hard up there. The Vet hospital here is good, so I come on down here.

You sick? asked Rodeo.

I got Agent Orange, you know? the man said. From the government. My own fucking government tried to kill me while I was in its very service. Can you believe that shit?

Not much I can't believe about the government of this country, mister, Rodeo said.

Rodeo knocked off his beer then waggled his finger between the man and himself. The bartender refreshed the mugs and made change for three beers and a shot out of Rodeo's twenty and placed the money on the bar.

Much obliged. The man's voice was slurred. But don't get me started on Bureaucracy. Clusterfuck is what it is. Ought to blow the whole caboodle to shit and start over.

I sometimes feel that it's hard to get anything done through regular government channels, Rodeo said.

'Struth. Not but one man man enough in government around here to get shit done and that's the Tea Party fellow Randy Miller and the liberals are trying to kill him outright.

That a fact? asked Rodeo.

'Struth, said the barhound. All over the Internet, idn't it? Assassination plot on Randy Miller 'cause he's running for Congress and that scares the shit out of them liberals. Ronald told me all about it.

Rodeo leaned forward. The Viet Vet tilted his head and looked down his long nose at Rodeo.

You Mescan? he asked Rodeo.

My mother was Italian-American. Her people came to this country from Sicily in the 1800s, said Rodeo. I'm Black Irish on my daddy's side. His people came over during the Famine, way back when. Daddy was a roughneck in the East Texas Oil Fields and he served in WW Two, Infantry, Indian-Head Division. Rodeo told these practiced lies easily.

No shit, the man said. Your old man was in the Second? Landed on Normandy?

Rodeo nodded though this was also not true.

What's your name son?

Rodeo looked around the bar carefully to make sure nobody there actually knew him. Early, Rodeo said. Bill Early.

Olin, the man said. He didn't supply a last name or offer a handshake.

Who is this "Ronald" you're talking about? Rodeo asked. He reached into his pocket for his billfold but the bartender unceremoniously shut Rodeo's party down.

Y'all are cut off and out of here, the woman said. She stared at Rodeo with her one good eye. Rodeo shrugged and pushed his half-empty mug toward the old man who killed it.

Let's move on, Olin, Rodeo said. Buffet's not the only place we can drink.

'Sonly place I'll drink. Olin wobbled off his barstool and without a backwards glance stalked out the door.

Rodeo watched him leave.

You're next, cowboy, the bartender said.

I'm looking for a friend of Olin's, Rodeo said. He slid the photo of the solo hunter out of his billfold and placed it atop the money on the bar. "Ronald Rocha" is who I'm looking for.

The bartender looked at the blurry photo quickly, put her hand over it and pulled it into the wet sink, soaked it for a few seconds and then shredded it in Rodeo's face.

You need to drift, Cowpoke, she said. And you might not want to drift back this way.

Rodeo claimed his change without leaving

a tip and left the bar. He walked around the neighborhood for ten minutes looking for Olin, didn't find him, so headed back to Arizona Motel.

Rodeo sat alone on the edge of the Arizona Motel pool and watched his dog swim laps for no reason. Rodeo heard the truck before he saw it, the throaty rumble rolling into the parking lot like the prelude to a storm. Sirena ran the black Chevy 4×4 fast over the speed bumps and parked right under the ramada of the bar-b-que near the pool in the middle of the horseshoe of the motel. Rachmaninoff's "Moscow Bells" were muted abruptly when she shut the truck down.

The dog swam to the pool's edge, struggled up the steps and ran to the chain-link fence where he stood panting as he pressed his nose against the gate wire like he was trying to escape jail.

Hello, boy, said Sirena Rae Molina. You been missing me?

Rodeo's former girlfriend unlatched the gate, bent down and rubbed the old dog's head until his tail almost wagged out of joint. She stood up and let the gate shut behind her as she stepped onto the pool deck. Rodeo could hear her undressing but he did not turn around to see how far she would go toward naked. A sleeveless pearl-buttoned shirt landed nearby enough for him to smell her scent of White Shoulders as his bad hopes rose against his best intentions. Her boots hit the deck and then a buckle-bunny belt that once had been his.

She stepped into the pool. Her blue-jean cutoffs were trimmed short so her butt cheeks showed on the bottom side to complement the g-string whale tail showing off on the top side and the wife-beater she wore was cut ragged just below her breasts as if she had torn it with her sharp, white teeth.

Sirena swam to the deep end under water and then surfaced and rolled onto her back and floated for a minute then breast-stroked back to the shallow end wall of the pool where she folded her elbows on the concrete, turned toward the man and his dog and rested her head on her arms. Rodeo had to restrain the dog from jumping back into the pool.

Rodeo's white feet in the water kicked like fish struggling against a strong hook, a short line and a heavy sinker. Rodeo let the dog loose and the dog scuttled to the woman and started to lick her face. She giggled and played with the dog until she got bored and then she thumped him firmly on the nose with a blood red fingernail and the dog moved away a few feet and circled three times, lay down and whined for more of the woman's attention.

Your dog still loves me, Sirena said.

That dog never had any sense, Rodeo said. That's why I got him.

He always loved you the most, Ro, so maybe you are right about that dog. I'm sure you'll break his old heart one day too just like you broke my heart, you mean old mule rider. Sirena sighed out dramatically. Left me all by myself, didn't you?

I'm sure you hooked up with somebody the night I moved back to Vista Montana. Rodeo looked at Sirena's profile.

Because I need company, the woman said. She looked at the sky as if at an audience, then looked at Rodeo.

Rodeo looked away from his ex, looked at the swimming pool.

I was upset because you dumped me, shitheel, Sirena said. And I don't like to get dumped.

I didn't dump you, Sirena. Rodeo steadied himself on the shallow edge of the deep pool. I told you you had some serious psychological issues and when you threatened to kill me in my sleep I suggested you and me might be well served with some time apart and when I moved back to my place you tracked me down in the desert and damned near shot my dog to death.

I was high, Sirena said. You know I wouldn't hurt that stupid dog on purpose. He loves me.

She cooed at the dog near Rodeo but the man held the dog down.

I know sensible behavior often seems crazy to you, Sirena Rae. And I know how you treat things you love, Rodeo said. My dog still has shotgun pellets in his ass.

The dog whined as Sirena shook out her big head of hair.

If I am crazy it's because I have PTSD from what my daddy did to me when I was little and everybody knows that.

I don't know that, Rodeo said.

The woman raised herself up and eased her wet breasts onto the hot concrete. My momma was, you know, she said.

Was what?

Bone deep crazy. Sirena sighed. Went from Hollywood Playboy Centerfold to Arizona Desert Lunatic in ten short years. But Daddy pushed her to that.

I didn't know your momma, Sirena, said Rodeo. But I know Ray. And I know he's generally sensible, so I doubt what you say.

What do you think about me, Ro?

I think you want something and while I don't know what it is exactly you want from me I doubt it's any good for me. And I doubt what you want from me is talking psychology about your family which you probably been doing in rehab therapy for weeks.

Sirena steamed on the concrete. I thought you loved me once, Ro. Wasn't that true? You were my knight in shining armor once, weren't you? The woman did not seem to be engaged in a real conversation as much as following a script she had already written.

I don't think so, said Rodeo. He looked at Sirena, who looked like one million dollars. I think you are a woman who's got a very poor self-image and some bad daddy issues and many chemical addictions who lives a high-risk lifestyle and latches onto men for a while now and again when it suits you because you think they might help your poor self-image and then you build these men all up and make out like they're great but then when these men don't solve your problems you treat them like shit and try to shoot their dogs. Rodeo took in and let out a deep breath, glared at Sirena.

You obviously been waiting a while to

back that truck up and unload that pile of shit, Garnet. Sirena smiled a prizewinning smile. You read one of your momma's library books or something, cowboy?

Yes, I did, Rodeo said. He looked back at the swimming pool. The water in front of him was calm but the traffic behind him was raucous. I read up on psychology a lot after you almost killed my dog. And what I read described you just perfect.

You think I'm borderline, don't you?

The woman said this like she knew what the man was talking about.

I know you go through men like hotcakes, every one of them your knight in shining armor until you start hating them then you turn them into enemies who are the root of all your evils.

Admit it, Ro . . . Sirena laughed her coffee and cigarettes laugh. If I were a man, going through women like you say I go through men you'd just think I was a Big Swinging Dick, wouldn't you?

You're not a man, Sirena, said Rodeo.

Sirena shifted nearer to Rodeo and cupped a hand to make some waves. I think that's been established between us, the woman said. She looked at his crotch and licked her thick lips.

Rodeo stood as best he could, navigating

his tumescence until he was wrapped in his thin motel towel. Sirena leaned over the pool edge, pulled her cowgirl shirt to her and extracted a pack of Marlboro Reds and a Zippo from the pocket, lit a cigarette and moved to the steps where she leaned back against the wall of the pool. Her silicone breasts floated in the chlorinated water. She ashed her cigarette into the pool.

I might be at BoonDocks later on, Sirena said. Buy a girl a beer for old time sakes?

When Rodeo moved toward the gate the dog reluctantly followed him. Rodeo stopped at the gate. Did you actually want anything, Sirena? Other than jerking my chain?

Sirena smoked and shrugged.

You used to like it when I jerked your chain, cowboy. In fact you liked everything I did to you with chains.

I used to like a lot of things, Sirena.

But now you don't like anything? the woman asked. Not even Sirena anymore?

Nope. Not anymore.

You're no fun, Rodeo.

I never was fun enough for you, Sirena. You need fun on a whole other level.

I guess that's in my blood. Momma was wild and crazy. Sirena looked at the blue sky. And Daddy was crazy too, in his day.

And wild. Mean and wild. Sirena blew more smoke from her cigarette and then paused and looked into the smoke she'd sent. He was asking about you the other day, Ro. I think he still imagines you might one day be his son-in-law and run the old rancho and be sheriff just like him, just like in the movies.

I doubt any of that is true, Sirena.

Well, Daddy is in a state and he's sure nervous about something.

There's a lot for Apache Ray to be nervous about, said Rodeo. You not the least of it.

He thinks the murders in Los Jarros are all related, Sirena said.

Related to what? Rodeo asked.

To each other, stupid. Daddy thinks the murders have all been done by the same person. And he thinks he knows who the serial killer in Los Jarros is.

Serial killer, said Rodeo. He shook his head. That's bullshit.

It's not.

You are full of shit, Sirena.

Sirena's shrug was theatrical.

Who is it then? asked Rodeo. Or who does Ray think it is?

Sirena turned and flicked her cigarette into the deep end of the pool where it hissed out and floated like the trash it was. She spoke to Rodeo in her baby doll voice.

Daddy won't tell me anything, Ro. Since I got back he won't hardly talk to me at all. But he's worried that somebody is killing Indians in Los Jarros. She held up one digit at a time until all her fingers were up and her thumbs outspread. One little Indian at a time. Until we are all gone.

Since your daddy's "Indian" status was mostly advertising bullshit you got no reason to worry, said Rodeo. And I doubt you're on any Real Indian list, Sirena.

I might be on some other lists, though, right, Ro? Maybe for best blow jobs or ass-fucking or something like that? She smiled again at her ex. Don't I look good enough for some list like that?

Rodeo stared at her since at the moment Sirena glowed with rehab tan and was taut from weeks of a healthy diet and no booze or drugs. Her honey hair was naturally bleached ash blond now, her eyes were clear. Her body, always exceptional by any standards, seemed now simply perfect even if a good bit of it was fake.

You are no Indian, Sirena Rae.

I'm as Indian as you.

Rodeo grunted.

Fuck you, Mestizo. You're not half the man I am because you don't have half the

170

cojones I got.

I wouldn't argue that, Sirena.

She ignored Rodeo and seemed to think deeply for a moment. Even if somebody is killing Indians, I'm too tough to die anyway, said Sirena.

She started to rise from the water but before she could get her whole show going Rodeo turned and walked back to his room. He did not look over his shoulder as he unlocked his door and stepped into #116. He could not help but leave the door unlocked though.

Though Arizona Motel did not have Wi-Fi in the rooms, the manager did have it in the apartment that adjoined the office space and guests were allowed to poach his signal in the "loungette." The same motley crew was assembled there today, slouched on the cheap, mock-Imperial settee and in the spray-painted gold armchairs, all smoking cigarettes and ashing on the new polyester Persian throw rugs despite NO SMOKING signs posted on every wall.

Two elderly Anglo men were sitting together on the love seat huddled over a battered and dirty laptop arguing over free porn sites. An old Hispanic man was reading the Bible on his Kindle, cursing in Span-

171

ish as he tried to manipulate electronic pages that, he complained loudly, kept flipping inexplicably from Genesis right to Revelations, from creation to destruction. An old Anglo woman knitted what looked to be mittens for a child. Zander Jone played pool by himself, waiting for a mark. The pool shark seemed constructed of pool cues himself and articulated as a puppet, his cheap straw hat perched on the back of his head as if he were an extra in a 1950's Western.

Game? Zander asked Rodeo.

You know I can't give you any match, Zander.

I'll play you for fun, man, said Zander. Professional courtesy, one rodeo star to another.

You never won more than entry fee at a county rodeo in your life, Zander, said Rodeo. And you never played pool for fun in your life either.

I'll play you for a ten-spot then and spot you two balls, Zander said. Your choice after break.

I'll play you for four dollars. Rodeo placed this amount on the table's rim. Since that'll buy you a Forty and get you out of my way for a while. Zander didn't even bother to put his money on the table. Rodeo sunk one

ball on break and then removed two un-
playable balls then managed to sink two in
a row before he missed badly.

Even a blind squirrel can find a couple of
nuts now and then, the hustler said.

Zander ran the table in two minutes,
pocketed his beer money, tipped his drug-
store cowboy hat at Rodeo and ambled
outdoors cool and humble as a true hustler.

Rodeo set up his laptop on the pool table.
RoseRite.com sold editorial services to
fledgling poets, though the photographs of
the proprietor of this virtual business could
have indicated another sort of service, one
less cerebral than sexual, though the site
did not seem to function as an actual escort
service.

The girl who owned the site was obviously
the pink-haired one in Samuel Rocha's
snapshots. There was a link from RoseRite
.com to Rosejewel.net, a site that sold
clunky, "artistic" custom jewelry that was
hard to imagine anyone ever wearing anywhere except at the Jewel and Mineral
Show. The Hotmail address on both sites
was a dead end and the contact phone
numbers on both sites had been disconnected. Rodeo used his cell phone to dial
the number on the back of the RoseRite
.com calling card.

This is the Kettle, open 24/7/365, a woman said.

Is Rose there? Rodeo asked.

She works mornings and this is not her number, the woman said.

The phone went dead but Rodeo at least had found a place to start.

"Ronald Rocha" did not achieve any hits on any search engines. Rodeo used the professional tracking service he regularly frequented and failed to find the man there either.

He might be able to locate the man through Veterans Administration if the man had actually been military but Rodeo didn't have any good contacts with any federal agency lately and except for Clint Overman he no longer had useful and dependable contacts with local or regional Law Enforcement. He worked for several different bail bond companies but these were simply small businesses. So since he had no significant contacts to explore or exploit, he was dependent on his own gray cells.

According to Olin at the Buffet Bar there was some connection between Ronald Rocha and Randy Miller, former Pima County judge and state senator and Tea Party candidate for Congress but Rodeo could not find any such link on the Internet. He did stumble upon blogs and amateurish Web sites that speculated on the supposed assassination attempts on Randy Miller, all of which could be traced to vigilante and right-wing groups in the Tombstone area.

Rodeo abandoned the Internet search and walked out into the dry heat, hefted the dog into the shotgun seat of the truck and then drove around the horseshoe parking lot. As he passed the swimming pool he saw hanging on the gate Sirena's cutoff blue jeans and the ripped undershirt. Catching the woman's scent the dog whined.

She shot you in the ass with a shotgun, Rodeo said. That doesn't make any difference to you does it? The dog whined again and the man rubbed the old dog's head. You never had good sense about women.

Rodeo drove to BoonDocks for dinner. The bar used to be a genuine downtown roadhouse but lately it had become more family-friendly. Still, Tucson being Tucson there was always some variety of regulars and drop-ins beyond what one might find elsewhere in a midtown saloon restaurant that was set amongst used car dealerships, pawn stores, and Laundromats, tire stores and gas stations and a rundown strip mall that boasted an A-1 Rent-All, Deseret Industries Thrift Store, Little Caesar's Pizza Parlor, Fry's supermarket and a discount store that advertised itself as "Everything For At Least A Dollar."

Only one Harley was parked in the shade on the north side of the building, both American and Confederate States of America flags bolted to the bike's rear panniers. There were also two beaten-down pickups side by side in the northside parking lot, one vehicle pointing east and the other west in a cowboy conference alignment. A near-new Suburban occupied the prime handicap space in palm tree shade near the rear door of the bar, the tailgate covered in MY CHILD IS AN HONORS STUDENT AT TRINITY CHRISTIAN ACADEMY bumper stickers. Other vehicles were scattered around the lot, dusty Crown Victorias and Cadillacs, pick-ups old and new, even a pink VW bug and a newish Mustang in University of Arizona crimson with Wildcat license plates.

Rodeo noted the faded green Toyota Land Cruiser, circa mid-1970s bumped up against the giant Chianti bottle that was a local landmark. A faded brassiere dangled from one of the grapes that hung from the concrete vine twined around the twenty-

foot-tall concrete-encased sculpture. Someone had spray-painted a gang symbol high
up on the neck of the statue but someone
else had pasted a NUKE THE GAY WHALES
FOR JESUS bumper sticker over the gang
mark.

Rodeo did not see the black 4×4 Sirena
had driven to Arizona Motel earlier that day.
He parked nearby the green Land Cruiser
and whistled the dog awake, lifted him out
of the truck and the man and his dog
entered the familiar gloom of BoonDocks.

The restaurant part of the saloon was a
huge room with four-tops, pool tables, and
a bandstand and then in the middle of the
big room was a long horseshoe bar and then
with two-tops on the "bar" side and with
TVs in every conceivable place on all sides.
All the televisions were tuned to cable
sports channels or Fox News outlets. The
closed end of the bar near the door was
covered in quarter poker machines that paid
out in free games. From the kitchen directly
behind the open end of the bar came the
smell of fried potatoes and seared steak.

Above the bottle shelves hung dozens of
small galvanized pails hanging from screw-
hooks, the pails just big enough to hold a
few packs of cigarettes, a lighter and small
personal items, condoms and calling cards,

car keys and combs. These hanging buckets were like the personal lockers of the regulars and were earned only after months of regular patronage, to be removed when regular bar attendance flagged. All the pails were decorated — painted, stickered, glittered, stenciled, grafittied — some created with obvious artistry and care while others were clearly the work of drunks with too much time and super glue on their hands. Many were decorated with the logos of sports teams from all over the country, representing the homelands of the retirees who had relocated to Tucson in general and BoonDocks in particular, or else with insignia of the various branches of the Armed Services, mostly Marines even though the Air Force actually dominated the town.

Rodeo's preferred seat at the bar near the outside door was occupied by a stack of textbooks and a legal pad, so he took a seat midway down the on the saloon side of the bar. The dog slunk under his master's boots, circled three times and went to sleep. Rodeo swiveled on his barstool and scanned the eastside wall to find his photo where it had been for almost fifteen years. The cover shot from *American Rodeo* magazine pictured Rodeo in his most famous flying dismount from the saddle bronc Nun Ridden Bad 13 during the final round of the PRCA World Championship he had won. The other memorabilia on that wall featured the Boon-Docks' proprietor, Tank Hage, Jr., in his glory days as a linebacker and a steer wrestler.

Feeling nostalgic?

A big, fat, tanned Anglo man Rodeo's age extended a hand over the bar and Rodeo turned and shook the hand firmly and let it go quickly before his fingers got crushed. The bartender reached into an old zinc-lined deep cooler and extracted a Schlitz can, wiped the cold frost off with the long tail of his short-sleeved cowboy shirt, popped the top and set it in front of Rodeo.

Some days more than others, Tank, Rodeo said. He drank off a quarter of his beer and set the can down, looking at his old high school pal.

You tending bar at your own place these days, Tank? I thought those days were over for you.

Waiting for the new girl, the bar owner said. He looked around as if this new girl might appear at any moment and from any direction. She's been a bit of a problem. Tank seemed distracted.

How's things besides late employees?

asked Rodeo.

Fine, said the big man. Though my chiropractor costs me almost half as much as my wife's Platinum American Express card. When the bar owner stretched his back one of the pearl snap buttons on his shirt popped open around his big, hard belly as his back cracked. He rubbed the razor-cut stubble on the base of his bull neck. Some headaches the neurologist can't figure out, the man said. Probably from all the concussions. Though he says it might be psychological. The bar owner shook his head as if it stung and then shook out one of his legs and flexed an arm. Had my right knee scoped again and one of the pins replaced in my elbow but the orthopedist says otherwise I'm good for another five years.

Good for what?

I guess that's the question, buddy. Tank shook his head like a wounded bull. My wife's psychotherapist she sent me to says I might have seasonal affective disorder.

Well, since it's no seasons in Tucson but monsoon season that shouldn't bother you too much, Tank. Buck Up and Bear Down.

No pain, no gain, said Tank. Idn't that what the coaches at Tucson High always told us?

I didn't listen to those coaches very much,

said Rodeo.

Well I did which is why I was All-State and you weren't, buddy. The bar owner sighed deeply and stretched his back until it cracked. But now I'm suffering for it.

I'm glad you don't complain about it, Rodeo said.

No complaints from me any old steer wrestler who played football hard don't have, said Tank. The man looked past Rodeo and all around the bar and then looked back at Rodeo. How 'bout you, cowboy? Holdin' it up or just holdin' it?

I don't have the money for an orthopedist or neurologist or chiropractor or psycho-therapist to build a conversation around, I'm afraid, Tank. How's business?

Going more for the dinner crowd around here. Even got a goaddamned kid's menu. Tank shifted on his feet as if he could not get comfortable. Tried to get something going last year with a new chicken shack franchise but we had problems getting the wings up from Mexico and that collapsed on me as a clusterfuck. Need some fiduciary infusion, but can't get it . . . Same ol' shit.

How's the family, Tank?

Fine. When Tank Hage shrugged he winced. Same ol' shit there too. I'm on my way out right now to watch another goddamned soccer tournament the girls are playing second string in. Kevin didn't make All-Stars in Little League again this year. The man shook his head. They're all Honors Roll every year so at least that's something I guess.

You take your victories where you can, Rodeo said. Tank looked down at his own big hands on the wet bar he owned, nodded.

I was by your mom's place recently, said Rodeo. How's Eryn doing these days?

Eryn's fine, I guess, Tank said. She eats painkillers all day and drinks like a fish all night and has something to say about everything and everybody as per usual. The bar owner looked around again as if waiting for something to happen. Still has her fingers in everything in the world and won't stay out of my personal business. But she's sharp as a tack when she wants to be and still tight as Dick's Hatband about her money. But what can you do about your own mother?

I'm not sure I had a lot of options with Grace, Rodeo said.

There's always options, buddy. Just most of them bad. Tank glanced around again and wiped sweat off his face with a bar towel.

How's Annabeth, Tank?

The wife's all right. Tank redirected the conversation quickly. How's your people? Your crazy preacher uncle and all them? How's that old dog of yours? He still got a motor on him?

My people are the same as usual. The clan in the Whites are still crazy. I heard my daddy is in West Texas living in sin with somebody new. Rodeo sipped his beer. But the dog is still running. Underfoot here.

Tank Hage tapped a finger on the bar in departure. First one's on the house, buddy. I gotta run now. Dad duty calls. But I'll get the new girl to take care of you. Don't be a stranger. Tank seemed in a hurry as he held out his beefy hand again and Rodeo shook it again. Good to see you, Rodeo.

Tell Annabeth I said howdy, Tank.

Rodeo's former high school teammate grunted and exited out the back bar space through the kitchen as a pretty woman entered it, the middle-aged bar owner and the young bartender scrupulously avoiding eye contact. The "new girl" had an obvious baby bump. She wiped the wood in front of Rodeo with a clean bar towel.

Rodeo scanned the pails hanging from the ceiling and found that his old "rodeo"-themed pail was missing, though his ex-wife's pail still hung seductively. Deb Mabry had not been in the saloon or even lived in Tucson in many years but her bar bucket remained hanging and though her cheerleading décolletage under the découpage was faded hers was still one of the best of the lot.

Rodeo looked at the bartender and then looked at the bottles arrayed behind her.

Deb Mabry had always been a Top Shelf type who would not drink well brands or ever settle for second best at anything if she had any choice. So she had stayed with him when he was on top but then dumped Rodeo when he wasn't. Her one perfect year, Deb's dream season had come when she was an Arizona Cardinals' cheerleader and her then-husband, Rodeo Grace Garnet, had celebrated a full stellar season on the pro rodeo circuit and won his PRCA World Champion buckle. But when Rodeo had broken his back later that season his wife had moved to another high shelf and Rodeo's life had moved on too, more or less.

You need something? the new bartender asked.

He ordered a Steak Special "well-done-burnt" to get something solid into his system. The bartender, who introduced herself as "Barbi-with-only-the 'I' in it" and looked exactly like that, took his order and moved back to the kitchen. Rodeo nursed his beer as he examined the bar buckets and waited for his steak.

Sirena's bucket was right beside Deb Mabry's for some reason and was clearly the sexiest if not the most artistic bucket on the ceiling, highlighting as it did Sirena's many years of professional pole dancing and erotic photo shoots.

As Rodeo's steak appeared, a man removed the textbooks from his barstool and reoccupied the seat at the end of the bar in front of the legal pad.

He and Rodeo exchanged a look and the man raised an eyebrow.

I know you, the man said. He advanced toward Rodeo over a barstool. I am seeing a study group filled with freshmen and one cowboy.

You were in the Anthropology Department at the U, Rodeo said. I think you ran a study group in Native American Studies I was taking last year.

Tinley Burke, the man said. I was a graduate student at the U and then I was an adjunct professor there for a while. Must have been that.

Rodeo Grace Garnet.

When the men shook hands Rodeo noticed the tremor in the man's grip. Burke then fumbled with a pill bottle on the bar, obviously struggling with the childproof cap. Rodeo reached over and offered his hand, twisted the bottle open. The professor nodded his thanks and tilted the contents of the bottle onto the bartop, sorted through a wide variety of pills and selected two. There were many well-known prescription medications in that single bottle with several deadly combinations potentiating. Burke stood up on his barstool and deposited the pill bottle in his own bucket that was customized with postcards from exotic locales and Polaroid photos of what looked to be ancient Indian artifacts and human bones, mementoes of travel and death.

The professor sat back down on his barstool and seemed to drift as his medicine took effect. He stared at his notes on the legal pad. Rodeo ignored the man politely, finished his steak in ten minutes and pushed the plate back, waved at the bartender for his bill. Barbi came over and slipped a handwritten note in front of Rodeo, said nothing and just walked away.

"Still sorry about your dog, Ro. Your tab's on me tonight. Remember the Copper Queen!?" The note was unsigned but obviously from Sirena. Rodeo folded it into his shirt pocket. He stood, whistled up his dog and nodded at his nearest barmate in parting.

Can you give me a lift home? Tinley Burke was leaning off his barstool almost horizontally. As a favor? From a former student to a former teacher?

Do you live at Eryn Hage's place now? On Convent? Rodeo asked the professor.

The man raised an eyebrow. How do you know where I live?

I recognized the Land Cruiser outside, Rodeo said. I saw it parked in front of Eryn's rent place recently and thought you might be connected to it.

Yes, the man said. I am connected to it as you say. You headed that direction? I'm drunk and need a ride home. Did I say that already?

Rodeo nodded. Tinley Burke put a twenty on the bar, put his car keys into his personal bucket, packed up his textbooks and notes under his arm and the men left the saloon together.

Neither man said much on the fifteen-minute drive but when they arrived at Burke's apartment on Convent Avenue the man invited Rodeo inside for a drink.

Not to say anything, Professor, but it may be that you had enough for one night.

You sound like my old therapist, Burke said. Or my sister. He fell out of the truck as he exited and Rodeo hurried around to help his old teacher and his books into the apartment.

The rental apartment was an adobe shotgun shack with the front room a booklined study, the middle room a bedroom with a kitchen and a bathroom in the back. Burke moved unsteadily toward the back of the house. Rodeo did not follow him but examined the small front room. The books on the shelves were arranged by category. Most concerned Native American culture, death and dying or the history of crime or psychopathology. There were a number of Indian artifacts arrayed on the shelves as well. A desk against a wall was empty but for an old Apple laptop with a thick manuscript atop it, as if there to keep the lid of the computer from flying up. *Paths of Death: A Serial Killer Thriller* by Tinley Burke was printed on the cover page. As Rodeo pondered this title, the author retched loudly from the rear of the apartment, so Rodeo saw himself out.

The next morning Rodeo skipped his usual

visit to the motel lobby because he hadn't paid his room bill yet. He drove to the Kettle, left the sleeping dog in the truck and established himself in a corner booth from which he could keep an eye on the whole of the restaurant and on his truck. His waitress was efficient and minimalistic with her service. "Rose" was easy to spot as she flirted with the men she served and paid little attention to the women.

Rodeo ate his breakfast slowly and studied the placemat, a cartoon map of Southwestern America, recognizing most of the highlighted spots as venues he had worked back in his rodeoing days or fun places he had road-tripped to with Deb or Sirena. He had an extra cup of coffee, which he didn't need, and drank two glasses of water with two packets of BC analgesic powder which he did need. When the waitress appeared with his check he asked her if she had had a busy morning.

Yep, she said.

You always work morning shift?

Yep.

Lots of girls on mornings? asked Rodeo.

Three of us, the waitress said. She jerked her head around the room like he could have seen that for himself.

I hated morning shift myself, said Rodeo.

Not exactly a morning person.

Takes all kinds, said the waitress.

Four to noon never suited me. Rodeo's "winning smile" bounced off the waitress.

Well, we get off this shift at ten, so it's not too bad.

All right then, said Rodeo. You have a good one.

You have one too, mister.

Rodeo left a small tip, paid cash and got a receipt from the cashier. He returned to his truck and sat in it for a few minutes thinking. Then he drove the long block back to the parallel park alongside the Santa Cruz and the public parking lot and restrooms there. Billy was not in obvious residence in that vicinity, so Rodeo returned to the place on the hillside where the dog had taken him the day before. He continued his drive north on Mission and turned off into Barrio Hollywood, wound his way through several residential streets and to the A-Mountain Road.

There were no vehicles in the parking lot but his. Rodeo parked and left the dog in the truck, headed down the southeastern side of the big hill to the "sniper's nest" where Rodeo glassed the surrounding hillside and the plain below with his big Leica binoculars. On the other side of the river workers toiled in the indigenous plant nursery in straw coolie hats. In the small corral beside that nursery a pair of miserable-looking horses stood stock still, side by side in the shade of the cobbled-together ramada. Another horse lay on its side in the dust seeming to be dead since nothing alive in the world looks as dead as a sleeping horse. In the fountain area a Goth kid sat in the heat staring at the riverbed under the bridge. Billy was still nowhere in sight. An unmuffled motorcycle sped down Mission Road and cut left on Starr Pass Road but otherwise there was no traffic for a long minute. Rodeo could not read the brand of the dirt bike as it passed.

Across Starr Pass Road, due south on Ajo Way was the Pima County Juvenile Detention Center where Samuel Esau Rocha had spent his incarceration for selling marijuana to high school and middle school students.

Rodeo analyzed the scene. The chain-link fence with razor wire coils atop would make it hard to hit targets inside the prison barrier. But the yard of the Juvenile Detention Center might be a tempting target for some random long rifle shots. Construction was ongoing on the west wing of the prison but should be completed shortly since the "grand opening" of the wing was planned for early autumn. For several minutes Rodeo watched dump trucks moving into and out of the fenced yard, young men in orange jumpsuits milling in the exercise area.

Rodeo looked back up the hill behind him. He could not see the parking lot, so he was out of sight of that space. Though this spot on the hillside was not as good a vantage point as the parking lot above, it did provide good sightlines east and southeast, as well as a significantly shorter and easier shot at Mission Road and Starr Pass Road traffic than from the Overlook and also provided more cover.

From where he stood there was good visibility of Mission Road for a quarter-mile stretch and Starr Pass Road for twice that distance with the bridge occupying a hundred of that eight hundred yards in the farthest left quadrant of the half mile of Starr Pass Road that was within rifle range. Rodeo guesstimated the shot from where he stood to the middle of the bridge to be in the quarter- to half-mile range. From that angle it would not be difficult for any decent marksman to hit a vehicle but to hit a pedestrian walking across Starr Pass Road bridge, especially in gloomy light, would require a professional.

From the reports in the paper and from TPD Detective Overman, Rodeo knew the kid had been discovered by a horseback rider under some brush near the west bank of the river. Since horses and ATVs were regularly ridden in the common community property of the dry riverbed, police investigators had not been able to identify exactly where Sam had fallen nor had they been able to discover amidst all the hoof and tire tracks how Sam had gotten from under the bridge to his final resting place under the creosote bushes at least twenty-five yards away from any possible landing spot.

Rodeo sidled between cholla and teddy bear cactuses to the edge of the packed dirt circle where he had stood the day before.

The sniper's nest had been swept clean. No trash was left, not even a cigarette butt. The shell casing was gone and some care had been made to clear the area of rocks and pebbles.

Rodeo returned to the Overlook and sat on that edge of the bench seat with his legs stretched out beyond the open door using the warm dog as a backrest. He extracted his note pad and pen and wrote —

1. Sam fell off bridge — himself — or was pushed?

2. shot up close and personal in a drive-by — gang — was Sam ganged-up?
3. long-range assassination — uncle, expert marksman, Gulf sniper estb. maybe Sam was squealing on different planned hit by RR and RR killed him to keep him quiet?

Rodeo aimed his binoculars at the bridge again and watched the traffic for a while. Four vehicles sped across the bridge, a couple going east and a couple going west, and then the bridge completely cleared. He counted Mississippis to seventeen and a solo car crossed going west and then slowed and stopped at the traffic light where Starr Pass Road intersected with Mission. Another twenty Mississippis passed before the bridge was occupied again, traffic going both ways meeting on the bridge. At one point the bridge was vacant for over thirty seconds.

Rodeo's cell phone buzzed in his shirt pocket and he answered it.

Is this the Garnet boy I hired? I was just calling the number you gave me to call. The one on the card you left on my table when you stole my money.

Yes ma'am, Mrs. Rocha. This is Rodeo

Garnet, Rodeo said. And I left you a receipt for what we agreed would be my minimum day's rate plus minimal expenses.

You stole from me.

It's all in the contract you signed, Mrs. Rocha. Rodeo sounded businesslike.

Aren't you Buck Garnet's son?

The woman seemed and sounded drunk or confused or both.

Yes ma'am. Are you calling from your home phone, Mrs. Rocha?

No. I'm on this cell thing that he used. It still has time on it and I'm going to use it.

You're using Sam's cell phone? Could I have access to that phone, Mrs. Rocha?

No. What do you want that for? she asked.

It might have some potential contacts in it, some clues to his death.

It's my telephone! the old woman shouted. I paid for it. It never was his. He just used it. You just do your job. Now that you stole my money do your job.

Rodeo had already done as thorough an Internet search as he was capable of, visited the police officer in charge of the investigation, interviewed a potential witness the police had not interviewed and visited the site of the boy's death. By professional standards that was enough to justify a day's pay. For some private investigators that

195

amount of work would have constituted a week's paycheck and he himself had had clients willing to spend ten times that amount just to find a missing child who was staying with friends or off on a drug-fueled road trip.

All right, Mrs. Rocha, said Rodeo. I'm doing my job.

Well, I just called that motel where you said you were going to stay and they said you weren't even registered. Are you even in town here?

I am in Tucson, Mrs. Rocha, Rodeo said. And I been working for you since yesterday.

I only paid for one day! the old woman yelled. You can't charge me for yesterday on top of everything else. I won't stand for it.

What time would you like me to come by and present the report I'm working on for you, Mrs. Rocha? Rodeo moved off the truck seat and shut the door behind him, moved around the driver's side and opened that door.

I don't want a report! I'm not paying you for any report. I can get a report from the newspapers. You're supposed to be working, not reporting, the woman said.

All right, Mrs. Rocha. Rodeo got in the pickup and slammed the door. I'll check Samuel's parents out.

I didn't say to check them out, the woman said. Leave them alone. Good riddance to them.

Rodeo started the truck and put his cell phone on the dashboard, put the truck in reverse and backed out of his parking space.

Mrs. Rocha, you're breaking up . . . What? Repeat that please, Mrs. Rocha. I can't hear you.

He put the phone back to his ear.

Worthless, the woman said. Corrupt and worthless.

Rodeo terminated the call before his client could.

Near nine o'clock Rodeo drove slowly through the parking lot of the Kettle and spotted through the restaurant's front plate glass a Kool-Aid hairdo bobbing near the salad bar. The PI still had an hour until Rose's shift was over, so he found the address of Samuel's parents. The old woman's handwriting on the notepaper was cramped but dramatic, the cursive practically gouged into the paper as if Katherine Rocha had meant to excise the address from her memory more than make it clear.

Rodeo called the number Mrs. Rocha had given him for her son, Alonzo Rocha, but the phone was shunted to an officially recorded message that indicated the number was no longer in service. Rodeo entered the address of Sam's parents into his GPS and headed west toward the Tucson Mountains.

Alonzo Rocha's house was near Katherine Rocha's house, north instead of south on Mark Street, but not separated but by two hundred yards. The residence of Samuel's parents was concrete block painted industrial gray with an aluminum porch, two picture windows on either side of a metal door and a dirt yard covered in weeds and trash. It was a small and untidy house though not any smaller or more untidy than some of its neighbors. A car so stripped of parts the make and model were not recognizable was propped on spare tires in the side yard. A mailbox tilted precariously on a splintered landscaping timber wedged into a stack of cinder blocks near the road in front of the house.

Rodeo parked on the dirt sidewalk and bade his dog stay put. He opened the mailbox as he passed it but did not pause to look inside, walked directly to the house. He knocked and the reinforced metal door rattled against its several protected hinges as if someone or something heavy was slamming into it. Rodeo waited, knocked again. The vertical blinds on the front windows were closed but as Rodeo moved away from the door a huge dog thrust its head through the metal blinds and rammed it against the window glass. Rodeo jumped back as the pit bull rattled the panes and began to bark hoarsely. Rodeo's own dog started howling from the pickup.

Cállate! Sintete! When Rodeo yelled his own dog immediately quieted as did the watchdog in the house.

A side window of the house next door opened and a man yelled at Rodeo as aggressively as Rodeo had yelled at the dogs. Cállate! Que quieres aqui!?

Rodeo walked to the neighbor's house with his hands held open to his sides.

Estoy buscando La Familia Rocha, Rodeo said. I'm looking for La Familia Rocha, señor. Necessito hablar con Alonzo Rocha. I need to talk to the Rochas who live next door.

The man in the window was old and wary.

Que me quieres? the old man asked. La Migra? Policia?

I just want to talk to you, señor, Rodeo said. Estoy un investigador privado, he said.

Que? the old man asked.

Estoy un "private investigator," Rodeo said. Like on the telenovelas. Usted hablas Ingles?

Espanol aqui solimente! Nada mas! Lega! The man slammed his window shut.

Rodeo walked back around the Rocha house, trying to peer into windows but the ferocious pit bull followed him from room to room, slamming his thick head into the window glass anytime Rodeo got near. The windowpanes were covered with dog drool and in places severely cracked. Rodeo could see through the cracked blinds that the house seemed deserted but for the pit bull though some furniture, appliances and fixtures were still inside. Rodeo proceeded to the other side of the house and knocked on another neighbor's door.

A middle-aged woman appeared from a back room, wiping her hands on a dishtowel. She brought the smells of pozole and pig's feet with her as she stopped three feet from the heavy screen door and inclined her head.

Buenas, señor. Que desea?

Puedo hablar con Señor ó Señora Rocha? Donde esta la familia Rocha?

They left, the woman said. She frowned. I don't know where they went. We weren't friends, just vecinos, neighbors.

I am a private investigator, investigating the death of their son, said Rodeo. And I thought they might speak to me about Samuel.

Esta muerto, said the woman. He's dead, señor.

I know that, said Rodeo. I am trying to find out how and why Samuel Rocha died.

No se, señor.

But you know where Samuel's parents are? Rodeo asked.

No, señor. I only know they left. The little girl died tambien. Somebody killed her too, back in the spring — around the time of Cinco de Mayo. The woman pointed down Mark Street toward Starr Pass Road. There was a shrine there for a long time but I think the City they finally took it all away. She brushed at her eyes. She used to play near the road all the time when her parents were drinking and she would even walk across the big road to go to her abuela's house on the other side. Six years old, can you believe it.

Rodeo shook his head sadly.

I said, "This will lead to tragedy." The woman wiped her eyes with the back of a hand.

And it did, said Rodeo.

Eso verdad, pero it does not seem right. Children play in the streets all night around here and so they should have more streetlights. The woman sniffed and shrugged. Quien sabe, señor? Who knows God's will?

Rodeo shook his head. He waited a moment then asked more questions.

So Alonzo and his wife have moved away from here?

Elizabet the wife left first with someone. A tribal policeman, I think came for her and she did not return. And then Alonzo he left after that, but he comes back sometimes for a night or two.

Do you remember when Elizabet left?

Right after the little one, Farrah's funeral. Alonzo he comes and goes since Samuel died.

They left permanente this time, you think?

The woman shrugged. Quien sabe? Sometimes people leave and then come back and sometimes they don't. I haven't seen Alonzo all this week.

There's a dog in their house, Rodeo said.

The dog didn't leave, I guess, the woman said.

Rodeo shook his head. How long has that dog been locked up in that house?

It's not my house, señor, the woman said. How would I know how long? Perdoneme. I have to cook now. She turned back to the interior gloom of her house.

Rodeo knocked on four more doors. No

one else knew when or where the Rochas had gone. No one knew anything about the dog in the house.

On his way back to the truck Rodeo casually pulled the Rocha's mail out of the box and took it to his truck. The bulk of the USPS mail was third class junk, so the only envelope that interested the private investigator was from Tucson Power and Electric, which indicated that service was now terminated at this address.

Rodeo called Animal Control and anonymously reported a dog locked in a vacant house. He gave the address.

It's a very large pit bull with a very bad attitude, he said. Probably half starved, so come armed and be prepared.

On his way back to the Kettle, Rodeo stopped again at the Circle K near Katherine Rocha's house because he saw a Reservation Police cruiser parked in the shade beside the convenience store. A cop was sitting in the car, so Rodeo parked beside it cowboy conference style, turned off his truck's engine, leaned out his window and lifted a hand in greeting. For a long moment the cop inside the vehicle ignored Rodeo but then the window went slowly down.

Rodeo did not recognize the policeman.

What can I do for you, guy? The Reservation cop sounded bored but wary.

My name is Rodeo Grace Garnet and I am a private investigator looking into the death of Samuel Rocha, the local kid who fell off the Starr Pass Road bridge near the end of July.

The policeman's broad face was blank.

And I was just wondering if you knew anything about it? Rodeo asked.

Knew what about it?

Just knew about it in a general way, said Rodeo. Who did the kid hang out with? Who killed him?

The officer seemed to consider the question seriously.

Who did you say you were?

Garnet. Rodeo Garnet. Clint Overman, Lead Detective with the City Police knows me. And I talked to Officer Monjano before about this, so he knows me too.

I'm sure a lot of people know you, guy, but I'm not one of them.

The cop rolled up his window and pulled away from the store without looking at Rodeo again. Rodeo used the public telephone bracketed to the wall of the building to call the nearest police station.

Tohono O'odham Police Department, a

dispatcher answered.

May I speak with Officer Monjano? Carlos Monjano?

Who's calling please?

Mr. Bill Early, said Rodeo. I might have some information for Officer Monjano on a case he's working.

Hold please.

Rodeo waited for almost half a minute.

Mr. Early, the dispatcher said. Officer Monjano is not available currently. I will connect you with another officer. Hold please.

Rodeo hung up, went back to his truck and sat for a long moment just thinking. He glanced in his rearview. Across the street another Res cruiser was parked on the shoulder of Starr Pass Road, the cop inside talking into his cell phone. After a minute the cop pulled his cruiser off slowly. Rodeo went inside the store and poured and drank a cup of Latin Flavors coffee and tossed the Styrofoam cup in the garbage, then squirted an extra-large Icee and paid for that, returned to his truck and headed west on Starr Pass Road toward the Casino.

After he had gone only a quarter of a mile he checked his rearview mirror and saw a police cruiser behind him. He sped up and turned his truck into the big parking lot of the Casino. He braked behind a tour bus and glanced around but the cop car did not seem to be following him.

He drank his Icee and waited five minutes then dumped the Icee cup on the parking lot and drove back onto Starr Pass Road to the Kettle where he once again drove the truck through the restaurant parking lot slowly. He spotted the pink hairdo still working inside the restaurant, so he circled around the La Quinta and parked in the shade of a palm tree near the motel's swimming pool in view of the main entrance of the restaurant. He pulled out his cell phone and punched 2ARRWS.

What's up, brother?

I think I found a sniper's nest, said Rodeo. On A-Mountain.

Luis said nothing for a moment.

Who's he shooting at from Sentinel Peak? Luis asked this as if Luis knew who "he" was.

Maybe the potential Congressman Randy Miller I heard from a drunk at The Buffet, Rodeo said. And I found some evidence that would indicate Samuel was in the tow of Ronald.

So?

So maybe Samuel found out about Ronald's plan and was going to snitch on his "uncle" and Ronald popped the kid while he was walking across the Starr Pass Road bridge.

Luis was silent for a long moment. You got the evidence?

I got some snapshots of the nest, but I never called it in and by the time I got back the place was clean, real clean.

If you can't prove it to Police, then don't say it out loud to anybody else, brother. Not about Ronald Rocha.

I don't even know if Ronald Rocha knows I'm looking for him.

If you know about Ronald it's a good bet he knows about you, brother. Ronald he has contacts all over your town and into the desert where you live. Including well-placed types like Randy Miller.

What do I do, Luis? You got me into this boondoggle.

Just get out of your deal in Tuxson and be finished with this, Rodeo. I think you're in over your head now.

You know how I am, Luis.

I know how you are, said Luis. You got a job to do and all that bullshit. But this is fast getting to be a Bad Job. So just give the old lady back her quarters and I'll cover you on that deal and forgive your day's pay in back money you owe me, so you won't be at no loss whatsoever by just coming back home to The Hole. I made a mistake setting you up with this job.

I'm trying to figure out why you did, Luis.

Luis said nothing but stayed on the line.

Because you thought Ronald Rocha might have killed Samuel Rocha. You thought that all along, Rodeo said. You heard about the kid being dead. And since Sam was shot off a bridge and since you knew the kid was connected up with Ronald Rocha, your sharpshooting, elk-hunting buddy who likes to kill things long distance, you figured it was Ronald that hit him.

I think Ronald he likes to kill things all ways, said Luis.

So you thought maybe this fella Ronald maybe might have killed the kid, so you wanted me to dig around and find out if your powwow compadre was murdering people who knew about what he was planning, people like Samuel. So you set me up to work for Mrs. Rocha. That's why the old woman is not even interested in this investigation, because you're the one that's interested in pursuing it. How about that scenario, Luis?

The way you put it it's hard to figure out how much of that scenario is right, Luis said.

I don't need an exact percentage Luis. Just give me a guesstimate, said Rodeo.

Only a little bit right, Luis said. The old Rocha woman and her clans are some distant way related to Silk and one of her thousand clans and I seen this dead kid . . . Luis paused. I just saw Sam around some so yeah, I wondered. But the old woman she called out here about you, Rodeo, Luis said. Second Wife she got the feeling talking to the old woman that the old woman she just wanted to get you in her hire for some reason but I don't know the reason.

Luis paused. Rodeo said nothing.

I didn't see the real harm, brother. I just thought working for the old Rocha woman might work out as a day or two wage for you and get me a little of the money you owe me back in the till. Things are tight at The Store just like they are everywhere else, you know. I carry your credit every month and it doesn't add up for me lately.

You didn't think I would find anything, said Rodeo. You thought I would just make a few calls, collect my day's rate and that would be that. That's what you thought.

I didn't think you would find something new since the TPD didn't find nothing, said Luis. I should have known better knowing you. But now that you're getting closer to

Ronald I'm not sure about this whole deal.

What's the old woman's motivation in this, Luis?

You know what they say about motivations, brother. You can't never tell about them sometimes. Pigs and dogs behave for food but horses and humans have minds of their own.

But Katherine Rocha called about me specific?

The old woman she called around looking for you specific.

Why me?

I guess she knew about you from when you were a kid or something, said Luis. I don't know. She knows your people anyway and she finds Silk. Then when Second Wife she talks to me about it I realize like I said that I know this Rocha kid a little too from the hunt that time in the Whites, said Luis. And more lately from Black Mountain.

Samuel was at sweat lodge? asked Rodeo.

Yeah, he was coming to sweat for a little while. I remember because this kid he blacked out one night after only three stones or so and we had to pass him around the circle hand to hand to get him out the right way and Ronald followed the kid out of the lodge even though Ronald he could take twenty stones and not break a sweat. And that's the last time I saw either Ronald or the kid.

When was this? asked Rodeo.

Back in the late spring or early summer.

Rodeo considered the information. Before or after Cinco de Mayo time?

After probably, said Luis. Why?

Samuel's little sister, Farrah, was killed on May third.

Pues?

So this little girl gets killed in a hit-and-run and then the little girl's brother starts going to sweat lodge to clean up his spirit, so maybe the kid ran over his own sister, Rodeo said.

Luis said nothing.

What's the logical problem with this scenario, Luis?

The problem with this problem is not the logic of it, brother, said Luis. It's that people ain't logical. And this problem it's not your problem. And Ronald Rocha might be involved with it.

So?

So it's some types of people you don't want to have problems with or even have problems around and Ronald is one of those types, said Luis.

What's his reputation? asked Rodeo.

He was some sort of sniper who also did

interrogations in the Gulf War maybe, said Luis. Totally dedicated. A hard guy with skills. Randy Miller was his CO and Randy Miller is a hard guy too, I heard. And they are both "special."

How are they special?

Butt buddies special.

Randy Miller is married, said Rodeo. He was a County Judge and a State Senator. He's running for Congress from Seventh District. He's got kids, I heard.

Lots of special guys are married with kids, brother. Especially when they are political. Where you been all your life?

Rodeo digested this new information.

I know you won't come home just on my say-so, brother, said Luis. And I know you don't want to quit on a thing until it's done to your own satisfaction. But I also know you will quit on something when the logic goes bad against you.

I try to be wise about such, Luis.

Then be wise in this situation, little brother. Be very wise on this one.

I'm well armed and alert at all times, Luis, said Rodeo.

Rodeo hung up without saying good-bye as the young waitress Rodeo was waiting for walked out the front door of the Kettle like her crazy hair was on fire.

■ ■ ■ ■

Rodeo held out a hand a few feet in front of the waitress to slow her down.

Rose?

The young woman stopped suddenly on the sidewalk outside the restaurant and looked down at the name tag on her polyester outfit which read EVELYN and then looked Rodeo over from head to foot and shook her head aggressively. Rodeo lowered his arm.

Rose's not my real name, the young woman said. The jewelry in her ear and her nose twinkled in the harsh glare of the sun. Sweat watered the rose tattoos on her forearms and wrists. And I don't do that kind of work anymore.

What kind of work is that? Rodeo asked.

The young woman ignored the question.

I just quit this fucking place too, the young woman said. She threw a bad finger over a shoulder at the Kettle though no one seemed to be paying any attention to her from inside the restaurant.

Waiting tables is a bitch, Rodeo said.

The waitress shrugged at him.

What's your other work? Rodeo asked.

She ignored this question again and asked

one of her own. How did you find me?

Internet.

I can't get that fucking "RoseRite" site off the Web, she said. A guy made it for me and now it seems like I'm stuck with it for the rest of my life.

Did Samuel Rocha make it for you? asked Rodeo.

Rose squinted her eyes which were pretty but unnaturally bright blue as manmade jewels.

That kid wasn't smart enough to do something like that, she said. He didn't even have a computer or a smart phone, can you believe that? She smiled very slightly and looked up at her interrogator. How do . . . did you know Sam? she asked.

I didn't know him, Rodeo said. Not while he was alive anyway. Maybe I'm getting to know him now that he's dead.

I don't know what that means, Rose said.

Rodeo showed his ID and explained his business in broad terms. The young woman examined his credentials and listened intently.

Can we go someplace, Rodeo Grace Garnet? she asked. It's roasting out here.

Back inside the Kettle? Rodeo suggested.

No. I hate that fucking place and it hates me, the young woman said. She folded her

214

arms across her chest. I didn't actually quit yet, but I try to quit it every fucking day. She inclined her head toward another restaurant, a Waffle House attached to a Howard Johnson's across the street. The pair walked in silence across Starr Pass Road and entered the restaurant and took a booth by a window. Rodeo ordered coffee and a slice of pie from a harried waitress who smacked her chewing gum like she was punishing it.

What kinda pie you want, honey? the waitress asked. She wore no name tag and seemed to be in a big hurry. We got all kinds a pie.

Anything will do, said Rodeo.

Anything-will-do means apple, the waitress said. So a coffee and a slice a apple pie for the gentleman. And for the lady? The waitress glared at the girl in her Kettle uniform.

Just water.

Right. Just water for the lady. The waitress moved off in a huff.

I hate this fucking town, Rose said.

Why do you stay here? asked Rodeo.

Because of the Gem Show, you know. The young woman held up her tattooed wrist from which dangled an extravagant bracelet. I'm a jeweler, so I stay in Tucson so I can be around my business.

Rodeo nodded. During the winter the Tucson Gem and Mineral Show attracted tens of thousands of buyers and sellers of precious and semiprecious gemstones and minerals from around the world and a host of jewelry makers, wholesale buyers and retailers and a lot of hustlers as well.

The jewelry I saw on your Web site looked pretty . . . Rodeo searched for a word. He chose one he had heard recently. Special.

Thanks. The woman adjusted the bracelet on her wrist. I do have a special talent, I guess. People tell me I do at least.

Special talent usually demonstrates itself without much advertisement, Rodeo said.

The young woman looked again at her own jewelry and then looked out the plate glass window until Rodeo's coffee and pie arrived but with no water for either patron. The girl pulled a water bottle out of her sling bag, took a long tug.

Well, what can I tell you, Rodeo Grace Garnet, Private Investigator?

I guess we could start with your real name. He nodded at her name tag.

Evelyn, she said. I am Evelyn Dolores Handy. Kind of rolls off the tongue doesn't it?

It could in the right circumstances, Rodeo said.

The young woman stared out the window. Call me Rose, I guess. Everybody does.

Rodeo waited for a moment until the young woman turned back toward him.

How'd you find me? she asked. The cops never did.

Should they have found you, Rose? The cops?

The young woman shrugged at her interrogator again.

I was going through Samuel's paperback book collection, Rodeo said. And the word Rose was in a margin here and there. Your Web site address, RoseRite.com, turned up too.

Along with some hearts and flowers probably, Rose said. When she turned and squinted at Rodeo her eyes slitted like a snake's. Little Sam had a total crush on me.

But a crush not reciprocated? asked Rodeo.

Not at all reciprocated, said Rose. She turned her head coquettishly. How old do you think I am?

Twenty-six. Twenty-seven.

Her face fell. Well, Sam was nineteen, the woman said. He was an okay kid, but no thank you.

You like older men? asked Rodeo.

I don't like men at all, said Rose.

Rodeo waited for a minute before he spoke again.

And Samuel? Did he like older men?

Sam liked whoever paid attention to him I think, Rose said. His parents never did. He did not exist to them. They lived only for that Little Miss Pageant Doll they called a daughter.

Farrah?

Yeah, Rose said. Can you believe it? Little Mexican kid called Farrah. The waitress shook her head. They dyed her hair and gave her contacts to make her eyes blue. Five fucking years old.

I guess your hair is naturally pink and your eyes are naturally blue, said Rodeo. The young woman blushed. Rodeo shifted the conversation.

Did you know anyone that Samuel hung out with?

We didn't hang with the same crowd, Rose said. My friends are college kids or Downtowners mostly. Fine Arts people, hippy people, Fourth Avenue people, you know.

Patchouli and dreadlocks, Kierkegaard and world music types?

Rose frowned. I guess so, if you want to stereotype.

Is a cliché the same as a stereotype? Rodeo asked.

Rose shrugged as if she understood the distinction.

But you wouldn't really hang with some kid like Samuel, right?

Little Sam . . .

His name was Samuel Esau Rocha, said Rodeo.

Whatever, Rose said. She stared at Rodeo.

Rodeo played the contest until the young woman turned to the window again.

Sam didn't really hang with anybody I know, Rose said.

Who did he hang with then?

He sold dope to little middle school brats and the high school rats but he was not even cool enough for any of them and so he hated them and he hated Nerds and he hated Goths and he hated Chollos and . . . Rose stared at Rodeo. Sam hated Redneck Indian Cowboys from the Res the most.

I been called a lot worse, Rodeo said. He sipped his coffee. Go on, Rose.

And he hated his family, especially his grandmother. That bitchwitch.

That's a lot of hating, Rodeo said.

But he wasn't even a serious hater, you know. He was just . . . He was just sort of nothing, you know?

I don't know much about Samuel, Rose, but by his poetry and what people say about him, said Rodeo. And now he's dead. That's why you need to tell me about him.

He wasn't any kind of person, said Rose. The woman seemed frustrated. He had no real identity. He was sort of like a generic dispossessed teenager. Not ugly but not really that cute except for those huge dark eyes of his. Not smart but not retarded. Rose paused. He wasn't even serious about not being serious, you know what I mean?

Not really, said Rodeo.

Well, like he didn't even care that much about dope or destruction or pulling down the hegemony. Sam didn't stand for anything or even do anything.

Samuel liked to read and write poetry, go to concerts, Rodeo said. Samuel liked you, Rose.

A lot of people like me. Rose folded her arms under her breasts to make them bigger. I have tits. A lot of people appreciate a good set of tits, didn't you know that, cowboy?

Rodeo sipped his coffee and looked into his cup. I do know that, Rose.

Well then.

But you didn't like Samuel? Rodeo asked.

He only read dumb kid shit like Harry

Potter or crazy conspiracy books. And he only went to concerts to fit in. He would go to anything at the Rialto if there would be some crowd he could pretend to be with. And he went out because he hated staying home with that old bitchwitch of a grandmother he seemed chained to.

Rodeo nodded slightly to encourage the young woman to continue.

You found his books, so I guess you searched his room or something? Rose asked.

I did.

Well, did you find some huge collection of CDs or a guitar or turntables or anything that would tell you he really loved music? Rose asked. Even a harmonica?

You didn't like Samuel, Rodeo said.

He was a loser.

Rodeo stared at Rose until she looked at him and then looked away again.

Should I feel guilty about that? Rose asked.

I don't know you good enough to know what you need to feel guilty about, Rose, Rodeo said. But every sane person has something to feel guilty about.

Well, I don't feel guilty about anything, Rose said. I don't believe in it.

If you say so, Rose. Rodeo redirected the

221

line of questioning from the existential to the practical. How did you and Samuel meet?

He hired me, said Rose.

Hired you to do what?

Not what you think, she said.

What do you think I think? Rodeo tried to keep his face neutral.

Rose looked beyond the parking lot at the white blue sky.

Rose hesitated. I used to do some things.

Like what kind of things, Rose?

After college I was trying to save money for my jewelry business, you know. It was really important to me, my art was.

How so?

My art defined me, she said. I thought it did at least, you know. I thought if I didn't make it as an artiste of some sort then I wasn't anything. I wanted to be known for my art. My family wouldn't support me and my art so . . .

Rodeo looked at the traffic that crawled along a feeder road from a disemboweled interstate that fed his hometown with traffic.

You're judging me, Rose said. She glared at Rodeo. You shouldn't do that, you know. You shouldn't judge me.

I'm not judging you, Rose.

You're judging me with your eyes.

I'm not even looking at you, Rose, said Rodeo. Maybe you're looking at yourself.

The young woman laughed from deep down in her throat.

Does that part of your life have anything to do with Samuel? Rodeo asked.

No.

Well then, Rose, I am seriously not interested in it. Rodeo looked at the young woman. Not at all.

Rose looked at him and then looked at his pie.

You gonna eat that pie?

Rodeo slid his pie in front of Rose and she cut off a slice with his fork and put it in her mouth and chewed and swallowed carefully.

I didn't find any jewelry in Samuel's room, Rodeo said.

He never bought any from me. He wasn't interested in my jewelry. He was seriously not interested in it. Nor in sex either if that's what you got stuck in your brain.

You and Samuel never made out?

It's none of your business.

So you helped Samuel with his poetry?

I've actually got a college degree in creative writing from ASU, la de da . . .

Rodeo said nothing.

. . . so I ran a little one-line ad in the Personals of the *Tucson Weekly* — "Need Help With Your Poetry?" He called and we hooked up.

So, Samuel took your ad serious, Rodeo said.

I guess he did, Rose said.

How was it? Samuel's poetry?

Rose shrugged. Typical teenage angst and ennui, you know. I wrote that crap too when I was young. But there wasn't much I could do for him. He had it in his mind that this shit he was writing would get published and he'd get a scholarship to a creative writing program somewhere like I did and get out of his hellhole. But that wasn't going to happen for him, you know.

You told Samuel that? That it wasn't going to happen for him though it happened for you?

No. Rose seemed indignant. Why should I? I'm not a stuck-up bitch. He was paying me to help him and I actually tried to help him but he wouldn't take my advice, so I finally gave up.

How did he pay you, Rose?

What do you mean?

What did he pay you with?

Dope when he had it, Rose said. Sometimes quarter rolls and dollar coins he stole from his gran. I didn't charge him that much. I wasn't trying to rip him off.

Did you have any other customers for this editing service of yours? Rodeo asked.

Some old fuckers called me up, you know, and I met them but they just wanted me to suck their dicks while they read their bad poetry to me like that would be a treat for me.

And you weren't in that business anymore, right, Rose?

Rose put down her fork and glared at Rodeo.

I get the feeling you don't like me, Rodeo Grace Garnet, she said. Is that right?

It's not really my business to like or dislike people, Rodeo said.

I understand that, you know, Rose said. I really do. I know how business is. Sometimes you have to do business with people you don't like, don't you? She pushed the pie plate away from her and then brushed her hands together. But I am not really doing any business with you here, you know. So now I need to be moving on. Thank you for the pie and see you around.

Rodeo reached across the table and grabbed the young woman's wrist. After years of clinching a bridle rope against tons and tons of torque Rodeo's grip was unnaturally strong. Rose grunted in pain.

That's not a good thing to do to me, the young woman said.

Sorry, Rose. Rodeo let go of the woman. It's just that you might be through with me but I'm not through with you.

You can't intimidate me, you know. Rose gathered up her big hobo handbag but Rodeo reached into his pocket and pulled out his wallet, thumbed out a twenty and slid it over next to her half-eaten pie.

Let me hire you for a quick editorial job then, Rose.

Rose glared at Rodeo but then glanced around and then took the money and pushed the bill into her bag and sat back in the booth.

You got three minutes, mister. She said this in a practiced way.

I found a few of Samuel's poems, Rodeo said. In a notebook hidden under his mattress.

I bet that's not all he was hiding under there from his grandmother, Rose said.

Samuel wrote a poem about Black Mountain. Did you help him with that one, Rose?

Yeah.

What did it mean? Rodeo asked.

The editor wrinkled her brow.

I think he got assraped or something, she

said. By an Indian? Or by the spirit of his dead ancestors supposedly or something? She looked at Rodeo for confirmation. Rodeo shrugged. Well, that's what I read as the literal line under the bullshit. I told him to just do a straight narrative poem of something like that. Make it real.

Maybe it was real and he wrote the poem to make it unreal, Rodeo said.

Maybe. Rose shrugged again. Anyway he wouldn't listen to me, so that was that.

Rose fixed her eyes on the half-eaten pie on the table.

There was another one, about death and a little girl . . .

Yeah, I remember that one too. Obviously about his sister. I told him the same thing, to make it straight, just describe it straight.

Was he describing something he did? Rodeo asked.

Rose sat up straighter on the booth seat.

He felt really guilty about his little sister, you know. Rose sighed and looked directly at Rodeo. But he wrote about guilt a lot, all the time. And his poetry about it was never pretty or unique.

Guilt is not pretty, Rodeo said. But it is usually unique.

Well, it was very fucking tiring, this kid's guilt. Rose paused. But he didn't run over his sister, I know that.

How do you know that, Rose?

Because he didn't even have a car to drive the night the little pageant queen got killed in a hit-and-run.

How would you know that, Rose?

She hesitated. Because he was here that night, she said. He walked here and then some guy picked him up on a dirt bike right here in the Howard Johnson's parking lot the next morning.

Samuel was here at HoJos, in the motel, the night his sister got killed? Rodeo asked.

Yeah. I rented a room and was having a pay party and I invited him because I knew he would bring some smoke.

What's a pay party?

People pay a flat fee at the door to party. I buy a keg and spread the word.

You make money on that?

I always break even and get to party for free. I invite a few minor dealers who will bring some smoke or whatever so kids can score if they want. It's a win/win for everybody.

So Samuel was here all that night? The night his sister got killed?

Yeah. He was supposed to leave but he didn't, Rose said. He stayed all night. Crashed on the floor. I remember stepping over him the next morning.

Why was he supposed to leave? asked Rodeo.

What?

You said, "he was supposed to leave." Why was Samuel supposed to leave? Were you kicking him out?

No, I'm not a bitch, the young woman said. I told you that. It was a party. I wasn't kicking him out. But his grandmother, who is a bitch, called him pretty early on that night and he was supposed to go pick her up from the Casino and take her back to her house but he blew it off.

Did Samuel usually drive his grandmother around?

Sam and his grandmother had a deal, Rose said. His parents didn't want him in their house, never had once his sister the beauty queen was born, I guess, and he never had enough money or balls to move out on his own. So he lived with that old lady and in exchange for rent he did errands for her and when his grannie got drunk at the Casino he would go get her and drive her back in her car.

So Samuel's grandmother would drive herself to the Casino?

She always drove herself out there, Rose said. She hated for him to have that shit car even for a while. And then she'd get drunk playing slots and later on call him and he'd come get her.

How did Samuel get to the Casino?

He walked all over town, said Rose. He could walk all day. He liked to walk around. He said it cleared his head. Even in the middle of the summer he'd be walking for hours and hours. He was crazy that way.

And Samuel walked from his house to this HoJos on the night his sister got killed?

He walked here, partied, passed out and stayed the night on the floor, said Rose. The next morning I think he made a local call on the room phone and then a little later I heard a dirt bike in the parking lot and looked out and saw him riding off with some dude.

Did you know the dude?

No clue.

What did he look like?

Skinny, old, terra-cotta tan like half the guys around here.

Rodeo looked directly at the young woman, nodded.

Thanks, Rose. I apologize for grabbing you, he said. That was out of line.

The young woman seemed shocked by this apology and disarmed.

That's okay, said Rose. I've been handled

a lot worse, you know.

I'm sorry about that too, Rose.

Rose looked at Rodeo as if she were trying to figure out what he meant.

You take care now, Rose.

Rodeo had dismissed this witness but it took her a few seconds to figure that out. When the young woman got the message, she slung her big bag over her shoulder and slid to the outside edge of the booth bench, stood and held out her hand. Rodeo shook it firmly and she returned his firm grip and left the building. Rodeo watched her walk across Starr Pass Road until she disappeared behind the Kettle. The Waffle House waitress appeared with a check.

How was that pie, honey? The rude waitress jammed Rodeo's check under the pie plate and looked at it on the wrong side of the table and then she looked at Rodeo. That pie work out for you all right, hon? I ask because sometimes it does with that particular pie but usually it doesn't. And I think that's because that pie it might look tastier than it really is, she said.

Rodeo looked away from the waitress, looked at the new supports of the old highway going up like monuments in the shimmering heat in the heart of Tucson, his hometown. The giant supports had vines with leaves carved into their sides, this bas relief now the color of sand would be painted green eventually. A motorcycle with a bad muffler cruised down the feeder road of the interstate and the thin, tanned rider looked toward the Waffle House. Rodeo followed the progress of the bike as it entered the shadows under the overpass. A streak of blue exhaust blew out from under the bridge as the bike roared out of sight. He said nothing.

Takes all kinds, the waitress said. She turned on a square heel and stalked away.

Rodeo picked up the check, tore off the perforated receipt on the bottom, walked to the cash register and paid and didn't leave a tip. He left Waffle House, the Kettle and Rose behind him, returned to his truck and drove with his dog to Fourth Avenue, back to the Buffet where he hoped to talk again with Olin or some other barhound like Olin who might know Ronald.

Rodeo had just switched off the engine of his pickup when he heard the roar of a dirt bike beside him and a rangy, tanned, shirtless man materialized on the passenger side of the truck, reached through the open window, grabbed Rodeo's dog by the collar, pulled the old dog up and his head back and aimed the blade of a skinning knife at the dog's throat.

Rodeo reached his right hand under his seat but the man shook his head.

Negative on gunplay and on creative thinking about the use of conventional resistant force, friend. I can only control this little bike between my legs for so long and then I have to cut and run, if you get my drift.

Don't kill my dog, Rodeo said.

The man managed the running dirt bike between his legs as he tilted up the dog's head and pressed the blade into the dog's throat hard enough to elicit a whine.

You are not leading this dance, friend. But we don't have to be stepping on each other's toes here. So like a slow dance put both your hands on the steering wheel though you are not now steering.

Rodeo looked around but since there was no one in sight he did as directed, put both his hands on the steering wheel of his truck.

I don't want to kill your dog and run away from you. But I will.

The man pressed his knife against the throat of Rodeo's dog. I will kill your dog right here right now and then kill you just on principle. This is something I can do and that you will both be powerless to resist, the motorcycle man said. Do you understand that, friend?

Rodeo nodded.

I'll make things simple for you then, friend. As I keep this knife blade pressed against the throat of your old dog you will keep both your hands on the wheel of this piece of shit truck of yours or else you, boy and dog, die together. I can kill you both in one motion. This is a simple task for me and these are simple instructions for you, so I won't repeat myself.

Rodeo nodded again. The man turned off his motorcycle but the noise in Rodeo's head did not diminish.

You're Ronald Rocha, Rodeo said.

I am he, the man said. But don't look at me. Look only forward at your hands on what is now the wheel of your life or else your dog is dead as only a beginning to your torment, friend.

Rodeo stared at his own hands. They were trembling.

I can't see how you and me are going to be friends, Ronald, said Rodeo.

When every man is friend to every man and all are equal in the world then nobody is a friend to anybody and then I will be the Last Man and the end times will have arrived.

You alone, Ronald?

To be truly alone a man must be a god, the man said. Do you understand me?

Not really, Ronald.

Let's start with something simpler for you then, Mr. Garnet.

Ronald Rocha looked around and made eye contact with some pedestrians but they moved on. He pressed the blade against the dog's neck and the dog whined.

A man's dog is always the easiest soft spot to exploit since killing a man's dog only amounts to destruction of property in most states including the Fair State of Arizona.

Do not kill my dog, Ronald. There's no point in that.

If I need to kill something in this world I usually find a reason for killing it, friend.

The man drew the blade against the dog's throat just hard enough to draw blood. The dog did not now make a sound, did not even whimper gripped with terror and on the verge of nervous collapse as he was.

What do you want with me, Ronald?

Since I am both the cause and the effect of human relations I create a lot of useful contact points in the universe and one of these points of illumination informed me that you were pursuing me and that course of action must cease, said the man.

Were you planning on shooting someone from that sniper's nest on A-Mountain, Ronald?

My plans are my plans, friend.

Did you kill Samuel Rocha because he knew something about an assassination you were planning on somebody? Or maybe a fake assassination? Maybe on Randy Miller?

I would follow Colonel Miller into Desert Hell again without question. And I loved Sammy Rocha.

So you didn't shoot Samuel off the bridge? Rodeo asked. And you were only going to fake an assassination attempt on Randy Miller to bolster his political career?

As I said, friend, my plans are my plans.

What do you want from me, Ronald?

I would like to kill the person who is responsible for my Sammy's death. But I do not know who that person is. I think you do know or will soon find out who that person is. And I want you to give me this information.

I thought for sure it was you, Ronald. So now that you said it isn't you, I don't know who killed your boyfriend.

But you are going to find out who killed Sammy, said Ronald Rocha. You are going to commit yourself to finding the person who is responsible.

If you'll just let my dog loose, Ronald, I'll do it for you.

The man on the motorcycle said nothing for a moment but then nodded.

I think you will, friend, said the man. And if not then you will pay in a variety of ways. None of them nice. For you or yours.

Ronald Rocha let go of the dog, sheaved his knife, kick-started his motorcycle and disappeared with a howl in a fog of blue exhaust.

The dog collapsed, his breathing irregular and weak. Rodeo reached behind the seat, grabbed a mechanic's rag and staunched the blood seeping from his dog's neck. He awkwardly shifted into first gear and barreled to the edge of the parking lot, where he paused since his vet was all the way across town on the east-side and he had no idea where another nearby veterinarian's office could be.

He swiped his eyes with a shirt sleeve, turned left and without checking for traffic, ran a stop sign onto Fourth Avenue and headed toward downtown. He roared through the underground tunnel under the railroad tracks and onto Congress and then made a sharp left that pulled the tires of the truck off the ground as he cut through the parking lot of the Rialto Theater and then accelerated across Broadway barely missing a city bus. The winos lined up outside at the blood bank and ranged around Armory Park stared at the old truck and horns honked around him but Rodeo did not slow until he shot a gap in Sixth Avenue traffic and came to a stop in front of the old Quonset hut. He jumped out of the truck and hurried to the passenger side, opened the door and lifted the dog from the seat, carried him into Tucson Famous Pets and Aquarium Design Center.

Summer Skye swept vitamins and brochures and pet magazines onto the floor to clear the counter space.

Put him down on his side so his snout is facing me, the vet said. Carefully.

Rodeo did as instructed.

What happened to him? she asked. Was he hit by a car? Does he have internal injuries? He has some pellet scars in his flank. Did he get shot? Where is he bleeding from?

His throat was cut, Rodeo said. He did not bother to explain and the former veterinarian did not ask for more explanation. She pulled back the blood-soaked mechanic's rag and then grabbed a roll of paper towels from under the counter and pressed the whole roll into the dog's neck.

It looks like the blood is just flowing from the cut outward, she said. His lungs sound clear. He's mainly in shock. Hold these towels firmly and don't move and don't panic. He can sense your emotional state, so emanate calm and love.

The former vet left the man with his dog and ran to the back of the store and into a storeroom at the back. She returned a minute later with an old-fashioned, bellowed doctor's house call bag.

I'm going to give him a sedative. Hold him steady.

Summer readied the hypodermic and started talking to the dog in a low, soothing voice.

Good boy. You're a good boy. What in the world happened to you, boy? You're such a good dog aren't you? Who would want to shoot you and slit your throat?

The dog raised his cloudy eyes toward the face of the woman and she plunged the needle into his hip. His eyes began to close and his trembling subsided and in a few minutes his breathing regularized and he seemed simply to be asleep.

Summer Skye straightened up from her hunched position and wiped the sweat off her brow. She looked over Rodeo's shoulder to face a small girl and her mother, the girl holding a dog's chew toy, the mother a bottle of vitamins. Without a word the mother guided her child away from Summer and the distressed animal on the counter top and they dropped their potential purchases on the floor and left the building, the little girl sobbing silently.

Great, said Summer. That kid's probably scarred for life now and they'll probably never come back to my store and that kid will never even want to have a pet.

Having pets is a bitch, said Rodeo.

Having pets is not a bitch, said Summer.

Rodeo's eyes teared up. Summer sighed, leaned over the counter and patted Rodeo on his shoulder.

So you owe me for that chew toy. Summer resumed her attendant position over Rodeo's dog. And that bottle of multivitamins those customers were going to buy you are going to buy a year's worth of them. Your old mutt needs them.

Whatever you say, Doc, said Rodeo. You can design an aquarium for me too. As long as it doesn't use much water.

Rodeo wiped at his eyes and his face with his shirt sleeve as Summer removed his hand and the roll of paper towels from the dog's neck. The woman tossed the soaked roll of paper towels into a trash can. She held Rodeo's trembling hand for a long moment, let it go, then looked at his dog's wound.

You got any pet insurance?

Rodeo shook his head.

Well, since he's probably not going to die of this wound you're getting the Cheap, she said.

Summer cleaned and dressed the dog's wound, applying multiple butterfly bandages. She sealed the wound with Super Glue, covered the wound site with sterile pads made fast to the dog's shoulder with duct tape.

Is he going to be okay? asked Rodeo.

I'll keep him here for a day or two, Summer Skye said.

I need to take him to my vet.

Vets are pricey and there's nothing anybody can do for this type of thing that I can't do here.

What does he need?

Just my TLC, peace and quiet and the right sounds and smells around him for a little while. What does he like to eat?

Bacon, said Rodeo. And he loves to drink. But since he's been sick I've had him on dry food and just a little Jack Daniel's "light" in his water bowl when he whines.

Bacon and booze it is then, said Summer Skye. Even though I'm a twelve-step semi-vegan. The veterinarian smiled at Rodeo. Where'd you two meet?

I won him by losing a hand of poker at the Eagle's Nest outside Gladewater Texas after the Round-up Rodeo about fifteen years ago. Though he's not much a prize.

Rodeo put a hand on the dog's neck. His eyes teared up despite his best intentions.

Do you have anybody else to cry about? Summer Skye asked.

Not at the moment.

Summer Skye removed Rodeo's hand from the dog.

Your pain won't help his healing, she said. He's better off with me for a while. You understand that, don't you?

Yes, I do.

And if he's healthy enough to heal he will. If he's not, he'll die and I'll make sure he's comfortable and you won't have to pay a fortune to cremate him. What's his main health problem?

Something in his gut. I'm not sure of the details because I don't want the details and I can't afford chemo for him anyway.

How did this current injury happen? Summer Skye asked. I've never seen such a fine cut made outside of surgery.

It's a long story, Doc, said Rodeo. I'm a private investigator on a case and this was collateral damage from an ongoing case. The less you know about it the better probably.

What about the shotgun pellets? Hunting accident?

Ex-girlfriend accident.

The woman did not press Rodeo for more information.

You sure you're okay with this, Dr. Skye?

You don't trust me?

I don't trust anybody particularly, said Rodeo. But some people I think are competent and others not so much. You seem competent to me.

Thanks.

Thank you, Dr. Skye. I appreciate you. You don't know how much.

Yes, I do. I've had lots of old dogs in my care.

Well, I've only had this one, said Rodeo. And I don't know what I'm going to do when this one's gone.

Get another one, she said.

I doubt I will.

Summer Skye shrugged. Most people say that but then most people do. Out with the old, in with the new. Dog people always just get another dog.

I doubt I will, said Rodeo. After this one. He's special. Rodeo rested a hand on his dog.

That's what everybody says and that's part of what got to me and made me quit my practice. Either pet owners were so distraught over their pets' illnesses and deaths they just infected me with their sorrow or else they were so casual about it like, whatever, sell me a live one to replace the dead one.

Are those the only options — total devastation or callousness? Rodeo asked.

I see your point, she said. Go the middle way.

If you don't aim too high or aim too low you'll often at least hit the target, said Rodeo. If not the bull's-eye.

The ex-vet wiped at her blue eyes.

I do get wrapped up in things to a debilitating degree sometimes, she said.

Doesn't Hudson help?

Hudson?

Your girlfriend? asked Rodeo.

Oh, you remember that Hudson. Summer smiled at Rodeo. You've got a really good memory.

For some things, Rodeo said.

Hudson's not really the nurturing type.

Sorry to hear that.

No worries. Hudson is my sugar momma and she's okay with that so I guess I'm okay with that too.

Neither person said anything as the dog breathed regularly but raggedly between them.

Stay with him while I go get his place set up in the back, Summer said. Then I'm going to ask you to leave for a while.

I'd rather stay, Rodeo said.

You're too close to him, the woman said. I mean, that's good. It's obvious you love him a lot. But you've got nervous parent vibe. He'll pick up on your anxiety if you hang around and that won't help him. He just needs calm around him right now. And some doctoring. Trust me, I used to be a doctor.

When his triage place was ready they moved the dog to the back room, and then Rodeo reluctantly headed for the exit. Summer let the man out the front door and gave him her contact info. He stored both her cell phone and the store's phone numbers in his own phone.

Don't worry about him, she said. He'll sense your worry and guilt, even from long distance and that won't help him heal.

He wouldn't be in this position if it

245

weren't for me, Rodeo said.

He's lived a long time and from the looks of him has lived pretty well. You're probably responsible for that too.

Rodeo reached his hand out and the woman shook it.

You done me the biggest favor here, Doc, said Rodeo. I owe you.

You seem like the type who'll pay me back, said the woman. So I'll take care of your dog for a couple of days gratis and call you when he gets well or if he's going to die.

Rodeo handed over his calling card.

Summer Skye examined the calling card then looked at Rodeo.

Go get some rest, Rodeo, she said. You look like you need it.

Actually I got some work to do, Rodeo said.

Well, take it from a used-to-be doctor who had a major nervous breakdown. The ex-vet paused and looked at Rodeo full in the face. Don't lose your head about something that might turn out to be okay later on, she said. Sometimes we make a big deal out of something when making a little deal out of something would have served us just as well.

I don't think it's like that right now, Rodeo said.

He walked farther down the path, got in his truck and lifted a farewell hand as Summer Skye closed the door of her shop. He started the truck and reached toward the shotgun seat. His hand hovered over the empty space for a moment. He frowned and put his hand back on the steering wheel.

Rodeo drove to Santa Cruz River Park and parked nearby the indigenous plants nursery. He walked to the public restrooms and then to the fountain but didn't see Billy. He sat on Billy's bench for a few minutes and then strolled to the nursery, where he talked to four plant workers who were just finishing their lunch break. Though Billy was a familiar local character none of them knew the homeless man. None of them had been interviewed by TPD about the death of Samuel Rocha.

How about a late 1960's model Chevrolet Impala, bright green with spinning rims and copper Historic Vehicle plates? Rodeo asked.

There was some hesitation on this question since lowriders were common in the area, but none of the nursery employees admitted they had ever seen any sour-apple-colored Chevy Impala in the vicinity of the nursery on a particular day in late July.

Rodeo drove to nearby Parade Liquor.

■ ■ ■ ■

The human crows again were all aligned on the guardrail across the street from the convenience store, this time with the addition of the Zander Jone. Rodeo parked in front of the store, went in and bought a twelve pack of Milwaukee Ice and a box of Black & Mild little cigars on his credit card and carried his purchases out of the store and across the road where he sat down next to the pool hustler, popped the tab on a beer and drank it down like he needed it. The regulars just stared at him.

Fella, it's cops all around here, idn't it, the Indian woman said. You gonna get us all in trouble, fella.

Rodeo ignored the warning.

Y'all know that homeless fella named Billy? he asked. Stays sometimes down by the river, at the jogging path park near the water fountain by the bathrooms?

Yeah, said Zander. I seen him around here for a long time. He's from El Paso. Used to be a singer with some band over there he says. His sister's a nun or something.

Yeah, fella, the Indian woman said. Billy he's always talking about El Paso. El Paso, El Paso. She shook her head. He really wants to go back to El Paso.

Anybody seen him today?

Billy's gone, fella, the Indian woman said. He's not at Armory Park. And he ain't in the River. I been all over today, fella, and Billy he's gone.

Y'all know where he sleeps at? Rodeo asked the group.

One of the Indian men waved a hand over his shoulder toward a drainage ditch. He stays on a ledge over there. But I don't sleep around him because he stinks so bad, so I don't know if he was there last night or not.

Rodeo nodded and said nothing more. The crows started shifting on the rail.

Fella, what are you going to do with all that beer? the Indian woman asked.

What I don't drink right now I'm going to give to y'all if you all will keep an eye out for Billy and give me a call if you see him.

We'll do it, fella! The woman pulled a welfare cell phone out of her shirt front and waited, finger poised for Rodeo's number. He gave it to her and she dutifully punched it in and repeated it back to him.

I'll give these cigars to somebody if they'll show me specifically where Billy stays nights, Rodeo said.

I would show you, fella, for sure, the fat woman said. But if I left for the smokes I wouldn't get no beer, not one can.

I'll go with you, Rodeo, Zander said. I don't need no bribe to do another rodeo cowboy a favor.

Zander stood and hitched up his belt and his cronies stared at him with respect.

We ain't going no place, fella, said the fat Indian woman. So you can give me the cigars and I'll hold them for Zander.

Rodeo gave the woman the cigars and Zander shook his head as if he had just missed an easy layup shot in a high stakes pool game. He led Rodeo the hundred yards to the concrete culvert and showed him where Billy kept his night camp. The place was a riot of junk.

Whew . . . Zander made a show of putting his forearm over his mouth. It really stinks down in there. Rodeo reached into his pocket, thumbed out four of Katherine Rocha's dollar bills from his wallet and slipped the money to Zander in full view of the other Parade Liquor crowd.

I appreciate you, Zander, said Rodeo. You know how to do another rodeo man a favor and I won't forget that. See you back at the barn.

Zander tipped his dime-store straw, pocketed the money with a flourish and headed jauntily back to his companions. Rodeo scrambled into Billy's den kicking carefully through his stuff, cautious of needles, snakes, scorpions. When he uncovered a bundle of envelopes he picked it up and examined it.

Not but one envelope was addressed to anyone named "Billy" or "William" so they had been stolen or found by the homeless man. Some of it seemed the type of thing he would steal or keep if found, things that seemed to have value and yet did not — fake checks from fast loan businesses, fake credit and ID cards from AARP or Citibank and the like. Only one bit of mail stood out as personal. The envelope was pliable from folding and yellowed as old newsprint and smelled of Billy or of something equally pungent and human. The USPS cancellation mark was indecipherable but the stamp was clearly from the 23rd Summer Olympic Games at Los Angeles. The return address was partially smudged but legible as "Mrs. Thomas O'Neal, 726 South Ambrose Street, El Paso, Texas." The addressee was WILLIAM O'NEAL: C/O CROSSROADS MISSION: NOGALES, ARIZONA. Rodeo read the letter.

Dear Billy Boy,

You are my Darling Dear Boy, always, always. I wish you would come Home to me. Your father is gone now for almost ten years and you know that. We miss you so.

Our Jane is working hard at Saint Ignacio. Sister enjoys her duties and prays for you daily. We both miss you so. Sister sends her Best Regards.

I can send you A Ticket Home, Dear Billy. You know I cannot send you plain money because you might use it for drugs and alcohol and only aid That Devil's Work.

But I can send you a bus ticket for Home.

You know how much we love you, both Sister and I. Your father loved you too as your Father in Heaven loves you. You must forgive your earthly father or in the End Times Our Father in Heaven will not forgive you.

Your loving Mother in Christ,
Mrs. Thomas O'Neal

Rodeo stared at this mother's missive for a while. He then refolded Billy's letter and slipped it back into the envelope that had long contained it. He hesitated but slipped the envelope into his shirt pocket. He sorted through the rest of Billy's mail stash and trash and found a small sheet of lined notebook paper from a spiral notebook.

You will never know how much I know
You miss your El Paso. But lost is where
    we go,

When we look for Home. If home is just a
    poem
Then I hope there's a sky-lit word dome

Behind your wasted eyes flared with death
And vision quest poems clouded on your
    beer breath.

My homes are drunks that crushed and
    betrayed
Our sibling dreams. But I still dream her
    golden hair

Floating across the sky, then landing,
    twining,
Her golden braid wrapped around me
    where I am standing,

But the bitchwitch is saying in her wasted
    slur
You are worthless, how did this occur.

And I say, you.
I saw, you.

To: Billy
From: Samuel Rocha, Poet

Rodeo folded up Samuel's poem to Billy and tucked it into his pocket. There was a variety of third class mail coming from several different sources and aimed at different destinations, offices and residences. Two envelopes were addressed to Erica Hernandez, the sitting U.S. Congressperson from Arizona District 7 who lived in South Tucson very near Starr Pass Road, one addressed to her home and one to her office. These envelopes were unopened but the addresses were circled with a Sharpie as if these locations were the object of the theft of them.

There was also a folded flier advertising an upcoming dedication ceremony for the new West Wing of the Juvenile Detention Center, a ceremony that would feature Representative Hernandez as keynote speaker and Former Arizona House Speaker Judge Randy Miller as Master of Ceremonies.

Three envelopes seemed cleaner, more recent and official. One was from C-23 Auto Paint and Body Shop, "In Bisbee

Since 1982." Another was from American Country Home and Auto Insurance Company and another from Verizon. These envelopes were held together with a rusty paper clip and all were addressed to Mrs. Katherine Rocha at 72602 Mark Street, Tucson, Arizona.

Rodeo sat in his truck and reread the letter from Billy's mother, then reexamined the rest of the mail he had lifted from the homeless man's nesting place. The phone bill addressed to Katherine Rocha indicated that an overdue payment for cell phone service had been received. The letter from American Country Home and Auto Insurance was a reminder that she only carried liability coverage on her vehicle and so was not entitled to reimbursement for any repairs. The bill from the auto repair shop in Bisbee was dated May 6 of that year and showed six hours of labor at $270.00 plus $425.00 for parts, including a used front panel and one new headlight set. There was a separate bill from the same company in the same envelope for a paint job in the amount of $607.37.

Rodeo called the C-23 Auto Paint and Body Shop in Bisbee and introduced himself as Bill Early, Insurance Claims Adjustor from American Country Home and Auto Insurance Company.

HowcanIhepya? the woman on the other end asked.

I am checking on an invoice that originated from your place of business, Rodeo said.

What can I tell ya about it, sir?

I understood from our client . . . Rodeo paused and rattled the paper in his hand into his cell phone. One Katherine A. Rocha of Mark Street, Tucson, that she brought in her car on May 4 of this year but the invoice says service by your company was on May 6. He used his Anglo voice and spoke as officiously as he could. Was she mistaken about these dates?

I'm sure the car was brought in when she said, Mr. Early. But we woulda put on the invoice the date the work was completed so that'd be the confusion. We probably just didn't invoice the job until it was done, the woman said.

Our records are showing this was a front end repair and a full body paint job on a Buick LeSabre but there's no VIN number for the vehicle on this invoice, Rodeo said.

There was a pause. Wait a moment, Mr. Early, said the receptionist. Rodeo waited long enough to hear several Beatles songs sanitized into Hold Muzak. Then a man's voice came on the phone.

Who's this I'm speaking with? The voice was thick and gruff and had a Southern drawl.

Bill Early, Rodeo said. American Country Insurance.

What's your employee number?

We don't use employee numbers at American Country, said Rodeo.

I know everybody in American Country, said the garage man. And there's no such person as you in it.

The garage man hung up. Rodeo headed to Bisbee, Arizona.

Rodeo found a Del Taco in the new section of Bisbee, and took his laptop into the fast food restaurant, ordered a Number Three Combo and ate a very late lunch or early dinner. He accessed their free Wi-Fi and used Google Maps to locate C-23 Auto Paint and Body Shop, which was just on the edge of Old Bisbee. Rodeo finished his meal quickly then drove his old truck to and past the garage on a moving reconnaissance. The office was closed for business but the garage doors were up and work still ongoing at C-23.

In the "show-off" spot in front of the paint

and body shop was parked a beautifully restored late 1960's Chevrolet Impala modified as a lowrider with silver spinning rims and sparkling sour-apple green paint job. The car described by Billy.

Also parked in front of the shop was a well-restored Firebird from the mid 1970s. The Firebird had both FOR SALE and LA VENTA signs wedged under its windshield wipers.

Rodeo pulled into a parking slot in downtown and unloaded his camera gear, binocs and sighting scope from the lockbox and put this equipment on the front seat, relocked the toolbox. He retraced his route, parking in a fairly protected space in a pullout a quarter mile from the C-23 shop. He leaned back on the bench seat and aimed the camera out the driver's side window. He took a dozen photos of the green-apple Impala including close-ups of the copper Arizona license plates. He also wrote down the plate numbers — HTX8 — in his notebook. There was no FOR SALE/LA VENTA sign on the lowrider Impala.

He evaluated the situation for five minutes. There were several men still busy in the work bays. Rodeo focused his lens on the FOR SALE and LA VENTA signs on the Firebird and dialed the contact phone number listed on both signs.

This is Jessie Storm, wassssssupp?

I'm interested in your Firebird, amigo. Rodeo spoke quickly and in his Mexican voice. If you can get off work you could meet me at the Brewery Lane Saloon in about ten minutes.

You could come by the shop.

Buyers set the scene, man, Rodeo said. You snooze you lose.

Two minutes later a young Anglo man walked alone out of the auto body shop with a spring in his step, pulled the FOR SALE/La Venta signs off the windshield of the Firebird and left rubber on the road as he drove to the center of Old Bisbee. Rodeo waited five minutes then drove to Brewery Lane Saloon and parked a few spots from the Firebird. He stored his gear back in the lockbox while he waited long enough for the young mechanic to get impatient but not so long that he would leave. Rodeo moved to the saloon, stood for a few seconds in front of the plate glass window pretending to adjust his hat so he had time to locate his mark. He saw the young mechanic sitting near the server's station and walked directly to a barstool one removed from the man. He pulled out his wallet, slapped down a twenty, looked around. There were

259

four other customers in the saloon as 4–6 Happy Hour was winding down.

The mechanic turned and eyeballed Rodeo for a long moment.

You looking for somebody? the mechanic asked.

I didn't know this was that kind of bar. Rodeo used his regular voice and the mechanic listened to it then blushed.

A bartender appeared and jerked his head up at Rodeo.

A Jack Black and Bud back for me, Rodeo said. He waved rather grandly at the mechanic. You got mechanical knowledge, buddy?

Say what? asked the mechanic.

I said I see by your outfit that you are a mechanic.

Yeah.

Rodeo jerked a thumb at the mechanic and then looked at the bartender.

Give the kid a shot and a beer too, Rodeo said.

The bartender slid the twenty off the bar and set two shots and two draft Budweisers with small change in front of Rodeo and the mechanic and disappeared into the kitchen again.

I know you, mister? asked the mechanic.

I hope not since I don't know you and so

if you know me then I am getting old and losing my memory of people. Rodeo threw back his JD and slammed the shot glass on the bar then turned to the mechanic in a bar buddy way. But I'll just be straight with you, buddy, Rodeo said. I got an old beat-to-shit Ford 150 that I just need a professional opinion about. And since I see by that patch on your coveralls that you come from C-23, which I heard is a pretty good shop around here, I was wondering since I bought you that round you maybe might give me your professional opinion about whether I should junk my old ride or fix it.

The mechanic stared at Rodeo. He looked around the saloon and looked at his cheap plastic watch and then shrugged.

All right, he said.

Rodeo described his own pickup at great length and then folded his arms.

First off, replace your points and plugs if you been runnin' on 'em a long time, then replace all your alternator wires, the mechanic said. Could be you're shortin' out on occasion just 'cause you got a old wire with a bad casin' and when the truck jiggles that wire it's hittin' up against the block sometimes and that causes you to stall out. Otherwise get a rebuild if you're so in love with the truck.

It was my mother's, Rodeo said.

Well then, said the mechanic. Do the right thing by it. Good truck's never failed if it was put together right and maintained right. Ought to last a man a lifetime if he don't live too long.

Much obliged, said Rodeo.

Just common sense, said the mechanic.

The pair sat in silence for several minutes. The mechanic glanced around nervously.

Rodeo nodded at the patch on the mechanic's pocket. How you like C-23? he asked.

It's all right. We mostly do regular stuff. It's Bisbee, you know. Small town shit. But I'm good at the work and it's something I can do. I wadn't no good at school but I got a good eye and a good hand for bodywork. The owner is a asshole from Arkansas but his wife who runs the place is sweet as pie.

You do much custom work? asked Rodeo. I saw a green-apple Impala on the street in front of your shop that looked like a pretty nice ride.

Yeah, that's Xavier Monjano's ride. Sweet idn't it?

'68? asked Rodeo.

'67.

Rodeo sipped his beer as if he was in no hurry.

"Monjano" sounds familiar to me. Rodeo attempted a casual tone. Is Xavier Monjano a Tucson guy?

Xavier's got a buncha cousins in Tucson, the mechanic said. The one I know is a Indian cop, I think. Which is funny when you think about it.

Why? Are the Monjanos characters? asked Rodeo.

Monjanos they got a variety of solutions to various problems if that's what you're askin', the mechanic said. Xavier's supposed to be paying ten cents in Florence but he split back to Chihuahua, what I heard. I don't know nothing about it. They don't let me ride with them, so I don't really know them.

Xavier's people wanna sell that car for six thousand? Rodeo lowballed the price.

Get real. The mechanic shook his head in an exaggerated way. That ride's got a cherry hemi in it and them rims alone cost six or seven bucks a piece and that custom paint cost four, so six wouldn't touch that automobile. The mechanic looked around the room again then turned to his beer and drank some, wiped the foam off his mouth with the back of his dirty hand. Anyway Xavier loves that ride and if somebody sold it out from under him while he was gone that'd be two cut-off balls for somebody.

Who takes care of Xavier's ride while Xavier's back in Old Mexico?

One of his cousins, the mechanic said. The Indian cop from Tucson. But he has to keep Xavier's ride up here in Bisbee. That's the deal, I guess.

You got a name for the cousin? asked Rodeo. Maybe I could negotiate with him on price?

The mechanic looked Rodeo over from head to toe and shook his head. I'll tell you the fella's name is Carlos Monjano but they call him Caps and if you want to talk to him about Xavier's ride Caps comes up here almost every week since Xavier's run off and takes the ride out. The mechanic finished his beer. But you're wasting your time on that Impala, mister. They ain't gonna sell it for any price. The mechanic nursed his shot of liquor as if he meant to make it last. He turned abruptly toward Rodeo. I got a ride for sale though, mister. The young man pointed out the window at the Pontiac. That Firebird out there. It's clean as a whistle and runs like a top.

Rodeo shook his head. Sorry to disappoint, buddy, but you know how it is with old guys and their old pickups. We ain't looking to lay down no serious rubber no more. Just trying to keep running what we already got.

The mechanic nodded glumly.

Where you from, buddy?

I'm from Vail right down the road a bit. You?

Tucson, born and bred. Rodeo took a sip of his Bud. You get much Tucson business at C-23? he asked.

Sometimes we do but mostly it's just Locals. Too far to drive over here.

I think an old friend of mine did bring her car over here though. Rodeo said this as if he were just recalling it. She said there was a good place over here to get quality work done cheaper than Tucson prices.

The young man raised his eyebrows. I did do a front fender and panel job with paint a couple of months ago, he said. Some dumbass tacked a spoiler on a classic Le Sabre and that was a pain in the ass to deal with during paint. The mechanic frowned. Waste of brain space for whoever did that.

That might have been the ride, Rodeo said. I think it was in May or June she brought it over here. Old lady though and batty as hell, so she probably wouldn't recall right. I think her car was for shit anyway. Nothing a skilled technician like you would probably work on.

I do as good a job on a shitty car as on a fine ride, mister, the mechanic said. And charge the same too, more or less. That's the mark of a professional. The young man pulled on an earlobe. And I do remember that car, now you say it. A Buick LeSabre, '84, I think. Nice ride, actually. Clean insides and real low miles, I remember. But I don't remember it was a old lady's.

Whose was it? Rodeo rotated his shot glass on the bar and stared at it.

Some kid's I think and he probably had put the spoiler on hisself which is plain stupid. Got to let a professional do professional work or it's just gonna be a mess, you know?

I agree, said Rodeo. Amateurs should let professionals just do the work for them. Did you say anything to the kid about ruining the ride?

I don't say shit to nobody about nothing, mister, the mechanic said. I clock in, I clock out and I just do my job every day. That's the American Way. The mechanic looked at Rodeo again very carefully as if he had just realized he had betrayed his own code of conduct. You 5-0, Mister?

I am much worse than 5-0 because Police is nine-to-five, five days a week but me and my people are twenty-four hours a day three hundred and sixty-five days a year, Rodeo said. He smiled at the mechanic and then leaned over and pulled out his big wallet and slid a school photo of Samuel Rocha in front of him.

The mechanic squinted at the small photo.

This the kid who brought that LeSabre in? asked Rodeo. I'll give you three seconds to answer. Yes or no are your only options on this question.

Yes.

Is this kid related to the Monjanos somehow? asked Rodeo.

Yes. The mechanic's eyelids fluttered and his upper lip beaded with sweat. No. I mean I don't know if he is or he isn't.

I worded that question badly, Rodeo said. So relax and just tell me what you know about this kid in the photograph and tell me quick. When Rodeo shifted his eyes from the mechanic the young man lurched off his barstool to make a run for the door. But Rodeo grabbed the mechanic's hand and folded his thumb down until the man coughed and his eyes turned ruby and ran. Rodeo looked quickly around the bar. No one seemed interested in them, so he guided the young man back onto the barstool.

The pain will stop if you're straight with me and there probably won't be much damage, Rodeo said. Otherwise I break your thumb and you pay the hospital bill and lose six weeks of work.

The mechanic's face was sheened with sweat. All I know is that maybe this kid that brought in the old Buick was related to the Monjanos, he said. But I wouldn't know how, mister. Serious. I wouldn't know how he was related even if he was. I swear that to you, mister.

You don't have to swear to me, buddy, said Rodeo. But you do need to make sure to tell the Indian cop — Carlos Monjano, the one they call Caps — that Rodeo Grace Garnet saw that shiny green Impala on Starr Pass Road the day Samuel Rocha got shot. Can you remember those three names and keep them together?

Caps Monjano . . . the mechanic said. He gulped air as tears slid down his pale face. Samuel Rocha . . . Rodeo Garnet . . .

Rodeo let go of his fierce grip gently, pulled a calling card from his wallet and placed it on the bar with a ten-dollar bill.

Just convey that message, buddy.

The mechanic rubbed at his sore thumb and wiped at the sweat on his face. They told me in school they always killed the messenger first thing.

Well, like you said, buddy, you didn't do

too good in school did you? said Rodeo. So if I was you I wouldn't worry too much about those old school lessons.

The mechanic nodded and looked at his damaged hand as if it were a new addition to his body.

I work on necks too, buddy, Rodeo said. Tell Caps Monjano that if you feel like it.

The mechanic shook his head as he watched Rodeo leave. I ain't telling anybody a word more than I have to ever again, he said.

It was full dark when Rodeo stopped at a pay phone at a Circle K on the outskirts of Tucson and thumbed in some quarters. He found the number stored for the Tohono O'odham Reservation Police in his cell phone and dialed it on the pay phone. He covered the speaker with the front of his shirt and tried to flush out Carlos "Caps" Monjano as the killer of Samuel Rocha.

I'd like to speak with Officer Carlos Monjano, the one they call Caps. He said this in his regular voice but rushed it.

Officer Monjano is not available, sir. How can someone else help you?

Just tell Caps Monjano I'm interested in his cousin's ride, that Impala over in Bisbee that I just found out about. Tell him I saw that green car going over the Santa Cruz River bridge at Starr Pass Road a couple of months ago and it looked like a good car for a drive-by.

Rodeo skipped the motel lobby when he arrived at the Arizona Motel and went right to #116 where he called Magpies Pizza on the house phone and ordered a large, plain cheese. He turned on the AC full blast. He took a lukewarm shower, got naked in bed and pulled the thinnest sheet in the world over himself. The room phone rang.

Rodeo, my friend, said the motel manager. I need to have some words with you.

Don't hassle me for money right now, Abi, and don't make me remind you of what you owe me for finding your sister's cousin's son, said Rodeo.

Yes yes, Rodeo, said the motel manager. My family and I are aware continually of all that you have done to keep some Indian Indians safe in Tucson. But I was just wondering if you cared to watch some pornographic movies this evening with me? I just received my new Pornflix Blu-ray DVDs which when watched are supposed to be better than actual sexual relations.

You ever think about having sex with an actual person other than yourself, Abi?

I think of nothing else, my friend.

Well, no thanks on the pornfest, Abi. But thanks for asking. I am just going to watch the news and I got a Magpies incoming, said Rodeo.

Do you want me to pay for your pizza when it is arriving?

Sure Abi. Put it on my tab and bring it over when it gets here. If I'm asleep don't wake me up and just put the pizza on the table near the door.

Rodeo dialed Summer Skye's cell phone but got shunted to voice mail and then disconnected. He dialed Tucson Famous Pets and Aquarium Design Center, but got a message machine. He left a message for his dog.

Hang in there, he said. We'll be on the road again and flush again soon.

Rodeo fell asleep during the first bit of KGUN ten o'clock news on a TV chained to a metal rack mounted on an eroding wall. The whole enterprise seemed ready to collapse under the slightest pressure.

. . . Randy Miller was running for U.S. Congress on the Tea Party ticket. A major battle between the Sinaloa marijuana growers' cartel and rival enforcement gangs from Tamaulipas had left downtown Nogales,

Mexico with major property damage, two civilians, two Narcos and two Federales dead. Tombstone vigilantes had constructed their own surveillance aircraft to patrol AMexican borders, said aircraft piloted by monkeys released from Arizona State University biomed studies under pressure from PETA. Another murder in Los Jarros County had been discovered on Agua Seco Road. The Tucson Unified School District was under fire from a coalition of evangelical Christians for sponsoring "unchristian" events like yoga and field trips to see the Dalai Lama. At the insistence of his third wife the basketball coach of the University of Arizona was having a second brain scan . . .

Rodeo woke up with his hands bound to the headboard of the bed with a pair of his own disposable handcuffs. Sirena stood over him pulling apart the snaps on her cowgirl shirt. The woman reeked of alcohol and looked fit to kill.

Who let you in the room?

Your boy Abi the Sheik let me in, Sirena said. And I paid the Magpies delivery boy for your pizza. And now I'm going to make you come in my mouth and then you will spank me for being such a bad, bad girl . . .

The image of the TV was blurred but the sound still blared.

Rodeo struggled up through layers of sleep and saw a jumble of beer cans and one-shot liquor bottles, cold pizza, ripped stockings and underwear and a hash pipe. He rubbed his head in his hands as he stumbled into the shower as the TV droned on. When he was as clean as he could get and standing naked and barefoot in the motel room, he heard the news clearly.

"Ray Molina, longtime sheriff of Los Jarros County, Arizona is dead by gunshot wounds suffered . . ."

Rodeo noted the time on his phone as he punched out 2ARRWS. It was almost ten a.m. He poured four BC powders into a half-full Coca-Cola can and drank the concoction down.

It's fresh news to me too, brother. Luis said this without preamble. Rodeo put the phone on speaker mode, sat down on the bed and tried to get his clothes back on.

Where did it happen?

They found Apache Ray dead under the overpass, said Luis. Where that other one was. They think he was shot there.

What was the cause of death?

Two guesses and the first one don't count.

Shotgun, said Rodeo. Front or back?

Full frontal, Luis said. It was a mess they said.

Any leads?

Deputy Buenjose was by here this morning about seven, said Luis. Asking all kinds of shit.

Who found him?

The bread truck guy he found Ray at about five. Sheriff was killed last night probably between twelve and one Buenjose told me.

Who was on dispatch last night?

Deputy Pal Real was doing dispatch last night till midnight then it went on automatic. Just before midnight somebody called in a suspicious activity under the interstate overpass and Pal Real he put it over to Ray and I guess Ray he went out there to see about it hisself since they are so shorthanded at County Sheriff.

Ray went out there alone? asked Rodeo.

You know how Ray gets when he acts Apache.

Did the sheriff manage to call in from the scene?

He called in to say it was nothing there, Luis said. So must have been an ambush.

Why didn't Pal Real call Ray back, Luis? Why didn't anybody know Ray was MIA?

Pal Real was at the end of his shift and he didn't take the call too serious I guess since Ray had called in from the scene and said it was nothing. Or said it was nothing he couldn't handle.

There's a big difference between "nothing" and "nothing you can't handle," Luis.

You know how Ray was, brother. Ready, fire, aim. That's the way Ray always was.

I remember how Ray was, said Rodeo.

The men were silent for a few seconds.

I know you sideways liked each other, brother, said Luis. So for your sake I'm sorry to hear about Ray getting it like this.

Somebody ambushed him, Rodeo said. After Ray made the call back in to Pal Real.

Likely, said Luis.

So whoever killed Ray probably knew how he was and how he worked and how Los Jarros County Sheriff's Dispatch works.

Or doesn't work, said Luis.

Rodeo said nothing.

Police were looking for Sirena Rae, brother, said Luis.

Rodeo still said nothing.

You in this someway, Rodeo? Luis asked. Think plain, brother. It's me now, but it will be Police soon.

275

No. I'm not involved in this, Luis. Rodeo paused. Unless I'm Sirena's alibi. I was with her last night about the time Ray was probably killed.

That might not be a good thing for you, Luis said.

I can't see any of this being very good for me, Rodeo said. But Sirena and I were here not there.

You got witnesses?

Abichiek and probably the pizza delivery man.

That's convenient, said Luis.

Yes, said Rodeo. It is, isn't it, Luis?

Rodeo called Summer Skye.

Is my dog okay?

He's doing good, Summer said. I brought him home with me last night he was doing so good.

I tried to call last night but just got voice mail on your cell and message at the store.

The store phone redirects to my cell, Summer said. So he heard your message. Then he started whining, so I had to give him some Jameson.

You're not keeping him to be your drinking buddy, said Rodeo. And you shouldn't be trying to improve his tastes.

I'm not. Summer laughed slightly. He's a

good dog and all. But he really stinks and Hudson does not like dogs especially old stinky ones.

When can I pick him up?

For his sake give it another day or two. You all right?

Rodeo examined the scratches and abrasions Sirena had inflicted on him the night before. He looked at the TV screen where flashed the face of the dead sheriff of Los Jarros County.

I'm not good, he said. But I could be worse.

Rodeo was sitting in the truck drinking another analgesic and Coca-Cola cocktail when his cell phone buzzed.

Mr. Garnet? Rodeo Grace Garnet?

I am Rodeo Grace Garnet.

My name is Sisely Miller, Mr. Garnet. I'm Judge Randy Miller's wife and I need some help.

Rodeo started his truck. What can I do for you, Mrs. Miller?

I need your professional help. About my brother.

Who is your brother?

His name is Tinley Burke.

Rodeo switched off the pickup's engine.

I know your brother, Mrs. Miller. Slightly

at least. He was a professor of mine at the U. Rodeo omitted his taxiing Burke from BoonDocks to Eryn Hage's place on Convent Street the night before the last. What about Professor Burke, Mrs. Miller?

He's dead.

Rodeo sat back against the bench seat of his truck.

I'm sorry for your troubles, Mrs. Miller. What happened?

It's not important, the woman said.

Excuse me, Mrs. Miller?

I mean . . . The woman stopped. Rodeo could hear the familiar rattle of ice cubes in a drink. He's dead, Sisely Miller said. And it's terrible. The ice rattled again. But that's not what I am calling you about.

How can I help you, Mrs. Miller?

I need something found.

You need to slow down and explain the situation to me, Mrs. Miller.

Where should I start?

Just start at a good spot and go until you're finished.

All right. The woman sounded flustered, but she found a starting point and started talking. My brother and I had an appointment last evening. We were to meet for dinner at eight o'clock at the Riverpark Inn. He's never late and seldom misses appointments but he did last night. He did not respond to phone calls and I was worried, so this morning I went by his apartment. He didn't answer the door, so his landlord let me in and we found him dead and now I need some help, the woman said. Can you help me?

You called the police?

Yes, of course. In fact we called immediately. They are at his apartment right now.

How did you get my name and number, Mrs. Miller?

My husband, Judge Randy Miller contacted someone he knows in the Tucson Police Department. Someone he knew from a statewide committee or something like that. Overhill? Overdale?

Clint Overman? Rodeo asked.

That's right, she said. Detective Overman.

Is there some question about your brother's death you think I can answer that the police can't, Mrs. Miller? I don't know anything about it. What happened?

I guess he overdosed accidentally on prescription medication, the woman said. Actually my husband, Judge Miller, assures me that it will be ruled an "accidental overdose."

It's probably too soon to say that, isn't it,

Mrs. Miller?

My husband usually knows these things. The woman's voice sounded matter-of-fact.

What do you need me for then, Mrs. Miller?

I want you to find something. The woman hesitated. It's not a police matter. It's a private matter. I want you to find something of his for me. Something my brother had. Something he made. Can you just come see me? she asked. I can't do this over the phone. Meet me in the restaurant at the Riverpark Inn in about twenty minutes, she said. The woman hung up before Rodeo could agree or disagree.

Rodeo called Clint Overman at home.

You know what time it is? the TPD detective asked.

It's ten-thirty in the morning, Clint. Why aren't you at work?

I'm not at work. The man said this as if he were unsure of where he was. His voice was slurred.

I just need some information on Tinley Burke, Clint.

Who?

Tinley Burke. He's the brother-in-law of Randy Miller, Judge Junior of "The Millers," the Tea Party fella running for Congress.

I know who he is, said Overman. The cop's voice was belligerent. Me and good ol' Randy sat on some bullshit "stop crime or else" committee the current harebrained governor cooked up for the right-wing constituency to preserve Family Values. Overman hiccupped. Which I have no more since I have no family no more. Rodeo heard the crack of a beer can opening. Why you calling me about Family Values at this time of the morning?

Apparently Judge Miller called you for a referral for a private investigator and you referred me.

Oh yeah. Just a while ago. Randy called me looking for a PI, so I threw you the bone, Garnet. The detective's words tumbled together. So now you owe me and we're even and you can fuck off forever.

Rodeo drove to Convent Street and parked in front of the Dota house across the street from Tinley Burke's last known address. Tomas's riding lawnmower was gone but the ground was littered with empty beer cans. Rodeo watched the curtains rustle in the front room of the house then turned to look at Eryn Hage's place. There were several police cars, marked and unmarked, and an ambulance parked in the vicinity. A man in a sharkskin suit and bolo tie detached himself from the small crowd around Burke's front door and approached Rodeo. Rodeo nodded through his open window, pulled out his fat wallet, slid out his PI license and handed it over. The man examined it closely and then returned the investigator's license and stuck out his hand.

Jethro Haynes. Detective, TPD.

As the men shook hands the policeman looked closely at Rodeo's red and raw wrist. He leaned forward slightly to sneak a look into the cab of Rodeo's truck, then pulled out his leather-bound notepad and gold-plated pen.

What brings you here, Mr. Garnet?

The wife of Judge Randy Miller is trying to hire me to look into something for her about her brother. Rodeo inclined his hat toward the busy apartment.

She tell you where he lived?

Yes.

What do you know about this? the detective asked.

I know he's dead, said Rodeo.

The Millers don't think you can investigate Tinley Burke's death alongside TPD? The cop sounded skeptical. Because that is not going to happen. Not even for Judge Miller.

No. It would be a property reclamation job of work for me as I understand it. Something's lost Mrs. Miller wants found. But I hadn't met with her yet, so I wouldn't know what she wants found that's lost.

The detective took a few notes.

Are you otherwise acquainted with Tinley Burke?

Not especially, Rodeo said. Professor Burke was an old teacher of mine at the U.

What would you say if I said a witness has you on this scene night before last, with Mr. Burke?

Rodeo looked toward the Dota house to his right and watched a curtain slide back into place. He turned back to the police-man. I'd say Mama Dota doesn't miss much, so that does not surprise me.

Are you familiar with this 'hood?

This is a home 'hood for me, Rodeo said. I grew up around here and lived here somewhat last year.

So what were you doing here with Burke night before last? Partying?

I drove him home from BoonDocks.

Why's that?

He was intoxicated.

Were you intoxicated as well?

Not to speak of.

But you came back here from the bar to party with him to get drunk? And anyone else in this party?

I drove him home, got him in the house and left.

You performed a Samaritan's deed then?

He was drunk and asked me for a ride and since here is not too out of my way back to where I'm staying right now I gave him the ride.

Where are you staying?

Arizona Motel. Room 116.

Is that your last known address?

No. I got a place in El Hoyo, down in Los Jarros.

What are you doing in town then? Job?

Yes. Little day job. Nothing major.

Can I ask what that investigation is about?

Nothing to hide, but no. It's got nothing to do with this.

You never know, do you? asked the cop.

I guess that's why we need detectives, said Rodeo.

The cop smiled and wrote that down then continued with his interrogation.

What time did you bring Dr. Burke back to his domicile?

Maybe nine? Mama Dota would know by what telenovela she was watching. That's how she tells time.

Were you driving your vehicle or his? The cop gestured at Rodeo's old truck and at the Land Cruiser that was now parked in front of the apartment.

Mine, Rodeo said. He left his Toyota at BoonDocks. And no, I don't know how it got back here.

And you parked out back when you returned Dr. Burke home?

No, said Rodeo. Didn't know there was an out back to his place and Mama Dota would not have seen me if I had.

The cop smiled again and made another note.

Anybody else with you two in your truck or in the house when you dropped him off?

Not that I know of, said Rodeo. But I never moved out of the front room though, so there could have been someone else in the place I didn't see or hear. I didn't stay for long, maybe three or four minutes. He went to the back of the house and started barfing, so I left.

So your fingerprints will be in his domicile?

Rodeo took a minute before he answered. Should be on the door and no place else.

Are you certain about that?

No. But that's what I am recalling for the record.

Anything else? asked Detective Haynes. For the record?

Just what I said. I'm here because his sister wants to hire me to find something of his she thinks is missing.

Lost or stolen? asked Haynes.

I don't know yet. Do you?

The cop tapped on his leather notepad with his gold pen.

The sister was looking for a book manuscript or something of that sort, the cop said.

Did y'all find anything like that? asked Rodeo.

The cop looked over his shoulder at Tinley Burke's apartment then looked back at Rodeo.

Probably not.

Rodeo put his hand on the car keys but stopped himself from turning the engine over when the cop took a step forward.

You sure there's nothing else, Mr. Garnet?

The Professor asked me to open a pill bottle for him when we were at BoonDocks and I did, said Rodeo. Though I think he left that pill bottle at the saloon, in his bar bucket there, since the Land Cruiser is returned back here maybe the pill bottle will have been too. My prints are on file.

Only for your PI license or for something else?

Might be some variety of them for different things, said Rodeo.

You got witnesses to you opening the pill bottle at BoonDocks?

I'm sure somebody saw me open the bottle for him, Rodeo said. The bar wasn't busy but there was some custom. The bartender was "Barbi-with-just-the-i" or "Bambi-with-just-the-i."

Know what was in the scrip bottle? What kind of pills?

Cornucopia, Rodeo said. Pills what killed him?

Off the record and prematurely, I'm not saying. But the good Dr. Burke apparently was something of an expert mixocologist and he actually had scrips for almost everything we found in the house.

Almost?

There were a few undocumented oxys with Mexican markers on them. Burke did not have a prescription for oxycodone. Do you know where he could have gotten Mexican oxycodone, Mr. Garnet?

No.

The cop closed his notepad and smiled very slightly.

Well, I know who you are now, he said. So if we need you to make a statement we'll be in touch. And of course if you think of something or even better if you discover something that might be useful to Law Enforcement I know I can trust you to call TPD and ask for me directly.

Are you the new kid on the block, Mr. Haynes?

Depends on who you ask, the detective said.

Do you know what's happening with Clint Overman? Rodeo asked.

Yes, I do, said the cop. Detective Overman's moved to Shutter Island.

At the restaurant of the Riverpark Inn, Sisely Miller was waiting at one end of a long patio that was shaded by a beige-and-green awning and overlooked the grounds of the motel. Nearby the patio a kidney-shaped swimming pool sparkled in a manicured lawn and several attractive people in bathing suits were on chaise lounges sunning themselves to death. A couple were playing a heated game on the paddle tennis courts and A-Mountain was also visible from her perspective but Sisely Miller stared at the bottom of her Bloody Mary glass. No one else was on the patio of the restaurant.

Mrs. Miller?

When the woman jerked her head up her blond hair did not move a wisp. She didn't rise but leaned forward and offered her fingertips, shared a tremored grip with Rodeo.

You must be Rodeo Garnet.

Yes ma'am, said Rodeo. I must be.

Sit.

Rodeo took the seat opposite her and studied her as she looked past him trying to locate a waiter.

The woman was a size zero dressed in fashionable clothes appropriate for a well-tended early forty-something on a shopping and spa day. Her green eyes seemed slightly glazed under groomed eyebrows that were obviously but not obtrusively fighting against a facelift forehead. Her perfume was a delicate blend of citrus and smoke. The remnants of two Bloody Marys were in reach of her clear lacquered fingernails. She waved a command at a waiter and sat back folding her hands in her linen lap. She met Rodeo's gaze directly.

My husband of course is Randy Miller, who was a Pima County judge as was his father and grandfather, and then my husband was Speaker of the Arizona State House of Representatives and now he's a leading candidate for the United States House of Representatives running as an Independent. The woman seemed to be explaining something to an idiot.

I know who your husband is, Mrs. Miller, Rodeo said. My daddy was a hand for Randy's daddy, Judge Senior at Slash/M Rancho back in the 1970s.

Did you know Judge Miller back then? The woman seemed shocked by this possibility.

No. My mother and I stayed on the Res when my daddy worked and bunked down in Los Jarros. Rodeo frowned slightly. The Millers didn't mix with the Hands anyway, he said.

I seldom go down to the Miller Ranch, Sisely Miller said. I don't care for Los Jarros County.

Unless you like dirt and jackrabbits, it's not much reason to, Rodeo said. He paused a few seconds then started his client pitch. You said Clint Overman gave you my name, Mrs. Miller?

Judge Miller knows this Detective Overman from participation on a committee of some sort, she said. And they both are relatively close to the current governor.

I don't follow politics too much, said Rodeo.

Well, I must so I do, Sisely Burke Miller said. She puffed out a quick breath as if to revive herself in the heat. Suffice to say I needed someone local to help me and you are that person apparently. Are you professional?

If you pay me I am.

I guess I meant to ask if you are licensed and efficacious?

Rodeo narrowed his eyes. I am a licensed private investigator, yes ma'am. And whether I'm efficacious or not would depend on what effect you desire, Mrs. Miller.

The woman leaned back in her chair as the waiter put a fresh Bloody Mary next to the two empty glasses already on the table.

I'm not eating, she said. She glanced at Rodeo. But you may if you like. The woman sounded as if she were accustomed to giving orders.

I'll just have a big OJ and a glass of ice water, please, said Rodeo.

The waiter nodded and moved off. Sisely Miller watched him leave.

I like wait staff who speak English well or simply don't speak at all, Sisely Miller said. Is that very bad of me?

Depends on what language you need to speak in the circumstance you're in and what you might need from a waiter, said

Rodeo. And I don't know much about what's "bad," Mrs. Miller. I am mostly interested in what's useful to get a job done and earn a living.

You are a working man.

Yes ma'am. I am.

Rodeo's drinks appeared and he drank his water in a single go and then poured the orange juice over the ice and drank half of that.

Rough night? Sisely Miller asked. She raised a tweezed eyebrow at Rodeo's abraded wrists.

He pulled his shirtcuffs over the sexplay wounds but otherwise ignored the question.

Could we get to business now? asked the woman.

Your brother just died and you wanted me to do some recovery work for you that's got nothing to do with his death. That the long and short of it, Mrs. Miller?

It's abrupt. She cocked her small head. What is the job generally in your line of work, Mr. Garnet? She asked this as if she were actually curious.

I find out things that might be useful, Rodeo said. When I get lucky I find out things other people, often official people seem to have trouble finding out.

And you get paid for that?

I always get paid, Mrs. Miller. One way or another.

Sisely Burke took a drink then patted her lipstick dry with a paper napkin.

I'm not insensitive, you know. It's just that my brother was a burden and now this . . . Her voice cracked slightly.

You're under a lot of stress right now, Mrs. Miller.

I am always under a lot of stress. You cannot imagine. Sisely Miller used the napkin to wipe at her eyes though they did not appear to be moist. Still it's a terrible thing to say about my own brother, I know. Maybe especially since we were twins and you know what they say about twins.

Not really, Rodeo said.

We had a very special connection. She brushed her eyes again. Only I know how he truly was.

How was that, Mrs. Miller?

The woman crushed the napkin and dropped it on the tabletop. He had "issues."

What kind of issues?

Her small shoulders inside her silk blouse moved up and down. The Burkes of Santa Barbara are . . . She acted as if she were searching for a complex term. Prominently well-to-do, to say the least. And so my brother and I were trust fund babies and maybe because of that he remained forever the retarded adolescent. She paused. He also did not approve of my choice in husband.

Why not?

She did not answer this question immediately but seemed lost in thought. He considered my arrangement with Judge Miller as overly "strategic."

Rodeo waited for more. Sisely Miller seemed to stir herself with some effort before continuing.

I married well, at least. And had the children we needed to carry on the family fortune and took on some adult responsibilities over the years. My brother was . . .

She put a fisted little hand over her mouth as if she needed to physically stop herself from talking.

He was a good teacher, said Rodeo. I took one of his classes at the U of A and Professor Burke knew his archeology and related well to students.

He's dead, Sisely Miller said. She was not listening to Rodeo. She stared at her Bloody Mary. Rodeo stared at her.

He was always unstable. Just like our father. She said this more to herself than to Rodeo. He was always a danger . . . Her voice trailed off.

A danger to who? asked Rodeo.

I just meant my brother was dangerous to himself, Sisely Miller said. She waved a dismissive hand. With the pills and alcohol, I meant. The woman put a hand to her coiffed hair then put both hands flat on the table as if coming back to business. So there's no question about that. About his death, I mean. I know he overdosed on some combination of his addictions, killed himself with a few of his favorite things, as he called them. The woman paused and let out a tiny puff of breath. That's not why I've hired you.

You hadn't hired me yet, Mrs. Miller, Rodeo said. I'd need some fiduciary exchange before I'm hired.

Sisely Miller leaned back and killed her third obvious drink and then stirred the quickly melting ice cubes with a wilting celery stalk.

But I shall, she said. Because you must find something for me.

Find what, Mrs. Miller? Rodeo asked.

A manuscript, she said. My brother said he had completed it, so I imagine that was true as he always finished what he started.

Is it like a journal or something?

No. It is not a personal journal or a purloined letter or the like. It will be a book in manuscript form.

Rodeo raised his eyebrows in a question.

My brother wrote a memoir that I don't want getting into the wrong hands.

What would the "wrong hands" be, Mrs. Miller?

Any hands but mine, the woman said. Especially any hands that have newsprint on them, if you understand my meaning.

You want me to find something that the Press should not find, said Rodeo.

My husband is a front runner for an occupied seat from Arizona District Seven for U.S. Congress in the upcoming election . . . Mrs. Miller stopped abruptly as if this statement explained what needed explaining.

That's Erica Hernandez's seat, said Rodeo.

It is currently, said the politician's wife.

Rodeo finished his juice and set the glass down carefully on the glass tabletop.

I'm staying in a motel not far from where your brother was living and I know, knew him slightly from the University where I took one of his classes last year, Rodeo said. Night before last we were at a local bar and he needed a ride home, so I drove your brother to his apartment.

How was he?

He was in pretty bad shape, so I helped

him inside his place, said Rodeo. And I saw a laptop and a book manuscript on a desk in his living room.

Recovery of the laptop is of no concern.

Wouldn't the manuscript of this memoir book be stored in Professor Burke's computer?

No. Let me explain something to you. Sisely Burke Miller tapped her fingernail tip on the glass top of the table as if to get the attention of a dull student. My brother was eccentric in a variety of ways including being paranoiac about information and identity theft, so he only worked on one computer at a time, usually a laptop with the Wi-Fi and all the external portals deactivated. As he composed his books he printed them immediately.

What did he do with the hard copies?

It depended on the book, Sisely Miller said. His genre books he usually just had bound at Kinko's when he finished them and he kept these under his bed or in a closet or armoire. If you saw a manuscript unbound he was probably still working on it. She took a deep breath and let it out slowly as if practicing breathing.

But the more personal the story, the harder he tried to conceal it, she said. He stored these novels in a lockbox or even at times took them to his safe deposit box at the bank. As he grew more paranoid about someone stealing his ideas he distrusted even the best banks, so he began to hide the more personal books. Like buried treasure, he would say.

And the computer he worked on?

After every writing session he deleted all the files from the computer. He stored nothing electronically and backed nothing up, so he had no thumb drives, CDs or floppy disks. He had no Internet hookups in his apartments. If he needed to use the Internet he used it only on community computers at shared sites, usually at a public library. When he completed a book he incinerated the laptop he wrote it on so thoroughly that even expert forensic scientists could not retrieve his files. The woman paused. So you see why the laptop is irrelevant?

There's nothing on it that could be accessed or downloaded anyway, said Rodeo.

Not by any normal person, Sisely Miller said. And while my brother would have believed that the FBI or CIA or KGB was trying to pirate his brilliant ideas, I do not believe in such conspiracy theories. When she waved at the waiter the diamond in her ring bedazzled.

Do you think some regular person, a common thief, stole the manuscript when they stole the laptop? Rodeo asked.

It is possible but not likely, Sisely Miller said. She shifted in her seat. There was so much of more value in his apartment. Navajo rugs and collectible Indian artifacts, cameras, artwork, a silver service. His Patek Philippe cost thirty-five thousand dollars.

What?

His watch was still on his wrist, the woman said. And he usually had at least a thousand dollars in his wallet.

He didn't use credit cards because those are traceable, said Rodeo.

Correct. He even used prepaid cell phones so his calls couldn't be traced. Sisely Miller leaned back with relief as the waiter appeared again with a fresh red cocktail for her. When the waiter attempted to remove her empties she physically pushed his hand away as if she needed the dirty glasses to keep count of her consumption. Sisely Miller nodded at Rodeo as the waiter left chastened. So you understand the situation?

If the computer was taken along with the manuscript then whoever stole these was not a common burglar or petty thief looking for something to hock, but somebody who wanted the information or ideas in the computer or manuscript?

Correct. And that someone might have known my brother well enough to get into his apartment but probably did not know him well enough to know how my brother worked and so wouldn't know the laptop wasn't important, that only the manuscript was important. Sisely Miller tapped her fingertip on the tabletop again. What was the manuscript on his desk called?

Paths of Death: A Serial Killer Thriller.

That's an impossibly amateurish title and one he would use for his facile genre books but not for his memoir. The woman shook her head. He told me he was entitling the memoir *Running in the Dark.* So what you saw on his desk could not possibly be what I am looking for.

So, even if the manuscript and laptop I saw were stolen, you don't care, Mrs. Miller?

My brother was not a terrible writer but his books were drivel for the most part, she said. Nothing but clichéd themes and middle-aged men having affairs with beautiful dames and acting heroic and trying desperately to remain hip. He could never get anyone reputable to take him seriously, so whoever took *Paths of Death* is welcome to it.

300

That means I am probably looking for a manuscript that he hid, said Rodeo.

I am assuming so.

Did Professor Burke have any friends you knew of, Mrs. Miller? asked Rodeo. Anyone he would have confided in about the memoir you're looking for or who could have seen him hiding it?

He would confide in no one but me, the woman said. But he was dating someone. And she had been in his apartment.

How would you know that, Mrs. Miller?

I just know it.

But you don't know who it was?

She shook her head.

Did your brother have a lot of other houseguests?

Rarely. He was a very private person. Very reserved. He could be sociable when he was drinking but he did not like many people. He did not let many people inside his world, if you know what I mean?

I understand that, Rodeo said.

Will you work for me? the woman asked.

Rodeo turned and looked at A-Mountain then looked back at Sisely Miller. I wouldn't mind looking into this case for you, Mrs. Miller. Though it's no guarantees in this sort of thing. If this manuscript is just hidden I can probably find it but it could be a needle in a haystack deal and take days or weeks or months. Or it could be an elephant in a room and only take me an hour to find.

If it was stolen? Sisely Miller asked.

If this memoir was stolen by someone who wants to do harm to your husband's political career it's too late already, Mrs. Miller. They would have scanned it and it's already all over the Internet right now and there's nothing I can do for you about that.

I don't have a lot of options, Sisely Miller said. I have to try and find it.

Why don't you look for it yourself or have some of your husband's people do it? asked Rodeo.

It's not my husband's affair, she said.

Rodeo narrowed his eyes at her.

Judge Miller doesn't know what's in the memoir, does he? he asked.

The judge's wife held her tongue and also seemed to be holding her breath.

Judge Miller knows you're looking for something that was in your brother's apartment, said Rodeo. Something that might damage Judge Miller's political career if it got out. But Judge Miller doesn't know what it is, does he? Rodeo wrinkled his brow. He might even think it's just something incriminating about your brother, his brother-in-law, like a heroin stash or kiddie porn or illegally owned Indian artifacts. Rodeo looked at Mrs. Randy Miller. Does he even know it's a memoir about your family that you're desperately seeking?

No, she said. So you understand why I can't get my husband's "people" involved.

Rodeo nodded.

Sisely Miller studied Rodeo carefully. I was told you are "efficacious" as we discussed before. And generally trustworthy.

She stared at Rodeo but he did not move or say a word.

And since you clearly need the money, and as money is no object to me in this matter, I would suggest you take the job and get started.

Rodeo pulled a standard contract out of his back pocket and placed it on the table. Sisely Miller examined the contract cursorily as she tried to smooth the wrinkles out of it.

I . . . She started and stopped. Do we actually have to have a contract?

Not if you got cash money on you, Mrs. Miller, and like handshake deals.

When the woman spilled her Louis Vuitton handbag on the table it disgorged a box of Gitanes and a gold cigarette lighter, a tampon, keys, a pacifier, a cell phone, a condom, Tic Tacs and a thick roll of hundred-dollar bills bound with a rubber band. Sisely Miller raised her well-groomed eyebrows at her prospective hire.

Two thousand to get started, Rodeo said.

Sisely Miller peeled hundreds off the roll and then stacked it on the table and flattened it with a slightly shaky hand.

I just need your word that when you find the memoir you bring it directly to me. Not to Judge Miller or any of his minions. Certainly not to the Press in any version. And you don't copy it or read it. You don't show it to anyone. You don't use it to blackmail me, us, Judge Miller. You don't even speak about this, to anyone. Period.

If I turn up something that's to do with Law Enforcement, I'd have to let the police know about that, Mrs. Miller or I could lose my PI license.

I'm sure there's not anything like that in the manuscript, she said. This book, these ramblings are probably just my deluded brother's fantasies of what our relationship was and what our family was like. And his death by overdose is going to be enough to manage. For me. For our twins. For Judge Miller's campaign for Congress.

I need your contact information.

The woman slid a calling card onto the tabletop.

I'll start as soon as I can, Rodeo said.

You could start in his apartment immediately, Sisely Miller said.

If it's a crime scene I won't have access for a while.

It will not be a crime scene, the woman said. I will make Judge Miller see to that.

It's Eryn Hage's place. But I've known Eryn most of my life, said Rodeo. I could talk to her about getting into her place.

The rent is paid through the end of the year, said Sisely Miller. So the Hage woman has nothing to say about it.

Rodeo reached for the money on the table. When Sisely Miller removed her hand the hundred-dollar bills curled themselves back up into a loose but tidy roll that fit perfectly in Rodeo's pocket.

Rodeo went directly to Old Pueblo Credit Union and deposited most of Sisely Miller's cash into his almost-empty bank account, keeping only enough in his billfold to pay his motel bill and have some spending money for the next week and pay down his debt at Twin Arrows Trading Post pawn shop by ten percent. He then drove the several blocks back to his old neighborhood.

Eryn Hage had bought the long adobe

building she lived in during the 1970s, partly in order to preserve a Territorial-Era building when whole blocks of derelict but classic houses and stores, schools and small businesses were being razed to make room for the Tucson Convention Center complex, but mainly because back then the Barrio Historico or neighborhoods surrounding it were a place where a big house could be bought for a small price.

Eryn's domain was an old-fashioned quadruplex of four shotgun-style units built side by side by side by side. Each unit had a front room, a middle room and a back room that was a kitchen/pantry. Originally the residences had all housed whole families or extended families who shared bathroom facilities in the backyard but Eryn had remodeled over the years. She had combined two apartments to create her own residence and kept the apartment nearest her for her seven kids or one of her two dozen grandkids to use when they were between school semesters, prison stints, jobs or marriages and needed a free fall-back place in which to collect their thoughts for a few months before moving on to their next phase of annoying Eryn. Sometimes one of her four ex-husbands lived there as well.

The other apartment she rented at exorbitant rates to visiting professors or managers of the Major League Baseball teams who camped in Tucson for Spring Training or Gem and Mineral show vendors or buyers who needed a base of operations close to the interstate. Her place covered a double city lot with access in the back from Main Street as well as from the front on Convent. The swimming pool was directly behind the rental apartment and the whole compound was surrounded by a corrugated tin fence that was more decorative than protective.

Rodeo pressed the door buzzer and heard the cranky voice of Eryn Hage crackle through an intercom.

Lift up your hat and smile for the security camera.

Rodeo did as bid.

Johnny Jesus, the landlord said. You look old as dirt, Little Rodeo.

Rodeo tilted his hat back down as the gate buzzed open. He pushed through into a small courtyard and walked to the landlord's front door where half a dozen locks un-latched and a big hacienda door made of steel opened.

Howdy Eryn, he said.

The woman did not offer her hand but beckoned Rodeo to pass inside her adobe abode with the wave of a big plastic tumbler.

She locked the door behind them and walked unsteadily toward her expansive living room.

Have a seat, the woman said. But don't sit on the couch, I just had it cleaned.

Rodeo headed toward a straightbacked, carved Mexican chair near the dead fireplace. On the huge rough-timbered mantelpiece were museum quality Indian artifacts and even a whole human skull, many firearms, some vintage and some still in the packing grease. Random Christmas decorations were forgotten alongside dozens of antique photographs and tintypes. Rodeo stopped to study the photos. He was in a couple since he had been bosom buddies with one of Eryn's several sons, Tank. A particularly interesting photo on Eryn's mantel was the grainy photo taken of his own father, Buck Garnet, astride his paint pony facing Black Mountain. Eryn plopped down on the couch and took a noisy drink from her tumbler. She didn't offer Rodeo anything. Rodeo took off his hat as he sat.

How's your daddy? Eryn Hage asked this as her first question. Hear from Buck lately?

Best I can figure from various sources, Eryn, is that Buck's still alive and either back in West Texas living with an old army buddy and still cowboying on a rich man's hobby spread in Hudspeth County or up in the 'handle or near Sweetwater working on a windmill farm.

Cowboy Buck Garnet working on a windmill farm in Texas? Good Lord, what's the world coming to.

I couldn't say, Eryn.

The hostess sunk herself deeper into the leather couch and her reverie.

Buck's an old man now, she said. She assumed a wistful look. And I doubt he's much good at work anymore but he sure was a Hand back in the day.

Buck's only sixty-six, Eryn. How old are you these days?

I quit counting at seventy, she said. Her rheumy eyes searched the museum of memory on the mantel until they stalled on the photo of Buck on his pony near Black Mountain.

Those were the days, she said. I remember you riding sheep in the Indian Rodeos back then.

I remember falling off sheep and Buck yelling at me and Grace bawling, Rodeo said.

We all have our burdens, little cowboy, said the old lady. Don't whine about it.

Rodeo placed his hat crown-down on the floor.

Tank said he saw you lately? Eryn said.

Yes ma'am. Saw him yesterday at the bar.

You remember when we moved down here? Eryn asked. She gestured with her tumbler toward the photos and memorabilia as if with this wand she could recreate the past. When I divorced Tank Senior? You and Little Tank were so little. She took a drink and looked at the mantel trying to locate another specific image. I loaded up all those kids and all those animals and all our crap and moved lock stock and barrel off the ranch and into town and roasted a whole beeve for this goddamned neighborhood for my divorce celebration.

It was some party, Eryn.

The woman grimaced.

I was finding drunks around this place for days seemed like. Lost two of my kids for a week and one dog never did come back.

I remember, Eryn.

The woman focused on him. How you been, Little Rodeo Man?

Fine, said Rodeo. How you been, Eryn?

Better'n you from the looks of it. Looks like a couple of colostomy bags hanging up under your pretty eyes. Not hitting the bottle like your mother are you?

No ma'am.

All that High Indian on your mother's side

and the Low Irish on your daddy's . . . who knows what Buck was, she said. Mexican probably though he looked for all the world like an Italian opera singer.

Rodeo said nothing.

Just a wonder you turned out good's you did, Eryn Hage said.

I take that as a backhand compliment, said Rodeo. From you, Eryn.

The old woman squinted at him then laughed but then her face turned serious.

You know Tank, Jr. and Annabeth are divorcing?

Sorry to hear about that, Eryn.

The woman drank from her tumbler as if she were alone.

Where's your dogs at, Eryn? Rodeo asked.

Well, about two weeks ago MacArthur got loose in the garden and drank up all the saucers of beer I'd left out for the slugs to die in then he keeled over and never got righted again. So I guess you could say MacArthur drank himself to death just like a good Irishman. Skinny's in the hospital with some kinda liver troubles. But not from drinking. Still her liver is swelled up like a pate goose's. Some kind of intestinal worm or something.

Pookie?

Pookie died last year. When you were here

on Convent, living across the street with that awful Molina girl.

Rodeo stared at his hands.

I don't care how good-looking that girl is or how much money her daddy has, Sirena Rae Molina is just trash, Little Rodeo. And now her daddy's been murdered. The old woman looked cross-eyed at Rodeo. I guess you heard about Apache Ray?

I did, Eryn, Rodeo said. It was bad news to me.

The pair sat still and silent. Rodeo waited.

What can I do for you, Rodeo? Eryn finally asked. What's your business?

Let me in the far apartment, the one Tinley Burke was renting from you, Eryn.

Eryn nodded her chin into her chest. His sister talked to me about that, the landlord said. Told me you were working for her. Working for the Judge, actually is what she said. She likes to hold that Miller dagger on a thin string over your head, doesn't she. The question was rhetorical.

That all right if I snoop around then, Eryn?

You're a private investigator, aren't you? So that's what you do, I guess. Snoop around and annoy people. She shrugged. Since I know you, it's fine for you to go in there soon's the police are done. Hell, stay

312

till the end of the year, I don't care. Rent's paid and I could use some help around here now that that Burke fella's gone.

I appreciate it, Eryn, but I got my own place now.

Piece of shit house in the middle of no place, what I heard, she said.

Rodeo glared at the old woman but she did not notice. He started to work.

Mrs. Miller said you let her in the apartment this morning, Eryn? he asked.

That's right. I usually wouldn't intrude on my renters like that but the little woman insisted, so I let her in.

Where was Burke when y'all found him, Eryn?

On the bed in the middle room, Eryn said. Choked to death on his own vomit I imagined from the looks of him. I didn't get too close but I have seen like before.

Did Sisely Miller get close to him? Rodeo asked. Did she go in the house?

She didn't get close to him. In fact that woman went right past her brother in the middle room and looked all over the front room then she ran past me and out back and started dialing her phone, calling her husband from the sound of it. Didn't even call the police.

Who did call the police?

I did, Eryn said. I went back over to my place and called 911 and I just stayed right here in my own house after that. I don't know what she did over there and I do not care to know.

Did she say anything memorable to you?

Said something to me about something being stolen but I can't protect everything in the neighborhood, said Eryn Hage. There's a thief in almost every house around here, you know that. Most of them lawyers or doctors these days, so there's probably less retail theft now that the Mexicans are mostly gone but more wholesale theft now that the lawyers have moved in. The old woman took another drink. I tell my renters to get renter's insurance. That's what it's for.

How'd you feel about him, Eryn? Rodeo asked. Professor Burke?

The landlady shrugged. Not one way or the other, Eryn Hage said. He was real quiet at first when he moved in. Stayed inside his place mostly. Lately he'd been drunk a lot from what I see in the recycle bin but he never gave me any troubles that way and you know I lived around drunken cowboys and drunken Indians my whole life, so he wasn't any better or worse than any other man I ever had staying with me. He was houseproud and kept the place really nice what I could see of it. Kinda anal about keeping the place nice actually and even worked in the yard and kept up the pool. The woman wrinkled her brow. I thought at first that he was probably just queer. But then he had some woman over there time and again and I think they were going at it pretty good.

Do you know who this woman was, Eryn?

I didn't care, she said.

He took care of the property you said, Eryn? The in-law house and the storage sheds and such?

I don't get outside much anymore, so I gave him the run of the place, Eryn Hage said. He was cleaning up the outbuildings for me, he said. You know I got sixty years of accumulated junk around this place. His rent was paid upfront and he left me alone and I left him alone. You can't hear nothing much through this adobe, you know, so whatever he did or didn't do over there was none of my business as long as he didn't damage my apartment.

You have no ideas about who visited him?

I had some ideas but I don't know or care about any business that went on over there that's not my business.

Anything else you can think of, Eryn?

asked Rodeo. Anybody been lurking about or any yelling in the days or screaming in the nights?

General Patton could be shooting mules in my living room and I wouldn't stir after I take my pills in the evening.

What are you taking, Eryn?

Oxycodone, she said. You want some? Your broke back still acting up on you?

She reached to the side table and picked up an unlabeled prescription bottle and shook it at Rodeo as if it were a rattle.

No thanks, Eryn, Rodeo said. He waited a beat. You give any Mexican oxys to Tinley Burke?

The woman looked at the pharmacy bottle. Oh, you know. Now and again. She shrugged and put the orange plastic bottle on her side table. I saw him out back last week or so and he complained he couldn't sleep lately and his back was stiff from carrying something or other, so I gave him a little handful.

Anything else about him, Eryn?

Like what?

Like anything peculiar, said Rodeo.

What's peculiar, Little Rodeo?

You know what peculiar is, Eryn.

Eryn Hage frowned. They had a peculiar relationship, the landlord said.

Rodeo waited but nothing more was immediately forthcoming from Eryn Hage.

Who did?

Him and that sister of his, said the landlord.

Peculiar in which direction, Eryn?

Just peculiar, she said. They were twins, you know.

Rodeo raised an eyebrow.

This is not my business, Eryn Hage said.

What's not your business, Eryn?

Whatever was going on over there, she said. The landlord gestured with her tumbler in the general direction of the rental unit on the north end of the house.

I'm not following you, Eryn.

You seen those kids of hers? asked Eryn Hage.

No, said Rodeo. Why you asking that, Eryn?

If you're investigating that Miller bunch then maybe you should take a look at those kids of Sisely Miller's and give Randy a once-over while you're at it.

What do you mean, Eryn?

Even though I appreciate his politics, Randy's queer as a three-dollar bill and those kids of hers are a couple of inbred mongoloids if I ever saw them.

Sisely Miller's kids aren't by Judge Miller?

asked Rodeo. You think Judge Miller has a wife and kids as cover?

You just cover your own ass if you are working for the Millers is all I'm saying, Little Rodeo. The old woman stood and started toward the front of her house. Rodeo put on his hat and obediently followed the old woman into the foyer and walked through the door she opened.

Good to see you, Little Rodeo, Eryn Hage said. I'll call the TPD about getting you back into my place to snoop around.

I'm not sure you can speed that wheel, Eryn. Rodeo had turned to go, so Eryn spoke to his back.

You have no idea what an old lady is capable of doing in this world, Little Rodeo, the old woman said. You have no idea at all.

Rodeo knocked at the front door of the only other house on that block, a massive adobe nearly as large as Eryn Hage's. THE BLUE HOUSE was painted above a front door that was as thick as a bank vault's. This huge adobe house was painted periwinkle blue. With the August Arizona sun shining the residence resembled a child's crooked drawing of a generic house on a summer's day except for the two pink plastic flamingos in flagrante delicto near the crumbling front steps.

Multiple locks clicked as Rodeo tilted his hat back and stared up at another security camera. The heavy door opened and a thin middle-aged man in a kimono appeared. There was not a single hair on this man's head, face or body to be seen. His features were delicate and his skin glowed in a medium shade of brown but his eyes were hard and black.

Howdy, Egg.

The man looked at Rodeo from head to toe.

You look like shit, Hot Rod.

That seems to be the standard opinion of me today, Egberto.

The hairless man stepped aside and Rodeo entered the adobe house and Egberto locked the safe door shut behind them.

And why are you here after months and months of us not seeing you?

Just in the neighborhood.

Bullshit.

Seeking neighborhood gossip then, Rodeo said.

That makes more sense for you, Egberto said. The man moved toward the back of the house and Rodeo followed. I am not seeing people at the moment since I have a show to get ready for. But you are welcome to an audience with the Porn Lord if he's seeing people today.

How is Richard? Rodeo asked. I heard he was sick.

Going going . . . The host waved a hand backwards and forwards. Some days he is the same old Richard Dick as of old and some days he isn't.

Which is better?

Egberto stopped in the middle of a big room, turned to Rodeo and shrugged theatrically.

The bad news is that Richard Dick is not the man he used to be. Egberto's smile demonstrated perfect teeth. But that's the good news too.

How is it today with him?

Richard is not feeling well of late but he got some new hash to smoke today. So it might be a good day for you, Rod. He misses company.

I thought you were his company, Egg.

I am, said Egberto. But you know how active he always was. Flitting and fucking here and there and everywhere. Richard Dick was never a one-man woman or a one-woman man.

The man turned and continued through a maze of interconnected rooms that were decorated solely with huge tapestry pillows and prayer rugs on the polished and stained concrete floors and oversized modernist paintings on the original adobe walls. Complicated culinary smells filled the air from the nearby kitchen.

What's cooking, Egg?

Egberto did not stop but spoke over his shoulder. Hatch peppers stuffed with home-made elk sausage. But Richard doesn't eat much anymore and you won't be here long enough to have lunch will you?

I won't be here that long, Egberto.

Egberto led Rodeo past a huge Martín Montoya horse painting and a Jorge Frick color study and to a vintage pole ladder stuck through a hole in the middle of the ceiling of a small back room where he stopped and turned around. Rodeo stopped and looked up the ladder but Egberto stayed in place in front of it.

How's your whore fiend Sirena these days, Rod? Egberto asked.

Sirena and I don't keep in touch, said Rodeo.

Egberto gave Rodeo a skeptical look but shrugged.

Well, I know since Miss Prissy Tits is out of rehab she's been boning the Professor next door, Egberto said. Though I gather he kicked the OD bucket today or yesterday or recently.

I don't know who she was dating, Rodeo said. Not me.

Is that what you came to find out, Rod? Are you being a jealous man? Sirena can make a normal man a jealous man, you know. Even I was jealous of the bitch when Richard was fucking her.

The bald man put a hand on a rung of the ladder. I have endured as much from that bitch as have you.

We're both grown men, Egg. We make decisions.

The bald man looked at Rodeo carefully.

I did not make the decision for Sirena to move in here and try to take my place. I went along with the decision but I hardly think I made it.

You could have left, Rodeo said.

Egberto shook his head. That's the difference between you and me, Rod, the man said. I couldn't leave.

Send our dear friend up the ladder now, please, Egberto! A cracked and thin voice came through the crawl hole in the ceiling as a wisp of gray smoke.

Egberto left the room. Rodeo climbed the ladder of converging poles and emerged on a lush rooftop garden decorated Moroccan style and rimmed by terra-cotta pots overflowing with large and healthy paddle plants, sharkskin agaves, topsy turvies, cherry coke and silver sawblades and multiple varieties of aloe and variegated and plain palms. A confederacy of satellite dishes were arrayed protectively around the rim of the garden. Rodeo stuck his head through the crawl hole.

Howdy, Richard.

An emaciated and terminally tan Anglo man in cutoff khakis used a little glass pipe to gesture at a low, cushioned bench. A faded-to-pink tank top promoting The University of Arizona Women's Water Polo team was draped on the man as if on wire hangers. Thinned and dyed black hair hung in lank ringlets to his shoulders. Richard Dick smiled genially and then coughed convulsively, cleared his throat and relit his pipe. Once Rodeo was on the roof and seated the host bowed toward his guest from the oversized butterfly chair he seemed encased in.

I thought I recognized that gorgeous baritone. You want some very excellent hashish, Rod? I made it myself.

You know I don't smoke it, Richard.

Richard Dick chuckled in his throat. It

shocks me sometimes, Rod, that you still like me knowing how much you despise me.

I don't despise you, Richard. I just don't like the pretend "porn star name" you and Egberto gave me.

True, it does not follow the rules of pet's name plus mother's maiden name, but your pet has no name and "Rod Grace" has a nasty but angelic ring to it. The porn king sniffed his stained fingertips. And you should have worked for me when I was doing fuck films, Rod. You had the right résumé, so to speak.

I don't think so, Richard.

And yet Sirena Rae, the love of your life, worked for me for many years.

Sirena Rae was never the love of my life, Rodeo said. She was a girlfriend. And you had lots of women working for you, on the pole and in front of the camera. I have never been sure why she took root so much with you.

Really? Did you never fuck the woman? The porn king laughed hoarsely and stared at Rodeo's exposed and abraded wrists. She had a dance scholarship to the University of Arizona. Did you know that?

Her daddy says she had an academic scholarship for geniuses to Arizona State.

At which university a pole dancer who can

324

read probably would be a genius. Richard Dick laughed until he coughed. Sirena does draw that allegiance from some of us deluded fools. But Egberto is correct in this. She does not deserve our beloved attentions. Brilliant and fuckable as she is, she's a shooting star.

She's just a woman, said Rodeo. The world is half full of them as you know better than me since you use women for your living.

Richard Dick coughed against the smoke escaping from him. Actually I use men's desires for women to make my living, he said. But it remains that Sirena was one of my best "Dick's Girls." Sirena had a national following, as you know. She traveled the strip club circuit much as you used to travel the rodeo circuit.

I don't see me riding saddle broncs for a living and Sirena riding poles for a living as equivalent, Richard, Rodeo said.

Probably because a good stripper or porn star always makes more money than a good rodeo cowboy. Though their careers probably end as sadly. As did yours.

Rodeo unfolded himself from the settee and moved to the terrace wall that faced the property line of Eryn Hage. He peered toward Eryn's house but little could be seen through the thickness of mesquite tree branches from the Hage side but a glimmer of the swimming pool. Rodeo kept his back to his host.

Sirena's father was just murdered, Rodeo said.

She probably killed Apache Ray herself, Richard Dick said. She certainly threatened to often enough when she lived with us.

I'm sure Sirena's a suspect but I imagine the sheriff's death was more likely a drug hit or maybe some unofficial payback for something the sheriff did or didn't do in his official capacities, said Rodeo.

You don't suspect Sirena?

Ray ran a pretty clean county and that can make a sheriff a lot of real enemies.

You didn't answer my question, Rod.

The ones you love are usually the ones that kill you in the end, Richard. I do believe that.

And you know Ray was loaded. And you know as well as I do that Sirena hates, hated her father and loves money, said Richard Dick. And she's too lazy to ever do any real work.

I don't know much about the Molina finances, Rodeo said. I do know that Sirena Rae and her father had a complex relationship. And she is the laziest woman I ever met.

Sirena would hire somebody to brush her pretty teeth for her if she could afford to. Richard Dick smiled at his joke but then frowned at something else. During one of her confessional phases when she was living with us, Sirena told me Ray molested her when she was a kid. Do you believe that, Rod?

She did become a stripper, Rodeo said. But I'm not in any position to judge the relationship Ray and Sirena had, Richard. Ray always seemed pretty solid to me. Rodeo looked over his shoulder at his host then looked back into the trees.

Sirena told me once that Apache Ray wanted you to be his son-in-law, Rod. And that's why she hooked up with you in the first place, to please her father. So maybe your "relationship" with her was part of her bad daddy complex?

Water under the bridge, Rodeo said. He turned toward his host. You spend a lot of time on this rooftop, Richard. You ever see anybody over there at Eryn's rental place, in the northside apartment?

Ah, now we come to the real reason for your visit, said Richard Dick. He sounded disappointed. Information, the blood of your industry. You come to drink my blood.

Rodeo turned to look at his host and raised an eyebrow.

You know I seldom stir from my throne once I am ensconced, so there's little I can tell you even if I cared to, Rod.

But you pay attention, Rodeo said.

Truly, I still do, Richard Dick said. I'm not sure why I persist in doing so, but I do.

So?

So at times I might have smelled a slight scent of White Shoulders, perhaps? Orange blossoms? And of cigarettes, foreign and domestic. And heard distant strains of Rachmaninoff, Brahms, Bach. And sounds of pleasure and of pain.

Rodeo steadied himself against the balustrade of the rooftop terrace.

When, Richard?

You know that in my opiate haze time and space and memory are often irrelevant, Rod. And if you or anyone else, official or otherwise, would expect me to testify to any of this recollection of mine in any court of law in America . . . The man waved a liver-speckled hand in the air to dismiss his testimony.

I'm not looking for a court appearance, Richard. Rodeo turned back to look at Tinley Burke's apartment. But you think it was

Sirena over there?

My sense of smell is still excellent. The man stared at the sky for a while and then sniffed his fingertips as if he had lost a memory in them and could recall it with enough focus. Richard Dick's Sense of Smell . . . The man sniffed his fingertips again as a strange habit. I'm still good on this most primary sense. He nodded to himself. So I'm sure it was Sirena over there at least on several occasions during the last few weeks or months.

When?

I confuse my days, Rod. And even the hours of my days. I am an unreliable witness in extremis.

How long was she going over there, Richard? Rodeo turned back to look into the local treetops. How long was Sirena over at the Professor's?

Only for several weeks, said the man. She always parked in the back. She was driving something large and rumbly.

You think Burke had other women while he was in residence at Eryn's?

By scent I would say that there was at least one other woman who visited regularly, said Richard. Once or twice a month from the time he moved in. Always at night.

What was the other woman's scent, Richard?

Jil Sander of some sort, I would say. And she smoked cigarettes, but not Sirena's Marlboros.

Was this woman coming to see Tinley Burke when Sirena was over there too?

Not at the same hours, but during the same weeks, yes.

Rodeo turned to his host and leaned his hip on the low wall, crossed his arms on his chest.

Did you know Burke's second woman?

Richard Dick shook his head. But both the unknown woman and Sirena parked in the back where they couldn't be seen coming or going.

You think it was his sister that was the Professor's other visitor?

You have such a prurient mind, Rod. I like that. When Richard Dick shook his head his long ringlets moved like fringe. I don't know your Professor's sister. I did not even know Tinley Burke except to recognize his voice.

Who was he talking to?

Eryn, usually about the garden or grounds. Occasionally himself. Sometimes I could hear him sobbing on his back porch when he was obviously in his cups or muttering as he rummaged through Eryn's old mother-in-law shack in her backyard. The man on his rooftop sat contemplatively for a minute. But it may have been his sister. I do like that thought, I must admit.

His sister, Sisely is her name, is married, Rodeo said. To Randy Miller, the former judge.

Well . . . there's married and there's married. Richard Dick relit his pipe once again and waved a hand through thick smoke. Though currently a prominent member of the Tea Party I believe the good Judge Randy Miller used to be a rather circumspect member of the Tea Bag Party. I would consider that ironic but that it's not. Richard Dick squinted toward the open trapdoor in the ceiling of his house. You could ask Egberto about Randy Miller, he said. I believe Egg might have . . . serviced Judge Junior back when Egg was still in the escort industry. Richard Dick paused. Though I would prefer that henceforward you not drag my consort and myself into any cesspool you might be currently trolling through. The days the Egg and the Dick have together are regrettably limited and we would prefer to spend these final days alone. Or entertaining real friends.

Thanks for the information, Richard, said Rodeo. I appreciate it.

We would truly welcome a real social call from you, Rod. Egg has become quite the chef lately. I believe his chicken enchiladas would compete favorably with Mi Nidito's. Richard smiled slightly then grimaced. But if you mean to ever return for a real social call you should probably phone to make an appointment. Richard Dick inclined his head toward the ladder in the hole in the ceiling of his house, clearly dismissing his guest. Take care descending, my Hot Rod. It's a desert down there.

The sun was tilting west fast as Rodeo's old Ford 150 rattled over the ribs of the gutted dirt road named Elm Street. Even though Rodeo had only been gone a couple of days, his place felt more deserted without his dog in tow. He parked and went to the storage shed where he started his generator. Then he unloaded his gear into the casita, turned on his AC unit and the swamp cooler in the house and went back outside and crawled up the ladder onto his roof with binoculars and his rabbit rifle, a notch-scoped Savage rimfire .22.

This was the best time of the day to see bobcat and coyote and peccaries around his place and even an occasional coati-mundi but Rodeo saw nothing this evening not even the hares and jackrabbits. A flash high on the nearby hillside caught his eye and he aimed the binoculars up into the Theatine Mountain range. He scanned the long trail up the side of the hill toward La Entrada but could identify nothing.

He slid down the aluminum ladder and reentered the house which had cooled by now to tolerable temperature. He took a short tepid shower, put clean sheets on his single-sized bed and locked his place down. He cleaned and reloaded his 9mm Glock and put it under his bed then spun the cylinder on the S&W .38 and put his father's revolver atop his mother's Bible before he crawled naked under the thin sheet and went to sleep.

Rodeo slept soundly until false dawn when he sat up in his narrow bed and read some passages from the Book of Luke. He left and made his bed, sponged his head and torso over the kitchen sink and then dressed in loose Wranglers and a long-sleeved khaki shirt. He swept his floors and dumped the dust outside then cooked a frittata with brown eggs and Spam and with a Hatch green chile pod cut over it as salsa. He made a fresh pot of cowboy coffee and ate and drank quickly.

Rodeo put two cans of ranch beans, a small sack of cracked Green Valley pecans, three snack-sized bags of Fritos and a plastic milk jug full of water in a thick plastic trash bag and stuffed the trash bag into the bottom of his father's old GI rucksack. He set the pack on his shoulders and snugged the straps then checked the speed-load in his holstered snake gun, a Colt .357 Trooper. He clipped his father's old Schrade Safety Push-button knife to his belt, slung his binoculars and canteen around his neck. He tried to call Summer Skye on his cell phone but couldn't get any reception so he set a stained straw Stetson on his head and headed uphill toward La Entrada.

Since he was not slowed by his decrepit dog, Rodeo marched steadily up the small mountain and didn't stop until he was within a hundred yards of the cave. There he announced his presence loudly in both English and Spanish and then waited for five minutes so that any Undocumented Aliens or others hiding or resting in La Entrada would have time to collect their gear and move off.

In all the time he had been supplying the cave, Rodeo had never seen a person in La Entrada though he had seen plenty of proof of human existence, including discarded clothing and sleeping bags, trash bags, blown-out boots, cigarette butts and even human excrement dumped on the floor of the shallow cave and piss stains on the walls.

So Rodeo was shocked to see the man with one hip resting on the metal footlocker and both feet firmly planted in the ground dirt of the cave, with the black graphite stock of a scoped rifle pressed to his shoulder and the side of his face and with the barrel of that sniper's gun aimed directly at Rodeo's chest.

In this beautiful weapon of destruction are handmade soft-point thirty-caliber two-hundred-gram bullets, said Ronald Rocha. Each bullet with a ballistic coefficiency of point four four eight.

Rodeo was so surprised he did not even reach for his side-arm.

You probably do not know what that means.

I don't know ordnance too good, Rodeo said.

It means, friend, that when I squeeze this hair trigger with sufficient force your heart will be exploded beyond your spine and your spine will be dust and you will not even know you are dying you will be so dead already.

I believe you, Ronald.

Then extract that revolver from your rightside holster with two fingers of your left hand and toss the gun off the cliff with your left hand, Ronald said.

This is a vintage .357 Trooper with a custom grip, Ronald. This gun would cost fifteen hundred dollars at auction. Couldn't we just unload it?

This situation you're in right now is not about negotiation *for* you, friend, said the marksman. But it is rather about simple obedience *from* you.

Rodeo unholstered and then tossed his revolver. The big gun clattered down steep stones with a loud noise.

Now the knife.

This knife was my daddy's and I cannot replace it.

I have got sentimental attachments to things I cannot replace too, friend, said Ronald Rocha. Some days I think these attachments are too numerous to name and remember and might overwhelm me until I am crushed by the weight of them. Yet I have seen these mementos, these physical artifacts of emotional connections, including physical bodies, tossed and gone to dust in an instant. And lost. Forever. But not forgotten.

So you know what I'm talking about then, Ronald, said Rodeo. You know the value that some things have.

The man with the rifle shrugged. We honor things by our memory of them as we honor people lost to us through revenge. That is the law of the desert.

Rodeo did not speak.

I'm saying lose the little knife or die for it, simple as that, Ronald said. This is not a negotiation. I don't have to negotiate with you about this simple decision which comes down to keeping the thing or keeping your life. And I am not saying that one choice is better than the other, friend. You have free will to choose. I am happy for you to die for the little knife.

Rodeo pitched the pocket knife off the cliff and that drop scarcely made a sound.

Now take off your pack and those binoculars real slow and toss them over the side too.

With some effort Rodeo managed to sling the heavy pack and his expensive binoculars and all the else he had packed for his normal day over the edge.

Now turn around and roll up both your pants legs to the knees.

Rodeo did.

Now pull up your shirttails all the way up

to your neck.

Rodeo pulled his shirttails out of his Wranglers and up.

Now turn back around and face me and drop your pants and u-trous to your boot tops.

Rodeo did so. Ronald Rocha smiled slightly.

You just got to admire a man sometimes, said Ronald Rocha. He stared at Rodeo for a long moment.

Whatever you say, Ronald, said Rodeo.

Then have a seat is what I say now, Ronald said. On the ground. And with bare ass on empty hands and with back against hard rock. And do everything real slow because I am a little twitchy right now, friend. And I read you as a hero type, so do not make me kill you right now because I love to kill heroes. You're not going to be a hero today, are you, friend?

I'm never a hero, Ronald, Rodeo said.

No, you are not a hero, friend. I was wrong to say that. Because I don't think Indians are heroes, do you? That's something I never saw on TV.

Whatever you say, Ronald.

I served my country, but I don't think I was a hero.

I am not any sort of hero either, Ronald,

so don't kill me about that.

Just follow directions and sit on your hands then, friend.

Rodeo sat down awkwardly on his bare ass with his bare hands.

I like the way you can follow directions, said Ronald.

It's a habit of mine, said Rodeo. My daddy hit me when I disobeyed him, Ronald. So I never did unless I had to.

Ronald stared at Rodeo and then moved forward to press the muzzle of his rifle gently up one of Rodeo's nostrils.

I do not believe that about you, friend. I bet you fought your father from the get-go. And I bet you also had some harsh criticisms of that man, your father, criticisms you never expressed out loud to him. Is this the case?

Rodeo nodded his head against the pressure of the rifle barrel up his nose.

And I think you got something to say about your father right now, do you not, friend? What do you think about your father, friend?

Ronald lowered the point of the gun and pressed it gently into Rodeo's breastbone.

My daddy was, probably still is, an asshole, Rodeo said.

What else, my friend?

He's sane, said Rodeo. Shitty but sane.

Ronald Rocha glared at Rodeo.

So if your father is sane, what does that make me, friend?

The rifle butt slammed into Rodeo's forehead so quickly he did not even have time to think about raising his arms in self defense.

Rodeo awoke upright, still leaning with his back against the cave wall. Rodeo's hands were bound behind his back with duct tape. Ronald Rocha was sitting very near him in an Indian squat the barrel of his black sniper rifle pressed into Rodeo's chest exactly above his heart. With his free hand Ronald poured Fritos into his mouth from a small foil snack bag.

Rodeo looked at the rifle then at Ronald. The man seemed calm but Rodeo did not move anything but his eyes. The rifle did not waver any more than the man holding it.

I love Fritos, Ronald said. He crushed and tossed away the Fritos bag that wafted away on an updraft. Fritos are like AMexica, a blending of the worst of two cultures that somehow works and tastes right but creates dangerous side effects. What do you say about that, friend?

Fritos don't sit well with me, Rodeo said.

Ronald smiled slightly.

You persist in your nature? Is that how it is with you, friend?

No, Rodeo said. I don't know how it is with me, Ronald. That's how it is with me.

Your parents must be very proud of you, of your moral ambivalence and lack of heroic expertise, friend.

My mother is dead and my daddy fucked half the women in southern Arizona then abandoned us and went back to Texas, said Rodeo. I'm not too concerned about the opinion of my parents anymore, Ronald.

I killed my parents before they could kill me and I doubt anyone will ever find their bones because I ground them up and ate them. And that's how that is with me.

Rodeo nodded.

But we are not getting friendly with each other now, friend. I am not here to be your friend, friend. You are not going to talk me into or out of anything I want to do with your use of pathos and ethos and logos. And if you persist in trying to be some kind of smart-ass detective I can and will make you suffer so much that you will fuck your own dead mother. You will unearth her and fuck her back to death and be glad to do that just to avoid me. Do you understand what I am saying, friend? I am the reason for this. I am the reason for all of this. You are not the reason. You got that?

Yes, Ronald. I got it.

I just want your attention, friend? Do I have that?

Yes, you got my attention, Ronald. Undivided.

Ronald Rocha licked the salt off his chapped lips.

Good because I am not going to remind you on how stupid you are anymore, friend. Because I studied up on you, so I know you are smart enough so you can find and kill a man nobody else could find to kill like Charles Constance. And you killed him with your hands, which is harder than some people might think.

I appreciate the compliment, Ronald. Coming from you.

Okay then. Let's not play dumb with each other anymore.

I won't, Ronald. I'm not playing dumb anymore.

So you got some news for me about my Sammy then, friend?

Not yet, said Rodeo.

Now there you go, friend. You said you weren't going to play dumb and then at the first opportunity that is exactly what you do. Ronald scanned the cave. And this would be a bad way for you to go out, friend. Trussed up in your own hideaway place. Dying of thirst. And you think some of your Mexicans coming along here will save you but they would just take the food and water you have freighted up this mountain for them and then leave you here to die of thirst which will be a profound irony if not an important one. Ronald looked at Rodeo. You know your Mexicans would do that to you, don't you?

They are not my Mexicans, Rodeo said. But they probably would. Immigrants don't like trouble.

So you are not doing good deeds, stocking this earthly storehouse so that your storehouse in your Father's Heaven will be stocked?

Bringing food and water up here is just a hobby that occupies some of my time because I am underemployed, Ronald, said Rodeo. Like most good deeds most people do it's just a hobby.

Ronald cracked a smile. He tilted his head around the cave at the supplies stored behind him then looked at Rodeo. I see now that you do think things out, friend. You have reasons for your actions and understand them and do not overestimate the worth of them. You are a selfish man though some would call you selfless and you know this. Ronald nodded profoundly. I like that about you, friend. You know how it is with yourself and so you make a world where what you think makes sense makes sense, even when you are wrong about what you think makes sense. And you know that.

It might be like that with me, Ronald.

And so I imagine since you know yourself so good and you think you and me are so similar then you see how it is with me right now, said Ronald. And so now you got something to tell me, right? About my Sammy's bad death?

Like I said, Ronald. Not yet.

So you will not tell me what I really need to know so I can get my revenge? Ronald asked.

I got no trouble telling you what you need to know whenever I really know it, Ronald, said Rodeo. But I can't tell you who killed Samuel Rocha until I'm sure who is most responsible for his death. Because I know you are going to kill that person in cold blood. I know that's what you really want, Ronald. Revenge, plain and simple and hard for the person who suffers it from you. You want to torture the person who killed your Sammy and then look them in the eye as you kill them in cold blood. So you see how I have to be right about it, don't you, Ronald? You see how I have to be sure about it or I will be responsible for the torture and murder of an Innocent and I don't want that sort of blood on my hands, not Innocents' blood.

As you say, friend, there will be much suffering first. Ronald moved to Rodeo and lifted Rodeo's chin with the thumb of his free hand and locked eyes with him. Is this suffering what you have a problem with, friend? Knowing what I know about you, I do not see how it could be since you once beat a man to death with your bare hands. That could not have been pleasant for him.

Rodeo shook his head to loose his captor's thumb.

So what is the problem, friend? Why won't you tell me who killed my Sammy?

What if the person really most responsible for Samuel's death is not someone you'd expect, Ronald? asked Rodeo. What if it's not some gangbanger or some punk you can kill easy? Or another soldier? Or a cop? What if it is someone you would not have suspected? Someone you cannot anticipate and relish torturing and killing?

If it is the Pope and the Virgin of Guadalupe and Baby Jesus or even myself that killed my Sammy, friend, then I will kill all of them.

Ronald turned his eyes away for a moment and then returned them misty to Rodeo's dry eyes.

I will do what I have to do to whoever I have to do it to including myself, said the man. Because this is my code. This is the code that I have known all my life and created with my life. This is the code of my desert. The code of all deserts. That all are the same in my eyes, friend. And there is perfect equality only when each eye that is lost is replaced by another that is lost.

I understand an eye for an eye, Ronald.

It makes no matter whether you do or whether you don't, friend. Your understanding of the situation is not relevant because you are not Me. And that is what makes all the difference between the world of the Master and the world of the slaves, said Ronald. That is what separates man from superman. Ronald leaned his head toward Rodeo. That I do as I please is as I please, friend.

I hadn't worked out all this philosophy as good as you have, Ronald, Rodeo said. So life might be a little more complicated for me than it is for you. But just on a practical level I need a few days to finish my investigation, so give me a few days to clear up Samuel's death. Give me some time to figure out this particular situation in the correct and accurate way.

What is correct and accurate on one day is correct and accurate a thousand years before now and a thousand years from now, friend, said Ronald Rocha. He rolled his eyes toward the roof of the shallow cave and then rolled them back down. But gods can be generous, so I will give you three days. And then I will kill somebody. Somebody you still love. Or somebody related to you maybe in the White Mountains. Or I will establish myself on your mountain here and just kill somebody on your property. Or kill your dog.

All right, Ronald. I got you.

And if you test my patience beyond that then I will keep on killing the Innocents around you until you will wish yourself dead and then eventually I will kill you too, friend. Slowly. Because I will know that you are undependable and simply not competent, so there will not be any continuing need for you in my life or in this world which amounts to the same thing. But you will not know the day or the hour that I come as death to you. So you will be plagued all your life, what is left of it, by that thought that nags you — where is he? when will he come? You understand that, friend? If you cannot help me, I will destroy the world you live in and then I will kill you slowly.

I got it, Ronald. I got it.

The man stared at Rodeo then looked away. When you find out who was responsible for my Sammy's death leave the name and contact information in this storage box right up here, right in this Indian cave of ours, said Ronald. Because we are Indians this will be our sacred space.

When I'm sure, when I am dead certain who killed your Sammy then I will leave you the name of that killer, Ronald. I promise. But I got to figure it out first.

I wish I could do it myself, said Ronald. But even the gods have limitations. And so there are things I know how to do, said Ronald. I can be invisible, for instance. Once apprehended, I can make people confess to crimes and even to desires. I can kill a human or a beast from a mile or more distance. These are things I know how to do that the Colonel taught me to do in the Gulf War and these are my warrior's powers that all the other gods of war envy. But if you make people speak in tongues and have not the ear to hear what they say, then what they have to say is useless.

Did you get Billy to talk to you before you killed him?

Ronald Rocha squinted.

The Billys of this world are expendable too, friend. They are not protected by their ignorance.

He saw you and Samuel on A-Mountain shooting your rifle.

You can discover things. This is clear, friend.

So you'll let me do the discovering and then you'll do the judgment and execution?

To each worker his work, said Ronald. That will work for me, friend, said Ronald. And you do not care about any of this anyway, do you? In your heart, you do not mind if detection is your business and revenge mine.

No, Ronald, Rodeo said. I don't really care.

The captor stared at his captive for a long time.

I believe that might be true of you, friend, said Ronald. I believe it might.

Rodeo closed his eyes for a moment then opened them again. The gun was no longer trained on him. Ronald Rocha had turned away from him and was looking at the desert.

Did it feel good, friend? To kill a man with your bare hands?

It was just something I did, Ronald.

Something you had to do.

No, just something I did.

Do you have regrets about that? asked Ronald. That revenge?

No, Rodeo said. I beat to death a serial killer and I have no regrets about that, Ronald. Rodeo paused. But my lack of remorse does not mean that I did the right thing.

Ronald moved and stood on the edge of the cliff with the big rifle propped on his thin hip and stared out toward Mexico which was but one hard day's walk away for a strong man.

You know anything about this place? Ronald kept his back to Rodeo.

Back in the day it was a lookout vantage. What used to be some Western Apache tribe, maybe the Chiricahua would put a couple of braves up here to watch out for raiding parties coming up from the south and send up smoke signals if they saw somebody coming to attack their tribe.

You think they loved each other up here, those Indian braves?

May be, Ronald, said Rodeo. It's lonely up here and no witnesses to speak of.

Ronald Rocha continued to look out over the desert. Yes, he said. It is lonely up here. He held his face up to the sun and spread his arms wide at the blueblister sky. If Rodeo could have moved himself enough he could have pushed the man right off the cliff but he could not move himself enough.

But it's still good to feel the sun warming your skin, isn't it, friend? asked Ronald Rocha.

Some days that's good enough, Ronald, said Rodeo.

Ronald Rocha lowered his arms and his rifle and turned to face his captive.

I am leaving now and leaving you alive, friend, he said. For the moment.

I appreciate that, Ronald.

But you know now that I am always with you, friend. You are always going to know this about me. Forever. Because that is the worst torture to any man. That I am in his mind forever.

Yes, Ronald. I'm always going to know this about you.

All right then. You perform your professional task now, friend. And when you have made the discovery I desire then you return here and put a piece of paper in this provision box of yours and on that piece of paper is going to be the name of the person responsible for the death of my Sammy. And I will give you three days to do this. To present me with the accurate and correct object of my revenge. Or seventy-two hours from now I start killing Innocents.

Ronald stuck a hand in a pocket of his desert camo pants, extracted a cheap pocketknife and tossed it onto the dirt near Rodeo's feet. He went back to the metal provisions box and lifted it open with the toe of his GI desert boot and looked over the provisions there and let the lid of the trunk fall back down.

You got anymore Fritos, friend? he asked.

In the pack, Rodeo said. The one you made me throw off the cliff, Ronald.

I'll go get them then, Ronald said.

Rodeo drove to Twin Arrows but there were too many cars and motorcycles in the parking lot and one that looked like an unmarked police car, so he kept driving until he reached the Boulder Turn-Out where he parked. He was dressed in clean Wranglers and a fresh starched shirt but his hands were still shaking visibly. His wrists oozed blood into the cuffs of his shirt and his face was flushed and swelling. He held a bag of melting frozen okra to the bridge of his nose and had his fourth beer wedged between his legs. He stared through the cracked and dirty windshield at a triangular cloud moving like a flatiron pressing the sheet of the sky.

He dialed 2ARRWS.

I'm taking care of business for a change and making some money, said Luis. So be in a hurry, brother. What's going on? Where you at? People been asking around about you.

I'm around about. And I got a question for you, Luis.

That's a change of pace.

How would you flush out somebody you think did a drive-by?

What you got going on?

While I'm doing the job for the old lady Katherine Rocha you set me up with, I met this homeless guy who saw a certain car in the area of Starr Pass Road bridge where Samuel Rocha probably got shot in a drive-by. I followed a lead and found the car in Bisbee and it's connected up to a Res cop named Carlos Monjano who might be the biological father of Samuel's little sister, a child named Farrah.

I think I know this guy some, Luis said. Caps Monjano, he goes to sweat lodge sometimes. Macho guy? Big? Frown face?

That's him. And he's the real father of the

little girl that got killed in the hit-and-run back in the spring around Cinco de Mayo time.

So you were thinking it was Ronald that killed Samuel Rocha, but that's not what you're thinking now?

No. Ronald did not do it.

What convinced you of that?

A long story I don't have time to tell.

That's a lot of work for a day's pay, brother.

Sometimes it's like that in my business, Rodeo said. Sometimes it goes the other way.

So what are you thinking now, brother?

I am thinking that from one perspective it might look like Samuel killed his own little sister, Farrah, in the hit-and-run back in early May, Rodeo said.

Why you think so?

Because he lived just a couple of blocks from the accident site. The car he usually drove had a front end repair and full body paint job up in Bisbee the day or so after little Farrah was killed. And right after little Farrah gets killed her big brother starts attending sweat lodge to purge his spirit.

Did the kid really hit-and-run his own little sister?

A witness I found says no. A girlfriend of

his named Rose, a waitress at the Kettle on Starr Pass Road, says Samuel couldn't have done it because he was with her at the time of Farrah's death.

What are you saying then, brother?

I'm saying that if a person only knew these three things about Samuel and this situation — Samuel's home location nearby Farrah's house, the front end damage to his car that gets repairs started the very day after Farrah is killed and that Samuel is acting guilty in sweat lodge — and you didn't find this witness, the waitress from the Kettle, then it would be logical to conclude that Samuel is guilty of the hit-and-run that killed his little sister Farrah Katherine Rocha. And if you are looking to revenge her death then Samuel would be your target.

So you think this tribal cop, Caps Monjano, he would want to revenge the little girl's death?

Yes. I think the biological father of Farrah, Carlos Monjano, found out that the big brother of his daughter Farrah, Samuel Rocha, had brought an old Buick LeSabre into a body shop in Bisbee to have the front end repaired and get a total cover paint job. Then I think this cop Monjano found out that Samuel had started going to sweat lodge for healing right after his little sister was killed. You said Caps Monjano goes to sweat sometimes, so he would know who's showing up and praying and what they are praying about. Monjano just didn't find Rose — like I did — to alibi Samuel. So when he did the math on this problem he didn't have all the figures. Without Rose, Samuel looks good for the hit-and-run, so Caps Monjano borrows his gangster cousin's low-rider from Bisbee, drives to Tucson and cruises where he knows Samuel usually is, drives by, pops him and the kid falls off the bridge.

Or he gets a gangster friend to do it for him.

I think Caps would do it himself, Rodeo said. He pushed a pregnant girlfriend of his down the stairs at Sun Devil stadium, so I don't think he'd have much trouble stalking a kid and taking a pot shot at him in a drive-by on a near-empty road.

Call Hot Tips about Monjano then and sic Police on him. See if the asshole runs for it. Luis said this without hesitation. You got coverage that way and if it rolls the right way you might get some reward money to use to pay me back some of the money you owe me and then I can be your friend again. And this way won't involve no gun-n-ammo show which you know I oppose on principle after my experiences in Vietnam that cost me forty percent of my fingers and half of my peace of mind.

You're confirming what I think, said Rodeo.

That's what friends are for, brother, said Luis.

Rodeo drove down Agua Seco Road and onto the interstate and headed toward Tucson until he parked at a 69 Truckers' Stop. Rodeo left his old pickup between two other beat-up trucks, traded his straw Stetson for a greasy gimme cap with a bill so rolled it was almost a tube and put on a pair of wraparound sunglasses to hide his bruises. He entered the store and walked directly to the restroom where he locked himself in a stall for ten minutes and took a huge shit. He then exited the men's room and sidled up to the banks of pay phones near the truckers' pay showers, wiped some coins clean on his shirttail, fed them by their edges into the pay phone and dialed the Tohono O'odham Police Department.

I need to leave an important message for Officer Carlos "Caps" Monjano. Rodeo said this in a low voice before the dispatcher could begin her introductory spiel.

Speak up, please. May I have your name?

Just make sure this is being recorded . . . Rodeo waited a count of three and then said in a rush . . . Tell Carlos Monjano that there was a witness on the Santa Cruz River bridge who saw him shoot Samuel Rocha from a green Impala with copper Arizona historical vehicle plates, HTX8. And tell him that Ronald Rocha, the uncle of the deceased is going to kill him, kill Carlos "Caps" Monjano as soon as possible to revenge Samuel's death. This information will also be going to all statewide and federal law enforcement agencies, so make sure Monjano understands that.

Rodeo hung up and wiped his prints from the phone with his shirttail as casually as he could. He returned to his truck and drove another five miles to another large truck stop and performed the same routine but this time calling the Anonymous Tips Hotline for Southern Arizona.

He listened to an electronic voice and then pressed the buttons on the phone that represented the option with the most anonymity and that offered payment for information leading to the arrest and conviction of any at-large felon. He memorized the code provided him by the system and then spoke clearly into a receiver that would automatically scramble his voice so it could not ever be identified or used as evidence in any court of law.

A Tohono O'odham Police Officer named Carlos Monjano shot Samuel Rocha on the Santa Cruz River bridge, Rodeo said. Monjano was driving a green Chevrolet Impala and that car is parked at C-23 Auto Body and Paint Shop in Bisbee. The license plate is a historical vehicle copper and the number is HTX8. Officer Monjano may or may not have acted alone. Monjano shot Samuel Rocha because he thought Samuel Rocha had killed his cousin's child, a little girl named Farrah Katherine Rocha in a hit-and-run on May 3 of this year. But that child, Farrah Katherine Rocha is actually the biological child of Carlos Monjano. DNA tests will prove this. The DNA of Carlos Monjano will be on file with the Tohono O'odham Police Department.

Rodeo hung up and wiped the phone, returned to his truck and dialed Summer Skye's cell phone number on his own cell phone.

My dog still alive?

He's eating bacon and drinking Jameson as we speak or I'd let you talk to him, Summer said.

After all these years together, me and that

dog have got nothing to talk about anymore, Doc.

Rodeo parked in front of the apartment that Tinley Burke had rented from Eryn Hage. The yellow crime scene tape was gone but someone had spray-painted DOA on the door. Rodeo called the TPD, identified himself and asked to speak with Detective Haynes.

What can I do for you, Mr. Garnet?

You can tell me where you're at on the Tinley Burke case, Rodeo said.

Because?

Because I'm working for Tinley Burke's sister, Sisely Burke Miller, whose husband is Judge Randy Miller, who might be a Congressman soon or governor one day and who has had dinner with all the important people in this great state of Arizona including your chief, said Rodeo. And I doubt there's anything to keep under wraps anyway that would kill you to tell me.

There was a short silence on the Tucson Police Department end of the line. Let me call you back, Garnet.

You got my number?

I got everybody's number now, said Detective Haynes.

Rodeo hung up and then just sat in his

truck. Weaving down the avenue away from the Dota house and heading in the direction of Midtown Liquors was Tomas on his lawn tractor. Otherwise Convent street was quiet as a nun.

Rodeo massaged his temples until the cell phone buzzed in his shirt pocket.

Preliminary autopsy reports on Burke indicate a drug overdose exacerbated by over-consumption of alcohol was responsible for his death, said Officer Haynes. You need anything else?

You know what killed him specifically?

Probably a bad mixocology as I had earlier suggested, the cop said. ME says maybe a big dose of oxycodone tipped the scale since oxy seemed to be the only thing in Dr. Burke that he didn't have a scrip for. Throw something strong like that into your regular drug regimen and it can kill you even if you been working your routine 'scrip mix safely for a while.

Know where Burke got the oxy? Rodeo asked.

No, we don't. Do you, Garnet?

No idea, Rodeo said.

Now is there anything else I can do for you and the powers-that-be?

When can I get into Tinley Burke's apartment? asked Rodeo.

Why do you need to be in there?

Because that's what Sisely Miller wants me to do. Get into her brother's place and give it a thorough search.

A thorough search for what?

That would be my client's business, said Rodeo. My client is Mrs. Judge Randy Miller.

I get it, said Detective Haynes. No need to be subtle. But Miller's people indicated that there was no problem with a ruling of accidental-by-overdose of prescription medicine on the brother-in-law.

There's not any problem with an OD by prescription drugs for Tinley Burke, Rodeo said. And I'm not investigating Professor Burke's death anyway, so that's no trouble for you and me. Sisely Burke Judge Miller just wants me to do something personal I'd rather not discuss.

Get in there then if you can find somebody to let you in, said the detective. TPD don't care. This is an OD — the guy had enough pills and booze in him to kill a palomino pony — so we at TPD are moving on and nobody I care about thinks any different.

Did you find anything or take anything out of the apartment? asked Rodeo.

The death looked like a classic OD so we only took some prints from the pill bottles we found and a few liquor bottles, wrapped up the bedspread he died on and that was that. There was no sign of foul play. We snooped around a bit but didn't toss the place since his sister was right there and there seemed no point. We took our pictures, bagged the body and moved on, said Detective Haynes. Prelim autopsy and toxicology was done at record speed at someone's . . . Randy Miller's, I guess . . . insistence and we at TPD are done with this on the investigation side. You got any more questions? No, you don't. You don't have any more questions, said Jethro Haynes. And after this courtesy, all nonpolice parties can kiss my ass on this particular case. You especially, Garnet, because there's a change of guard around here so you don't have any special status at TPD anymore. You get that?

I get it, Jethro.

Okay, then, Garnet. Good hunting. And of course if you find something useful you will call the Tucson Police Department and Detective Haynes will now be the man to take your call.

Rodeo went to Eryn Hage's complex and was buzzed in immediately. The woman did not acknowledge Rodeo's two black eyes but instead handed him the keys to her rental and motioned him out her back door.

Drag that bad mattress out of his place if you want to help me out, Little Rodeo. Should be a Queen back there in the Outback Studio to replace it with since every time one of my kids or grandkids moves I get stuck with half their crap.

I'll do my best with this situation, Eryn.

If your broke back goes out I got some good pain pills.

Oxys from Mexico? asked Rodeo.

Better than booze and no calories, the woman said.

The stench from the vomit and the feces Tinley Burke had finally released into the world was so nauseating Rodeo hurried into the bathroom of the rental apartment and found some Vick's VapoRub in the medicine cabinet and swabbed his nose with the camphor then turned on the bathroom blower. He went then into the kitchen and turned on the stove ventilator then proceeded through the apartment opening all windows not painted shut throughout the three rooms and then he turned on the swamp cooler to Full High.

Rodeo found Lysol under the sink and exhausted the aerosol can into Tinley Burke's last known address. When he tossed the aerosol can into the trash can under the kitchen sink he discovered latex gloves for dishwashing. Rodeo slipped these gloves on before he dragged the soiled mattress out of Tinley Burke's apartment and to the garbage pickup spot at the back of Erin Hage's property where he slit the mattress in likely places with his pocketknife to check for things hidden.

Rodeo found nothing.

While Tinley Burke's apartment ventilated, Rodeo went to the pool house — a post-and-beam mother-in-law studio built on a concrete slab with a set of French doors facing a porch with a tin shed-roof over it — to look for a replacement mattress.

Rodeo peered through the French doors at the standard assortment of furniture and domestic junk old people collected from and stored for younger people — futon racks and futons, folding chairs and dining room chairs and kitchen chairs and bean bag chairs and video game chairs, turntables and occasional tables and dining room tables and drafting tables, computer desks and computers and word processors and typewriters, ceiling fans, oscillating fans, box fans, standing lamps and desk lamps and lava lamps, suitcases and suit bags and duffel bags and grocery store bags and boxing bags and shipping boxes, hot plates, electric woks and crock pots, popcorn makers, microwaves and mini fridges.

Rodeo espied a tall stack of mattresses overarching all this junk and so he tried the handle of the French doors. The studio was unlocked.

Rodeo rummaged the large room in a general way picking through various antiques and human bones, crockery, glassware, textbooks, yearbooks, CDs, records and tapes. When he found an eight track of Brother Dave *Live in Houston* he pocketed it.

When he happened upon a collection of Indian artifacts stored in ten compartmentalized wooden boxes, he stopped still in his boots.

Each archeology site box was identified with a typed label — Navajo, Tarahumara, Hopi, Apache, Yuman, Havasupai, O'odham, Seri, Paiute, Yaqui.

Rodeo recognized his tribe, Yaqui.

With his rubber kitchen gloves still on, Rodeo examined and handled the artifacts in the storage boxes — the rattles and combs, ironwood trinkets, potsherds, trading beads, bits of leather thong, bound feathers, arrowheads — then he used his cell phone to call Eryn Hage.

He described the wooden storage boxes and the contents in the compartments of the boxes.

Don't sound familiar to me, said the homeowner. But you know I bought and sold artifacts for years when that was still a thing to do. And I got hundreds of pieces of Indian crap out there in the studio from my days as a dealer and a lot of burial crap we found on the ranch I never even tried to catalogue or sell once the market went down and the Government Indians and University Professors took over and turned the world politically correct. Rodeo heard the rattle of ice in beverage. But Burke was an archaeologist or claimed to be, so he probably has all kinds of stuff back there too. Arrowheads, potsherds, who knows what? Probably some skulls and bones out there related to you by blood, Little Rodeo.

Did you tell Professor Burke he could be out here, Eryn? In your outbuildings and such?

He had free rein and keys to everything on this place except my house proper, the landlady said. He maintained the pump house for the pool and was cleaning out all the Tuff Bilts and the greenhouse and the bar-b-que ramada. He drained the Koi pond and resurfaced it. He reorganized my garage and even fed the chickens for me so I wouldn't have to make the trip to the back of my place since it seems like a mile to the rear gate and to the trash bins and recycle bins, so I seldom go out there anymore, Eryn Hage said. And as soon's those chickens die that's it for me keeping livestock. My ranching days are over. The woman sounded drunk or stoned or both. Same with dogs. I am tired to death of dogs, so once Skinny dies that's it with me and dogs because I have paid all the pet health insurance I am ever going to pay and once Skinny kicks the bucket and I bury her I buried the last dog I am going to bury because I'm too old to take care of any animal but myself. Eryn took a noisy drink. I saw you hauling off that old mattress, Little Rodeo. Are you going to put a new one back on the bed for me and make up that bed? There's fresh linens in the bathroom closet.

I'll take care of everything I can take care of, Eryn, Rodeo said. But it will take me a little while. So if I'm here for a little while don't panic.

I hadn't panicked since Oprah Winfrey invented mad cow disease, Eryn Hage said.

So take your time, Little Rodeo. Nice to have a real cowboy man around my place again. You being here reminds me of the old days on the Ranch, she said. And come over to the house and get a pill if you need one. Oxys are better'n booze and no calories.

Rodeo carefully moved the stack of artifact boxes until he had a clear angle to the mattress pile. There were twins on top of a queen on top of a king. Rodeo levered the twins off the queen and when he did he saw a bound manuscript.

He picked up *Running in the Dark, a Memoir by Tinley Burke,* held the book in his hands staring at it for almost a minute. And then he took off his gloves, settled into a bean bag chair, propped his boots on a stack of Norton Anthologies and started to read.

With the bed on his back his eyes were downcast, so he noticed on the haul to the apartment a number of different shoe prints in the dust and some cigarette butts. He knew Eryn would not have allowed smoking in her rental, so some of these could have been discards from Burke though Eryn had described her renter as a neat freak. Several of the discards were Marlboro Reds stained by various shades of lipstick on the filters.

There were also several Gitane butts. He carried the queen into the rental unit and placed it on the bed frame. He did not make up the bed.

He returned to the pool house and retrieved *Running in the Dark,* returned to Burke's apartment.

Even though his job for Sisely Miller was technically finished, Rodeo searched the apartment now seeking evidence of old crimes.

He started at the back of the apartment, in the small bathroom and examined the contents of the medicine cabinet. There were no drugs, prescription or nonprescription, and nothing else unusual beyond three large tubes of personal lubricant. The room was clean but not clinically so. Rodeo inspected the drain cover in the bathtub and found a few long hairs, all shades of blond. There was a used tampon in the trash can, nothing hidden in the water tank of the toilet.

In the kitchen Rodeo searched the cabinets where cans and boxes were organized and aligned — SpaghettiOs and mac-and-cheese, chili, beans, canned tomatoes, boxes of pasta. Dishware occupied the rest of the cabinet space and was mostly new Fiesta dinnerware and Jadeite. The pots and pans were in the storage area in the antique gas stove and were all copper. The silverware was all silver.

In the main compartment of the refrigerator was soda pop and seltzer water, Bloody Mary mixer, condiments, salad dressing, olives, pickles, capers with the liquid poured off. There was no fresh food at all. The freezer held two bottles of Stoli vodka, one still sealed and one three-quarters empty. A liter bottle of Jägermeister was about half empty. There were frozen Tony's single-sized pizzas, an assortment of expensive Omaha steaks, Jimmy Dean breakfast snacks, Lean Cuisines and several cans of frozen juice concentrate. One of the orange juice cans was not as frosted as the others and obviously a fake can used as a hideaway for small valuables.

Rodeo pulled out the fake OJ can and unscrewed the top. Inside was a single spent shell casing. He tipped it out onto the kitchen table and identified it as from a .38. He replaced the brass cartridge in the OJ security can using a tine of a silver fork and put it back in the freezer.

Rodeo sat for a while at the kitchen table and scanned the room. The low ceiling was braced by three rough-cut vigas and with a ceiling of ocotillo with the dried fibrous wood closely packed, bound with baling wire and shellacked. Decorative plates hung on one wall, probably Eryn's as they all had Western themes and seemed to have been in place for a long time judging by how the wall paint had faded around their perimeters.

But one plate seemed newly hung. Rodeo put his rubber gloves back on now and removed this plate from the wall and flipped it over. Taped to the back of a Grand Canyon commemorative plate was a Polaroid Instamatic snapshot of a Dairy Queen somewhere in the desert. Though the location was not identified, Rodeo guessed it had been taken in Sells, Arizona near where one of the Los Jarros victims had been shot with a .38.

Rodeo replaced the plate and moved to the front room that had served as Tinley Burke's living room and study. Rodeo found a Polaroid Instamatic amongst a small collection of cameras displayed on a bookshelf but it was empty. None of the other cameras had film in them and none of these cameras was digital. Rodeo checked behind and under all the furniture in that room but found no child pornography or drug stash.

He moved to the bedroom to do a quick check on the furniture there. Except for the several pairs of plastic handcuffs, personal lubricant and a hunting knife in the bedside table there was nothing of note in the sleeping quarters so Rodeo moved back into the study and settled down in front of the bookcase.

He scanned the shelves quickly and paused at *The Old Man and the Sea.* He noticed that this version of Ernest Hemingway's very short classic was much longer than usual so he slid the book out of the shelf. It was a fake book, a realistic-looking hideaway for larger valuables, hollowed out and holding a gun, a short-barreled .38 Police Special, old and not well maintained with what looked like very old dried blood spatter rusting on the barrel and the body and staining the white pearl handle.

He sat looking at the gun for a few minutes then he called Sisely Miller.

Yes, the woman answered immediately. Have you found it?

No ma'am, Rodeo said. Professor Burke had access to all the outbuildings on Eryn's property, so it's a bigger project than I thought it would be. Maybe might take a few days.

Are you calling for more money then?

Not yet, Mrs. Miller. Though that might become necessary at some point.

Then why are you calling me?

I just wanted to know about your brother's gun.

What makes you think he had a gun? Sisely Miller sounded very suspicious.

Not much doubt about it, Mrs. Miller, Rodeo said. I'm looking at it right now. Smith and Wesson, pearl-handled .38 revolver. Maybe twenty-five or so years old I'd say. He paused. And it really needs a clean.

So what if my brother does, did have a gun? What's that to you?

Well, if this gun was used in the commission of a crime, then that'd be police business, Mrs. Miller.

What crime? My brother didn't commit any crime here.

Suicide is a crime in most states, Rodeo said.

He overdosed. On prescription medications. That's a very different matter than suicide.

I didn't say I was talking about Professor Burke's suicide, Rodeo said. He waited long seconds for Sisely Miller to respond.

Have you found the memoir, she asked.

No. Not yet, said Rodeo. But you said something when we met at Riverpark Inn about your father having committed suicide and I am looking at a gun that has blood on it.

Sisely Miller did not speak for a moment, but Rodeo could hear her breathing deeply. She then sighed loud enough to be heard. It's public record anyway, she said. You could look it up in the Santa Barbara and LA papers from twenty-five years ago. My father committed suicide when we were teenagers and my brother . . . She hesitated. My brother discovered the body. But the gun was never recovered by the police.

So, your brother kept that gun? The one your father used to commit suicide?

It is possible. I have never seen it, but as I said he was very secretive and liked to bury his treasures.

All right, Mrs. Miller. I'll not bother you anymore about this. I'll call when I'm done with the investigation. He disconnected without saying good-bye. His phone rang but he let Sisely Miller get redirected to voice mail.

He closed the hollowed-out book on the .38 and put it back where he had found it and started a close search of each book, starting at the top shelf with archeology.

After an hour Rodeo had read down to a shelf height at which a man seated at the desk would have an easy reach from his chair to the bookshelf. And the books in this area were obviously the most used. Rodeo identified and examined the book most clearly dog-eared. *Paths of Life: American Indians of the Southwest and Northern Mexico* was a nontechnical reference book published by the University of Arizona Press describing and analyzing the cultures of the ten major tribes of Native Americans in the Southwest. As he read the table of contents Rodeo felt a cold hand press his chest.

An hour later Rodeo knocked on Eryn Hage's back door. She called him in. Eryn was sitting on the cowhide couch staring at the mantelpiece. She nodded Rodeo into the straight-back chair near the hearth but seemed to be lost in serious reverie or simply stoned. Rodeo cleared his throat and she looked at him then.

Jesus Christ, you look like you got run over by a bull, she said. That just happen out back? You drop something on yourself?

Something sort of got dropped on me recently, Eryn, Rodeo said. It's nothing.

You know your daddy came in my house one day and looked about like you do right now. When I asked him what happened he said he got drunk and fell off a tractor and the tractor ran right over him. Right over his pretty face. The woman stared again at Buck's photo on the mantelpiece. He left right after that. I guess he recovered?

I guess he did, Rodeo said.

You got things straightened up in my rental, Little Rodeo? Eryn asked.

Somewhat, Eryn.

You staying around then?

I don't think so, Eryn. I could be here a little while longer but I maybe might have already wrapped things up for Sisely Miller. At least as best as I can.

Eryn Hage suddenly seemed sober.

Hard to make a living when you work by the hour and work that quick, the old rancher said.

Sometimes it's like that in my business, Rodeo said. Sometimes it's the other way around.

Well, whatever you were doing for that Miller woman, charge her double your regular rate because the Millers have more money than the Pope and I guess her people do too from the looks of her and the way she acts, said Eryn Hage.

What do you mean, Eryn? How does Sisely Miller look and act?

Like money, the old woman said. Like a Power Player.

How'd Burke get here to your place then, Eryn? Rodeo asked. No offense, but this place is not exactly the Ritz.

His sister just rang my doorbell one day. Eryn took a drink. I let her in since she knew some people I knew and she's not bigger than a fried pie except for her plastic tits. Her Chanel suits weigh more than she does. Said she'd heard about my place for rent from some Gem and Mineral people I might have known once and she wanted a place for her brother to stay. I know the Millers have their in-town family home nearby the courthouse. Had that since forever, of course. Millers were around here even before the Hages were.

So it was Burke's sister that actually got Professor Burke in your rental here? Rodeo asked.

She said her brother wanted someplace private, I guess. With a back way in. Like I told you, the little girl said she was Randy Miller's wife and I know Randy from Tea Party rallies and I know the Millers who've been in south Arizona as long as dirt has been, so it seemed all right. Millers are good people even if some of them are peculiar.

What does that mean, Eryn?

Nothing. That's just the way it is with

378

families. Always have the weird one now and again.

What do you think of Randy Miller?

If he doesn't get himself assassinated then Randy will be our next Congressman from District Seven if I have anything to do with it. Then he'll probably run for President before he gets too much older or somebody lands some mud on him.

Who says Randy Miller has been threatened, Eryn? Who would assassinate Randy Miller?

Some radical leftist crackpot what I heard. It's all over the Internet, the woman said. She waved her plastic tumbler. You know Randy scares hell out of all them over at the University, all those liberal intellectual types with their heads up their asses.

What about Sisely Miller, Eryn? asked Rodeo. What did you make of her?

Well, the little lady carries cash. Which is probably not too smart these days. But it was good for me because she gave me cash money for twelve months, double for Gem Show time and a big damage deposit so I didn't care if she moved the Ayatollah Khomeini into the rental as long as he didn't smoke. Like I said, I can't hear much of anything that goes on in that far apartment. The man kept to himself and so I had no complaints until he killed himself. Truth told I hardly ever saw him. I thought his sister might be the crazy one to tell more truth.

How so? asked Rodeo.

She seemed to have an agenda, said Eryn Hage.

Of what sort?

Nothing in particular. She's just not up-front and seems sort of manipulative if you know what I mean. I don't like sneaky people. I just wasn't raised that way. Your mother was like that.

Like what, Eryn?

Working on their men behind the scenes. Not upfront about things.

You think Sisely Miller was like that?

I think she had an agenda with Randy, is what I think.

Like what?

She needed a husband, he needed a wife. Some people are like that.

What was the relationship between Sisely and Tinley?

Before he moved in that sister of his came over here and made out like her brother was some sort of basketcase.

Was he? asked Rodeo.

When I met the man he seemed to be just quiet. Maybe he was a little weird. I thought he was queer but then when I was on the back patio one night I heard him banging away at some screaming woman.

Did you see the woman, Eryn?

No, she said. I didn't see her. I heard her. But I don't meddle with my rentals.

But his sister told you that Professor Burke was crazy?

She didn't say it outright. She said it like, "if you could keep an eye on him and give me a call if he needs anything, Judge Miller and I would appreciate it," like that. As if I'm going to spy on my own renter or something. I didn't care what he did as long's he left me out of it.

Did you ever visit with him, Eryn?

He just kept to himself mostly, but when you talked to him he would talk and be friendly enough. Seemed normal for the most part. Just that he wanted to talk about things that weren't regular, you know.

Things like what, Eryn?

Well, not about the weather or horses. My men always wanted to talk about weather or horses. Or dogs or cattle . . .

Politics? Did Professor Burke talk about Randy Miller or politics?

Not about politics, Eryn said. About life stuff, you know. About feelings, whatever the hell those are. And about how I felt being old and being a single woman and what's the meaning of life kind of crap. The old woman jiggled the ice cubes in her drink and shook her head. Not interested, I told him. Life is life. You live and you die and work in between. So he left me alone after those first few conversations.

Was Burke acting different lately?

Seemed downer than usual, Eryn Hage said. But he wadn't hardly a bundle of joy to begin with. Just seemed preoccupied is all. I know he lost his job at the U and so I thought he probably just missed the teaching work. I gathered from his sister that he didn't need the money but men need to have work.

Anything strange happen while he lived over there in your place?

Strange like what?

Just anything out of the ordinary beyond what a regular drunk would do?

Eryn scrunched her brow. Now you come to say that . . . Eryn nodded. I'd been off to Scottsdale on some business a couple of weeks ago . . . I don't know when . . . the old woman drifted off.

Go on, Eryn, said Rodeo. What was out of the ordinary when you came back home here?

Just that there were three dead cats —

bang, bang, bang — laid out side by side by side right in the middle of the street right in front of my place, right out there on Convent.

Were they roadkills?

It'd be unlikely that three of those skittish feral cats we got taking over the neighborhood would all get run over right in the same place and line themselves up all in a row like that wouldn't it? Don't be stupid. Somebody put them there.

Anybody got a grudge against you, Eryn?

Half the neighborhood has a grudge against me, the old woman said. And the other half thinks I am the saint of Convent Street.

You wouldn't remember when this happened, when you saw these cats, would you?

Not a clue but to say like I did that it was a little while ago. If you're pressing me I don't even remember where I was coming back from, tell the truth, could have been a Tea Party rally in Tempe. In fact, I might have seen her there. Randy was the keynote speaker. Why? You working for the SPCA now? Good riddance I say about dead cats. I hate them. Ruining the neighborhood and you can't shoot them anymore.

You don't know how they died?

No idea. Why should I? Just seemed weird is all.

Eryn, I'm gonna go back over to Burke's place . . .

It's not his place. It's my place.

Rodeo stood.

Make me a fresh drink, will you, Little Rodeo?

Eryn Hage held up her plastic tumbler. Rodeo took it to the kitchen and dumped out the old drink's residue. He reloaded the glass with ice from a bag in the freezer and poured it almost to the top with Diet Coke from a two liter bottle then added about one teaspoon of gin to the top just for taste, just as he'd made his mother's drinks whenever he could, mostly ice, mostly mixer with just the smell of alcohol on top to convince her.

He handed the drink to Eryn and told her to drink it slow because he had made it strong and then left the old woman to herself.

He went back to Burke's apartment and spent a little more time with *Paths of Life: American Indians of the Southwest and Northern Mexico.* He looked for the fictional manuscript that probably had been inspired by that nonfiction, Tinley Burke's serial killer book, *Paths of Death* but could not find it.

When he had constructed a good scenario of the action, Rodeo called Sirena's cell phone. The phone number was not accepting voice mail so he called the Molina home in the desert where she would be staying now that her father was dead and gone. But Ray's voice answered on the third ring as the message machine activated.

"This is Sheriff Ray Molina. If you got an emergency and get this message then call 911. If you need information, call 411. If you got information then come by the sheriff's during office hours like a good citizen." The message was then repeated in bad Spanish.

Rodeo waited for the beep. I just thought you might like to know that I found a thumb drive with a copy of Professor Burke's serial killer novel at BoonDocks, in his trinket bucket where you never thought to look, Rodeo said. In this story a crazy man bases serial murders on an academic book and kills members of all the ten tribes of Indians in the Southwest. That sounds sort of familiar doesn't it? Like you said at the swimming pool, there's a serial killer loose in Los Jarros County. And it seems like this would be a good way to hide the one murder out of the ten that was actually the motivated one. Like the Apache? You might want to take a look at Tinley's writing. It's a pretty good read. Rodeo hung up.

Rodeo then dialed Twin Arrows.

Luis, stay at the store, he said. I'll be there in an hour and a half.

Where else would I be? asked Luis.

Rodeo's cell phone rang during the drive to Twin Arrows. He did not recognize the number but he picked up anyway.

Mr. Rodeo Garnet? This is Paul Bercich and I am a Special Investigator attached to the Major Crimes department of the State Police. We'd like to talk to you. The sooner the better.

Are you holding her? Rodeo asked.

Who's that?

Sirena Rae Molina, said Rodeo. Have you arrested Sirena? Is that what this is about?

Paul Bercich cleared his throat. Well, I guess we can skip some of the music and go right to the dancing. No, we're not holding her. Her lawyer flew right in and swooped her up just like the eagle snatches up the snake on the Mexican flag.

Who's her lawyer? Rodeo asked.

Jarred Willis, Bercich said.

Rodeo's mouth felt dry. Maybe sooner

would be better than later, he said.

Sooner's good for me, said Paul Bercich. We are in Los Jarros County right now. How about we meet you at that store nearby your place?

I'm headed to Twin Arrows Trading Post right now, Rodeo said.

See you there in an hour.

A black Crown Victoria with a whip antenna and polarized windows was parked back-end to the hitching post at the northside end of the store. Rodeo parked near the door and thought he saw in the back seat of the car a dark face under a white hat. He exited his truck, but as he was moving toward the Crown Vic to check it out a man he didn't know appeared at the door of the store.

Hello there, the man said. You Rodeo Garnet?

Yessir.

The man strode toward Rodeo with his right hand outstretched, his other hand flashing a badge in a leather folder. The man was middle-aged with a hard paunch, talked like an Anglo but seemed Mexican. There was a bulge under his left armpit and another under his jacket near his right hip. His cowboy boots were pointy-toed and high-heeled. His hair was slicked straight back with gel and he gave off a strong scent of deodorant.

Paul Bercich, Special Investigations Unit, State Police.

Rodeo shook the man's hand. His grip was strong and his hand was dry.

Mr. Bercich, said Rodeo.

Come on inside then, said Paul Bercich. We've been waiting for you. Got some questions.

The cop held the door open and let Rodeo pass inside. Luis was in his usual place behind the counter. A thick slice of adipocerous meatloaf and a cup of coffee were already in Rodeo's spot on the counter, with more coffee brewing on the ring behind the bar.

Sa'p a'i masma, Luis.

How ya' doin', Rodeo?

Rodeo crinkled his brow at this strange greeting.

You know how it is, Luis . . . Rodeo said. Could be better, could be worse.

Silk made meatloaf if you want to risk it, Luis said. The captain here declined but I know you got a cast-iron stomach and you know how Second Wife Silky gets riled up when you won't eat her food since you're such her favorite.

Rodeo took his usual seat and the policeman remained standing. Rodeo cut and sluiced a slice of meatloaf into his mouth. It tasted like copper.

Where's your dog at? Luis asked. What do you think about that meatloaf Silk herself made for you?

Dog's in the hospital, said Rodeo. And if I eat a whole slice of Silk's meatloaf I might be there too.

I married for sex, Rodeo.

Luis laughed very loud and casually slid right on his rolling barstool.

I'm sure marrying for sex made sense to you twenty years ago, Luis, Rodeo said. But I don't know how much sense that makes for you nowadays.

You disrespect me like that again and I'm never bringing you any more provisions from Casa Encarnacion, Luis said. In fact, brother, this is the last fucking favor I ever do you.

Rodeo turned and looked directly at the policeman who was still standing, leaning slightly toward his left side to clear up his gun hand, backed against the clothing carousel.

Luis's wife is the worst cook in Southern Arizona, Mister Bercich, Rodeo said. That's why Luis married her. To keep his slim figure. You wanted to talk to me?

When the man's face twitched Rodeo simply hit the floor.

The roar of Luis's sawed-off shotgun was deafening. Both plate glass windows of the trading post shattered under a barrage of automatic weapon fire from outside. Rodeo hugged the wood floor. He looked over to his left and saw the "Special Investigator Paul Bercich" dead a few feet from him, staring with the one eye he had remaining in a pool of his own blood, his hand still on his holstered sidearm.

Luis!

Just stay down, brother!

Luis had moved along the counter and laid his shotgun on the glass teeth of the broken window, angled it north. He fired off three rounds as the black Crown Victoria sedan squealed away from the scene.

Rodeo's ears were ringing, so he could only hear a murmur from his friend as Luis talked into what must have been his cell phone. Luis backed away from the window and Rodeo could vaguely hear him jacking more shells into his shotgun.

State's on the way! Luis shouted. I'm going to check the back door!

A handgun clattered down beside Rodeo's head. He picked it up and recognized it as one of his own he'd put in hock. He checked the load and scrambled to the front door, peeked through the thick screen. There seemed to be no one around but he slammed back the screen door and fired off three quick rounds. He winced when he realized he had bounced the final round off the shank of his own truck. Luis crab-walked to Rodeo and sat down Indian-style beside him near the front door.

And they say America didn't learn nothing in the Vietnam War, Luis said.

It's old competent assholes like you that make me glad about the Vietnam War, said Rodeo. I had my head up my ass, Luis.

Like I said, brother, this is the last favor I ever do for you. Luis wiped his face with the sleeve of his denim shirt. I'm serious this time.

Neither man said another word until several minutes later they heard a man's voice booming through a loudspeaker. "THIS IS THE STATE POLICE. COME OUT WITH YOUR HANDS UP!"

Sounds like here's your Mormon boy-friend from State Traffic come to see you again, Luis said. You should give him a dance this time.

Rodeo and Luis walked out of Twin Arrows Trading Post side by side with their hands high to the sky where Officer Theodore Anderton was waiting for them.

I think I will give him a dance this time, Rodeo said.

An EMT applied a bandage to Rodeo's head where a glass shard had penetrated just above his eye. The smell of blood was heavy in the air. The young med-tech was gray in the face. Theodore Anderton looked at the carnage. Rodeo shifted on his barstool as antiseptic stung his face.

You need to keep ice packs on those bruises for a while, he said. And you'll need some stitches if you don't want a bad scar.

I know all about ice packs and bruises and bad scars, said Rodeo.

Painkillers?

Rodeo nodded toward the beer cooler, which still promised FREE BEER TOMORROW. I can self-medicate, he said. The med-tech nodded, packed his bag and left. Rodeo resettled on his usual barstool.

So what tipped you? Theodore Anderton asked.

Rodeo nodded toward Luis, who was again on his rolling stool behind the counter.

Ask Rambo over there.

Instinct, Luis said.

No such thing as instinct, said Officer Anderton. So let's call it intuition.

Two in-country tours in 'Nam then. That teaches intuition.

Officer Anderton looked at Luis's forearm on the countertop, at the tattoo there.

USMC? the trooper asked. "Kill 'em all and let God sort 'em out." That sort of thing, Mr. Encarnacion?

That'll work for me, Luis said.

But you didn't know that the dead man was not from Special Investigations since we have all sorts. You could have killed an innocent man, Mr. Encarnacion.

Or an innocent man could have killed me, Luis said. And either way it wouldn't be the first time something like that happened in this bad country.

The state cop looked at Rodeo.

The whole situation was sketchy, Rodeo said. I shoulda seen it too. The car was parked too far from the building and parked assbackwards and there was a man in the back seat. The fella who came out to me on the porch was over armed. His boots were wrong. His sports coat was wrong. His badge was flashed too quick. His English was good but his accent was wrong for around here. He smelled wrong. His name didn't fit his face. He wasn't Local and he wasn't Government Issue. The man was twitchy.

And now that man is dead, said Anderton.

Fuck him, said Luis. And the horse he rode in on.

So who is he? Anderton asked. His ID is fake and the car he came in is gone.

APB? asked Rodeo.

We have an "all points" on, said Anderton.

Rodeo shrugged. He looked Norteno, but he sounded like he was from someplace else. Maybe Texas? Rodeo looked at Luis.

There was a couple of them in here yesterday, Luis said. Not this one, but same look, driving the same type car maybe.

They buy anything? asked the cop.

About twenty dollars' worth of tourist junk.

That what tipped you to them? asked the cop. That why you had an armed response ready?

I always have an armed response ready, said Luis. But yeah. Only reason for guys dressed up like that to stop at a place like this is to buy gas, cigarettes, snuff or beer. They wouldn't be buying no tourist souvenirs.

Could they be Federation Cartel hitmen?

Anderton posed the question to the room.

They could be, said Rodeo. But the one who talked and fronted acted like he could have been Police at one point in time, so maybe he's one of the former Federales who turned bad and works now for Gulf Cartel.

How'd he get your phone number? Anderton asked Rodeo. You said he called you to arrange this meet.

Rodeo's in the Yellow Pages all over AMexica, Luis said. Wouldn't take no genius to figure out his phone number.

They probably got my cell number from my ex-girlfriend, Rodeo said. Or my lawyer. I'm pretty sure it was one of them that set me up.

Anderton shook his head. You should think about getting a new dating service and a new lawyer, Mr. Garnet. Theodore Anderton glanced at Luis.

Don't look at me, said Luis. The storekeep pointed one of his blunted fingers at Rodeo. These criminals and lawyers are his friends, not mine. I just sell cheap beer and Indian blankets for a living.

Why not just ambush you as they did Sheriff Molina? asked the state cop.

I don't know, said Rodeo. I think they knew where my house was so that would not have been any trouble for them to drop

395

me at my place. So I can only guess they wanted to get both me and Luis at the same time and someplace public so we'd be sure to be found. So Twin Arrows would be the place for that.

Why murder either of you?

The person who is paying for these hits knows that I understand the plan of action and also knows that if I had told anybody what I know it would be Luis. So why not kill me and Luis both here in a scene that looks like a drug cartel shootout and then kill several birds with this one stone and offer at least a couple of good motives besides the real one for our deaths.

There was a good bit of cocaine in the dead man, Paul Bercich's coat pocket. Maybe he meant to plant that?

Maybe, said Rodeo.

Is there a drug angle around here? In Los Jarros County? asked Ted Anderton.

No more here than elsewhere, said Rodeo. Luis doesn't deal drugs out of Twin Arrows. Nor do I deal drugs. You can look, which I am certain you will, Officer Anderton. But you won't find anything on that. So my suggestion would be to let that go and look elsewhere. That's just my advice.

Sheriff Molina? He's got a million-dollar home and a high-cost lifestyle as I understand it.

Ray made his real money selling old trucks to new Mexican-Americans, Rodeo said. And I think his wife, Sirena's mother, had some money. She was an Asquith and they were an old Arizona family.

Why was he a small county sheriff then?

We all have ideas about ourselves, Mr. Anderton. I think Ray's idea about himself was that he was not a used car salesman but a Western lawman. Rodeo shook his head. And he was a pretty good one I'd say. For all his faults, Ray Molina ran a clean county as far's that's possible. But y'all wouldn't know Ray was clean. And the News and the Papers and Internet are already speculating that the sheriff's murder was a possible drug hit and a TV report like that is all that's needed to create a drug angle that could link me and my business as a Private Investigator and Bounty Hunter to Luis the local store owner to the local sheriff Ray and then to some drug cartel that could be running dope right through the middle of Los Jarros County, Arizona.

And your deaths as well as Sheriff Molina's could be tied to the other recent murders in Los Jarros County, said Anderton.

And we could all be tied up to the other

murder victims recently in Los Jarros. Rodeo nodded. Ray was an Apache, Luis is Tohono O'odham and I'm Pascua Yaqui, so that's another two dead Indian men in Los Jarros County, two more pieces in the serial killer puzzle and that's another angle to confuse the picture about me and Luis getting killed.

The cop furrowed his smooth brow.

What are you doing here anyway, Officer Anderton? Rodeo asked. Were you on traffic patrol?

State Police have created a special team to work the Native-American murders in Los Jarros County and I pulled some strings to get on this Special Investigations crew.

This dead man who called himself "Bercich" identified himself as from "Major Crimes" on the phone and told me he was with the "Special Investigations Unit" when he introduced himself here, said Rodeo. So my guess is that whoever sent this "Paul Bercich" and his cohorts down here to kill me and Luis wanted to get the work finished here in Los Jarros, get all the murders they needed done before State took over Law Enforcement in this matter from the Sheriff's Department. It was well known that Sheriff Molina's department was seriously short-handed at the moment and not really capable of handling Major Crimes. Rodeo wiped some blood out of his eye.

But how would outsiders know that? Anderton asked. This attempt today on yourself and Mr. Encarnacion was a professional hit, but it seems informed by at least some official or insider knowledge.

Maybe "Bercich" is really a cop somewhere, said Luis. It's happened before. A rogue cop with contacts.

I am sure this "Bercich" is not with any law enforcement agency in Arizona, said Anderton. But we'll know that soon enough for certain. Assuming that he is not, it would seem clear that he might have a conduit somewhere in State Law Enforcement. Would you have any idea who that information conduit might be?

Maybe it's you, said Luis. The storekeep stared at the policeman. Since this is finally your break, idn't it? Getting in on a Major Crime has got you out of Traffic, hadn't it?

If you want to look at it like that, Mr. Encarnacion, Anderton said. Is that the way you care to look at it? For the record?

For the record, I just want to go home, Luis said. Second Wife is sitting over there in my trailer with some policewoman and the Snowballs they don't understand dykes and they don't like Police and Silk she don't like Rodeo to begin with and since he's to blame for all of this in her eye I probably won't get laid for two months now.

Maybe you and your wife should go someplace to spend the rest of the night, Anderton said. SIU has established a base of operations in Jarros and are at the Lazy 8 there. We could get you two a room at the motel for a while? You as well, Mr. Garnet. It might not be safe here at the moment.

Who's dead here? Luis asked. And who's alive?

Officer Anderton smiled slightly. I see your point, Mr. Encarnacion. But we'll leave a patrol car here all night and State Police will continue to be a presence in this area until the serial killings of Native-Americans in this area are solved.

Then tell them cops to stay out of my yard unless they want more "armed response," Luis said. And unless you got a warrant you don't go no place but around here at the store. The storekeep turned off the coffee burner and moved slowly around the counter. He lifted a hand toward Rodeo, and neither man said anything more to one another. Luis left the building through what was left of the front door.

Anderton followed Luis out to the dirt parking lot to give instructions to one of his crime scene colleagues. After the stretcher came in and the bagged dead man went out, Rodeo left the store proper to stand on the porch, where Theodore Anderton joined him.

Are you okay, Mr. Garnet?

I'm fine, Officer. I appreciate you asking.

Theodore Anderton leaned over the hitching post and looked up at the sky.

It's special out here in the desert, he said. This is how it was in the Holy Lands. You can actually smell the sand. Like the ancient Hebrews must have.

Smells like blood and dirt to me, Rodeo said.

The men watched the CSI crews at work around and about the trading post. When flashlights strafed and illuminated small areas these small lights made the rest of the desert seem very dark.

Do you know what's going on around here, Mr. Garnet? Have you solved the crimes?

Rodeo grimaced as he smiled slightly. I appreciate you thinking I could, Mr. Anderton. And yes. I think I do know what's going on around here. And I think I know how and why the Indian men have been murdered around here, including Sheriff Molina. I just don't know yet what she

401

needed me for.

Rodeo retrieved the academic book from his truck. Anderton brought in another State Patrolman as Rodeo moved behind the glass-topped counter of the Trading Post.

Just you and me, Mr. Anderton.

That's a violation of protocol for reception of oral evidence unless you want what you say recorded.

What I am going to visit with you about is not evidence of any kind, said Rodeo. He poured himself a cup of cold cowboy coffee and took a sip. It's just visiting, Officer. And I suspect you've broken rules before. Like those photos you seem to have gotten ahold of. The ones of the evidence, the Indian artifacts found at crime scenes.

Anderton put his hand on his second's shoulder and guided him toward the door with whispered instruction. The second cop touched his walkie-talkie and left. Anderton shut what was left of the saloon door behind him and turned toward Rodeo.

Any other stipulations, Mr. Garnet?

Pull the walkie off your belt and your cell phone out of your shirt pocket and bury them in those blankets over against the far wall.

Anderton frowned but then did as instructed.

You want a coffee, Officer, or do you have your own water bottle in your vehicle?

I'll take a coffee, said Anderton. He took Rodeo's usual barstool. Black. And in as dirty a cup as you have, please.

Rodeo poured a cup and slid it in front of the Statie. You weren't Marines I gather, Mr. Anderton?

Nossir. I was Regular Army. In the MP, which made sense as my father had served in Vietnam as an MP and then on the State Police Force in Utah for thirty years.

Raised in Utah?

Yes, I was raised in Heber City, said Anderton. And then I studied for two years at a community college, worked one year as Security at the Gateway Mall, then I performed my two years of service for my church, LDS.

Where did you go on your Mission?

Amsterdam, Holland, the Mormon said. He smiled. With zero converts. Then I signed up and did three tours with the Army, mostly Iraq, with no kills but numerous GI arrests. When I mustered out I wasn't ready to go back to school, so I let myself get recruited into AZDPS Highway because I found out in Iraq that I like the desert. I have been in Arizona for four years. No wife or wives, no children, not homosexual. No personal or personnel issues. So now you know who you are dealing with.

The facts of a man's life seldom tell me much about the kind of man he is, said Rodeo.

I have studied your background, Mr. Garnet, so I hope that is true for you. Because some of your past actions indicate that you seem to have little respect for the rule of law.

As with Charlie Constance . . . ? That what you're talking about?

For one, most notable instance, sir.

I generally get the job done. Rodeo slid the University of Arizona publication *Paths of Life* over the countertop. This is the key to your quest, Mr. Anderton. Just open up the book at the beginning and start reading the list of tribe names from the table of contents, Rodeo said.

Tarahumaras . . . Anderton said aloud. What sort of tribe is that?

Mexican Indians, from what I read, said Rodeo. So are the Seris. And it was a Seri man killed out at my place.

Or made to look like a Seri anyway, said Anderton. The evidence found under that vic's body was obviously a plant. But some-

404

one at the University confirmed that it was ironwood and that's the material the Seris from Kino Bay prefer to use to manufacture their tourist ware. And they especially like to carve sea turtles so that was a wing of a sea turtle under that vic near your property.

So we got a dead Seri Indian as one victim, said Rodeo.

The first vic under the interstate bridge was positively identified as Navajo, said Anderton. The trooper more closely examined the book Rodeo had given him since the cop now obviously understood his task.

And that fella in the barditch at the Turn-Out? asked Rodeo.

Hopi. We got a DNA match off him through Prison Systems' data bank. He was a registered sex offender.

And then Ray was an Apache, Rodeo said. In an advertising sort of way if not by blood.

And then there was a killing just within hours of Sheriff Molina's, probably just after the sheriff's murder, on Well's End Road, said Anderton. There was a fragment of a woven basket found on that crime scene though it's yet to be identified as regards place of origin.

So we got the Dine dead under the bridge and then later Apache Ray in the same location, said Rodeo. So that's a Navajo and an

Apache. Then we got a Hopi in the Turn-Out near the county line and the little Seri at my place. And if Luis had been killed that would be the O'odham. And me, I would count in the toll of dead Indians as the Pascua Yaqui. Rodeo paused. That would make Indians from six of the ten major tribes of AMexica all dead in Los Jarros within the last few weeks, Rodeo said. And so who have we got left, Officer?

The Tarahumaras, Yumans, Paiutes and Havasupai, said Anderton.

The kid who was murdered near the Dairy Queen in Sells was from Lake Havasu, said Rodeo. So that kid might count as the Havasupai. Rodeo paused.

Or he could have been just a drive-by, said Anderton. Since he was killed with a .38 and not as the others with a shotgun.

Or that Havasupai kid could have been the "practice run" for our serial killer, said Rodeo. No easier way to kill somebody than a drive-by. It's simple, no blood spatter on you, expelled cartridges, if there are any, stay in your vehicle and you just drive away. If you're just looking for a target, any random person to kill, you just troll around until you get somebody in the right circumstances, on a lonely road on a bridge and cap them.

It seems like you have thought this out to some degree, said Anderton.

A case I'm working. Rodeo did not give any details of the Samuel Rocha case.

Anderton did not press Rodeo but checked the crude map in the front of *Paths of Life.* If that vic in Sells, the young man near the Dairy Queen, was Havasupai then that would represent the seventh of the ten tribes mentioned in this book. He tapped his manicured fingerend on *Paths of Life.* Plus the unidentified victim who was killed on Well's End Road very shortly after Sheriff Molina was ambushed under the bridge of the interstate.

What tribe was that victim? Rodeo asked.

No specific identification has been made on that vic, but he was Native-American. Anderton scrunched his smooth brow. So there is a serial killer at large in Los Jarros County, Arizona.

A for-profit serial killer, said Rodeo.

What's the profit angle?

If you're a student of crime, Mr. Anderton, you'll remember the Tylenol Murders.

The cop nodded. Seven people were poisoned when they took capsules laced with potassium cyanide, the cop said. The case has never been solved. The main theory was that the serial killings were part of a plot to extort money from the parent company of Tylenol.

But let's say if you wanted to kill just one person but had no compunction about killing a few more people in order to obscure the real victim, wouldn't a setup like that be handy? asked Rodeo. Say a man poisons a lot of bottles of aspirin in several locations so that when his wife turns up dead from poisoned aspirin she is just one victim amongst many, said Rodeo. Suspicion is spread around and that creates reasonable doubt.

Multiple murders are perpetrated to conceal the one real target murder. And even if the murderer is properly identified and prosecuted there might be enough reasonable doubt to sway a naïve jury, said Anderton.

But once you know that only one of the victims was the main target, the job of law enforcement becomes a simple murder investigation, Rodeo said.

And that means we look at the family and the finances of the principal vic, said the SIU cop.

I doubt any but one of the dead men or potential dead men around here had a pot to piss in, Rodeo said. Me included. Several of them rotted right beside a road and nobody even missed them.

Except for Sheriff Molina, said the Statie.

And Sirena and her daddy have some history and I don't know exactly what it is but it's not good. And that's what all this is about. Sirena wants the land, the rancho, the cars and trucks and she wants the cattle and cash money and stocks and bonds and the life insurance on Ray. And she wants all this on her own, without her daddy around.

Are there no other relations?

Her momma killed herself by OD, said Rodeo. Or got herself killed by OD.

Anderton considered this for a moment.

Knowing Sheriff Molina's habits why not just doctor his alcohol with a fatal dose of barbiturates?

That's probably about how her mother died, said Rodeo. So I imagine Sirena didn't want to run the risk of both her parents dying the same way. Sheriff Molina couldn't overdose himself since her mother had already done that. And Ray could hold his liquor.

Did Ms. Molina murder her mother too?

I wouldn't put it past her, said Rodeo. Since it would have been very simple to do and Sirena Rae doesn't suffer from conventional morality or normal fealty.

You really think Sheriff Molina's daughter

409

is capable of all the recent murders in Los Jarros County?

I would imagine that Sirena probably hired a sicario to do her dirty work for her. A contract killer paid per hit. She wouldn't do it herself, said Rodeo. Except maybe the drive-by of the Havasupai kid in Sells near the Dairy Queen. She could have done that one since it was clean and easy pistol work from a truck.

Why would she do that one murder and not the rest? Do you think that young Havasupai man was her "practice run" and after that she lost her nerve and hired out the rest to a professional hit man?

No. I think if she did the drive-by it was not practice for her, but a way to create evidence to frame a patsy she had.

Who would that be?

Rodeo shrugged as if he didn't know.

But the way I imagine it, Sirena finds out that her patsy has a gun, a .38 to be exact, she steals it from the patsy's house, kills the Havasupai kid with it, puts the gun back in the patsy's house. There again, if she has to go to trial she gets her lawyer, Willis Jarred, to get a court order to search the patsy's house, they find the .38, ballistics links it to the murder of the Havasupai kid near the Dairy Queen in Sells and she's got more "reasonable doubt" on her side since here's another likely murder suspect, the patsy.

I am very impressed, Mr. Garnet. Anderton looked stunned. Where did she get the hitman?

She probably brought a sicario across the border. And unless he gets caught in the act or acts real stupid, there's no way to catch him.

Ms. Molina has those sorts of contacts?

This bad country down here is full of contract hitmen ready to kill pretty much anybody for a thousand bucks a pop, Rodeo said. And since the freelancers just work for money, they have no allegiances to drug cartels or political entities or governments and so they leave no traces. They are real professionals, said Rodeo. So whoever hires them is not running all that much risk on that end.

Rodeo sighed out a big breath as he collected his thoughts. My best guess would be that her lawyer probably set up a meet for her with some cartel people he did business with. Willis Jarred defends half the bad guys in AMexica. And once her sicario is gone away from Los Jarros — and he's probably hiking back across the desert to Mexico with a pocket full of cash money right about now — then Sirena's pretty much home free.

She's still taking a serious risk, Mr. Garnet. You make a good case and so might the prosecuting attorney were she privy to what you know, so an acquittal for Ms. Molina is not at all guaranteed, said Anderton. I don't think an entirely sane person would take such risks.

I'm not a psychologist, Rodeo said. But I know Sirena and have studied her and I think she's a borderline personality disorder. Which means she has a natural predilection for taking high risks, even very high risks most people, even most murderers would not take. Risk-taking is bone deep with her. And she is very smart. So "reasonable doubt" would satisfy her.

Rodeo looked out the broken window to see if anyone from Law Enforcement was lurking. Anderton readjusted himself on his barstool, pretended to take a drink of the World's Worst Coffee.

How did Ms. Molina get the Native-American victims into Los Jarros County? Some are not local.

Well, Ray was local and Luis and I were local too, said Rodeo. As for the other victims, if the men came from Mexico, like the little Seri man nearby my place, then

412

she hired them like everybody else around here hires Undocumented Aliens, but instead of putting them to work she kills them or has them killed. You said one of the victims was a registered sex offender and those guys will go anywhere for the promise of sex, so she used a public computer and found that guy on a Internet chat room for perverts. The sheriff said that his deputy, Pal Real, found out that the kid from Lake Havasu was something of a porn addict maybe. So Sirena could have also hooked up with him on the Internet. She chats him up for a while and gets him to come down to Los Jarros to visit his O'odham cousins and meet her. She sets up an appointment with him at the Dairy Queen at a specific time so she knows where he's going to be. Then she shoots the poor kid in a drive-by. Haven't you ever seen "To Catch a Predator"? Men will go anyplace for sex with a teenaged girl, so she just takes on that persona and they would come down here like flies to shit. She could arrange these hook-ups using public library computers or powwow fliers or personals in the *Tucson Weekly* that couldn't be legally traced to her.

And then she and her sicario murder all

these Native-American men? Anderton asked.

Yes, Mr. Anderton. And then somewhere along the way her daddy, Apache Ray Molina, is killed in the mix so that the sheriff gets bundled in with the rest of the dead Indians in Los Jarros County in any investigation, said Rodeo. Hitman goes home to Mexico. Probably by sneaking back across the border the same way he came in, maybe even through my backyard since La Entrada is one of the most difficult points of ingress. Border Patrol don't care about people going back to Mexico.

We could catch him, this sicario.

You could. But you won't. And even if you do, unless he gets totally stupid and confesses, which he won't, there's no real, decisive physical evidence to connect Sirena to any of this. So what if the sicario has American money on him? He won't crack . . . and why would he? He only has American cash money on him and that's not much of a crime. He just gets deported. If you think she leaves her fingerprints on any of this then you don't know Sirena.

But Ms. Molina is still the prime suspect for her father's death, said Anderton. There's no question about that. We always look first at the family.

And you will find nothing, said Rodeo. Just like I said. Sirena has an airtight alibi for the time of Ray's death.

You.

Her sicario was killing her daddy when she was having sex with me, said Rodeo.

Ms. Molina's statement has already been taken, Anderton said. And I'm sure someone will be contacting you shortly for yours, Mr. Garnet, in order to substantiate hers. I'm not quite sure why they haven't yet.

I been out of pocket, said Rodeo.

You'll be called to testify, Mr. Garnet, said Anderton. At least at the Grand Jury hearing.

Rodeo nodded.

But even if Ms. Molina hired someone, some sicario to perform these murders, including her own father's, she could still be indicted and convicted of conspiracy for multiple murders and do at least ten to twenty, Anderton said.

Look at the percentages Sirena actually faces, Rodeo said. If y'all can't catch the hitman or hitmen that Sirena hired to do the shootings and get them to confess, then all you will ever have is hearsay and circumstantial evidence. And if Sirena's plan here at Twin Arrows had worked out for her, and me and Luis were dead now, then you wouldn't even have my speculations — which I'm pretty sure are accurate but I couldn't ever prove — that Sirena used contacts her lawyer set her up with to hire a Mexican hitman, lured Indian men to Los Jarros on the Internet or by hiring Undocumented Aliens who fit the profile she needed and then had them all murdered just to obscure or confuse the murder of her father, Ray. Rodeo took a breath of cooling desert air and wiped blood drip off his lips with the back of his hand. And then she set up some patsy to take the fall for this.

Where did she get the idea? From the book we were reading, *Paths of Life*?

Her plan is probably based on a novel that is based on *Paths of Life*, Rodeo said. The novel is a "serial killer thriller" the patsy wrote. In the book a serial killer probably kills a member of each of the ten major Indian tribes in the Southwest, for what reason I wouldn't know. Sirena took this fiction and turned it into reality. Then she can use this patsy's novel, and his own .38, to frame him for the murders of Indian men in Los Jarros including Sheriff Apache Ray. And juries around here don't give a shit about motive. All they want is means and physical evidence. All the physical evidence would be on the patsy, not on Sirena. I'm sure Sirena didn't leave physical evidence that any regular cop would find or that couldn't be spun into nothing by a good lawyer, said Rodeo.

But where is this patsy? Anderton seemed suddenly agitated.

Dead.

She killed him too?

Nope. Just he died.

Anderton was quiet for minute. So this scenario is completely your speculation, Mr. Garnet?

Rodeo said nothing for a while. Yep. I could find evidence against the patsy, but I know he's innocent and that would only help Sirena's defense, so I won't find that evidence.

If you could find that serial killer book and establish some links between Sirena and the patsy, then there might be a case.

The "serial killer thriller" is gone baby gone, said Rodeo. I think Sirena saw the book at the patsy's house maybe, read enough of it to get the gist and that gave her the idea of killing ten Indians. She sets up her patsy by planting evidence in his house and once the killings are done, including her father's — and not Ray's as the last one either, that would be too obvious — she plans on leading Police to the patsy's door. Rodeo took in a deep breath, winced in pain, continued. But the patsy died before Sirena was done with him. He died before Ray, her daddy, the principal target of all this, was murdered. The murders had to continue to Ray's and past Ray's, so a few more Indians had to be killed. But now the prime suspect, Sirena's patsy, is dead. So she had to steal the serial killer thriller because if found it'd really be a rompa cabeza for her.

Anderton stared at Rodeo his mouth nearly agape.

So the serial killer thriller is now burnt to ashes, I am sure. And the computer it was written on is destroyed completely. And I don't think there will be any reliable witnesses that Sirena and this patsy had an intimate relationship. They might have known each other in public, at a bar for instance, but Sirena wouldn't tell anybody she was dating this patsy. And he was too private to tell anyone. Rodeo sighed. So as I said, Mr. Anderton, all this is just me talking. I couldn't prove anything, not against Sirena at least. She's too careful to catch.

Do you still think she'll get away with it, Mr. Garnet?

She will, because even if Sirena somehow goes to trial, if she gets the right hairstyle, the right outfit and a good lawyer she can establish reasonable doubt and then the Molina estate is all hers, eventually.

And Ms. Molina has a good lawyer.

Jarred Willis has some very bad habits, said Rodeo. But he's the best trial lawyer in southern Arizona with beaucoups of connections. His father was a national senator from Arizona back in the 1970s and his mother ran the Arizona Chapter of the American Red Cross for twenty years and Jarred himself is Tucson High and the University of Arizona with a JD from James Rogers Law School and an MBA from ASU plus a year on a Fulbright.

Mr. Willis sounds expensive, said Anderton.

Apache Ray Molina was one of the richest working men in southern Arizona, said Rodeo. And when Ray married into the Asquith rancho his small Mexican fortune just multiplied into an Anglo fortune. So whenever probate clears, Sirena Rae will have more money than she can burn in a bonfire. I'm sure Willis will get his cut of that fortune. There's not many lawyers who wouldn't take the risk for that sort of backside payoff.

The men shared a silence for a minute that Anderton broke.

Why did she murder that Seri man on your property?

Rodeo shrugged and shook his head.

Just to jam me up maybe? She was vindictive that way and I had dumped her. Rodeo shook his head. Maybe she was just trying to get me involved because nobody in the Los Jarros County Sheriff's Department thought there was a serial killing going on in this county, said Rodeo. And she needed to get Police interested this case. And she needed the cases to be linked for her plan to work. And that was the problem for her, said Rodeo. Because even though she or her hitman or hitmen left their victims on the roadsides, the bodies of the dead Indians were not being discovered. Nobody cared about these men particularly so nobody was looking for them. And even when they were discovered no one was putting all the killings in Los Jarros together to make them into the serial killing spree she needed.

And that's why she had the Seri man killed by your property line, Anderton said. To get you involved, sir? Because of your background with a serial killer, with the Charles Constance Case?

May be like that, said Rodeo. Because if I had to defend myself or if I just got involved in the killings in Los Jarros, then because of my reputation the media would surely start screaming about another serial killing spree in Los Jarros County.

Anderton cleared his throat. I did have a similar idea to yours, Mr. Garnet. If you might remember?

I'll admit you were linking these deaths in Los Jarros into a serial killing, but you thought the serial killer was me, Officer Anderton. Rodeo shook his head. And if Sirena had known about your interest in the murders down here in Los Jarros County then she probably would have found a way to get you in the mix to speed the wheel for her. And maybe then she would have left me alone. Or just killed me as the Pascua Yaqui victim on the list of dead Indians just out of spite. I wouldn't put it past her. She could carry a grudge.

But Ms. Molina did not even know I existed, said the cop.

No, she didn't, Rodeo said. You are not a Regular around here and don't have a local reputation so you haven't much been in this story. And anyway Sirena knows I'm not stupid and so she must have figured that eventually I'd have worked out her plan. So that's why she put a hit on me. And since she knows that I often confide in Luis she thought she'd manage to get us both out of the picture and get in two more dead Indians with appropriate tribal affiliations on her list. If she was going to have some drugs planted at Twin Arrows that would make it look like Luis and me were involved in a narco shootout and just muddy the waters more.

Do you believe that the patsy you described had any idea about her plans? asked Anderton. Do you think this man actually killed someone? That he actually started this chain of murders?

I don't know, said Rodeo. He might have murdered the kid in Sells near the DQ. It's the only murder in Los Jarros recently not done by shotgun. Maybe that kid was a test kill. But like I said, I think it was Sirena did that to frame him up.

Ms. Molina seems sociopathic, said Anderton.

You see why I broke up with the girl, don't you? asked Rodeo.

Early the next day Rodeo knocked on the big yellow door in the middle of the Old Pueblo.

Come!

Rodeo stepped into the office of Jarred Willis, Esq., put two cans of beer, one Green and one Blue, on the desk, and then sat down in the distressed leather armchair for distressed clients. Willis got up, locking the wooden doors of his office and the secondary, steel-reinforced inner doors as well. He turned on the overhead lights and then moved around to close the heavy wooden shutters on both deep front windows and the back window. He turned on a white noise machine that emitted a static hiss and then stepped over to Rodeo.

Stand up, he said.

Rodeo stood and raised his hands as his lawyer frisked him thoroughly, even taking off Rodeo's cowboy hat to examine the interior of it and sliding his finger between Rodeo's belt and his Levi's.

Sit, the lawyer said.

Rodeo sat back down. Jarred took his own seat and leaned forward to snag the Foster's Bitter, pop the top and take a long swig. He nodded at Rodeo and at the Blue on the desk untouched.

Not drinking?

Rodeo shook his head. It's all for you, Jarred, he said.

That's the way I like it, Tonto. The lawyer drank, sat back and stared at Rodeo's face.

Have you gone back to riding broncs, Tonto? I hadn't seen you this beat up since your Indian Rodeo days.

Rodeo ignored this and began his own interrogation.

Since you conspired to have me killed are you at least willing to tell me what's going on with Sirena, Jarred? Since we're in lock-down mode here anyway? Or for old time's sake?

The lawyer took another long swig of beer even though it was still early in the day.

You were Mr. Sports Hero at Tucson High, Chief, said Jarred Willis. And you were getting nasty with Deborah Mabry, the prettiest girl in school, and the only girl that I loved. And you and me were friends and you knew that I had a total crush on Deb and you rubbed it in my face that she was yours and not mine. I was the geek on the debate team who couldn't even get a handjob.

We were kids, Jarred. And your daddy gave you a hundred dollars a week allowance so you could have paid for a handjob. Probably could have gotten one from Deb if you'd spent that hundred taking her to Tucson Inn or someplace fancy like that, she was so "top-shelf" about everything.

The lawyer looked thoughtful.

Well then, your butt buddy, Tank, used to beat the shit out of me too, said Jarred Willis. There was that too.

I admit that Tank did kick the shit out of quite a few people, said Rodeo. But he even beat the shit out of me a few times.

The lawyer put down his beer and held up his hands. I'm just saying "old time's sake" doesn't mean to me what it does to you, Tonto.

Rodeo moved to leave. The lawyer waved the private investigator back into his seat and leaned forward and squinted his eyes to examine the damage to Rodeo's face, which was significant, then he leaned back in his captain's chair.

But there's no harm in confirming what you think you already know, said Jarred Willis, Esquire. And we are in lock-down mode here, hermetically sealed. So, shoot.

How much did Sirena pay you? Rodeo asked.

That seems an odd first question, said the lawyer.

I was just wondering how you think Sirena's going to pay you anything, Rodeo said. She hasn't got a pot to piss in. She still owes me rent money.

She's getting considerable monies advanced against her projected future fortune.

Advanced from who?

From certain parties that will remain nameless.

So how much are you getting, Jarred?

The lawyer held up five fingers.

Rodeo shook his head.

She's giving you half a million for this boondoggle?

It's not a boondoggle if it works out, Chief. It's business.

What does she get for that kind of money? Rodeo asked.

Theoretically, the lawyer said. And this is only theoretical, mind you, I established some first-level contacts and agreed to shepherd her through a trial by a jury of her peers if it comes to that.

Sirena paid you, or says she's going to pay you, five hundred grand to set her up with what? asked Rodeo. A narco hitman, a sicario and a legal defense?

I believe it is actually a little more complex than that, said the lawyer.

She's doing a deal with somebody major criminal, isn't she, said Rodeo. Some narcos, probably someone you lawyer for, helped her set up the hits to get rid of Sheriff Ray and then they take a big cut of her inheritance.

Even more complex than that, Chief.

Rodeo scratched at the dried blood on his face. With Ray gone Los Jarros County will be even more the Wild West, won't it, said

Rodeo. And then Federation Cartel will have even more direct access to Arizona's southernmost county than they already have once Ray, who was actually a pretty good lawman, is gone and they got a puppet sheriff like Deputy Buenjose Contreras in place. And you have those cartel contacts, Jarred? Through defending local drug lords?

I don't care what anybody else says about you, Chief. You are just not as dumb as you look.

I appreciate that, Jarred. Coming from you.

Nothing personal in this, Tonto.

So you helped set me up?

No. What has happened to you is collateral damage. Jarred held up a pledging hand. I just made some introductions between established and potential business clients for her, the lawyer said. That's it. As I understood it, Chief, you were not included in this package deal. She pulled you in on her own for reasons of her own.

But you knew Sirena was going to kill her daddy? asked Rodeo.

One might assume that has been in that girl's plans from the beginning of her life, Willis Jarred said. And frankly some people weren't going to live much longer anyway. Ray was in an unhealthy state and probably would have been derelicting his official duties to an even more egregious level shortly and then wasting away in Margaritaville, just losing more and more money from his sizable estate of which I am executor . . .

But you approved her plan, said Rodeo.

It's not my job to approve or disapprove anybody's plans, Chief, said the lawyer. I'm just a businessman whose job is to make profit off current conditions. Just like you, Rodeo. Just like you.

I know it's like that with you, Jarred, said Rodeo. So I really can't even hold it against you, can I?

The lawyer shrugged. How you think of me is up to you, Chief. I just recognized that if you put two mean wildcats in one small cage, one of them is going to die in that cage. And if you are betting on cats then you probably ought to bet on the younger and stronger cat and not the older and weaker one, if you get my drift.

You're approaching this all very philosophically, Jarred.

Like I said, Chief, I'm just a businessman. My conscience is clear.

It probably is. Rodeo smiled slightly. Your ass is probably totally covered in this and your conscience is probably totally clear. Your mother would be proud.

My mother has Alzheimer's and yours is dead by suicide and neither of us has any kids we claim, Chief, so I don't really give a shit. I'm just a pragmatist. Again, just like you. So don't try to judge me.

I see your point, Jarred.

My point is go fuck yourself. Jarred Willis said this in a level tone. I'm a lawyer. That's what I am. The lawyer wiped a bit of beer spillage from his silk shirt with his silk tie. I just do what lawyers do. And if you think you are going to make me feel guilty, go fuck yourself is my point.

Why did Sirena send the hitmen to Twin Arrows?

I don't know, Chief. She's still pissed at you maybe and she never did like your butt buddy Luis, so . . .

I don't know anything that would stand up in court, said Rodeo. There's no real proof of anything against her.

So it was a nice plan, wasn't it?

She is pretty smart, said Rodeo.

Smart is who gets away with it, Chief. Simple as that.

But why was I involved at all, Jarred? asked Rodeo. What was the point in that?

You'd have to ask her why she used you as an alibi for the time Ray was whacked. She could have picked just about any man in town. She could have picked an off-duty cop, a judge, a fucking priest. The Pope would fuck her probably. I don't know why she picked you. Maybe she likes your big swinging dick. Maybe it's just like that.

And the body on my property line?

No idea about that either, Chief. Jarred Willis held up his open hands. When you called me after you found that dead man near your gates . . . Shit, I was your lawyer at that time and I gave you good lawyerly advice on your last retainer nickel. I told you to stay out of it. I told you too, Chief. I even suggested you extend your vacation this year. Willis shook his head. But of course you did not listen to your lawyer.

Did you fuck her too, Jarred?

The lawyer stood and walked to the heavy closed doors.

I'll claim lawyer-client privilege on that one, Chief. Jarred unlocked and opened the door, beckoned his visitor to leave. But membership does have its privileges.

Rodeo exited the office and stopped on the steps but didn't turn to look at Jarred Willis, Esq.

Sirena's going to get away with it, isn't she, Jarred? Rodeo asked.

Might do, Chief, said the lawyer. She's got a good lawyer.

■ ■ ■ ■

The next morning Rodeo arose even earlier than usual, took a sink bath and dressed in his hiking clothes. He packed his camping gear and the dog's food and medications into the truck, but he left all his guns in the safe. He cleaned his house thoroughly, made a pot of strong cowboy coffee, then sat at his kitchen table and composed the note to Ronald Rocha.

Rodeo printed in block letters: CARLOS MONJANO, TOHONO O'ODHAM PO-LICE DEPARTMENT, TUCSON, ARI-ZONA, BIOLOGICAL FATHER OF FAR-RAH KATHERINE ROCHA, THOUGHT SAMUEL KILLED FARRAH IN A HIT-AND-RUN SO HE SHOT SAMUEL OFF STARR PASS ROAD BRIDGE IN A DRIVE-BY. Rodeo folded the note into his shirt pocket, filled a blanket-sided canteen with tap water and then sat on the concrete steps of his house until false dawn, when he started walking to La Entrada.

Rodeo's cell phone buzzed in his shirt pocket as he was on his way to pick up his dog at Tucson Famous Pets and Aquarium Design Center. TPDS showed as the caller.

Mr. Garnet, this is Jethro Haynes.

What can I do for you, Detective Haynes?

Border Patrol took Carlos Monjano into custody about four a.m. today while he was attempting a crossing north to south. We think Monjano was on his way to Chihuahua, where apparently he has relatives who are involved with the Federation Drug Cartel. Just thought you'd like to know that.

Why would that interest me?

88CRIME got an anonymous tip which indicated that Carlos Monjano was the person who shot Samuel Rocha in a drive-by and I know you were investigating Samuel Rocha's death.

Did Monjano confess to shooting Samuel Rocha?

No. But he had his gun with him. Fired a few shots and one hit a Border Patrol. Not smart. We probably wouldn't have had anything on him substantial, just the tip off the hotline, but since he shot a cop we got him in custody for as long as we like and we can sweat him. And of course if we can find a slug in the riverbed then we have his gun and if they match up we'll probably have him for the death of Samuel Rocha as well.

Hard for a man to get rid of his guns, said Rodeo. And hard not to use them when he has them. That's the trouble with guns, idn't it?

I don't see any trouble with guns, said the police detective.

Anything else, Detective Haynes?

I've taken over the investigation of Samuel Rocha's death and have got a new CSI team coming in from Phoenix, said the TPD detective. And they think that with new intelligence and a computer model they can better project the slug flight after they reconstruct the drive-by scene on the Starr Pass Road bridge, so I'm putting men in the Santa Cruz riverbed with metal detectors.

What about the car Monjano might have been using for the drive-by?

The tipster directed us to a garage in Bisbee, so I've got people over there combing a green 1967 Impala and we have an eyewitness now who will testify under oath, a young mechanic named Jesse Storm, that Monjano did at least drive the car out of the garage on the day Samuel Rocha was shot. In fact, when we re-tracked on Detective Overman's original investigation into the death of Samuel Rocha we found quite a few gaps.

Clint's been under terrible pressure these

last several years, said Rodeo. Go easy on him.

Not to criticize a fellow police officer, said Haynes. But a man has to do his job or quit it. Simple as that, Mr. Garnet. The detective did not wait for comment on his statement. I just cannot work out how Carlos Monjano was certain that Samuel Rocha killed the little girl in a hit-and-run.

I'm not sure Monjano was certain that Samuel did kill Farrah, said Rodeo. But I think he was going to make someone responsible for the death of his biological child and Samuel was the best bet for having been responsible for that hit-and-run. I guess when he thought someone was on to him and he ran for Mexico when he got flushed that proves he killed Samuel enough for me.

But do you think Samuel Rocha did run over and kill his own sister?

Rodeo did not answer that question. I just followed the leads, Mr. Haynes, he said. I found a man who saw a lowrider car in the vicinity of the Starr Pass Road bridge around the time of Sam's death. I found that car in Bisbee at an auto body shop that had also probably repaired damage to the car Sam Rocha often drove, front end damage of the sort that would occur if the car had run into or over something or someone. Shortly after little Farrah's death, her brother Samuel starts attending sweat lodge, probably because he felt guilty about something and needed his spirit cleansed. What would you assume?

There was a pause on the TPD end of the line. Rodeo waited.

Sometimes things work out unexpectedly well, don't they, Mr. Garnet?

Not so's I've ever noticed, Mr. Haynes.

He's been whining for you since before daylight, Summer Skye said. She smiled. He knew you were coming. He knows something is up.

This old dog loves to travel, said Rodeo. He can smell it when we are about the hit the road and we are about to hit the road right now.

Rodeo had the dog in his arms and the dog was licking the man's bruised face without cease.

The vet hung her skinny arms over the sidewall of Rodeo's pickup. She did not even ask about Rodeo's face.

How is he, Doc? Rodeo asked.

His flesh wound will heal up fine, she said. And he seems to be recovered from the shock. She paused. But eventually, if you want him to live much longer he'll need some real professional help.

Rodeo nodded.

I just never have the money, he said.

Well, he's a happy dog, said Summer Skye. That's the important thing. She drummed her fingers on a tent bag in the bed of the truck. Where are you two going with all this camping stuff?

Rodeo loaded the dog into his familiar depression on the shotgun seat and as excited as the dog was to begin with from seeing his master, once back home on the bench seat he was asleep in seconds. Rodeo slammed the door shut and walked around to his side, got in the truck and spoke through the open window. Summer moved away from the truck.

We're running some errands around town, he said. Tying up a loose end over on the Res and then out to the Foothills to deliver a package and try and make some real money. Maybe enough to pay for some canine chemo. He started the truck. And then we are going to El Paso to deliver an old letter if we can find out who to deliver it to. Rodeo looked through the cracked and dirty front windscreen. And then I think we're headed to Far West Texas, maybe Hudspeth County or up into the Panhandle, maybe out to where the big windmill farms grow.

You got family over there?

Maybe I do, Rodeo said. I'm not too sure anymore. He held out his hand and Summer Skye shook it hard and let it go quick.

Thanks, Doc, Rodeo said. I appreciate you a lot.

Just stay safe, Summer Skye said. I'm sending out positive vibrations for you two.

Rodeo smiled and nodded as the vet backed away from his truck and lifted her hand. Rodeo and his dog headed to the Res.

Rodeo left the dog sleeping in the truck and let himself in through the gate of Katherine Rocha's place, knocking on her screen door hard enough to make it rattle. The old woman took some time to answer but eventually she opened the wood door and peered out through her Mexican screen door and then unlocked it. Rodeo passed inside and followed her as she went straight to the kitchen where she poured four fingers of Christian Brothers Brandy into a tumbler and took a spasmodic gulp. She turned her soured face at Rodeo, who had followed her silently.

Did you bring me my money back you stole?

Rodeo shook his head but said nothing.

I heard they arrested Carlos Monjano for killing the kid so I guess you didn't amount to much did you? said Katherine Rocha.

Rodeo stared at the woman as sweat began to form on his brow. Katherine Rocha's hand shook liquor onto the floor. She stared down at the sweet brandy stain on her linoleum.

How did you hear this about Carlos Monjano? Rodeo asked.

I heard it, the old woman said. My ears still work, don't they.

The police did not say anything like that about Officer Carlos Monjano, said Rodeo. They didn't say this Tribe cop, Monjano, had killed your grandson. You might have heard on the News that Carlos Monjano has been arrested but I know for a fact that you did not hear from the News why Farrah's biological father has been arrested.

The jelly jar shattered on the floor as the old woman wobbled against the sink.

I think you ought to have a seat, Mrs. Rocha.

I can stand on my own two feet in my own kitchen without some half-breed telling me what to do, the old woman said. Her voice was brittle and frail but still mean.

Rodeo pulled out a kitchen chair and

waited. The old woman sat down hard and kneaded her eyeball sockets with swollen knuckles. Rodeo backed away to the door-jamb and leaned slightly there to keep his knees from shaking. He wiped his face with his hand.

What I couldn't figure out was why you hired me in the first place, Rodeo said.

I told you why. I wanted you to do some work, to find who killed the boy. But you failed at that didn't you.

Rodeo continued as if the woman had not spoken.

You obviously didn't care about Samuel. You thought your grandson was a piece of trash. And I'm not sure anybody cared about the kid but one man.

You don't know anything! You're an idiot. Just like your mother. And no account. Just like your father.

You know Ronald Rocha, Mrs. Rocha?

He's crazy! She spat the word. That man is Corruption!

I wouldn't argue with you on either count about that estimation, said Rodeo. He waited a few seconds before continuing. But Ronald did love Samuel. And he still does. He grieves for the boy when no one else does.

You don't know anything . . . The old

woman's voice was now very weak.

And Ronald, more than anything in the world, wants to know who is responsible for Samuel's death, said Rodeo.

You know who! The old woman practically yelled this. You found out, didn't you? She was his child and so Carlos did it out of revenge! It's over. The police just got Carlos Monjano. No thanks to you.

No, Mrs. Rocha. Rodeo spoke quietly. The police have in custody the man who shot Samuel and caused his death. Though you'd have no way to know that but unless you just guessed it.

The old woman said nothing.

But Carlos Monjano, Farrah's biological father, is not the one *most responsible* for Samuel Rocha's death. You are.

The woman sat still like a stone. Rodeo waited, but Katherine Rocha did not move, seemed scarcely to breathe. He continued.

You and Samuel had an arrangement, Mrs. Rocha. Your grandson was supposed to pick you up from the Casino after you had spent the afternoon playing slots and getting drunk. He would walk all the way out there and then drive you home.

He was worthless. She whispered this as if she did not want to be heard.

You called Samuel that late afternoon or

early evening in May, May the third, but he didn't answer. He was at a party and he didn't answer your call. He stayed at the party and there are plenty of witnesses to that. Maybe you waited but then you got impatient. You should have just called a taxi or gotten a ride from someone else but you were too cheap to do that and I doubt you have a friend in the world. So you just drove yourself home that night, even drunk as you were.

The woman sat, stared at her hands on the table.

You ran over Farrah, Rodeo said. You didn't mean to of course but you did. She was probably walking the couple of blocks to your house, her abuela's house where she knew she would be doted on because she was the favored child. Maybe her parents were drunk at home or out partying and not paying any attention to her. Neighbors said the kids play outside in this neighborhood at night, in the dark. Or maybe for some reason you just turned left on Mark Street toward your son's house instead of turning right toward your own house. You were drunk and confused. And Farrah was playing in the street as she often did and you hit her with your car.

The old woman remained frozen.

And you knew you did this, Mrs. Rocha, said Rodeo. You knew you had run over her as soon as you did it, didn't you? But you didn't want to take responsibility for that so you didn't even stop. You just drove back to your house. Nobody much in that neighborhood notices anything anyway and you know that. And you tried to forget it, what you'd done. Because somehow in your mind it wasn't your fault, was it? It was not your fault because nothing bad that's ever happened to you in your whole life has ever been your fault.

The woman said nothing.

I don't know how you hid the car from the police. I don't know why they didn't question you more thoroughly, said Rodeo. The man in charge of the investigation was just not doing his job properly. That detective from Tucson Police assigned to Farrah's death was just not doing his job. And you're just an old woman no one would suspect. So you got away with it.

Rodeo waited, but his scenario earned no reaction from the old woman at all.

The next day you told Samuel to drive your car somewhere, not in Tucson, and get it fixed, maybe even before the police had arrived. You didn't tell him what had happened, you just sent him on this errand for you. Samuel knew of a shop in Bisbee maybe because Carlos Monjano had talked about this place to Samuel's father, Alonzo, or someone local around here. Or maybe it was just bad luck for Samuel to wind up at C-23 Auto Body where Carlos Monjano was known to frequent.

The old woman still did not move.

You have lots of cash on hand so you gave Samuel some cash and told him to clean the car up and get the damage to your car repaired, even if it was slight, and then to destroy the receipt once the work was done. But Samuel knew what had really happened. It wouldn't take a genius to figure that out just by the circumstances and your nervousness about the deal. So he didn't destroy the receipt. I don't know why he kept it. Maybe he would use it against you later for blackmail or maybe he was going to give it to the police or maybe it was just a memento. Maybe he just forgot about it. But for whatever reason he kept it and that receipt was the clue that led me to Carlos Monjano. Rodeo wiped his face. Samuel probably died with that receipt in his pocket. And he had not told anyone about what had happened. But I'm sure he had figured out who was responsible for his sister's death. You.

The old woman shook her head.

His half sister, she said. She was just his half sister. The old woman's voice was scarcely audible.

Rodeo waited but Katherine Rocha said no more.

Your hit-and-run was not discovered but Carlos Monjano started snooping around, looking for the person who had killed his biological child, Farrah. He told me he knew you and he was always around you and Alonzo's family, taking Farrah to Little Miss Pageants, playing his godfather role. So in passing one day you might have even hinted to him that it was Samuel who was driving around in your car that night, that Samuel might have been driving over that night to see his parents a few blocks from your own house. That's what you did, isn't it?

The woman did not deny or confirm anything.

So Carlos Monjano killed Samuel because he thought that Samuel had run over Farrah. Monjano shot Samuel in a drive-by just based on this idea that you put in his brain and without any real evidence. Rodeo closed and opened his eyes slowly, but the old woman remained still as a statue in front of him.

I don't know what your motivations in all this are, Mrs. Rocha, Rodeo said. Maybe you did this because you knew Carlos Monjano and knew how mean he was and knew he was seeking revenge, so once Carlos Monjano had put the blame on Samuel then you felt somehow like you would be in the clear for what you'd done. The cops didn't care about the hit-and-run, the cops didn't care about the drive-by. So once Carlos Monjano was satisfied he had identified his child's killer then you were safe. You probably didn't think he would kill Samuel but I'm not sure you cared that much.

The old woman began to rub her knotted and mottled hands together as if she were washing them.

But it's been gnawing at you, hadn't it, Mrs. Rocha? The guilt has gotten to you, hasn't it?

The woman bowed her head.

Or else you just couldn't rest easy thinking someone would find out what you did? asked Rodeo. And that's why you hired me. Just to put your mind completely at rest. Because if a private investigator could not connect you to your granddaughter's hit-and-run then you were really home free. You just had to know if you were ever going to be a suspect. It was gnawing at you that you might be. Not knowing was driving you crazy.

The old woman's breathing became labored.

Or else you really did want someone to know about what you did, Rodeo said. You wanted at least one person in the world to know what you did. You couldn't tell anyone else because you had no one else — no priest, no friend or family to confess to. So you hired me to be your confessor.

You're stupid, the old woman said. You are just guessing at things you don't know about.

That may be, Mrs. Rocha. But I figured out your crime and I think Samuel had figured it out too and whether you felt guilt or not, he did. He was racked with guilt about his little sister's death, Rodeo said. Maybe he was guilty because he didn't come to pick you up when you were drunk at the Casino. Or maybe he was guilty because he knew what had happened but couldn't or wouldn't tell anybody. Maybe he was just a guilty kid in general. I didn't know Samuel. But the boy kept your secret, Mrs. Rocha. I don't know why Samuel didn't rat you out, but he didn't. He died with your secret.

I didn't do anything, the old woman said.

Carlos Monjano killed the wrong person, Rodeo said. He should have killed you, Mrs. Rocha.

You're stupid trash. The old woman's voice was weak but she looked directly at Rodeo until he looked away. And a thief. Just like your mother.

Rodeo pushed himself away from the wall. I came here today to let you know that your deeds are coming back on you, Mrs. Rocha. Because now Samuel's only friend in the world, Ronald Rocha, knows your part in this, in Samuel's killing. And you know Ronald Rocha, so you know how he is. Rodeo's legs began to shake slightly. Ronald Rocha means to avenge his Sammy's death and kill the person most responsible for that boy's death, said Rodeo. And that person is you, Mrs. Rocha.

He doesn't know anything, she said. You're lying.

Rodeo did not confirm or deny this.

How does he know? the old woman asked.

He knows because I told him.

Rodeo steered his beat-up old truck down a long, winding gravel driveway and parked behind a Hummer in front of the Southwestern-style McMansion in the northern Foothills area of Tucson that his

447

GPS had led him to. The house door opened before he could ring the bell and Sisely Miller stood in the doorway with little twin boys clinging to her tailored pants legs. Rodeo exited the truck and started toward the house, staring at the children. It was impossible to tell who they looked like since both children had Down's syndrome. She pushed them away from her, back through the open door where the nanny swept them away.

You said on the phone you found it, Sisely Miller said. The woman was flushed and seemed tightly wound. You found what I was looking for?

I have the hard copy of your brother's memoir, Mrs. Miller. I think *Running in the Dark* is what you don't want people to read.

Sisely Miller squinted at Rodeo and crossed her arms. She didn't say anything for several long seconds.

Where is it then?

It's safe.

Safe? The woman now glared at Rodeo. Are you extorting me?

No ma'am, Rodeo said. It's just that I incurred some equipment losses and personal injuries during the investigation so my charges are somewhat over just my day rate and regular expenses.

The woman tilted her head like a bird

448

ready for flight or fight.

How much more do you want?

Three thousand, Rodeo said.

Three thousand! The relief was evident on the woman's face. She uncrossed her arms and laughed at Rodeo. When she put her hand politely over her mouth the ring on her finger refracted light on his face. Forgive me, Mr. Garnet. I forgot what sort of socioeconomic level you are in.

Rodeo blushed.

I have three thousand in my purse upstairs. She turned toward the house and spoke over her shoulder. I assume you'd prefer cash, wouldn't you?

I assume you would too, Mrs. Miller.

The woman disappeared into the house. Rodeo leaned against his truck for ten minutes until Randy Miller strode through the open front door of the small mansion and down the marble stairs, extending his hand before he even reached the bottom.

Randy Miller appeared to be in his late fifties, fat in the body but with tight neck and face skin, a sprayed-on tan and dyed hair that was almost maroon.

Randy Miller, the man said. My friends call me Judge Junior.

Rodeo Grace Garnet, sir. Rodeo sniffed

orange blossom aftershave and cigarette smoke.

Pleasure, friend. The politician gripped Rodeo's hand in a hard vice. Rodeo flinched but Miller did not let go of Rodeo's hand as he surveyed Rodeo's face. My Sissy said you incurred some losses and personal injuries during your investigation for her. Did I get that right?

Yessir. A Colt .357, a pair of Leica binoculars, a custom Schrade knife and my backpack. Rodeo named the objects lost by Ronald Rocha. Plus some face and tooth damage.

Randy Miller shook his head as he let go of Rodeo's hand.

All that to find what? Randy Miller asked.

That'd be for your wife to tell you, Mr. Miller.

I'm asking you to tell me. The judge's voice was polite but steely.

Rodeo shook his head.

The way it works in my business, Mr. Miller, is that I make a deal with a specific person and then I report to that person. That's why they call them "private" investigations.

The judge assessed Rodeo for a long moment.

In my experience, the way it works out is

that weak people desire the power and the money of the strong people, said Judge Miller. Just as you are doing now, friend. The judge tilted his head and looked directly into Rodeo's blackened brown eyes. The strong thrive in the Foothills while the weak live in the barrios and shacks out in the middle of the desert. And that's the way the world works around here, isn't it, friend?

Mostly it is, said Rodeo.

Well, now that the assumptions of our mutually shared paradigm are established, where exactly is this thing you have recovered that my Sissy is so worried about?

In the truck. But it goes to Mrs. Miller.

Randy Miller jerked his head toward the door of his big house and Sisely Miller appeared there. She looked crestfallen, even smaller than a size zero, fearful. When Rodeo lifted an eyebrow and inclined his hat toward her she nodded her permission at him then folded her arms across her chest again and backed into the shadows of her home.

Rodeo unlocked the various locks on the strongbox in the bed of his truck and then extracted the manuscript and handed it to Randy Miller, who looked at it cursorily and nodded.

This is it? This is what all the fuss is about?

It's what Mrs. Miller asked me to recover, Rodeo said. It's what I recovered.

Randy Miller tucked the manuscript under his arm as if it were unimportant.

I understand from my Sissy that she has already paid you two thousand dollars for this . . . Judge Miller tapped the manuscript under his arm. And now you are asking for another three thousand. I have a little problem with that.

You won't when you read Tinley Burke's memoir, Mr. Miller.

The politician narrowed his eyes at the private investigator.

I don't quite see how it is with you, friend. I don't quite see your whole angle here.

My daddy said that sometimes the smart man just pays up and doesn't make a big fuss on principle about every little thing, said Rodeo. And in the long run that can just be the cheaper way out of a jam, Mr. Miller.

Randy Miller stared at Rodeo then nodded and managed the manuscript as he pulled a large roll of high denomination bills out of a gabardine pants pocket. I will do business with you just this once, for my Sissy's sake, the judge said. He handed Rodeo three one-thousand-dollar bills and Rodeo stared at the face of Grover Cleveland for a second then folded the money into his shirt pocket. The judge tucked the manuscript back under his arm.

What is your real agenda here, friend?

Rodeo stared at the judge, who locked eyes.

You know a man named Ronald Rocha, don't you, Judge Miller? This abrupt question made the judge flinch. A single bead of scalp sweat coursed down his face and he brushed at it with his free hand. Ronald worked for y'all on Slash/M rancho down in Los Jarros, I think. And he served under you in the Gulf War. You know Ronald, Mr. Miller. Covert type. Torture expert. Sniper. A helluva shot from what I hear.

Randy Miller wiped away the gloss of sweat now on his full upper lip with the back of a white hand.

Is that what this is really all about, friend? Politics?

Nossir, said Rodeo. I guess it's more along the lines of what I know about, what information I have.

And what intelligence would you possess that would be of interest to me? What information do you possess that I might have a need for?

I'm not selling information at the moment, Judge Miller.

Then what is your concern here, friend?

Erica Hernandez, Rodeo said. The sitting congressman from District Seven. Your opponent in the November elections.

Judge Miller raised both eyebrows.

I don't want to see her assassinated by Ronald Rocha. Rodeo said this plainly and did not wipe the sweat off his face. And I don't want there to be a fake assassination attempt on you that might unfairly alter the outcome of this next election.

And when and where was this supposed assassination or faux assassination attempt to take place? Randy Miller asked this as if he wanted the information.

Weren't you going to give some sort of speech at the Juvenile Detention Center in South Tucson next month? asked Rodeo. Dedicating the new wing? Rolling in your caravan down Starr Pass Road in easy range of A-Mountain?

When Randy Miller squinted at Rodeo the skin on his whole face tightened. Perhaps I underestimated you, Mr. Garnet.

It's happened that way before, Mr. Miller, Rodeo said.

Are you working for someone I know or should get to know?

I'm not working for anybody at the moment except your wife, said Rodeo. And

454

Mrs. Miller has paid me to do a specific job of work for her and I did that job and she can trust me about that, said Rodeo.

The judge pulled the manuscript from under his arm and examined it more closely now, pursed his lips then squinted at Rodeo.

You have a license for your private investigation service, Mr. Garnet?

You can have your people look it up, Mr. Miller.

I think I will do that, Randy Miller said. Do you want anything else from me and my family?

I didn't call y'all, Mr. Miller, said Rodeo. Y'all called me.

It won't happen again, I assure you, said the judge. In fact, I don't imagine your business phone will be ringing much at all in the future.

Suit yourself about that, Mr. Miller.

Rodeo got in his pickup and slammed the door shut. As he backed out, he looked at Randy Miller out the side window and over his elbow.

Good luck in your run for Congress, Mr. Miller. Though I think it's a long shot.

I think I've got a fine shot at it, friend.

Rodeo drove east as fast as his old Ford 150 would go, which still kept him well under the posted speed limits on I-10. He didn't slow down but for gasoline until he was in Texas and did not park until he turned off the truck in a Pay-and-Lock parking lot in downtown El Paso. He rented a room for a night at the Gardner Hotel, the downtown El Paso equivalent of Tucson's Arizona Motel, which catered mostly to male pensioners, hitchhikers and European hostelers looking to slum. He paid the extra fee for his dog and led him up shaky wooden stairs to a barely furnished room with cracked window glass and the stench of old cigar smoke. The dog, exhausted from his long driving trip, simply circled three times and curled up near the foot of the sagging bed.

Rodeo used the El Paso telephone directory to find his next destination. There were dozens of O'Neals but only one labeled Mrs. Thom. O'Neal. He dialed the number but it was disconnected. He tore the page out of the phone book and left the dog sleeping in the hotel.

The neighborhood of Mrs. Thomas O'Neal was near the University of Texas at El Paso, and Rodeo's GPS guided him to a modest but freshly painted frame house planted in a neatly kept yard. He pressed the doorbell but no one answered. He moved to one of the similar-looking houses aside the O'Neal residence and rang the electric bell. An elderly man appeared behind an aluminum screen door and peered myopically at his unexpected and very bruised and disheveled caller.

How can I help you, sir?

I'm looking for the Mrs. O'Neal that lives next door, Rodeo said. Mrs. Thomas O'Neal, I think.

What's your business with Mrs. O'Neal, sir?

I have a letter from her son I thought she might like to have.

Her son?

Her son Billy, said Rodeo.

Well, sir, Mrs. O'Neal has been passed on now for a number of years. And her son, well I don't know that he has been around here for twenty years or more.

Does . . . did Mrs. O'Neal have a daughter who was a nun?

A nun? The old man stared at Rodeo. No. Miss Jane O'Neal is a nurse. Are you sure you even know the O'Neals, sir? The man sounded suspicious.

Nossir, said Rodeo. I didn't mean to trouble you with what has probably turned out to be a wild goose chase.

The old man shut his door and locked it

several times. Rodeo walked back to his truck and drove to a liquor store where he bought a six-pack of Tecate in cans, two limes, a pack of Marlboro Reds, a Party Size bag of Fritos, a plastic tub of Hidden Valley Ranch Dip and a pint of Jim Beam. He asked for his change in quarters and after he deposited his vice in the truck stationed himself at the pay phone bolted to the front of the convenience store.

He asked to speak directly with Detective Haynes and was put on hold by the Tucson Police Department dispatcher.

Jethro Haynes.

Rodeo Garnet.

Well, I guess you heard the news then, Garnet.

No, I hadn't heard any news.

Carlos Monjano cracked in The Box, said the Tucson Police Department detective. Once we threatened to exhume that little girl of his for DNA tests to prove that he was the real father he confessed to the drive-by. Monjano did not want us disturbing his little sleeping beauty queen's eternal rest, I guess.

The detective sounded pleased.

That little girl was his child, Detective, said Rodeo. Her name was Farrah Katherine Rocha.

The detective did not reply to this scold for a moment. It's a sad business I'm in, Mr. Garnet, the cop said. But it is a business and it will never go away, I'm afraid. I don't do the crimes, I just process them. Like yourself but in a more professional way.

I solve crimes, Detective, Rodeo said. I don't just process them. But I savvy your drift. And I know it gets to be like that, doesn't it? We all get to be like that about death and dying eventually, don't we?

It is inevitable, said the detective. But the bright side is I am getting a major collar and somebody else . . . who knows who? is making money from 88CRIME for the anonymous tips to the hotline. That is, if the good citizen who made the anonymous call might care to collect the money for that anonymous information.

Everybody has to make a living, Detective Haynes.

Yes they do, said the cop. Even private investigators.

I guess Clint Overman is not coming back to work anytime soon? asked Rodeo.

Detective Overman is currently on extended medical leave since he piled his pickup into a tree near a kid's soccer field and then left an abusive message on the governor's voice mail. Detective Haynes paused a beat. So I doubt that Mr. Overman is coming back in an official capacity to any position in Law Enforcement at TPD or in Arizona since you cannot make mistakes like that in any bureaucracy, said Haynes. So you deal with me now at TPD, Garnet, or you don't deal with Tucson Police at all.

I'm afraid I got some more business for you then, Detective. And this one's not coming in on the hotline because you will owe me personal for this one.

I'm not sure I want that sort of debt from someone like you, Garnet.

Suit yourself when you hear it, said Rodeo.

May I record this phone call?

No, said Rodeo. He spoke very quickly. 592 South Convent Avenue, said Rodeo. Refrigerator freezer and Grand Canyon commemorative plate. Look in the bookshelves and the back outbuildings too.

Tinley Burke's place?

Get in touch with Ted Anderton, late of State Highway Traffic now with Special Investigations Unit, Rodeo said. He'll explain it all to you. And tell the trooper that he owes me too.

Rodeo awoke the next morning bloated from salt, his head swollen from beer and bourbon and a beating and with his tongue fuzzed from half a pack of cigarettes. He had fallen asleep in his clothes, so he unpacked a clean outfit and took a long tepid shower and re-dressed himself. He then fed and watered and walked his dog and left the dog asleep in the lobby of the Gardner Hotel, a once-fine establishment that was now mostly occupied by old men who liked old dogs.

Rodeo snagged a Styrofoam cup of very bad coffee and a couple of local newspapers from the lobby and sat in a lawn chair on the sidewalk in front of the Gardner, one eye aimed at the street and the other eye scanning the police blotter and news sections of the newspapers. Several stories were noteworthy to the PI.

The postmortem indictment of Tinley Chance Burke, brother-in-law to Law and Order, Right Wing Tea Party frontman Randy Miller, former Pima County Judge, former Speaker of the Arizona State House of Representatives, current frontrunner in the November midterm elections for Erica Hernandez's District Seven Congressional Seat, had made the morning edition of the *El Paso Star-Telegram.*

Tinley Burke was being considered posthumously as potentially involved with the homicide of Winthrop Begay (of Lake Havasu, Arizona) in Sells, Arizona. Incriminating evidence of a wide variety had been discovered in and around the former rented domicile of the erstwhile University of Arizona adjunct professor. No direct response from Judge Randy Miller had been available by early morning press time but Miller's spokespeople had assured the press that Randy Miller would do what was correct and Christian in order to uphold conservative family values in this matter.

The murder of Ray "Apache Ray" Molina, Sheriff of Los Jarros County, Arizona, was on page four of the *Telegram*. The lawman's murder was still under investigation by Los Jarros County and Arizona State Law Enforcement. Ray Molina's next-of-kin, his daughter Sirena Rae Asquith Molina had been detained as a person of interest by the Special Investigations Unit of the State Police and questioned about her father's death, but had been released on her own recognizance and was, according to her lawyer, Jarred Willis, Esquire, uninvolved with this crime. Jarred Willis suggested Law Enforcement widen the net of their inquiries and perhaps recognize the half dozen murders of Native-American men during the last several weeks in Los Jarros County as potentially all being the handiwork of a single serial killer.

Rodeo's name was not mentioned in the Burke/Randy Miller article or in the article about the death of Los Jarros County Sheriff, Ray Molina.

There was no mention in that edition of the *Star-Telegram* of the case of Carlos Monjano in connection with the death of Samuel Rocha, though all the regional and national news outlets eventually picked up the Reservation cop's arrest. Eventually it became public that Carlos Monjano was the biological father of Farrah Katherine Rocha but her body was never exhumed.

When Katherine Rocha, the grandmother of Farrah and Samuel Rocha, died of a stroke in her house on the Pascua Yaqui Reservation, no mention was made in the regional or national press. Tucson papers and TV, however, did report that Katherine Rocha had probably been in her house dead on the kitchen floor for several days, in the last days of August heat, when she was discovered by a USPS mail carrier who noticed the stench while delivering junk mail.

463

■ ■ ■ ■

Rodeo used the local El Paso phone book and his cell phone to locate Jane O'Neal at Saint Ignacio Hospital but was told by the hospital telephone operator that nurses' shifts would not be divulged to anyone without proper clearance. When Rodeo was done with his several cups of coffee and his dog was through with his morning constitutional, they drove to the small, private hospital on the northside of El Paso.

At the Information Desk of Saint Ignacio, Rodeo was informed that Jane O'Neal was an ER nurse, so he found his way to the Emergency Room and asked for her.

I'm Jane O'Neal. Rodeo turned toward the voice behind him. The woman addressing him was plain featured, Anglo, scrubbed clean and dressed in white.

I have something from your brother to give to you, Rodeo said.

My brother? The woman raised a gray eyebrow over a granite eye.

Rodeo thrust the worn envelope and letter into the woman's hands. She took it and examined the old LA Olympics commemorative stamp on it and the address then extracted and unfolded the pungent letter with some care. When the woman had read the letter she seemed clearly perplexed.

I guess this is a letter my mother sent to my brother Billy, the nurse said. But that was years and years ago when I was only a kid.

I think Billy is dead. Rodeo blurted this out. I think someone murdered him because Billy witnessed practice for a fake assassination attempt . . .

The nurse interrupted Rodeo's ramble with a raised hand.

Billy's not dead, Jane O'Neil said. Billy is right here. In the hospital.

Rodeo rubbed his sore face with his hands. Could I see him?

What in the world for? Billy's sister asked. I don't even know who you are. And frankly, you don't look much better or sound much saner than Billy did when he was admitted here.

Rodeo nodded slowly.

I had a spot of trouble recently, Rodeo said.

You look injured, the nurse said. Her face softened and she beckoned toward a plastic chair. Were you in a car wreck or something?

You could say that, said Rodeo.

Let's sit you down and get you some water, the nurse said. Her voice was professionally kind now. How would that be?

Rodeo allowed himself to be led to a plastic chair. He took a paper cup of water and drank it down and handed the cup back to Nurse O'Neal.

And now I think you should explain yourself, the nurse said. Let's start with your name.

Rodeo. Rodeo Grace Garnet. I'm a private investigator from Tucson more or less. But I work all over the southwest.

What do you want from my brother?

I don't want anything from him, Miss O'Neal, Rodeo said. Billy was just part of an investigation I was doing lately. He witnessed something and when I looked all over his old haunts and couldn't find him I thought he probably got killed for some crime or potential crime he had witnessed.

A crime? Well, Billy will not be able to testify, his sister said. Don't think that you're going to haul my brother back to Tucson after all he's been through. We've just gotten him stabilized.

I don't care if he goes back or not, Miss O'Neal. I was just doing a good deed. Rodeo pointed at the worn letter in the woman's hand.

And where on earth did you get this letter from my mother to Billy?

I found it, Rodeo said. In his sleeping place. He lived on a concrete shelf above a drainage ditch near the Santa Cruz riverbed in Tucson. When I went looking for him I found some things of his. I thought he had been killed and . . . I don't know. I just thought seeing the letter, knowing that he had kept it all these years, might give his mother or you or whoever some . . . Rodeo shook his head and shrugged his shoulders.

Closure?

Yes. Rodeo sat back in his chair. I guess that's the word I'm looking for.

You seem sort of disappointed that Billy's not dead, the nurse said. She did not sound scolding but only honest.

No. I'm very glad Billy is alive, Rodeo said. And that he has a good sister to look after him. It just ruins a theory of mine and an idea I had about somebody I thought was a real bad guy who might not be so bad. And I am a little confused about all this myself now, said Rodeo.

Jane O'Neal put her hand on Rodeo's forearm.

You're a very sweet man to have thought about us in this way, the nurse said. To come all this way to bring an old letter back. To have thought about other people that way . . . Well, it's unusual. You see that, don't you?

I probably didn't do it for y'all, said Rodeo. I'm probably the one who needs some closure.

On what?

On a lot of things that are never going to get closed, said Rodeo.

The nurse considered this and then nodded.

Is there anything I can do for you before you leave? Would you like to see an ER doc or a physician's assistant? I can arrange that.

Could I see Billy? Rodeo asked. Could I visit for a minute with your brother?

Billy's sister considered this for a moment then nodded briskly.

Billy's still in the ICU. We are trying to detox him slowly enough so he doesn't go into shock. He's medicated heavily. He probably won't recognize you.

That's all right, Rodeo said. A lot of people don't.

Billy O'Neal seemed younger than Rodeo remembered, now a diseased and dissipated fifty instead of a diseased and dissipated sixty.

Who cleaned him up?

I did of course, his sister said. When Nurse O'Neal tucked the sheets more tightly around her brother he opened his eyes and smiled at her. He's a sweet boy, she said. He has just had some troubles during his life. But he's better now. He's home again. Isn't that right, Billy?

Better now . . . Billy's words were slurred but understandable. Home . . . Elpaso-texas . . .

How did he get here? asked Rodeo.

Billy shifted his gaze toward Rodeo when he heard the man's voice.

On Greyhound, the nurse said.

How was he capable of that?

I don't know, Jane O'Neal said. It's a miracle. He said some Indian man — the soldier Indian, Billy calls him — bought him a ticket and put him on the bus in Tucson. Billy had a tag pinned to his jacket with his name and El Paso written on it. He had a bag of Fritos in his hand and a ten-dollar bill in his pocket. People along the way helped him. Good Samaritans are not unheard of, even in these days.

How did he get to this hospital, to you?

When he got off the bus here in El Paso he was dazed and confused and a police officer took him to another hospital where they managed to get his name. An ER doc who knows me and knew vaguely that I had a lost brother transferred Billy here to Saint

Ignacio. The nurse brushed at her wet eyes. It really is a miracle, she said. The woman seemed to believe this. I had just started nursing school when he ran away, she said. I hadn't seen my brother since I was a teenager but I still recognized him. Didn't I, Billy? Jane O'Neal patted her sibling's arm. I did recognize my big brother.

Missedyou, Billy said. He smiled weakly.

Can I ask him a few questions? Rodeo asked.

Billy's head shifted again toward Rodeo's voice, though the patient seemed unable to focus on Rodeo's face.

Not if you're going to upset him.

I just want to ask him about Samuel Rocha, Sam, the kid that used to visit him at the River Park, the kid that fell off the bridge.

Well, you got all that in, didn't you? The nurse frowned.

I help him, Billy said. 'Member? I tol' you I help him.

Who did you help, Billy? his sister asked.

That boy. I took his letters and was gonna deliver his mail for him. His name was Sam but he was inna sand and so hot so I dragged him inna shade to cool and I forgot.

Rodeo sighed and rubbed his face with a hand.

What is it? Billy's sister asked. She moved from her brother's side to Rodeo's and pulled on Rodeo's arm. She lowered her voice. Tell me, the sister said. Did Billy hurt someone? If he hurt someone I have to know.

When Rodeo looked at the woman's hand on his arm she removed it. He shook his head.

Billy didn't do anything wrong, Rodeo said. He was just trying to do a good turn. Be a good Samaritan. It didn't work out like he planned. What he did didn't help Sam. Rodeo looked at the homeless man who had returned home. But Billy's a good boy. Take care of him now.

Rodeo moved toward the door.

I still gottaten, Billy said.

What did you say, Billy? his sister asked. She went to her brother and when she bent her face near his their family resemblance was unmistakable.

Tellimistillgottaten, Billy said. The man in the hospital bed looked at Rodeo. His words were slurred and his head drooped. Earnedit, didn't I?

Billy's sister looked sharply at Rodeo.

Rodeo stared at Billy, the person who had probably, actually killed Samuel Rocha by dragging the damaged and paralyzed kid

471

into brush in the Santa Cruz riverbed, where he was hidden from view and where Samuel had perished because no one had cared enough to miss him and look for him.

Billy earned ten dollars for helping me with one of my investigations, Rodeo said. He looked at the nurse. I gave Billy a job and he's just remembering that because it was probably the high point of his life in Tucson but for leaving the place. And a man needs a job of work sometimes.

Billy started blubbering then and his sister jerked her head at the door so I left the room, left the hospital, left El Paso and took my dog on a road trip in search of my own daddy.

And except for the Grand Jury hearing, me and the dog stayed out of Los Jarros County, Arizona, for a long while, a long enough while anyway to allow the Locals' opinions to settle and all of the spilled blood of the murdered to dry to dust and their dead flesh to cure to hide in this bad country I call Home, El Hoyo, The Hole.

Sirena Rae Molina never stood trial for the murder of her father or for conspiracy to murder her father or anyone. On the last day of August she was killed by a gunshot wound in the back, probably from very long range, while she was standing on the steps to the side door of my casita. The slug hit her in the left rib cage and slammed her against the Mexican screen door so hard she then fell back into the side yard with her arms outstretched as if on a cross. The images of her falling back and dying were captured by the game camera affixed to the roof of my house. The woman's flesh was in that Mexican screen door of mine for a long time, until it dried out completely and then flaked away as just a little more dirt in a desert of dirt.

When she was killed Sirena had been armed with one of her daddy's .38 caliber Police Special revolvers, drunk on her daddy's Jim Beam, high on his oxycodone and at the morning-end of an all-nighter that started with a couple of regular unknown cowboys at BoonDocks in Tucson who moved with Sirena onto the Dairy Queen at Sells and then to the Molina Rancho and then ended, finally, with Sirena, alone, at Vista Montana Estates around daybreak.

In the last live image of the woman, Sirena Rae is staring at the game camera affixed to my rooftop. The chief AZDPS-SIU-CSI investigator and the attending Los Jarros County ME, Dr. Emanuel Boxer, concurred that Sirena had been alive and most probably conscious for at least a short moment after she was hit by the .448-caliber slug. You can detect the slightest flutter of her eyelids in her death shot. Her mouth is open as if she is screaming but her lips do not move.

Sirena Rae was wearing work clothes and cowboy boots, leather gloves and one of her daddy's cowboy hats, an old Resistol Cattleman's that I had seen Ray wear many times when he was off duty. His initials were stamped on the hatband — R.A.M. I don't know what the "A" stood for but I don't think it stood for Apache. Sirena had a watering can in one hand, a burred copy of my housekey in the other and the loaded Los Jarros County Police Department .38 revolver on her hip. She bled to death in a few minutes.

During a routine patrol the next day, the interim Los Jarros County Sheriff, Buenjose Contreras, found her, though I never knew any Law Enforcement of any sort to have ever before come to my place on a routine patrol.

■ ■ ■ ■

Sirena's killer has never been found. I testified at the Grand Jury hearing and I don't believe I perjured myself overmuch since I had nothing much to say beyond the obvious that everybody Local would know. I don't know why Sirena was at my place using a copied key to get into my casita. I don't know why she was armed. I don't know why she watered the garden.

On the day of her death I was checked into the America's Best Value Inn in Van Horn, Texas and I had the cheese enchilada plate for both lunch and dinner at Chuy's. I paid cash at that Mexican restaurant both times that day and paid cash for my motel room and so did not leave any paper trail but there were plenty of witnesses to a large Indian or Native-American or Indio-Mexican or Mexican-American or Mexican or very tanned Anglo man staying at Best Value and having lunch and dinner at Chuy's in Van Horn, Texas, on the day Sirena Rae Molina was killed on a corduroy byway known as Elm Street, which is just off the Agua Seco Road and deep in the place known as El Hoyo which remains

475

smack in the middle of Los Jarros, the smallest and southernmost county of Arizona.

I didn't tell anybody official about Ronald because it wouldn't protect me to do so and somehow I think Ronald probably saved my life with his sharpshooting because Sirena Rae would have probably gotten to me eventually, one way or another.

But then Ronald will probably kill me one day that way too.

And I don't know why Ronald Rocha shot Sirena Rae and not someone else. Maybe dressed like she was, Ronald thought she was me and he was sore at me for giving him Carlos Monjano but then giving Carlos Monjano to the cops as well so he could not exact his own brand of revenge. Or maybe Ronald thought Sirena was someone that I cared about. Maybe he just wanted to jam me up.

Or maybe he killed her because sometimes a man like that just has to kill something.

The sicario made his exit from Los Jarros by retracing the route he had used to come into the country. The first night of his return journey he spent in the cave at La Entrada. In this shallow cave he rested and ate from the supplies in the metal footlocker just as he had been instructed to do on his ingress. There was the slight tang of fearful sweat and piss in the cave but he slept soundly, curled up in himself as an animal.

Early the next morning he started slowly to make his way back toward the border with food and water from the locker in a plastic trash bag slung over his shoulder. He kept to the shadows, even more cautious now of being caught on his egress from this country than he had been on his ingress since he now had money in his pockets, American dollars, one thousand for each man he had killed . . . the two under the bridge, the one at the Boulder Turn-Out, the one near the pile of bricks in the desert, the one on Wells End Road.

He had waited one week in the safe house but when he heard nothing from his jefe, as instructed he left with nothing but the money in his pocket and the clothes on his back, trusting there would be food and water in the shallow cave waiting for him when he achieved the gap in the rugged Theatine Mountains. From La Entrada the man kept to his conservative schedule, walking only in the shadows at dawn and at dusk.

His first day south of the cave he found the sniper rifle and picked it up and carried it for a while before he discarded it as too heavy and potentially incriminating. He wiped his fingerprints from the black graphite stock with his shirttails and threw the gun into a steepsided arroyo. The second day south of the cave he found the GI pack and the old Schrade pocketknife and the dry canteen. He rummaged the near-empty pack and found a bag of corn chips as the one thing useful, ate them and then buried the foil bag under some rocks and buried the pack under some other rocks and then moved on. He tucked the old pocketknife into his pants pockets but later discarded the knife into a steep-sided ditch. Later that day he found camo pants and soiled underwear and a desert brown T-shirt stained with blood and he simply walked past these.

His final day in Los Jarros the sicario found a dead man, naked and barefoot, on his back, staring at the sky, white foam dried around his mouth. The dead man's eyes were sockets picked empty by crows. Ronald Rocha clutched a photograph of a young brown-skinned man, Samuel Rocha, to his chest. The eyes of the boy in the photograph were dark and luminous as black clouds. As the sicario walked by the dead man he crossed himself, but only from habit.

Very near the border a line of quails like a convened row of nuns moved across the rough trail the man trudged upon and hurried under the cover of thick creosote bushes and because there was no sound from the air of hawks or no other movement or sound of other earthly predators about but him the sicario took this as a sign that he was now safe since he was the greatest predator.

But then a brace of hawks screeched as they sighted the quails and the man swiveled his head to watch the birds flying together for a while and then the pair singled themselves and parted as if they had not come to a decision to separate but had simply been separated by the fate of winds.

And then with a cry as long and piercing as a siren, one hawk lost altitude and departed the scene by just plunging down into an arroyo as if into the ground itself while the other one flew up, flew against everything . . . gravity land wind clouds even fate . . . and kept on silently until it was beyond sight and the sicario thought it was as if these birds of prey had split the world in two, the one claiming with her scream, the earth and the other claiming with his silence, the sky.

ACKNOWLEDGMENTS

This novel was not assembled by committee or built by workshop; but I do really appreciate the following:

Readers-of-Drafts: Mathew Madan (thanks for everything, Brother), Karen "KP" Peirce, Simone "Si" Gers, Seth Stroupe, Gene Jerskey, Theresa Jarnigan "T" Enos, Claudia (*Fort Starlight*) Zuluaga, Andrea "AG" Graham, Ben and Ann McKenzie.

Editing: Peter Joseph, Executive Editor, Thomas Dunne Books, with Melanie Fried and the Thomas Dunne/Minotaur/St. Martin's Crew — thanks for respecting my voice and my "rust."

The Tony Hillerman Prize and the Tony Hillerman Writers' Conference: Jean Schaumberg and Anne Hillerman — thanks for making us a part of this great family.

Research Assistance: Erin Lee Mock, Ph.D., James J. Helmer, M.D.

Promotion: Corinne Cooper and Michael Longstaff — Professional Presence: Communication Consulting, Tucson.

Poetry: Alexander Long (*Still Life; Light Here, Light There*) wrote the "Samuel" poems — thanks Bud, since you are better accidentally than I am on purpose.

General Support Crew: Marta Helmer, Ventura, CA; JB McKenzie Stroupe and her boyz — Sam, "Little" McKenzie, Seth, Ernie, assorted canines and All Related People — Aunt Juanita and Jarvie in Texas; Betty Brown in Topsham, and Anna, Eve, Robin on RoundTop, Rick Lathrop and Crew at LongWind, in Vermont; the Woodsides and "Brick" in New Hampshire; Professional and Staff Congress-City University of New York; Richard (late, but not forgotten) yoga guru, Tuxson (and beyond).

Locations: Lee Public Library, Gladewater Round-Up Rodeo Association Arena, Gladewater Books, Guadalupe's, The Fork and Gym 101, Gladewater, Texas; Chuy's Restaurant, Van Horn, Texas; Las Tortugas, Costa Rica; Lazy-8 Motel and Arizona Motel, The River-park Inn, Che's Lounge, BoonDocks, The Buffet, Pima Community College-Desert Vista and PCC-Downtown, Bookmans, Arizona State Musuem ("Paths of Life"), Tohono O'odham Nation, Pascua

Yaqui Reservation, San Xavier Mission School and THE University of Arizona, Tuxson; The Hilton Santa Fe Historic Plaza, Hotel St. Francis, Collected Works Bookstore, Santa Fe; Claudio's Barber Shop and Applebee's in East Harlem, Harlem Social and Riverside State Park in West Harlem, Molly's on Third, The Green Door in Hell's Kitchen, and all New York Public Libraries, NYC.

Every artist wants a respected peer who will "help the boy": my "Peer Guide" is Maximilian Werner (*Crooked Creek, Black River Dreams, Gravity Hill, Evolved*) — thanks Maxo, I owe you mucho.

I also thank the hundreds of student writers I have worked with — at the University of Arizona, Arizona State University, Pima Community College, Flowing Wells High School, Fairleigh Dickenson University-Metro and the City University of New York — who, by their patience with me and enthusiasm for what I love, have made me a better writer.

Most thanks to Kimberly Adilia Helmer, who not only endured me in the house while this book was being written and rewritten, but who also loves me the whole sky.

ABOUT THE AUTHOR

A native Texan, **C.B. McKenzie** has through-hiked the Appalachian Trail, modeled for Giorgio Armani, worked on an organic farm, earned a Ph.D. from the University of Arizona, and currently teaches Rhetoric at the City University of New York.